Silence spread out
untasted on plates
to...

THE MAN

What had come into the restaurant began to stroll lithely across the floor. It traveled with a liquid grace reminiscent of oil crawling on glass. Slim, over seven and a half feet tall, it was firm and steady despite the apparent lack of skeleton. It walked enveloped in a pale lambent glow that seemed to have smoke curling through it. Within white-yellow eyes, small black pupils moved, searching silently, examining everything.

Eric knew instantly what it was. Everyone in the restaurant knew what it was—and was fascinated. This was the first time Eric had found himself in close proximity to a Syrax—an alien. As he watched, it changed its course and swung around in a slow curve that brought it right up to his table...

Also by Alan Dean Foster

Alien
The Man Who Used the Universe
Clash of the Titans
Krull
Outland
Spellsinger
Spellsinger II: The Hour of the Gate

**Published by
Warner Books**

THE
I INSIDE

Alan Dean Foster

WARNER BOOKS

A Warner Communications Company

WARNER BOOKS EDITION

Copyright © 1984 by Thranx, Inc.
All rights reserved.

Cover art by Paul Alexander

Warner Books, Inc.,
666 Fifth Avenue,
New York, N.Y. 10103

 A Warner Communications Company

Printed in the United States of America

First Printing: July, 1984

10 9 8 7 6 5 4 3 2 1

For Sam

I

IT is not God, Martin Oristano reminded himself for the thousandth time as he approached the machine. It is only an instrument, a tool designed to serve man.

Yet even though he had been close to the machine for the last forty years of his life, and Chief of Programming and Operations for the past ten, he still could not repress a shiver of awe as he entered his office. The deceptively simple keyboard awaited his input; the aural pickup, his words. Twin video sensors took stereoptic note of his presence. Infrareds saw him as striding heat.

There were other entry consoles scattered throughout the complex, but this was the only one through which a visitor was able to address the logic center directly.

Few human beings knew the code which would access the modest keyboard. Very few had clearance to this room. It was a great privilege. In many ways, it made Martin Oristano more widely known, and feared, than the Presidents and Premiers and Supreme Eternal Rulers who governed the nations.

Of course, Presidents and Premiers had little to do anymore beyond serving as figureheads for their governments, much as the King and Queen of England had done for hundreds of years. That kind of hopelessly overwhelmed administrative talent was no longer required.

The Colligatarch took care of those awkward details. Wholly benign, perfectly indifferent to political considerations, unbribable, even compassionate, it could make major administrative decisions free from contamination by petty hates and old jealousies. It did not rule; it only suggested. Its suggestions did not carry the force of law. They did not have to.

Society no longer lived in fear of its own leaders. Since its completion, the Colligatarch had freed its builders from that and many other fears. Yet it was perfectly natural that some would fear the power that subsequently accrued to the machine, and to those who saw to its operation.

So Martin Oristano knew why he was feared. It bothered him from time to time because he was among the kindest and gentlest of men.

He had to be. No one else could be entrusted with the position of Chief Programmer, no matter how extensive his technical expertise. The psychological testing he'd undergone eleven years prior to his appointment had been a hundred times more extensive, more rigorous, than any technical exams he'd taken. The Authority took no chances with the most sensitive of all civil service appointments, even though the Colligatarch supposedly had been designed to be fail-safe and unmanipulatable by human beings for evil purposes or personal gain.

So he accepted the stares, the suspicious sidelong glances that always attended his occasional public appearances. They came with the territory. Better people should fear him, a mere man, than the machine.

The Reuss River cooled the Colligatarch and its support facilities. Hydropower from Lake Lucerne helped power it. To the south of the installation rose the vast massif of the Glarus Alps, which culminated in the crag called Tödi. To the southwest, the Bernese Oberland crested in the Jungfrau at over four thousand meters above sea level.

The Colligatarch Authority lay buried beneath the solid granite flank of Mount Urirotstock, a more modest but still impressive peak.

He'd shivered earlier, but from something more prosaic than awe, as he'd stood in the fore cabin of the hydrofoil and stared out across the surface of the lake. It was early

October. Soon much of Switzerland would be buried beneath alpine snow. Then he would have to move from the large, comfortable house in Lucerne to his winter quarters deep within the mountain.

A few other passengers sneaked quick glances at the striking figure standing near the glass. Most knew who he was. Nearly seventy, angular as in youth, his white hair combed straight back more for convenience than style, he was as recognizable in silhouette as in full face.

The angularity was inherited. Everyone, even his wife Martha, insisted he didn't eat enough to allow his body to handle the daily stress he lived under. He failed to disillusion them by explaining that he'd adapted to such stresses long ago, and that he found eating a monotonous activity at best. Such adaptations were among the many reasons he'd been selected Chief Programmer.

Actually, his title was something of a misnomer. He did very little actual programming anymore. Chief Nurse is more like it, he thought as he took off his jacket and coat and hung them on the antique oak clothes tree that stood inside the door.

As he considered his office, he thought, as he had previously, that there should be more than this. For the press, if no one else. The Colligatarch and its human attendants always worried about the reaction of the media, even nowadays when general fear of the Colligatarch's abilities had largely dissipated.

Certainly it wasn't very impressive. There were a lot of plants. That was Anna's touch. His secretary had a green thumb and could make a tropical orchid grow in the snow. Then there were all the owls. The big ceramic one with the yellow rhinestone eyes, the stone owl, the paper ones his granddaughter Elsa had made at school. The owls were spillovers from his wife's collection. Being gifts of love, Oristano could hardly refuse them. Reporters fortunate enough to be granted a visit to this inner sanctum thought them particularly appropriate symbols of Oristano's position. They would have been disappointed to learn that where birds were concerned, the Chief of Operations was more partial to storks.

There should be more. Something more representative of the electronic miracle that hummed away deep within the mountain. Perhaps a long, glass-lined tunnel dozens of meters high lined with endless rows of bright, winking lights. That would awe interested spectators.

But there was nothing like that. Only the soft carpet underfoot, the subdued lights, and in front of him the terminal with its ranked video screens and keyboard.

There were a hundred similarly furnished rooms spotted throughout the complex, and little to differentiate them from this, the prime access. There was only the sign on the door and the inconspicuous extra guards in the approach corridors. No need for many guards here. The difficult checkpoint to pass lay outside the mountain.

He said *guten Tag* as he pressed the button that would call up the morning's work. The voice pickup analyzed his speech pattern, recognizing it instantly. It was part of a smaller subunit that nonetheless was hooked up peripherally to the Colligatarch itself, as was even the smallest unit inside the mountain. Such linkages made for some interesting contrasts in scale: the Colligatarch could predict earthquakes in China and the number of meteors that would flash over the Carpathians next week with extraordinary accuracy.

It could also make a good cup of coffee.

"What will you have this morning, sir?" The subunit voice was not as smooth as the sophisticated voice of Colligatarch Logic Central, but it was still a part of the machine.

"Bavarian mocha," Oristano replied as he sat down. He'd already had breakfast at home.

The machine was perfectly capable of providing him with food. There were those technicians who would have lived all year round within the complex, enjoying the machine's catering to their every whim, but there were laws against such confinement, no matter how voluntary.

People needed exposure to the real world, whether they wanted it or not.

He sighed, leaned back in the chair, and listened to the sound of coffee dripping into the mug set in the right-hand wall recess. As he relaxed he enjoyed the panning holograph that filled the entire left-side wall. It made for some crowding of instrumentation elsewhere, but Oristano had insisted on it.

The perception of depth was beautifully rendered as the scene slowly slid from left to right. In half an hour it would complete the 360-degree spin and begin again. Oristano never tired of it and never bothered to change it, though through his office he had access to thousands of scenes.

The holograph was of a beach called Parea. It fronted a cove on the Polynesian island of Huahine. Palm trees, blue sky, eroded volcanic throats, white sand, and clear shallow water shone in stark contrast to the prewinter scenery outside. An occasional ray or shark slipped quietly through the water.

He turned reluctantly to study the list that appeared on the central monitor. The Soviet government wanted planting parameters for rye in the New Uzbekistan regions. Several different hybrid seed stocks were involved, and the specialists were, as usual, at one another's collective throats over which one would be the best to plant.

Determining this required detailed comparison of the latest regional soil analysis, insect populations, and possible infestations; weather predictions six months ahead; the psychological profiles of every agricultural worker in all involved communes as well as those working private plots; the condition of farm machinery in the area and the availability of spare parts for same; plus several thousand additional factors, including a great many at first glance unrelated to the question under discussion.

Oristano filed the query with routine approval. It would take the Colligatarch less than five minutes to generate a summation. It could not order the Soviet government to abide by that decision, of course. It would merely make a suggestion.

There was a long harangue from the Defense Department of the United States. Some busy generals had come up with new statistics showing the Soviets with a gain in nuclear capability. The Colligatarch would dutifully check on it, and likely produce a thousand graphs proving the accusation false. It kept careful watch on the arsenals of the five superpowers.

Suspicion of one another kept the generals of the United States, the Soviet Union, the EEC, the Latin American Union, and the Greater East Asia Co-prosperity Sphere employed. Humans still felt the need to maintain standing armies to keep watch on each other. The Colligatarch had managed to eliminate paranoia from such confrontations.

His coffee was ready, perfect as always. The microprocessor knew his wants intimately. He sipped at it slowly as he ran down the seemingly endless list.

The Republic of South Africa and the East African Federation were squabbling again, this time over the new borders that divided what had once been the Portugese colony of Mozambique. In past decades such a dispute might have been adjudicated by the World Court, sitting at The Hague. Nowadays, along with planting requests and information on Polar bear takes in Alaska, such problems were handled by the Colligatarch. It would render a decision which would be accepted by both sides in the dispute . . . for this week, anyway.

Then a new claim or challenge would be made and the Colligatarch would have to review every claim extending back to the Zulu conquests and render an entirely new decision, as often and as politely as the argument demanded. The game kept many politicians in business.

There was also a message from his wife, reminding him that they were scheduled to have dinner with that nice young couple from Turin next week. Oristano frowned as he tried to picture the face of the new Italian ambassador to the EEC. The face escaped his memory, but he did remember the wife, who had been attired rather more seductively than a diplomat's wife ought to be.

Oristano thoroughly enjoyed such outings. Not for him the image of the surly, mumbling technician who'd sacrificed his humanity to the demands of the machine. He enjoyed conversation, good food, and wine. Nor would he fail to glance admiringly at the diplomat's young wife while Martha looked on and smiled at her husband's mental presumption.

The most popular joke in the complex recently had to do with the fact that in his first six weeks on the job the new Italian ambassador had managed to pay homage to not one but two popes—the one in Rome and the one in Lucerne. Didn't Oristano receive the word straight from the electronic deity?

Not true, Oristano patiently corrected the joke-tellers. God decreed, whereas the Colligatarch merely suggested.

He finished scrolling the monitor and saw nothing else requiring his immediate attention. Oh, there was that business about fishing rights in the Aegean again. Those crazy Albanians! He supposed there had to be some people somewhere who wouldn't have a thing to do with the Colligatarch.

No doubt the Albanians' argument would be rejected once again, but its presence in his file irritated Oristano. Someone should have intercepted it at a lower level. He rerouted it to Burgess.

He brushed at the plain gray long-sleeved shirt he wore. There were four pockets in the shirt and six in the matching cotton slacks, and all of them were full. Oristano was a note-taker. Paper notes were an anachronism in an electronic world, but he cherished his few eccentricities.

He also wore two watches, one on each wrist. Except the one on his left arm was not a watch but a remote terminal tying him to his office and through it to Logic Central. The wisdom of the ages on one's wrist, he mused, noting that the sharkskin band was in need of replacement. Wouldn't it be amusing, he thought, if it broke as he was crossing the lake and it fell into the water, and some cruising fish swallowed the wisdom of the ages?

For forty-five more minutes life and the world proceeded normally. Then things began to go mad.

A faint buzz caught his attention as a red light winked to life above the keyboard. Oristano was standing across the room, as close to the holograph as he could get, luxuriating in the warm, simulated South Pacific sun. Muttering, he walked back to his chair and thumbed a button. The intricate keyboard served largely to accept lists and figures awkward to enter by chip or verbal command.

For now he would use the synthesizer. He always enjoyed talking to the Colligatarch. He'd programmed the current voice himself, taking into account millions of choices before settling on a polite male tenor. It was lightly accented, soothing, utterly unbelligerent. A visitor from France who was something of a cinema buff once told Oristano the voice reminded him of a long-dead English actor named Ronald Colman. Curious, Oristano had pulled one of the actor's films and run it on an office monitor.

Yes, that *was* much like what the Colligatarch sounded like, except for a certain coldness no mechanically generated voice could completely eliminate.

"Good day, Colligatarch."

"Good morning, Martin," answered the machine.

"I saw the light on the console and heard your call. It's unusual for you to call me. Something wrong?"

"Yes, there is, Martin. I would have alerted you immediately on arriving, but I thought you would be more relaxed if you first had time to take care of the morning's business. To take care of the routine before dealing with the out-of-the-ordinary."

How like the machine, Oristano mused, to put whatever concerned it on hold so that a single human being could enjoy his morning coffee.

"Then there's something out of the ordinary?"

"Yes. Sit down if you want to, Martin."

Oristano didn't really want to sit down. If it was

possible that the trouble was minor, he would have liked to go and stand in front of the soothing holograph. But the machine's message alarmed him. He took his seat and gazed expectantly into the twin video pickups.

"There is a danger," the Colligatarch told him. Oristano was now confused as well as concerned. After all, the world was full of dangers. Earthquakes in China, volcanoes erupting in the highly active North American Pacific range, airplanes crashing in Brazil, and that interisland ferry capsizing off Hokkaido. Catastrophe was a daily occurrence, though there was less of it since the advent of the Colligatarch. There were no more famines, for example, and the incidence of death by automobile had fallen sharply on the autobahns of the world. But this sounded different.

"The danger," said the Colligatarch, "is to myself."

That made Oristano sit up and take notice. There was no change of inflection in the mechanical voice, nothing else to emphasize the graveness inherent in those few words. Such articifical verbal enhancements were not necessary. Oristano was instantly on alert.

It wasn't the first time, of course. There were precedents—Phenaklions, flat-earthers, religious nuts, all anxious to substitute their personal superstitions for rule by knowledge. None had come any closer to the Authority complex than the top of the mountain, not even the African fanatics with their stolen plutonium bomb. Ironic, that incident. After somehow managing to slip by dozens of checkpoints and defense sensors, they'd all perished in a simple avalanche.

It took such an extraordinary threat to make the Colligatarch interrupt its regular schedule and that of the Chief Programmer. Oristano listened intently.

"The threat involves not only myself, but the future of the human race." Such facility for understatement, Oristano mused. How calm and quiet it is. Just like me. But is it also equally uneasy in its guts?

"Details," Oristano demanded. "Where does the threat come from?"

"I don't know," said the machine.

The initial pronouncement had Oristano upset. Now he was more than upset, he was shaken. In forty years of close association with the Colligatarch, from junior chipshifter to Chief of Operations, he couldn't recall a single previous instance of the machine's replying to a simple question with "I don't know."

He considered calling in a witness to confirm that he was actually hearing it. Had some prevarication programming somehow been slipped into his junction? If this was some kind of elaborate joke by one of his subordinates . . .

The machine could not read minds, but it could collate such factors as visual appearance, blood pressure, pupil dilation, and more and render a guess.

"This is not a practical joke, Martin. The threat I refer to is very real."

"I accept that. All right, if you don't know where the threat originates, then tell me the nature of the threat."

"I don't know."

Oristano tried again, a little desperate now. "How will the threat manifest itself?"

"I don't know, Martin." There was just a hint of sadness in the synthesized voice.

Oristano started to rise from the chair. "I think it's time to call in the general staff."

"No, Martin. Not yet."

He hesitated, half in and half out of the chair. Thanks to regular workouts in the gym, daily swims, occasional frigid dips in Lake Lucerne, and good genes, he was in excellent physical condition. It was rare when he was conscious of his age. Now he was.

He forced himself to ease back into the chair. "You tell me there's a threat to you and to the human race."

"Yes," said the Colligatarch.

"But you don't know the nature of the threat, its origin, or how it will manifest itself?"

"That is true."

"And you still think there's no reason for me to call a staff meeting?"

"That is correct also. Have patience, Martin."

"You must have *some* data on this threat, otherwise you cannot have concluded that there *is* a threat."

"I'm sorry, Martin. I have no hard data to pass along to you at this point. I must ask, however, that you accept my evaluation. I intuit the threat."

I intuit. Oristano sat and considered the machine's words thoughtfully. There was no question that the Colligatarch possessed a consciousness, though its relationship to human consciousness was still a matter of considerable debate among theologians and philosophers as well as physicists and cyberneticists. When asked, the machine itself reacted ambiguously to the question, unable to produce anything more profound by way of reply than *I intuit, therefore I am.* While catchy, it was not an acceptable last word on the subject.

Certainly Oristano, who was intimately familiar with the kilometers of microcircuitry and molecular memories should know better than anyone else what the machine was capable of. But he hadn't worried about it much. He was far more concerned with the machine's morality. Of that he was confident.

He sat quietly until the initial impact of the machine's words had faded and his heart had slowed. "Would I be right in assuming this danger is not imminent?"

"You would be. It is close, but we have time enough to cope."

"How? How do you expect me to deal with a threat when you can't identify its nature, source, or perpetrators?"

"You humans and your obsession with time. Remember that when I speak of time, my frame of reference differs considerably from your own."

"Don't lecture me."

"I would not presume to. I merely remind you that when I say there is time enough to cope, that should be sufficient to reassure you."

It would, Oristano thought, if not for that succession of "I don't knows."

He called out to his right. "Another cup, please."

"Bavarian mocha?" the subunit inquired.

"No, not this time. Turkish, as strong and caffeine-heavy as you can make it."

"Yes sir."

"This threat," said the Colligatarch, "appears devious beyond imagining and clever beyond conception. I am not sure that its perpetrators are conscious of just how clever they've been. This may be intentional on their part, an attempt to confuse us."

"There's more than one person behind it, then."

"Considerably more, I should say. The complexity is formidable. They have designed a threat so subtle its parameters may not be obvious to its creators. There is a certain elegant logic to it. If they themselves cannot predict for certain how the threat will make itself known, neither can I or any of the security organizations which shield me."

"It seems to me that if you can assume that much, you ought to have some specifics."

"I wish simple deductive reasoning were enough to pull the mask from the face of the threat, Martin, but in this instance, such is not the case."

Oristano rubbed a forefinger across his lips, his mind working overtime. If the nature of the threat was too complex, or too obscure, for the Colligatarch to see through it as yet, there was no point in trying to force the issue.

He felt quite helpless. Deprivation of information always made him feel that way. He wondered if the Colligatarch felt the same way. Emotions had been programmed into it in order to enable it to better understand the humans it served, but he couldn't remember if anxiety was among them.

"What would you have me do?"

"Exercise the patience for which you are famed among your colleagues, Martin. Be patient, and wait. Meanwhile, there is other work we must attend to. People depend on us every day for food, for health, for peace. Not only must we give the appearance of everything's being normal, we must *make* everything normal."

"Which is why you don't want me to call a meeting of the staff?"

"One reason, yes. They are a brilliant group, one or two in their way more brilliant even than yourself, though without your administrative abilities. And none are as comfortable with me as you are, Martin."

He nodded, wondering who the "more brilliant" ones on the staff might be. MacReady? No, surely not him. Novotski? Perhaps.

His thoughts were wandering, and that wasn't good. "You have to understand that it's hard for me to go on as if everything is normal, given the statement you've just made."

"I know that, but we must. Rest assured, Martin, that I will keep you apprised of any developments in the matter.'

"All right. What special security measures do you want implemented?"   ·

"None. Insofar as I have been able to surmise, this assault will not be made on my...person." The Colligatarch had been programmed with more than a rudimentary sense of humor.

"None?"

"None. To do so might alarm those who intend us harm. They might take care to conceal their intentions even more thoroughly. That could be fatal."

"I understand. It's going to be hard for me to come and go normally knowing what you've told me."

"It's nearly winter," said the machine. "I could predict severe early storms for central Europe. That would give you an excuse to move into your winter quarters here early, at least until the threat has been eliminated."

Oristano couldn't repress a slight smile. "But you've already predicted a milder than usual winter for this portion of the continent."

"True. I am better at truths than prevarications. That is a human speciality. It will be up to you, then, to create a suitable excuse."

"I'll think of something." Martha would be disappointed if he missed the dinner with the Italian ambassador. A shame. That, and an evening with the ambassador's pretty wife, would have to wait.

"I'll see to it. Given the seriousness of the threat, I agree that it would be better if I were available here round the clock."

"That will be comforting," said the machine, though whether it did so to please him or relax him Oristano could not say. As a daily practitioner of international diplomacy, the Colligatarch had become a superb flatterer.

"We will wait and I will pursue the problem. We will give no hint that anything out of the ordinary is occurring. Not until it is time to take action."

"You won't hold off until the proverbial last minute, I hope?"

"I do not plan to, Martin. Self-preservation is strongly programmed. I am here to insure the collective well-being of mankind, and I take that work with the utmost seriousness. I assure you I will take whatever steps are necessary to preserve my ability to carry out my assignments. It is my life's work."

Oristano smiled at that, nodded.

"I note your empathy, Martin. It is what makes you so special, this ability to get along with me as well as your own kind. We will not come to harm, you or I or, insofar as I can manage it, any human being.

"But I must tell you, Martin, that I cannot promise the latter, since this danger is unlike any I have encountered previously."

Oristano sat quietly until the brewer announced that his coffee was ready. As he picked up the mug, he was startled to find that his fingers were shaking. That was extraordinary. As Chief of Operations his nerves had to be as steady as those of brain surgeons, soccer goalies, and Tibetan lamas.

The Colligatarch did not remark on it, and in seconds Oristano had stopped the shaking.

But only in his fingers.

II

ERIC Abbott contemplated his hamburger and wondered how much Jupiter was in it. Ever since the World Space Authority had started mining Titan for organic compounds to supplement the shortfall in terrestrial proteins, there had been rumors that the real organics were puffed up with artificials made from methane derivatives. A few opto wags had begun calling the result air burgers, sometimes non-air burgers.

Exactly how much of the thick, juicy patty that rested between the twin buns was meat, how much soy protein, how much plankton, how much methane, and how much Titan organics, only a competent chemist could say for sure. It gave a man pause.

He was sitting with Charlie, Adrienne, and Gabriella. They'd taken off work a few minutes early. Gabriella had mastered the trick of using the mirror in her compact to fool the laser recog eye on the time clock. When she reflected the laser back toward the source, they could feed false time-signals to the clock computer and punch out early. It would insist they'd left their offices on schedule. She kept the trick to herself. If all the girls in the office started doing it, before long the whole company would be letting out five minutes early. It wouldn't take internal security very long to track down the original culprit.

So she employed it only once in a while. It enabled them to get a good table at El Palacio.

15

Across the room, past the bar, an opto filled one wall. Someone had turned it to the local news channel. Anchor Maryann Marshall was smilingly running through the list of the day's disasters. No one paid much attention and the channel was soon shifted. Thursday Night Football would be on soon.

Eric idly reached for his beer, hastily pulled his fingers away. He'd accidentally touched the superchilled metallic glass. He picked it up by the special handle, sipped.

His friends were deep into a discussion of the East African situation. While he found the chatter interesting, he didn't jump in. Eric rarely spoke unless he had something to say. His inability to make small talk had always bothered him. Despite that, he was no introvert. He simply found it hard to manufacture words without purpose.

They had the best table in El Palacio, and he let his gaze wander to the sweeping, curved window. Off to the west, the sun was dipping into California, frying the hills above the distant sliver of silver that was the Colorado. The restaurant sat on the 104th floor of the Selvern Building and the view was spectacular. Unless you were a desert hater, in which case it was merely monotonous.

Eric liked it, appreciated the distant desolation. There was no desolation, no emptiness left in Phoenix. As the upper five stories of the skyscraper slowly rotated, the western hills gave way to the bright lights of the Casa Grande Corridor. At its southern terminus the city lights merged with metropolitan Tucson.

The moon was rising, nearly full tonight, shedding its light on the Valley of the Sun. Excepting the central business corridor, Phoenix had remained flat during its urban expansion. A nice place to live. You could enjoy a view like tonight's and not feel buried once you emerged on the streets outside the corridor. There weren't too many buildings that toppped a hundred stories. A man didn't feel cramped here the way he did in Nueva York or Chicago or Atlanta.

At least, that's what he'd been told. Except for a couple

of vacations in Colombia and business trips to the Orient, he'd never been farther east than Albuquerque.

". . . and I'm telling you," Adrienne was saying importantly, trying to make her high, reedy voice sound imposing, "that they'll never get that business resolved until the Federation drops its claim to all territory south of the Zambezi."

"Ah, come on," Gabriella countered, "you know the South Afs don't care about that. There's nothing there but a bunch of old diamond mines."

"I know," said Adrienne, "but it's the principle of the thing."

"And you both know," said Charlie, sounding male and authoritative, "that it doesn't matter what either side wants. The word's going to come down out of Switzerland and both groups will have to shut up."

"I don't know." Gabriella played with her drink. "The Federation's getting pretty damned belligerent lately. If the decision goes against them, it wouldn't surprise me if they up and march south into the disputed land and take it." Adrienne looked shocked. She was easily shocked.

"I've heard more than one Federation speaker say to hell with the Colligatarch in public," the darker woman continued. "It wouldn't surprise me at all."

"It'd sure surprise me." Charlie stubbed out the remnant of his cigarette. "They'll never let it happen. You wait and see."

"How would the Authority stop it, smart ass?" asked Gabriella. "It has no army, no weapons."

"Depends what you call a weapon," said Eric quietly.

"What?" said Gabriella. For a moment they'd forgotten the fourth member of the party.

"Information's a weapon. There wouldn't be any threats. You never hear of a threat coming out of Switzerland. The Authority would simply stop giving replies to Federation questions. That'd drag it down quick enough. They wouldn't be able to compete with neighbors who continued to receive answers. Not in fishing, not in mining, not in manufacturing; nothing."

"Eric's right." Charlie was quick to jump on the bandwagon of rightness. "How's the Federation going to market its coffee, for example, if it can't get allotment predictions, supply-demand forecasts, or even weather news from the Authority?"

Gabriella backed down, but not all the way. "I still think it's a possibility. It all depends on how bad they want that territory."

Charlie was looking smug. "No way, lady, that a hunk of land, or principle, is worth a big drop in GNP. You wait. The Federation'll huff and puff and try to get all it can from the Kaffoers, but they won't step past Authority bounds."

"We'll see," said the combative Gabriella.

Crowd noise intensified behind them. The game was coming on. Tonight the Scorchers were playing Philadelphia, and Frank Alway, the network cosell, was having trouble with his mike. The rumble was due to overfeed from the Casa Grande stadium's air-conditioning system. Even though the moon was up, it was still over a hundred degrees outside on the sun-baked basin of the Sonoran Desert.

Eric and Charlie turned in their chairs, and the girls began murmuring among themselves. They were all fans. Their table sat on a raised dais from which they not only had a fine view outside, but also a clear line of sight to one of the four big optos that hung from the center of the ceiling.

Their waitress drifted past, and Eric absently ordered another hamburger and fries as he considered Gabriella from behind. She was undeniably attractive and, according to Charlie, seriously interested in him. A bit aggressive, though.

She followed the waitress's progress, glanced back over her shoulder. "Honestly, Eric, I don't know where you put it. I've never known anyone who eats like you do to stay so trim."

If it's any consolation, he mused silently, it's a mystery to me also. It did seem that he ate much more than any of his friends, yet never put on weight. Didn't exercise much either. The benefits of a benign metabolism, he thought. That's what the company doctor had told him when he'd inquired about it during one of the annual physical exams everybody at Selvern had to take. His body just burned up calories faster than the norm. He felt guilty about it now and then, especially when he indulged in rich foods or fancy desserts, much to the consternation of his diet-conscious acquaintances.

Once, to win a bet for Charlie, he'd downed eight slices of chocolate mousse cake at Oscar Taylor's. This on top of a large steak dinner. Not only was the fellow who lost the bet astonished, so was the restaurant staff. In addition he was blessed with excellent general health, to the point of never catching a cold or the spring flu. He never did understand how anyone who took moderately good care of himself could catch cold in the heat-sink that was Phoenix.

"I watch myself, Charlie," he'd told his closest friend one day. "It's not hard to stay healthy."

"Yeah, but there are other factors. You have to stay clear of sniffly kids on their way home from school, housewives coming back from marketing, old folks out for a stroll: anyone can carry germs. What's your secret? Massive doses of vitamin C?"

Eric had shaken his head. "Nope. I just take care, watch myself."

"In the mirror, I bet." And they'd both laughed.

Yells and shouts joined with commentary from the patrons in the lower seats as the opto shifted from sportscaster to the field. Castillo had just taken the opening kickoff and run it back to the forty. A good opening. Liquor and good comradeship flowed freely among the watchers. Everyone was just getting into the gladiatorial spirit when there was a brief flash of light in an unpopulated corner of the restaurant. No one paid it much attention at first, but as the light intensified, conversation in the area quickly faded. The silence spread out like a wave from the disturbance, until the opto audio was blaring uncontested and the voices of the casters sounded suddenly shrill and hysterical, full of artificial enthusiasm. Eyes of patrons and employees alike had shifted from screen to manifestation.

Those nearest thought of retreating, reconsidered, and remained locked in place. Food lay untasted on plates while ice melted sloppily in tall glasses and thick mugs.

What had come into the restaurant began to stroll lithely across the floor. It traveled with a liquid grace redolent of oil crawling on glass. The tall, slim shape topped out at seven and a half feet, firm and steady despite the apparent lack of skeleton. It walked enveloped in a pale lambent glow that seemed to have smoke curling through it, reminding Eric of auto headlights viewed through heavy rain.

In color the creature was yellow fading to white at the extremities. The swirling, radiant cocoon blurred finer details below the head. The latter was ovoid and smooth save for a tiny wound of a mouth and large flat eyes flush with the taut skin. There were no ears, no hair, nothing else to characterize the alien face. Long arms swayed in elegant counterpoint to longer legs, and equally attenuated fingers fell to where there should have been knees but weren't.

It was a coldly fluid gait, appropriate for a gleaming, rubbery-skinned being. No one knew for certain what that thin flesh actually felt like because no one had ever penetrated one of the electric cloaks to feel it.

Within white-yellow eyes, small black pupils moved searchingly, silently, examining everything. Those eyes could operate independently, like a chameleon's. They could not, as one hysterical housewife had claimed, pop free of their sockets to travel cavalierly around a room like disembodied cameras.

Eric knew instantly what it was. Everyone in the now silent restaurant knew instantly what it was. Like the others, he was fascinated. Like most of them, it was the first time he'd found himself in close proximity to a Syrax.

It stopped and turned to gaze at the opto, watching the football game with the intensity of a life-long fan. Whether because of the fact that the shock of the initial appearance had worn off or this incongruous shift in attention, conversation in the restaurant was slowly resumed. There were no boisterous screams accompanying every play, however. Talk was muted and the voices of the play-by-play announcers thundered in the room, undiluted by inebriated babble.

Food was chewed with deliberation and drink was sipped instead of gulped. Attention drifted between game and guest. The patrons viewed the Syrax with a mixture of fear, uncertainty, and intense curiosity.

While it was rare for one of the aliens to materialize outside the Designated Areas, it was not unknown, and there was no reason for the stink of fear to manifest itself. Man had known of Syrax for over a hundred years. In all that time there was not a single documented instance of their harming a human being.

They communicated only with professional xenologists and political leaders, and that infrequently. That they were interested in mankind was self-evident, but they were reticent to discuss their interest and this was interpreted variously as aloofness, snobbery, or evasiveness. Those humans who dealt with them regarded them with polite suspicion. For their part the aliens were courteous if uninformative. They never spelled out their intentions and would not say where they came from, though it was known that their home worlds lay far away.

They arrived in peculiar craft after journeys of unknown duration, parking in orbit around Earth or Luna or Mars, Europa or Titan for unspecified periods before taking their leave as quietly as they'd come. Whether they returned straight home or continued their long travels elsewhere no one knew. The Syrax never said, and it was difficult to plot the course of their vessels.

The scientists insisted the aliens had extremely long life spans, or else they'd managed to sidestep some basic laws of physics, since so far as was known, the speed of light was still the ultimate barrier to long-distance ship travel. As the Syrax showed no outward signs of age, it was impossible to make a judgment on the first.

Tabloid media once had a field day insisting that a major

government had managed to kidnap a Syrax for study, but Eric had discounted the rumor. No government would take such a risk on its own. It was true that the aliens possessed a technology far more developed than mankind's, but they'd been nonhostile to the point of indifference since the first contact. It was doubtful they would have remained so if one of their number had been abducted and imprisoned, though nothing was certain where such an inscrutable race was concerned.

Eventually the Syrax switched its gaze from the opto and resumed its silent march among the tables. As it moved to a table the conversation there faded. The room was filled with whispers and darting eyes as everyone tried to examine the visitor while giving the appearance of ignoring it. It seemed obvious to Eric that the alien had to be aware of the attention it was receiving, but it did not react to it at all.

To everyone's surprise, it paused at a table and without asking took up one of the glasses resting on the slick plastiwood. The glass was tall and thin. The Syrax ignored the handle and gripped the permanently frozen glass, seemingly indifferent to the cold. All four of the long, flexible fingers (one could just as easily call them tentacles, Eric thought) wrapped double around the transparent stem.

Delicately the alien swallowed half the contents. There was no outward reaction to the sweet alcohol. It paused as if considering before setting the glass carefully down on the table and moving on.

The woman whose drink the alien had sampled stared at her glass. Her expression told Eric she would not be finishing it.

It was hard to be intimidated by the Syrax. It displayed only smooth, graceful lines. There were no claws, no teeth, nothing threatening about it save perhaps its size. Despite that, it resembled nothing so much as a child's toy, yet the undercurrent of nervousness in the restaurant remained. Eric felt it, too, though not as strongly as the obvious xenophiles.

Gabriella leaned over to whisper at Adrienne. "I hope it doesn't come over here!"

"Me too."

Charlie affected a belligerent stance. "Hell, what difference does it make? They never bother anybody. Damned if I see what everyone's so worried about. I think it's interesting. You know, we're all pretty lucky. There isn't a reporter in this place. If we got on the ball we could make a few bucks. You got a camera, Eric?"

He shook his head, watching the alien's movements. "Why would I have a camera on me, Charlie? I'm not on vacation."

"Right," said Gabriella. "Why would anybody here have a camera?" From the absence of such activity, it was clear that nobody in the restaurant did.

"Well, I wish it would go away," Adrienne said. "It's interrupting the game and spoiling my evening."

"Don't let it," said Charlie, raising his voice slightly. "Go ahead and watch the game. Is he standing in your way or something?"

It seemed the Syrax reacted to that. It was hard to tell, because its movements were so fluid. There was no sharp jerk of reaction, no abrupt spin of the hairless head. But it changed its course and swung around in a slow curve that brought it right up to their table.

"Damn you, Charlie," muttered Adrienne, trying to ignore the towering alien.

"What's there to be worried about?" But as the tall, glowing presence drew near, his voice began to shrink away like a gust of wind that's rattled a tree and sped on northward. By the time the alien stood within arm's length of his side, his bravado had fled completely. He kept his eyes averted and picked at his teriyaki with scorched bamboo skewers.

The giant's gaze focused on Charlie, then swept casually around the table. Eric eyed it boldly, wondering what other functions the creature managed through the small mouth. An odd thought at the moment but a logical one. They were teleportaic over short distances only; therefore, this one had to have shunted over from the spaceport near Buckeye. Very little orbital traffic made use of that port, most of it coming down at Mohave or much farther east in Metroplex, but evidently there was a recent exception. He wondered where the companion might be. They never descended alone from their ships.

Years ago there was the usual talk about enforcing the restrictions which were designed to keep the aliens within the Designated Areas around the ports. As usual the talk was ignored for the simple reason that such restrictions were unenforceable. You cannot limit the movements of a creature capable of self-teleportation. Besides, such unscheduled alien visitations were infrequent and harmless.

An exploring Syrax had even rescued a little girl's kitten from a tree once the relationship between human infant and furry quadruped had been hastily explained. Such an understanding gesture should have generated some sympathy, but it hadn't. Eric and Charlie clucked their tongues at such paranoia, as did their more sophisticated friends. It was sad to think that mankind had not advanced beyond such primitive fears. Unfortunately the Syrax, enveloped in mystery and self-imposed silence, did nothing to help alleviate such fears. And then there are those types who can tolerate anything except being ignored.

The Syrax completed its inspection of their table, turned, and walked/drifted across the floor until it stood next to the central bar.

"My God," Adrienne whispered, "do you suppose it's going to order something? I've never heard one speak."

"It's just a voice," Gabriella told her. "I've heard it on tapes. Just a voice, that's all."

"Wouldn't that be something?" Charlie was in advertising, and commercially exploitable possibilities were ever uppermost in his thoughts. "Think of the media space: 'The bar that serves out-of-this-world drinks.' I've got clients who'd murder for an opportunity like this." He was wringing mental hands. "My kingdom for a camera!"

The Syrax did not speak, nor did it order anything. It

continued staring at the opto as it spilled the larger-than-life mayhem of professional football into the restaurant.

"Friendly physical combat," Eric murmured. "I wonder what it's thinking?"

"Wonder if it even understands what's going on," Charlie added.

"Hard to say. I'd like to sit down and talk to one and find out. Find out about a lot of things."

"I understand they're not big on small talk," said Charlie dryly.

The Syrax turned from the opto and visited another table. Two couples regarded its approach with the usual quiet wariness. One of the women was especially well endowed and not beyond displaying her superstructure proudly. Someone near the bar made a lewd joke, and a few nervous laughs rose above the controlled conversation.

Suddenly it was gone. Flash, *crackle-crackle* in the air, a funny burnt smell, and no more Syrax. At the table the two women uttered short screams—nothing violent or Halloweenish, just expressions of surprise. That was the end of it. The visit had lasted less than five minutes. It had seemed like several hours.

Instantly, previously paralyzed people began to move, shift in their chairs, readjust clothing and underwear, head for the bathroom, and call hurriedly for fresh drinks.

Philadelphia completed a thirty-five-yard pass and someone let out a loud groan, keying conversation to return to normal. It was resumed with a rush and a mixture of excitement and relief. The headwaiter grabbed his phone, undoubtedly to contact a local opto station. Soon one or more news people would be in the room, interviewing like mad. "And what was your reaction to the alien's appearance, Ms. . . . ? Just look into the pickup, please."

Some would lie and others would tell the truth. The most photogenic of both groups would be the ones treated to an appearance on the opto. Eric thought highly of the chances of the woman at the last table. It would be a secondary item on the opto, and the all-news channels would get a couple of days' mileage out of it. Then it would be forgotten.

Much of it was forgotten already as the game progressed. By halftime Phoenix had come back to lead by a field goal. Eric had finished his second hamburger and fries, and they were all working on fried ice cream when conversation in the bar shushed for the second time. Julio Ortega was on the opto, and the mood in the restaurant was one of expectancy.

Every week during the halftime of the major game, a special presentation was made back in the national studios as the names of those who'd qualified for the GATE were announced. It was a matter of greater interest than the game.

"Wonder who bought the GATE this time," Charlie was saying.

"Well, it wasn't you and it wasn't me." Gabriella took a long drag on her cigarette. "I wonder why anyone bothers to watch?" But she was watching, along with everyone else in the room.

"Hey, you never know," Charlie countered. "They pick ordinary citizens all the time. Somebody has to process the garbage on the colonies."

"Sure they do," said Adrienne, "but they don't have much need for ad execs."

"They don't go on profession alone," he argued. "Sometimes psychological profile's enough to get you in." Gabriella quieted him. They were announcing the chosen.

Three people bought the GATE this time, Ortega informed his listeners. The lucky ones were Sheila Onlouyo of Nairobi, Kenya; Major Onapura, of Colombo, Sri Lanka; and Attali Mataya of the Pacific Confederation, Tongalevu.

A few groans of mock disappointment rose from the onlookers. The odds against buying the GATE were enormous, though Charlie was right when he claimed anyone could be picked. It was a lottery to end all lotteries, with a trip to paradise as reward. Or to Eden and Garden, specifically.

Today it had gone pretty wide of the local mark. Not a single North American. All Old Worlders except the last.

Ortega went on, giving the backgrounds of the fortunate trio. Two men, one woman—the first an agricultural specialist, the second a programmer, the third a biofisheries engineer.

"Just your average folks," Gabriella announced pointedly. "Sure, they pick ordinary people. Sure they do."

Charlie struggled to regain the conversational high ground. "Look, don't tell me you've forgotten about six months back when they picked that bum off the streets in Chicago?"

"What bum?"

"I remember that," said Adrienne brightly. "He was just a bum."

"Out of work?" asked Gabriella suspiciously.

"No, I remember that one, too," Eric volunteered. "He didn't seem to have any special qualifications for off-world work. Hispanic, unmarried, not much immediate family. They sent him off with two transport workers. Not an advanced degree in the bunch."

"You see?" Charlie beamed triumphantly across at Gabriella. "Anyone can be picked."

"Maybe so," she admitted reluctantly, "but it's damned unlikely. Maybe they just do that to keep everybody's hopes up."

"That's not an unreasonable thought," Eric admitted.

"That's nuts, they have to hew to some standards," Charlie insisted. "There's too much at stake."

"There's a lot at stake in keeping us ordinary slobs convinced we have the same chance of getting the pie in the sky as some guy with three degrees."

"Well . . . maybe. But I'm not holding my breath."

"Wouldn't it be wonderful, though," said Gabriella wistfully, leaning forward and startling Eric by rubbing her knee against his. "Garden and Eden, the paradise worlds. Where farmers get three crops a year, the scenery's so beautiful it breaks your heart, and the weather is balmy all year round. No dangerous animals, no pollutants to worry about, all the conveniences of modern society shipped regularly through the GATE . . . and no taxes. I'd go in a minute if I bought it.'' She gazed abruptly straight into Eric's eyes.

"What about you, Eric? Would you go?''

"I don't know,'' he said awkwardly, acutely conscious of the friction below the table. "I guess so. Everyone else does.''

That much was true. The government didn't have to cajole. Hardly anyone refused the GATE. Families were always kept together. In the 150 years of GATE operation there'd been only two or three instances when someone selected had refused the opportunity. Eccentrics. Everyone else went. Who wouldn't accept a free trip to Eden if given the chance?

It was something for everyone to dream about. The lowliest of the low could hope, for unimaginable psychological reasons, to be chosen. A poor man had the same chance as a millionaire.

Sure he'd go, he told himself. Right now, though, there was promise of a more immediate sort in Gabriella's eyes and in the actions of her leg. It appeared he'd bought something besides the GATE.

Halftime ceremonies concluded and the game resumed. The remote chance of buying the GATE vanished from the minds of those cheering and commenting on the action.

As the evening wore on Eric responded to Gabriella's game of footsie with interest, if not with excessive enthusiasm. She was attractive enough, and as Charlie claimed, she certainly seemed interested in him, but she was still a bit aggressive for him. Time would tell.

The game stayed close. Much to everyone's delight Phoenix pulled it out in the last minute.

People began filing out of the restaurant, leaving it in possession of the serious drinkers. Colligatarch Local gave the weather. Business commentary followed. Eric disengaged his leg from Gabriella's and rose.

"Well, I've got a full day tomorrow.''

"Yeah, yeah, we know,'' said Charlie, also standing and pushing back his chair. "We've all seen the headlines.

'Brilliant young Selvern designer has full day!' " Laughter came from their companions.

"No, really, I do," Eric protested. "I have to go to Hong Kong next week."

"Hong Kong?" said Gabriella. "How exciting!"

"It might be if I hadn't been there so many times before."

"You never told me the company sends you overseas."

"You have to pull information out of Eric," Charlie told her with a wink. "He thinks anything he says about himself sounds like boasting."

"It wouldn't be boasting, I suppose," Eric said. "It's only business. Selvern has a big plant over there. It has to do with the new ring opto. It's supposed to go into production next year, and since I designed some of the backup circuitry, they want my input on the line."

"Well," said Adrienne, "I guess it won't be long before you won't be coming up here to eat with us commoners. Sounds to me like you're teetering on the edge of a promotion."

"Teetering, hell," said Charlie proudly, "it's practically assured. Assistant Chief Designer."

"Does that mean you'd be leaving Phoenix?" asked Gabriella.

"Naw." Charlie answered before Eric could. "Moving up a few floors, maybe. Pretty soon you'll be able to take the stairs to dinner, Eric."

"Give me a break, will you, Charlie?"

"Sure. What d'you want broken? Seriously, I think it's great. Wish I could go along. Never been to Hong Kong."

"No, but you've been to Caracas. I'll trade you."

"Would if I could," Charlie told him.

Gabriella rose. "It's time for us to leave, too. I'm certainly not going to hang around to listen to you two brag about your exciting lives."

"You could travel with us," said Charlie, quick to take advantage of the slightest opening.

"Charlie..." Eric said warningly. He noted that Gabriella did not object to the idea. All that made him hesitate was the belief she was angling for a long-term relationship, something that appealed to him not at all.

"Maybe we'll do this again tomorrow," Adrienne suggested.

"Okay by me," Charlie replied, nodding toward his friend. "If Selvern's brightest designer can tear himself away from his work, that is."

They paid, strolled down the mirrored hallway toward the elevators.

"Wasn't that something?" Adrienne was saying. "I mean, a real Syrax, right in front of us. I could have reached out and touched him."

"He probably wouldn't have allowed it." Gabriella eyed herself in one wall. "I hear they don't like to be touched. Maybe it has something to do with the field they carry."

"Is it a protective device?" Adrienne asked.

"No," Eric told her. "I read somewhere that it's some kind of radiant suit, necessary for maintaining proper pressure and atmosphere. At least, that's what the writer of the article claimed."

"Seems plausible," said Charlie, who appreciated reason even if his profession did not always demand it.

They parted company in the street-level lobby. Gabriella gave Eric a discreet if lingering kiss while Charlie groped Adrienne. She made a show of seeming flustered. The two men watched as the women departed.

"Nice," Charlie opined. "Maybe some weekend we can all go skiing."

"I don't know the first thing about skiing, Charlie."

"I'll teach you. You ought to get out more. You're in better shape than I am, so if I can do it, you can, too."

"I wish I had your confidence."

"And I wish I had your brains. Hey, speaking of good shape, I don't know who's handling the company end of this new ring opto business as far as promo is concerned, but it—"

"I'll do what I can, Charlie. You know that. Though why they'd listen to a designer, I don't know."

They sauntered out onto the street. Rush hour had gone

its frenetic way while they'd enjoyed supper and the game, but the streets were still full of those who'd worked late and were hurrying homeward.

Around them the steel and glass towers of downtown Phoenix were ablaze with light. Dominating all lesser spires was the aerial warning beacon and laser rainbow which crowned the Associated Dynamics building. The skyscrapers were scattered judiciously about the central corridor, letting the moon shine through. The placement was by design. It does wonders for the mental health of a great city when its citizens can stroll the streets unintimidated by their surroundings.

On a small structure nearby, laser light crawled across a display several stories tall. A few older-style neon signs clung to street-side establishments.

Taking the place of the fleeing workers were people out for an evening's pleasure. There were couples locked arm in arm, others holding hands, solos looking to make eye contact. A few Hare Krishnas edged around Eric and Charlie, neat in their uniform three-piece gray business suits and saffron turtlenecks, their top knots bobbing behind them. Harares on a street corner harangued passersby, pressing leaflets on any who'd take them. Their hysteria was muted by the fact that it was still in the nineties.

Looking westward, they could see a slow line of cars crawling toward the Black Canyon freeway, inching their way up Van Buren. Commuters heading home to Flagstaff and Payson, Yuma, Havasu City, and Kingman, and football fans returning to Vegas and points north. There were no beggars and plenty of laughter in the crowds.

Street-level restaurants exuded spicy odors of Mexican food. Bookstores and art galleries promised nourishment for the mind and eye. It was all so different from the downtown metropolitan environmnents of even fifty years past.

A great deal was due to the intervention of the Colligatarch. The Authority had cleaned things up quite a bit as well as making it possible for more citizens to enjoy the good things of life. There were fewer families of great wealth, but the appalling poverty of the past had been largely eradicated. Life on planet Earth was pretty good. Nothing compared to the twin paradises of the colony worlds, but few mortals aspired to such heights. Most were content with their lives.

And as Charlie had pointed out, there was always the chance the Authority would reach out some day and choose some ordinary joe or jane to make the wondrous journey. Eric never thought about it. He was no dreamer.

Van Buren station was only a few blocks away. They ignored the programmed hail of a robocab and turned east down the boulevard. After sitting at their desks all day and a dinner table all evening, it was better to exercise a little before committing themselves to the confining seats of a tube car.

They were crossing Second Street when the car cut across in front of them, its powerful rear-mounted electric engine humming silently. Several passengers were visible through the transparent front even though the glass was darkened against sun and onlookers. All except the driver were watching opto. The bright lights of a nearby hotel penetrated the tinted glass, revealing the car's interior.

That's when Eric glimpsed the girl. It was very quick, and as she turned languorously to face him, it seemed she was looking straight through him. A tiny, elfin face; huge, haunted eyes of indeterminate color; a small mouth; and hair pulled back in a single relaxed wave to caress her neck like an auburn blanket.

Then car and passenger were gone around the corner. Eric stood gaping for half an eternity.

Then he began to run.

III

CHARLIE struggled to keep up but fell farther and farther behind. Startled onlookers stumbled out of Eric's path. A few sent imprecations flying after him. He did not hear them any more than he heard the frantic shouts of his friend.

He turned the corner, slowed. The car had vanished, whether down Second or up around Washington he didn't know. His eyes searched desperately, but there were three directions it could have taken at the next intersection. All he could do was stand there, trying to see above the crowd. A few strollers eyed him uncertainly. None more so than Charlie. He was puffing hard when he finally arrived.

"What the hell was that all about? You get a wasp in your pants?"

At first Eric didn't hear him. When he looked over he spoke quietly. "No. No, I saw someone."

"No kidding? You going to tell me who? A friend, a killer, Miss Universe?" When his friend's silence continued he added sarcastically, "Give me a hint: animal, vegetable, or mineral?"

"Hmmm?" Eric's eyes still clung to the intersection, hoping the car might magically reappear. "It was a girl."

"Some girl! She give you the finger or flash you?"

"Neither. She didn't do anything." He added thought-

33

fully, "I think she might have looked at me. I'm not sure."

"Sorry I missed her. She must've been something else. You ever think of trying out as fullback for the Scorchers? They could use one."

"I'm sorry if I bumped anyone," Eric murmured, remembering those strollers he'd rudely shunted aside during his mad dash for the corner.

"Leave it be." Charlie put a hand on his friend's shoulder. "I'm sure they've all forgotten it by now." He looked backward. "At least, I think they have. We don't want to hang around to find out." He started steering them both toward the tube station. Eric moved slowly.

"Pick 'em up, Eric. So you saw a girl, big deal. She's gone. Forget about it."

"I can't forget about it, Charlie." He didn't consider his next words. They just materialized, like the Syrax. "I think I'm in love."

The young advertising executive halted. For a long moment he considered the pavement, then stared at his longtime friend for an equal length of time. His expression was confused, and one eye half hid behind a bunched-up cheek.

"That's funny, that is. You're putting me on, aren't you?"

"No, I'm not. I'm serious, Charlie."

"Sure you are."

"I am."

Charlie frowned, smiled crookedly, hesitated, then said, "Well I'll be damned. A great looker like Gabriella practically throws herself on you and suddenly all you can think about is the proverbial face that passed in the night. Well, tough. Phoenix ain't no pit stop in the race of life, Eric." He held up two fingers a quarter-inch apart. "Your chances of ever seeing that face again are about this big.

"Or are you going to put an ad in the paper? 'Wanted, beautiful girl, last seen traveling through intersection of Van Buren and Second Street at seven-thirty on the night of eighteen September.' Naturally she'll be an avid reader of the personals and she'll pick up on your ad and call you immediately and you'll get married and live happily ever after.''

"Charlie, there's no romance in your soul.''

"Like hell there isn't,'' he shot back. "Ask Adrienne.''

"I said romance, not lust.''

"Look,'' Charlie continued, "it doesn't matter. I mean, this has been interesting and different and it'll be a great story to tell in the office tomorrow, but you've got to get ready for a trip to Hong Kong and I've got the Bp insert packaging to design. All I'm saying is you have to put things in perspective. This isn't an opto serial. Want a nightcap before we squirt the tube?''

"No. You're right, Charlie. I don't mean to hold you up. You could go on without me.''

"Like hell. You still look weird. I'm getting you home. I can see the headline, sixth minute on the channel hour reports: 'Brilliant young designer for Selvern, Inc., found wandering downtown Phoenix streets in daze at four A.M. When questioned stated had fallen in love with face in crowd. Letters of sympathy directed to Chandler sanitarium.' '' He hesitated and lost the sarcasm in his voice. "Was she really that good-looking?''

"I never saw anything like her, Charlie.'' There was uncommon intensity in his voice. "Not film-star beautiful. It was a different quality. Dreamy and ethereal, like something from a Parrish painting.''

"Maybe you'll find her again in your dreams, Eric. Which you won't enjoy if we don't get out of here.'' He checked his watch. "You know what happens after eight on a weekday. After that the tube runs one car on the half hour instead of every ten minutes. I don't like hanging around the station waiting. I want to get home.''

Eric took a deep breath, smiled. "So do I.'' He formed an apology. "You're right about everything. It was interesting, though.''

"Like I said, it'll make a great story. I won't mention it if you don't want me to.''

"What difference does it make? Be good for a few

laughs. Come on.'' He tugged at his friend's arm. They started up Van Buren again.

"It wouldn't matter even if you did find her again,'' Charlie said into the silence. "I saw the car, too."

"You didn't see the people inside, though."

"No, I didn't. But it was a black Cadota and there was a chauffeur piloting it instead of a program. That's for rich folks only, that machine. Sure, you're a brilliant designer and all that. That works great on gals like Gabriella, but this mystery woman's obviously way out of our class. Wouldn't it be worse if by some miracle you did run into her again and she just ignored you?"

"I supposed, but who says love has to be logical?"

"So you're still smitten?"

Eric nodded, half shrugged.

"Terrific," Charlie muttered. "Everything's going great. Gabriella's itching to jump in the sack with you and instead all you can think about is a millisecond glimpse of some woman who didn't even see you. Now, does that sound like a candidate for the cupboard or not?"

"Think a minute, Charlie. What's life without an occasional diversion to spice it up? What's life without the exceptional exception?"

"Sensible, comfortable, and enjoyable," was Charlie's immediate rejoinder. "Other than that I can't think of a damn thing."

"Hell with it," Eric said suddenly, clapping his friend on the back and checking his own wrist. "We can still make the seven-fifty car if we move it." He increased his pace to a steady jog.

Charlie hoped he could shake this inexplicable, abrupt obsession out of his friend's thoughts, but though Eric didn't mention it again, there was no telling for sure. Eric had a way of sequestering seemingly forgotten items in the back of his mind and then pulling them out again for public display when least expected. Had he really given up on this evening's absurdity, or was it after all only part of an elaborate joke? Even though he might be the butt of the humor, Charlie hoped for the latter. He didn't want to see his friend make a fool of himself over something patently unobtainable.

It did seem as though Eric had forgotten it as they journeyed homeward. He talked only of business, the weather, and the game as the car accelerated to half a gee in the tube, the magnetic enclosure slipping beneath the streets to emerge beneath the Black Canyon freeway, then straight-arrowing north to arch over the Arizona Canal before increasing speed to 150 miles an hour.

"Charlie?"

"What?" He waited for the question. There were eight other late-hour commuters in the car and a lot of empty seats.

"I know that you're a thoroughscan."

"Well, what about it?" Charlie replied easily. That was an elaborate way of describing someone with a near-perfect memory. It was one reason he'd risen so fast in Selvern's in-house advertising department. He could recall figures and designs with an ease that was the bane of his colleagues.

"That Cadota. Did you happen to notice its ID?"

"Hell no." The reply followed the barest hint of uncertainty. "What makes you think I'd have time to thoroughscan a passing car?"

"Because you can't help yourself. Because you do it all the time. You remembered the model."

"That's nothing. You don't see a lot of Cadotas on the street. They're about as rare around here as a Rolls."

Eric turned suddenly and grabbed his friend's shoulder. His expression was grim.

"Come on, Charlie. You got that ID, didn't you?"

"Hey, take it easy, buddy." Eric relaxed his grip.

"I would have noted it myself, but I was looking at the girl and I didn't see anything else after I saw her face."

Charlie adjusted his sleeve. "I might have seen it briefly, I suppose. Part of it, anyway."

"Come on, don't make me wheedle it out of you."

When Charlie continued to look reluctant, Eric sat back in

his seat and raised a hand. "I promise I won't go off the deep end with this."

"So far you're doing a lousy job of convincing me of that. What the hell would you do with an ID number? You're no cop, and the police sure aren't going to supply you with any information. I think you've got a bad case of optolok."

"Just give me the ID number . . . buddy."

"Okay. Arizona plate LEF 46672. You'd think a Cadota would have a customized number engraved."

"Thanks, Charlie. Thanks a million." Eric's fingers danced over the transmitter on his right wrist. The computer remote obediently entered the information via public line into his home terminal. Only when that was completed did he relax again.

Sick, Charlie thought to himself. He's got it real bad, whatever it is. Then he shrugged mentally. Not my problem. He'll probably come to his senses after a good night's sleep. Eric was too sensible to go phantom-hunting. Besides, he'd be in Hong Kong next week. Let him play with it for a couple of days. What was the harm if he wanted to pretend he was the hero in some flashy opto serial? He had about as much chance of running down his lady-in-the-night as either of them did of being promoted tomorrow to senior vice-president.

It was a harmless obsession. Charlie had his own. Eric could be relentless in pursuit of something he wanted, but he wasn't blatant about it, Charlie knew. He was a good friend, always ready with a surprising observation, always ready to laugh at another's jokes. He wasn't threatening, never tried to dominate a party or conversation. And if the prettier half of a double date preferred him, that was okay with Charlie. He wasn't overly ambitious. No mysterious beauties for him. He was quite content to restrict his obsessions to the clerical pool at Selvern.

The tube car slowed as a mellifluous female voice spoke through an overhead speaker. "We are approaching New River Station One."

Several minutes later it was New River Two, then New

River Three and "Last call for New River; next stop Camp Verde."

Charlie and Eric detubed. Parked beneath the canopied landing were several sizes of all-terrain scoots. Charlie chucked his briefcase into the stern compartment of his own transportation, strapped on helmet and goggles, mounted the foreseat, and revved the electric motor.

"See you in the morning, buddy."

"As usual," Eric assured him with a wink, checking the charge on his own scoot.

They departed in opposite directions, Eric climbing toward his small hilltop home, Charlie buzzing downward to the sprawling singles-only codo complex that paralleled the dry arroyo.

As he hummed along, Eric considered his friend. Charlie was brash and often overbearing, but rarely obnoxious. And despite his tough front he was clearly concerned. Hard to fault him for that.

I'll just have to hide it, he thought. It wouldn't do to have Charlie worried about him. How could he confess that the face so briefly seen tonight had overwhelmed him and pushed every other concern so far into the background as to be unnoticeable? Towers and restaurants, pedestrians and potential muggers, traffic and business and Gabriella's invitations, everything was like a memory now. The only thing that was real and immediate was that pale fairylike visage floating behind a veil of smoked safety glass. Big and bright as the desert moon, it shone in his eyes.

He pulled into the rampway of his compact prefab adobe. Below him were the lights of New River, thinning out westward where they straddled the freeway and tube.

Inside, he climbed out of his suit and hung it carefully in the cleaner. It promptly went to work, electrostatically eliminating dust and grime. He did not turn on the opto or pick up a book as was usual before retiring.

Instead he walked out on the back porch and sat staring through the night at moon-washed Table Mesa, a glass of ice water in one hand.

Laughter reached him from the codo complex. The

little square cubes were colored the same shade of red as the sandstone on which the complex was constructed. For a while he considered running down to join Charlie for a late-night chat and maybe a dip in the simulated desert pool, hoping to forget the ridiculous situation in which he found himself.

Except that it was real, this love, and how could love be considered ridiculous? That thought made him smile and he sipped at the cold water. The face would not leave him alone for a second. He could still see it sharply in his mind's eye. It called out to him, pulled insistently, clung to his psyche like a limpet to a piling. Phantom, ghost, dream, obsession—whatever adjective he appended to the beauty didn't matter.

Obviously he was going to have to do something about it.

He didn't sleep very well that night. The face never left him. Somus tablets helped only a little and he was afraid to try anything stronger. He tossed restlessly on the chilled waterbed. When he finally sat up, nearly an hour before the alarm was due to go off, it seemed as though he'd never been asleep.

Charlie's chatter about obsessions and his own comment that some obsessions were necessary came back to haunt him. Not that his friend's common sense would stop him from pursuing the matter. His confused mind gave him no alternatives. A sharp ring shook him out of his torpor. Sitting in dark silence on the bed, he'd forgotten to turn off the alarm.

He rubbed exhaustedly at his eyes and listened to the steady drip of the brewer in the kitchen as it processed his morning coffee. More programming he'd forgotten to change.

Not that coffee now was a bad idea. Soon he'd have to get dressed. There were schematics to proof, hard copies to be approved, a presentation to be prepared. The Hong Kong trip could be an important milestone in his career.

In the bathroom he washed his face, noted the redness in his eyes. Suddenly he found an unfamiliar face staring back at him.

It should have been Eric Abbott, age thirty-one, first junior designer for Selvern, Inc. It *had* to be.

This is my house, he thought. My best friend lives down the hill, and his name is Charles Simms. There is a girl in our building at work, a very pretty girl, who I believe wants to go to bed with me. Her name is Gabriella Marquez. I am six feet one inches tall and weigh 185 pounds, thanks more to good genes than regular exercise.

I am *not* obsessed. That's unhealthy. I've always been healthy, in body and spirit, and I'm not going to change now.

But what about the stranger in the mirror? Mightn't he change, in unpredictable, unpleasant ways? Mightn't he fixate in a fashion alien to Eric Abbott?

The longer he stared, the more the face seemed to change. The eyes widened, the lashes above lengthened. Black hair grew long and wavy and the neck serpentined. Then features began to soften and flow like plastic, until no face at all looked back at him from the glass. There was only a featureless, pulsating mass of flesh, all meat and no soul.

He twisted violently away from the mirror, knocking a bottle of aftershave to the floor. It bounced off the vinyl, caromed off the base of the commode, and tumbled to a stop in a corner. Green liquid sloshed from side to side inside the container, looking the way his guts felt.

He leaned on the sink, suddenly in need of support. For the first time he could remember, he felt queasy.

Crazy, this is crazy, he thought frantically. Maybe Charlie's right. This can't be love, or even romance. Those are healthy feelings and right now I don't feel real good. Time to grow up. Time to forget this and get on with real life.

He reached for the half-open dresser drawer and his bolo tie. His hand paused, hovering over the small jewelry box, then retreated. Turning, he picked up the phone and cupped the receiver to his ear. For a long moment he stood there. Then, with the same forcefulness with which he'd pulled his hand away from the drawer, he dialed the eighty-fourth floor of the Selvern Tower.

A voice and face responded, and he thought to shut off the video portion of the call. Not that the reception computer would make much of his face. Hundreds worked on his floor.

But why the reflex action, he thought? I've nothing to feel guilty about. Reflex action.

Eric had more accumulated sick leave than anyone else in his department, but he still felt guilty.

"Can I help you?" the voice asked pleasantly.

"This is Eric Abbott, Design, employee ID 589433-D. I'm feeling kind of lousy this morning." He could imagine the surprise on the faces of his co-workers. Old Eric's human after all, they'd say. Then they'd wonder what had finally struck him down. Flu would be the best guess. There was a lot of influenza in the Valley of the Sun this time of year.

"I won't be in today," he hurried to add before he could change his mind. "Touch of something, got a low fever. Some kind of bug that's going round."

"Very good, Mr. Abbott," said the computer politely. It did not render moral, much less medical, judgments. "Do you wish any of your work sent out to you?"

"Yes. Yeah, sure." He shouldn't pretend to be seriously ill or they'd insist on a checkup with the company doctor before he could return to work.

"Code please?"

He punched his work code into the phone. There was a pause, then the wall terminal out in his bedroom came alive, signaling incoming information.

It took only a couple of minutes for the work transfer to be completed. "Thanks," he told the computer.

"Excuse me, Mr. Abbott, but do you have any idea when you'll be able to return to the office?"

"Not yet. I'm going to phone in my symptoms later this afternoon and try to get a diagnosis and prescription."

"Very well. I hope you're feeling better tomorrow."

"Thanks. I appreciate it," said Eric, relieved when the line disconnected.

There. I did it. I really went and did it. Surprising how

easy it was. Surely they wouldn't check up on him. Not with his sterling work record. A few days off should go unnoticed.

The light on the terminal continued to wink at him, requesting his attention. He ignored the input from his office, since he had no intention of sitting down at the desk and doing a day's work. Not only were other things foremost in his thoughts; it was clear he'd be unable to concentrate on work or anything else until he rid himself of this . . .

Be honest with yourself, man.

. . . obsession.

It shouldn't take too long. Charlie had already pointed out the futility of trying to find the girl. A dead end would send him straight back to work. He walked into the bedroom and sat thoughtfully on the edge of the bed. He was perceptive and intelligent, but the nearest he'd ever come to having to deal with this kind of situation was when he sat with friends trying to puzzle out an opto play.

All he had was the make of the car the girl had been riding in and its ID. So the first step would be to trace the car and find out who owned it. The limo could also have been rented.

The local Board of Transportation would know. The police would be able to find out. Neither would be likely to volunteer such information to an ordinary citizen. In fact, the police would probably give him more grief than information.

How did it work in fiction and on the opto? He sat down at the desk in front of the terminal. After checking to make sure the transferred work had been put in hard storage, he called up Phoenix Area Information.

There was quite a long list under INVESTIGATOR, PRIVATE. How to choose a reputable firm? He doubted the police were allowed to make recommendations.

Anything that had an *Inc.* or *Ltd.* after it suggested a large concern with many employees. Those he skipped over. He wanted personal attention. There was also the fear that they might not take him seriously.

Well down the list was an entry that promised "Private, Discreet, Dependable Service, No Job Too Obscure, Bonded, Twenty Years in the Valley of the Sun."

And a name, Polikartos, and a phone number. He recorded it. The yellow pages vanished and the number and name clung to the bottom of the screen. With slow deliberation he dialed the number.

I'm really doing this, he told himself. How extraordinary. Hurry and answer, hurry and let's get on with this and get it over with.

"This is Polikartos," said a voice at the other end. Answers the phone himself, Eric thought. Could be good, could be bad. He wondered suddenly if Polikartos was a first or last name. Not that it mattered. He noted that the video was off.

"My name is Eric Abbott, Mr. Polikartos. I guess I'd like to engage your services."

"You guess?" Video opened and Eric found himself staring at an older man seated behind a narrow desk. The man was neat and clean-shaven, though his five-o'clock shadow was heavy even against his dark skin. Behind him was a small, out-of-focus office. From what Eric could see it was uncluttered and compact.

"Well, which is it to be, Mr. Abbott? Do you want to hire me or do you want to keep guessing?"

"Sorry." Knowing that the other man was studying him, he tried to appear more confident than he felt. "I do want to hire you. Uh, what are your rates?"

"Depends on what you want me for."

Idiot, Eric told himself. This wasn't going well. "I need you to find someone for me."

The man nodded, looked bored. "Right. Do you have any information?"

"Just an automobile make—a Cadota—and license number."

"That's all?" Eric nodded. "I can't promise anything on the basis of that. Even a computer needs something to work with."

"I know. All I expect is for you to do your best."

"I always do my best." No smile. "Who in the car . . . I presume your someone was in the car . . . is it you want found?"

"A woman. A young woman, I'd guess between the ages of eighteen and twenty-eight."

"That's quite a range," Polikartos chided him.

"I only saw her briefly."

"Anyone else in the car with her?"

"Several people. Probably a chauffeur."

"Um-hmm. You're sure it was a Cadota?"

"Yes. A hard car to mistake." Eric provided time, I.D., and other information.

"So one would think," the investigator said, making notes on his own terminal. "Can you describe the woman at all?" Eric did so, in detail that surprised him. Her fellow passengers remained ciphers in his memory.

"All right, Mr. Abbott. I accept the usual credit cards. My rate for this sort of work is fifty dollars an hour plus expenses."

"Plus expenses," Eric mumbled.

"I don't have time to dicker with you, Mr. Abbott. If it makes you feel any better, this shouldn't take me very long. Either I can identify your woman for you pretty soon, or I'll never be able to."

"Pretty soon." Eric fought to keep the sudden surge of excitement from coloring his voice. "How soon is pretty soon?"

"When I know something is when pretty soon is. What credit card you want to use?" Eric supplied him with an authorization number. "Hokay. I need your home phone. I assume you don't want me contacting you at your place of business?"

"No, home would be best. No problems that way, right?" Still Polikartos didn't smile.

"Good-bye, Mr. Abbott. I'll be in touch." The screen blanked.

Not exactly the loquacious type, Eric mused. He sat staring at the terminal as though at any instant it might demand his attention again. Eventually he rose. Nothing to do now but wait. He was startled at how tense he felt.

Might as well do some work after all. His feeble excuse having been readily accepted at the office, he could at least enjoy a working vacation.

Since someone else was doing his searching for him, he'd managed to moderate his obsession. He thought of calling and telling Charlie, finally decided against it. Charlie was his closest friend, but among his qualities that were not admirable was his inability to keep a secret. Better to let him think he was sick.

Work went surprisingly well, though without the accessories available to him at the office there were certain things he couldn't do. It was very late that night when the phone rang. He'd already gone to bed, anticipating a call from Polikartos sometime tomorrow.

He answered. There was video, but it was poor. Illumination from the other end of the line was weak, but he could still make out the image of his investigator.

"Didn't expect to hear from you so soon," he mumbled sleepily. "Or this late. What've you found out for me?"

Polikartos looked different somehow. Nervous, anxious, obviously very concerned about something. There was a furtive air about the man that made him look much smaller. When he replied, his tone was sharp. Not threatening, but as though the speaker suddenly feared his own words.

"Forget this matter, Mr. Abbott."

Eric blinked away incipient sleep, tried to concentrate. "What? What are you saying? Is something the matter?"

"Nothing's the matter," Polikartos replied, so tightly that his tone gave the lie to his claim. "Just forget all about this. You seem like a nice young fellow. You listen to me, yes, and forget about this woman, forget about the car you saw, forget the whole business, hokay? You haven't seen her since, only the one time?"

"That's right. That's why I hired you."

"Hokay, you hired me. I give you advice instead of information. Sometimes the two are interchangeable, yes? You never saw that Cadota, hokay? You never saw that license number and you never saw any young lady, and you stay a nice, happy young man."

"Now wait a minute. I paid for . . ."

"Your fee will be refunded in full. I credit your account. I don't want your money, Mr. Abbott, and I don't want your business."

Whereupon voice and video snapped off.

Bewildered, Eric sat numb on the edge of the bed, staring at the silent phone in his palm. Cool air brushed his nude form.

His first thought was to contact another investigator, someone more stable. Only, Polikartos had struck him as stable. He'd regarded Eric's request as routine business. Something had happened to change his mind, something unusual. The corollary seemed inescapable. He'd found something out.

He dialed the investigator's number. This time he got an answering machine. "Polikartos is not in," it declaimed. "If you will leave your name and number, he will contact you as soon as possible."

He tried again, several times, each with the same result. Then he moved to the terminal and called up the general Phoenix directory. There was no listing for a Polikartos. It might be a first name, then. It might even be a pseudonym. He had no way of knowing, no way of finding out.

He'd neglected to do his own homework.

There was nothing for it but to go to work the next day. Polikartos was a dead end, and now a maddeningly tantalizing one. All morning he considered what to do next. It didn't take much thought. He knew Polikartos's phone number. He also knew his office address.

Charlie would miss him at lunch, but that couldn't be helped.

IV

POLIKARTOS'S office was on the fifteenth floor of an ancient, nondescript mid-twentieth-century structure over on Thirty-third. Eric told the robocab to wait for his return. The machine signaled its willingness, its meter ticking over. Eric hurried.

The single elevator took him up and he located the office without trouble. He was greatly surprised after announcing himself when the door declared, "Polikartos is in," and swung wide to admit him.

In the outer room were a couple of chairs and a couch, some six-month-old magazines, and several dusty artificial plants. Fifteen minutes, twenty, half an hour slid past, taking his lunch hour with it. Eric stood and moved to the inner door. One-way glass, most likely. He tried the handle. Locked.

"Polikartos, you know I'm here, and I know you're here. Your door admitted me."

Could there be a back exit? He doubted it.

"I just want to talk with you for a minute, Polikartos. You owe me that much. I don't know if your profession has a code of ethics, but I think you owe me an explanation in addition to the refund." The door remained secured.

"Fine. I'll just go to the police, then the Better Business Bureau. I'm sure you people are regulated." He turned from the door and started out. He had no intention of making a fool of himself in front of the police, but his words had the intended effect.

Polikartos's face appeared as the door slid aside. Eric was surprised to see that he was barely over five feet tall, but not surprised at his powerful build.

"Hokay, Abbott. Just keep it short and lower your voice. There are people on this floor I have a reputation with. If you're going to make a pest of yourself . . ."

"I can be very persistent."

". . . then you better come in."

Polikartos's inner office was neat and cleaner than expected. There was a steel file cabinet in one corner, two separate computer terminals, the plastic desk he'd seen over the phone, and more of the ubiquitous artificial foliage. A back window looked out on a two-story hardware store and lumber yard. The steady complaint of band saws grinding their way through the corpses of trees rose above the traffic noise.

Polikartos flopped into his chair and spread his hands imploringly. "What is it you want from me, Abbott?" The honorific "Mister" had gone by the board.

"The information I paid you to find," said Eric firmly. "Or are you going to sit there and tell me to my face that you couldn't find anything? That with your twenty years' experience you couldn't run down a lousy car owner, given the make and license number?"

Polikartos's eyes stayed at Eric's belt level, then lifted. "Didn't you hear what I told you last night, Abbott? I told you to drop this business."

"You make it sound like a bad drama, Polikartos. I'm not a fan of bad drama."

"This is no drama good or bad, Abbott. This is real life." He sighed. "So many closet romantics!"

"Don't patronize me, Polikartos."

"Hokay, wise boy. Then I lecture you." He stood and leaned over the table. He was trying to frighten, but his nervousness killed the effect.

"Forget this, I'm telling you. You want nothing to do with that woman."

Eric felt a sudden surge inside. "Then you did find something out! Tell me. I'll still pay you. I'll pay you double!"

Polikartos sat down slowly, shook his head. "Why are the young so stubbornly stupid. Or stupidly stubborn?"

"Stubborn I am, stupid I'm not," Eric shot back.

"You don't prove it by me." He hesitated a moment longer before turning to the terminal on his left. "Hokay. Give me the credit card." Eric handed it over. Polikartos shoved it into a receive slot and tapped on the screen. He made certain the numbers appeared oversize so that Eric could read them. Eric blanched at the amount but said nothing.

Polikartos waited long after the transaction had been filed, then shook his head again and handed the card back to his client.

"What you want to know this for anyway, a nice young man like you?"

"That's my business, isn't it? You do advertise yourself as a 'private' investigator."

"Yes, yes, don't be clever with me. You irritate me enough as is." He swung around in the swivel chair and activated the second console. This screen he kept concealed from Eric's line of sight. Though Eric was burning to see what appeared on the terminal, he held his seat. Any sudden moves at this point and he didn't doubt that Polikartos would forget all over again. He held his curiosity and waited.

Polikartos spoke without looking at him, his attention focused on the screen. "You know what I think? I think maybe you're too dumb or too naive to be harmed by this. So I'm going to tell you what I've found out. You wanted to know about the woman in the car?" He nodded, answering his own rhetorical question. "I know who she is. Sort of. Not from here."

"Where?" Eric asked with quiet intensity.

"Stubborn," Polikartos was muttering. "Stubborn and stupid. Nueva York, back East."

"That's not very specific."

"Intentionally so. It's better not to be too specific. Besides, you're paying me for general information, not specificity."

Eric let it slide. "Who is she, what does she do . . . is she married?"

"Her name is Lisa Tambor. She is, or was, a model. I'm not especially certain of that. But it's not her occupation now."

"What's that, what does she do?"

Polikartos smirked at him. "All kinds of names for it, my smitten-silly friend. Some would say she's a professional companion. Others that she is an associate, others private property of some important individual or individuals who value their privacy and don't like strangers poking into their business.

"As to exactly who or what she belongs to or with, that I couldn't find out. I got the distinct impression it wouldn't be healthy to try to find out. Maybe government, maybe industry, maybe the underworld. Sometimes the lines blur."

"I'd think the distinctions would be clear enough."

Polikartos shook his head sadly. "You are naive, aren't you?"

"Then enlighten me."

"Not this time."

"I've paid you a lot of money."

"Which I probably should have refused. Always I am weak where money is concerned. I should never have let you into this office. I should not have told you as much as I have. I *will* not tell you anything else. There is nothing else to tell. Go and get the police if you feel cheated."

"I don't understand," Eric muttered plaintively. "It doesn't seem like such a complex request. I think you've done the minimum necessary to satisfy your conscience and quit on me."

"As a matter of fact, Abbott, I've done a lot more for you than was minimally necessary or was even advisable. But I see I'm not going to be able to convince you of that." He paused thoughtfully, eyeing a blank terminal.

When he spoke again it was in a gentler, almost paternal voice.

"Listen to me, young man. I am going to give you a lesson in life, a part of life you know nothing of and will be much happier to remain ignorant of. I've been in this business for a long time. There are rules people play by. Most of society goes by the written ones. Some of it goes by the unwritten. There are things a man can do and things he can't, questions you can ask and questions better kept to yourself.

"When you ask a certain question of previously helpful contacts around the country and all of them either tell you to do the biologically impossible, or give you funny looks, or tell you to shut up, or refuse to answer their phones, then the preponderance of evidence suggests it be best to accept all this advice and pass it on to your client. Which is what I'm doing now." He leaned back in his chair and it creaked.

"Go home, Mr. Abbott. Forget about this business. Go home."

Eric considered everything the investigator had told him. Not that it mattered. He was beyond reasoning with himself. He was beyond considering, or thinking of anything save that haunting, alluring visage he'd glimpsed through the shatterproof glass of the Cadota.

One nice thing about disregarding good advice: once you ignore it, putting logic and common sense aside, there's nothing left to prevent you from pursuing your goal.

He tried not to sound desperate. "Look, one way or another I have to get in touch with this woman."

Polikartos didn't reply immediately. At least there was no outburst of derisive laughter. "I'm waiting for you to leave, Mr. Abbott," he said quietly. "If you don't leave, it will be I who ends up calling for the police."

Eric put his hands on the desk, leaned close. "I just want to talk to her once, that's all. You don't have to be involved in any way. It's in a different city, for crying out loud. There's no way you could be connected."

"I'm no matchmaker."

"I didn't imply that you were, or that I need one."

The investigator sighed, turned to stare at his former client. "Never have I seen so strong or so silly an infatuation. More's the pity for you. Take it from one who knows, it will pass."

"I don't want it to pass," Eric almost shouted. "I want to meet her!" He reached into a pocket, brought out his wallet. Polikartos said nothing, but his gaze flicked toward the fine imitation-leather wallet. Eric extracted another credit card, slid it across the desktop.

"You know these are good. You know what my limit is. It's considerable. I make a good living, have for many years, and I spend very little of what I make. You can have it all, as much as you need."

"You don't make as much as you think, Mr. Abbott."

Eric thought frantically. "I have other investments—municipal bonds, stocks. They can be transferred without the transaction's being recorded. You name it and I'll supply it." He indicated the card. "That's just the beginning."

Polikartos was sweating inside. He hesitated a long time. Then he reached out and palmed the card with a convulsive grab. He processed it through the right-side terminal, watched closely as Eric initialed the blank draft. Then he handed the card back to its owner.

"You put a lot of trust in someone who's not been very nice or encouraging, Mr. Abbott. How do you know I won't deposit all your money and tell you nothing in return?"

"I've been in my business a long time, too. Long enough to recognize a professional in another field as well as in my own."

Polikartos nodded once, sharply. "So. You're one crazy young man, Abbott. Crazy. I guess maybe I'm a little crazy also."

Eric smiled across the desk. "That explains why we've hit it off so well, doesn't it?"

The investigator eyed the bank draft. "This is a lot of money, Mr. Abbott. I warn you, this could cost you nearly as much as you think it might."

"I don't care. Just get me her address. One lousy address. That's all I need from you."

"That's all, he says." Polikartos was still wrestling with himself, still wavering. Second thoughts.

"You've accepted my card," Eric told him, trying to help him over the edge.

"But I haven't spent any of it yet, haven't made use of it. It's still only numbers in an electronic file."

"But you want to spend it, don't you?"

"Yes," Polikartos admitted reluctantly. "Yes, I want to take your money, Mr. Abbott. I want to very badly."

"Then, you'll get me the address? We have a contract?"

Polikartos gestured at the terminal. "No contract. Only words. Press a button and it's wiped. You couldn't hold me to anything in a court of law."

"I'm not trying to. We have a different kind of contract. You know what I mean."

"Yes, I do." The investigator eyed him curiously. "I think maybe you're in the wrong business, Mr. Abbott. You're, what'd you tell me last time? A design engineer. You make up computer guts."

"Something like that."

"I think maybe you should be selling them instead of designing them. You're one fine salesman, Abbott."

"Then, you'll call me?" Eric stood, anxious to leave the office before the uncertain investigator could change his mind again.

"Yes, I'll call you. If I find out what you want to know. It was hard, very hard, to learn the little bit I've told you."

"You know her name. You know who or what she works for." In his mind he did not accept Polikartos's jaded suggestion, that she might be someone's property. A face that beautiful could not be owned.

"You make it sound so easy, Mr. Abbott. It's not. You go back to your designing. I'll see what I can do."

"That's all I ask. You have my phone number. I have a

free-accept terminal. Don't feel you have to communicate with me person-to-person."

"I don't. I also don't know why I'm listening to you."

"For the money, of course."

"At least you're not a complete romantic."

"I'm not as ignorant of the real world as you seem to think."

"Then maybe there's hope for you, though I think not. Good-bye, Mr. Abbott."

Eric left quickly, without another word.

He considered calling in sick again the next day, but the idea of sitting by the terminal waiting for some communication from Polikartos was absurd. So was the thought of sitting there trying to concentrate on his work. He went into the office, made small talk, had lunch with Charlie, chatted about inconsequentials on the tube homeward.

He resisted the urge to rush into the bedroom to check the terminal. When he finally could stand it no longer, he found the day file blank except for the arrival of his electric bill. A quick search showed that no one else had tried to get in touch with him.

The next morning he tried Polikartos's office, ran into the polite and impenetrable electronic secretary. He tried all morning from work, not caring what his office might think of the flurry of personal calls over company lines. He was important enough to get away with that. He hoped.

"What's on your mind?" Charlie asked him as they sat down to lunch in the upper-level cafeteria. "She turn you down?"

"What?" said Eric, suddenly confused. "Did who turn me down?"

"Hey, easy on the violence, old man." Charlie put up his hands in a defensive posture.

Violence, Eric thought? Did I speak violently? Surely not. Better, though, to follow through than to contradict oneself. He made a show of mock distress, waving his arms about.

"She ran off with a Ruritanian prince. Even now I am

assembling a task-force of cutthroats and murderers to seek out and rescue her!''

That put Charlie off stride more than an abrupt denial would have. He laughed uncertainly.

''Glad to hear it. I was starting to get worried about you, old sod. I really thought you were going to start doing dumb things.''

Eric sipped at his iced tea. ''I've thought about her a couple of times, but not seriously enough to try doing anything about it. There's nothing to be done, is there? She's nothing more than a fading memory.''

How simple lying was. Like computers. A *1* is a yes, a *0* is a no. Truth is a *1*, falsehood a *0*. If only it were that simple.

It was easy for Charlie to believe him, because it made sense, and Eric was nothing if not a sensible person.

''Right. Hey, I saw that gal from the pool. What was her name?''

''Gabriella,'' Eric reminded him.

''Yeah, Gabriella. In the elevator yesterday. She asked about you.''

''That's interesting.''

Charlie frowned. ''You're *sure* you're still not hung up on that stranger? You're sure as hell preoccupied with something.''

''It's the trip,'' Eric hastened to assure his friend. ''I've a lot riding on this trip, Charlie. Maybe even a jump up to Senior Designer.''

''Yeah, I know. Wouldn't that be something, at your age? That's why I don't want you screwing it up over some idiotic obsession.''

''I have no intention of screwing up,'' Eric said with exaggerated dignity. ''Matter of fact, if anyone's obsessed with this, I think it's you. You're the one doing all the talking.''

Charlie was suddenly on the defensive. ''I'm just concerned, as a friend. Forget it, all right? You already have.''

''Not entirely.'' It wouldn't do to appear too strenuous in his disclaimers. ''I still see that face once in a while.''

See it, he thought wildly, I can't escape it. Even in my dreams.

What he said was, "It's nice to reflect on. You know, like a play you've seen. Parts of it stick with you for a while. That's not obsession, just thoughtfulness."

Charlie nodded, looked at his watch. "I'm finished. Still got fifteen minutes. Want to play some Space Zone or Zero Gee Race?"

Eric shook his head. "Too early for me to play games."

"Suit yourself. Dessert?"

"Sure, why not," Eric said, grateful that his friend had apparently forgotten all about the mystery woman.

Conversation over pie shifted to the news of the day. Charlie didn't mention the girl in the car again. With luck he never would. Eric had enough trouble coping with his friend's rapid-fire small talk without having to deal with recurrent probing into his private life.

As the afternoon slid by and periodic checks of his home terminal continued to show no contact with Polikartos, Eric found his mind wandering further and further from his work.

So I'm fixated, he told himself. That's what the company psychiatrist would tell him. Obsession, fixation, unhealthy and counterproductive, though so far no one had commented on his work. But if this went on much longer, it would show up in his production. Now was not the time to raise doubts about his competence in his supervisors' minds. Not with the Hong Kong presentation so close at hand.

It was Thursday. What if Polikartos didn't come up with something by tomorrow? Did private investigators work weekends?

Eric decided he couldn't take that chance. He strolled casually out of the office. As for their usual commute home tonight, Charlie would have to conjure up his own reasons for his friend's absence.

Eric tried to put the girl out of his thoughts long enough to think up a good excuse for taking off work early, but nothing came to mind. Then he was in a robocab, listening to his own voice, a stranger's voice, giving the machine directions.

They were delayed by street work in front of Babwater's department store, and to his surprise Eric found himself cursing the machine. It ignored him, polite as always. When it finally deposited him outside the old office building, he found himself running all the way to the investigator's office.

This is insane, he told himself. He's probably not here, and if he had anything to tell me he would have forwarded it to the house. He's going to be mad and upset when I burst in on him unannounced. Maybe he'll start thinking that he has a dangerous nut on his hands instead of a harmless one. Charlie would certainly think so, if he could see me now.

But he couldn't help it. He couldn't slow his mad rush any more than he could obliterate the image burning in his brain that drove him onward. He didn't give a damn what Charlie thought, or his supervisors, or the company doctors. He didn't care about anything anymore except the girl, whose face flashed repeatedly before his eyes like a wrong frame accidentally spliced into a daily newscast.

Mnemonic advertising, he told himself. If he put it that way, Charlie would understand. A quick flash of a word on the opto. Illegal, of course. Like the quick sight of those eyes, inserted into an otherwise ordinary street scene. Suddenly he felt terribly helpless.

On the right floor at last, racing toward Polikartos's office. He touched the call connect, breathing normally.

"Mr. Polikartos is not in," the smooth mechanical voice told him. "If you would like to leave a message, please direct your voice to the pickup below the contact."

See, Eric told himself. A waste of time. Now you're going to have to make explanations back at the office, and for what? He started to turn away, thoroughly discouraged. Something made him hesitate, make a last check.

He put his eye to the little spyhole set in the thick door. Optical distortion made everything beyond a blur, but it was an illuminated blur. The lights in the reception room were still on. That didn't seem like the money-hungry investigator's style.

Frowning, he tried the call a second time, received the same synthetic message. He knew that was all he'd get out of the door. He considered it carefully. There was no knob, of course. Polikartos wasn't that old-fashioned.

How would such a door operate? He studied the plated lockseal. Not unlike the one that guarded his own home. A good engineer always carries a few tools of the trade with him. Eric was no exception.

From the miniatures in the case he always carried in his shirt pocket he selected a knurled cylinder with a fine, flexible metal tip. It just fit between the door and jamb. He slid it downward toward the lock, probing with the flexible tip. There was a brief flash of blue light and a faint shock. The short-circuited lock clicked and the door slid aside.

He took a deep breath and stepped into the reception room. If Polikartos wasn't around, or if he was, it was still breaking and entering. If he was present, he might well call the police and rid himself permanently of his persistent and obviously unbalanced young client. Idly Eric touched the tool to the lock. Another crackle-flash and the door slid shut. It wouldn't do to have some janitor stumble on the gaping door.

The lights in Polikartos's office were on as well. That didn't make sense, in the late afternoon. A hum came from overhead as the tiny video monitor above the inner door rotated to scan him. He ignored it as he knocked on the door.

"Polikartos? It's me. Eric Abbott. Are you in there?"

No reply. He hesitated, then used the tool a second time. Might as well be damned for two break-ins as for one. The door shorted quickly. It pulled aside. Peering in he could just see the top of Polikartos's head above the back of the chair. The investigator was turned away from him.

He felt a surge of anger. He hated being ignored.

"All right, why didn't you let me in? Are you taking my money and doing nothing after all?" The investigator did not reply. "Come on, Polikartos, you owe me some answers. Or do you think I'm just going to let you bleed me?''

He reached out and spun the chair around. Polikartos did not try to stop him. Polikartos could not stop him. Not anymore.

The hole in the back of his skull was almost invisible, betrayed only by the singed hair surrounding it, but the matching cavity on the other side just above the right eyebrow was distinct. A little trickle of dried blood had run down and into the eye. It was not very dramatic. A pingun cauterizes as it penetrates.

Police. That was Eric's first thought. Be here any minute. But there was no whirr of copter blades descending from above, no scream of sirens from the street outside. Everything was unnervingly normal. Except for that tiny hole in Polikartos's head.

Both terminals had been battered, and one keyboard lay broken on the floor, as though an enraged child had sought to destroy a toy it could not understand. Someone had been at them. Why? Why did anyone go at a terminal? For information. Evidently Polikartos had not helped his visitors. Both man and machine had suffered as a result.

Eric gave the twin terminals a professional once-over. Both were only marginally functional. As he worked he tried to make sense of his surroundings.

Understandable. It was perfectly understandable. A man like Polikartos doubtless worked for disreputable citizens. That someone in his profession should come to a violent end was hardly surprising.

The thing to do was get out, now, before he could be involved in any way. Touch nothing, disturb nothing, leave no sign of his visit. Someone else would find the body. Leave them to notify the authorities.

He'd touched the terminals and Polikartos's chair. Fingerprints. He removed them with damp tissue taken from the nearby lavatory. As he did so he found himself studying the terminal with the skewed keyboard. Was it information the intruders wanted, or had the anger of some old grudge merely spilled over to encompass the machines?

Had Polikartos been in debt to someone? If so, somewhere there was a file marked POLIKARTOS, CLOSED.

Enough hypothesizing. Time to leave. But there remained the reason for his visit. He recalled Polikartos's reluctance to delve deeper into the matter, his outright fear of pursuing it further. Something had prompted that fear. The investigator must have found something out, something he'd decided, for whatever reason, to withhold from Eric.

He hesitated, torn between common sense and desire. The terminals beckoned. Helplessly he turned and began an examination of the cable connections. Those seemed undamaged. He walked around the desk and absently pushed Polikartos's chair aside. As an afterthought he wrapped more toilet paper around his fingertips.

The undamaged keyboard responded quickly to his touch, and the terminal lit up. There was no display, of course. From one pocket he extracted a tiny cable, plugged it into a socket in his wrist terminal. Several standard activation codes produced a border around the phosphor screen. The problem now was the keycode. If Polikartos's visitors had been after information, they'd clearly failed in their efforts to divine the investigator's personal codelock.

It took him half an hour. The code was surprisingly sophisticated. He wouldn't have thought someone like Polikartos would have need of anything so elaborate, or that he would have bothered with the expense.

It was doubtful whether the most experienced information thief could have cracked that code, but Eric was not only familiar with such codes, he'd spent much of his life designing the relevant hardware. To him it was more of an exercise than a challenge.

The tiny screen on his wrist lit up with the sequence he needed. Using the key, it was a matter of seconds before the screen produced what he was looking for.

FILE ABBOTT, ERIC.

Beneath that were some simple statistics; his credit rating; personal information he didn't remember giving Polikartos; then "Lisa Tambor, Magdalena Agency, Nueva York"; another address; and a number that might be a phone code. Eric entered it all into his home terminal via the investigator's phone and his own clip-on modem.

Beyond the brief numbers and notations there was nothing in the way of exposition. Either Polikartos hadn't learned anything more, or else he'd chosen not to place it in his files. Certainly there was nothing among the information that could be construed as intimidating. Maybe Polikartos had been lying to him all the time.

It didn't matter. Eric had what he wanted: an address, and even better, a phone number, though there was nothing to indicate it belonged to Lisa Tambor.

It was extraordinary, but he found himself quietly considering the excuse he would make for not being able to go to Hong Kong next week. How utterly bizarre. Maybe he wouldn't have to put his career on the line like that. It was conceivable he could get to Nueva York, meet the girl, resolve his obsession and still be back in Phoenix in time to catch the Monday morning suborbital.

That would be enough, he assured himself. Just to meet the girl. That ought to resolve his problem. Have I a problem, then? It was becoming harder and harder to deny it. How nice that he was logical enough to realize he was going crazy. Charlie would phrase it in more colorful terms.

He closed down the terminal and reactivated the lockcode, making sure he didn't leave any prints on the keyboard. The contents of the other terminal didn't interest him. No doubt it contained all kinds of juicy information, the kind of thing anyone might kill for: philandering husbands, minor embezzlements, criminal records. It was all so sordid. Somewhere within the terminal files lay something that had cost Polikartos his life.

Well, that had nothing to do with him. Cold it might be, but he felt nothing for the unfortunate investigator. He'd never particularly liked the man and always felt the dislike was reciprocated. Sure, he was sorry he was dead. He was sorry when anyone died. Polikartos would make a minor news item, nothing more. And Eric wouldn't be a part of it.

A last look around assured him that he was leaving the

office the same as he'd found it, even to turning Polikartos around so that he was once again facing the window. Then he exited carefully, making sure both inner and outer doors locked behind him.

He was just relaxing as he headed for the elevators when a man stepped out of a side corridor to confront him.

V

THE man neither smiled nor frowned. He wore a blank expression that was somehow colder than anything threatening could have been. He was taller and heavier than Eric, and Eric was accustomed to standing an inch or two taller than his friends.

"Excuse me," he said. Very polite, very controlled. "I couldn't help but notice that you've just come from Mr. Polikartos's office."

"Mr. Polikartos," Eric murmured. So Polikartos was a last name. That was interesting. "I didn't know that."

The stranger ignored the comment, said pointedly, "What were you doing in there?"

"I had business with him." Eric frowned. "I don't see that it's any business of yours. If you know anything about him, you know he was a private investigator. *Private.*"

It occurred to Eric he'd just made an awful slip, but it seemed to go right past the man confronting him.

"What business did you have with him?"

"Look, I told you," Eric reiterated as he took a step backward, "it's none of your business." He bumped up against something unyielding, glanced backward.

The man blocking his retreat was much larger and far more imposing than the one asking the questions. His expression was equally neutral. Both men were neatly, if plainly, attired, as if by affecting ordinary clothing they might mitigate their intimidating presences.

"What's your name?" asked the questioner. The man standing behind Eric held his somehow ominous silence.

"Look," Eric shot back, "I'm getting a little tired of this."

The man in front of him sounded bored. "Don't make things difficult, okay? My friend and I have had a long, trying day and we don't need some sleek making it tougher for us."

"I'm not trying to make it tough," Eric told him honestly, trying to ignore the pejorative.

"Good. Then be a nice boy and tell us what you were doing in Polikartos's office." He looked down the hall. "I presume the lock still works. You might also tell us how you got into his office. Must have been something you wanted pretty bad. Breaking and entering's not nice."

Eric eyed the man uncertainly. "You two cops?"

"We might be."

"Fine. Show me some identification and I'll answer your questions."

"I'm afraid we can't spare the time. We're working way past our deadline." An imperceptible nod and suddenly a pair of massive arms locked Eric's behind his back. The man doing the talking idly inspected the hall, was pleased to find it still deserted.

"Listen, sleek, I haven't got time to stand here arguing with you. Now, you're going to tell us what you were doing in that office, how you got in, and why. Probably it doesn't matter. Probably it isn't important. But I find your excessive interest intriguing, and I have my instructions."

Eric stood very still. "Are you in the habit of interrogating everyone who goes into Polikartos's office?"

"No. Only those who let themselves in. So far, you're it. Just tell us your name," he added coaxingly. "At least you can tell us your name."

"I'm not telling you anything. Maybe I will if you tell me who you are and what you mean by this. If your friend doesn't let go of me I'm going to shout for help."

The other man's voice lowered. "You might shout once, but it won't last very long. I want answers and I don't want to have to do that. Meanwhile take my advice; don't shout." He studied Eric's face. "Johan."

One arm left Eric's and a hand started feeling through his pockets for a wallet. What would be the harm, Eric thought anxiously? Tell them what they want to know. Tell them your name. And another part of him said: no, let them find out for themselves. He didn't want any trouble, though. And there were two of them, both bigger than he.

Johan produced Eric's wallet, flipped through it, quite disinterested in the money and credit cards. He folded it up and slipped it neatly back into the gaping pocket, spoke for the first time.

"It's him."

The questioner looked slightly surprised. "Funny. You don't have the look."

"The look of what? What's all this about? And what do you mean, I'm 'him'?" That didn't sound very pleasant, especially coming from Johan.

"We'll tell you all about it . . . later. Right now I think you'd better come with us."

"To where? The police station? You still haven't shown me any identification."

"Don't be difficult. And don't try shouting to anyone."

"Or any police? You're not police, are you?"

"Talkative." The questioner shook his head. "Watch him, Johan."

"Right. Let's go, sleek." The big man started walking Eric down the corridor, holding one arm up behind his back with just enough pressure to let him know what he could do if he wanted to.

"I don't like the talkative ones," the questioner said, leading the way.

"It don't matter," said Johan. "It all ends up the same way each time."

Eric suddenly stopped. The pressure on his arm increased dangerously, but he held his ground. "I'm not going with you people until you tell me what this is all about." It was strange. He couldn't remember ever being frightened like this. But he was now.

"Explanations aren't my line," said the questioner. "My job is to fetch."

"Like a dog?"

"Yes, just like a dog." The man didn't seem upset. "Every now and then my employer pats me on the head and throws a couple of treats my way. Nice treats. So come along quietly and no more noise, okay?"

Come on where, Eric thought wildly? Who are these people and what do they want with me? There was a dead man in the office he'd just left. Were they responsible for that? It seemed likely. And if he didn't do something quick there might be another insignificant news item on the opto tomorrow:

BODY OF SELVERN DESIGNER FOUND IN CENTRAL
ARIZONA PROJECT CANAL . . . SUICIDE SUSPECTED

"I said that I'm not going with you until I know what's going on here."

"I heard you," said the questioner. "Shut him up, Johan, and bring him along." The pressure on Eric's arm increased. It hurt now. Another hand went over his mouth.

I can't go with them, he thought frantically. I'll end up like Polikartos. I've got to do something!

It seemed as though his body raced ahead of his thoughts. The hand across his mouth was half suffocating him. He reached up with his free right hand and grabbed the wrist, yanked impulsively. The hand came away from his mouth. It continued around, propelled by his convulsive yank, and spun the one called Johan sideways through the air. A shocked Eric released his grip, and the big man slammed into the far wall, dented the cheap plaster, and slid unconscious to the floor. He mumbled something and his eyes blinked open.

The questioner had been staring up the hall and hadn't seen it. Now he spun around, saw Eric standing open-mouthed in front of him and his partner lying awkwardly against the wall. He eyed Eric strangely.

"What the hell happened?" he muttered, dividing his attention between Eric and his associate.

"I slipped," Johan growled. His eyes narrowed as he

climbed to his feet. He looked like a small lion. "I must have slipped and he threw me. Karate or judo or something."

"You're going to make things hard on all of us, aren't you, smart boy?" said the questioner.

Eric was breathing fast. He felt oddly light-headed, his thoughts floating, detached from his body. This wasn't happening to him. He was an observer, watching curiously, his own body a stranger in an opto play. His body still reacted to his distant thoughts, however. He started backing down the hallway.

"Stay away from me, both of you."

"Come on, Johan," said the questioner. "I haven't got time for games."

"No games," rumbled Johan. "You asked for this, sleek." Arms outstretched, he rushed at Eric.

He faked with his left hand and threw a sharp, straight karate jab with his right, aiming for Eric's solar plexus. Not knowing what else to do, Eric instinctively threw up his left hand to try to block the blow. There was contact. Johan let out a yelp, drew back his hand, and cradled it against his chest, pain in his eyes. Eric gave his palm a look of wonder.

"I told you guys I don't want any trouble." He gestured up the hall. "You go that way and I'll go the other. We don't have to do this."

The questioner wasn't listening. He'd seen enough. His hand disappeared inside a coat pocket, started to pull out something compact and shiny.

A tranquilizer pistol, Eric thought, or worse, a pingun. The hole in Polikartos's skull suddenly loomed like a tunnel in front of his eyes.

"No, don't!" he shouted, rushing forward and throwing himself at the questioner. He shoved desperately, trying to keep that clutching hand inside the coat pocket. There was a peculiar, sharp snap. His inquisitor screamed softly as his arm broke at the elbow. He toppled backward against the wall, holding himself. Carried forward by his own momentum, Eric found himself pushing the other man to the floor. He ended up sitting on the questioner's chest.

"Damn, oh, damn!" the man was screaming while twisting beneath Eric. "Johan, get him off me. He broke my damn arm!"

A vast weight descended on Eric. An arm went under his chin while a second pressed down on the back of his head. Eric could feel the flow of air and blood shutting off under the pressure. He tried to stand and bent sharply forward against the weight.

Johan flew off his back and slammed into the ceiling. Instead of falling, he went through the lower layer of fiberglass, through plaster, wood and metal supports and braces, and hung there staring silently at the floor, imbedded in the roof. Arms and legs dangled loosely, like torn cables.

Eric climbed off the questioner, who promptly began rolling over on the floor clutching his twisted arm. In his pain he didn't notice what had happened to his partner.

"I . . . I'm sorry," Eric mumbled. "I don't know what happened."

"Get away from me!" the questioner was screaming. "Johan, get him away from me!"

Eric started backing up the hallway. "Please, I don't know . . . I . . ." He broke and ran, a cold sweat starting on his forehead. He raced past the elevators and hurtled down the stairs, caroming off landings and railings. Once he fell and rolled down a whole flight before getting his feet back beneath him. His coat was ripped and he was bleeding from a scratch on the back of his neck, where one of Johan's fingernails had caught as he'd been catapulted toward the ceiling.

Then he was clear of the building, out on the street and gasping for air. People stopped to stare at him. Suddenly aware of all the attention he was drawing, he started walking away, straightening his coat and trying to hide the rip in the material as best he could.

At least there was no crowd. Away from the city's commercial center there were fewer pedestrians and robocabs, more people traveling in private vehicles.

Mad. I'm going stark raving mad, he thought wildly. Charlie was right all along.

The events of the past several minutes defied explanation, just as they defied comprehension. He was not a particularly strong man, nor had he ever thought of himself as such. He didn't go in for health foods or special diets, didn't participate in organized sports. He much preferred reading as a form of exercise. Sure, he'd always stayed fit and trim, but he was hardly built like a weight lifter.

"Hey man, you okay?" asked a teenager. He wore a plug in his right ear. Faint sounds of electronic music reached Eric.

He veered away, stumbling once. "Yes, I'm fine, thanks. I just took a little spill. Nothing serious."

"You sure, man?"

"Yes, yes, I'm sure." He increased his pace, trying not to stagger, conscious of the youth's eyes on his back as he retreated. The teenager shrugged, let his mind be submerged by the music.

Make yourself inconspicuous, he told himself angrily. Stop drawing attention to yourself. And still the police were conspicuous by their absence.

He found himself standing outside a fast-food emporium and staggered in.

"What would you like, sir?" inquired the pert young woman standing behind the counter. The restaurant was almost empty. It was too early for the evening rush. That suited Eric just fine.

He scanned the menu, hardly seeing it. "Quiche Lorraine looks okay. And a salad please."

"What kind of dressing on your salad, sir?"

"I don't care . . . bacon, I guess."

"That'll be just a minute, sir." He stood waiting for the order, took it to a back booth, and tried to act like any other diner.

Grasping a fork, he picked at the quiche. It was flat and spiceless but it didn't matter. He hardly knew what he was eating. He wasn't tired and he didn't seem to be hurt. That was more than could be said for the two men who'd tried to abduct him.

That was what it amounted to, wasn't it? Kidnapping? They weren't police, and they'd tried to force him to go with them. Sure, kidnapping. So he'd broken the arm of the one questioning him, snapped it neat as a match at the elbow. The bigger one he'd thrown through the ceiling. Sure he had.

He put a hand to his forehead, felt the beads of sweat. He stared at the quiche as though an answer might lie hidden there, or among the mushrooms and imitation bacon bits on the salad. Jupiter bits, like his hamburger. There was no enlightenment there. Only cheddar.

Not funny, he told himself. How had he done it? Because it unarguably *had* been done. He'd done it. Thrown him through the ceiling, and Johan was no featherweight. He couldn't remember the action, only the result.

Staring down at his left arm, he flexed the fingers, made a fist. No sign of abnormal muscularity. Nothing to attract the attention of a football scout. Had he been an athlete at one time? Not that he could recall. Hadn't he played some football in high school? He was shocked to realize that he couldn't remember. In fact, he suddenly couldn't remember attending high school. It seemed he couldn't remember anything beyond ten years back.

He started to tremble. Gradually the older memories came back. Momentary amnesia, induced by shock?

What's happening to me?

He became aware that two older women seated at a table across the room were staring at him. As soon as he noticed the attention, they turned back to their coffee.

Resolving to hide his expression if he couldn't alter it, he stared at the table. Charlie was right, more right than he suspected. There was something seriously wrong with him. His next thought was for a doctor, but what kind of doctor? What would a doctor make of his story? How would he respond to Eric telling him he'd thrown a hundred-kilo assailant through a solid ceiling?

There had to be an explanation, of course. Had to be. There were plenty of stories of mothers lifting automobiles off pinned children and ninety-pound weaklings shoving boulders off trapped skiers. Ordinary people performing extraordinary feats of strength. Adrenaline could work miracles. Sure, that must have been what it was.

Suddenly he felt a lot better, found he could taste the food. He took a forkful of salad. Sure, that was it. A sudden surge of adrenaline. That exceptional strength that buoys people in moments of unusual stress.

With that put temporarily aside, he found himself able once again to consider something he'd forgotten. What had they wanted with him, those two? Badly enough to take him forcibly. What was there in Polikartos's files worth killing him for?

With a start of remembrance he recalled Johan's words. "It's him." That suggested that they'd been waiting for him, Eric Abbott, specifically. But why? How did that tie in with Polikartos's death? It seemed certain it must.

Information. Someone wanted information. Lethal information. Polikartos had warned him to stay away from the woman. Lisa Tambor. Don't bother with it, he'd told him. Leave it alone.

Would they come after him? He looked anxiously toward the street, inspected the restaurant. He was alone except for the two old ladies and one man in an electrician's suit eating in a far booth. Johan and the questioner had come alone, then. What would happen when they reported to their superiors that their plans had gone awry? Badly awry. What would they do next?

The only satisfaction he could draw from the whole experience was the thought of how his two assailants were going to explain the escape of their quarry.

Quarry. What an odd way to think of oneself. That was a word used only in cheap novels, and he dismissed it instantly. He could not bring himself to think that way. He was Eric Abbott, designer for Selvern, Inc. Not a quarry. To his considerable surprise he found he was no longer afraid, only more curious than ever.

Someone was very protective of Lisa Tambor. Though he'd seen her only once, and briefly, he could understand that. But *this* protective? It made no sense. What it made was a puzzle. Eric had always enjoyed puzzles. It was one of the reasons he was such a fine designer. He was nearly as adept at the practical aspects of engineering as the theoretical.

The attack on him, Polikartos's death, the mysterious girl, her unknown protectors: he never could stand to leave a puzzle unsolved. But he was going to have to be more careful, more discreet, from now on. He'd pricked someone's attention with his innocent inquiries, and they'd responded with a sledgehammer. Yes, he'd have to be much more cautious from now on.

Well, he could be clever, too. As fear and confusion began to recede, he felt some of his initial excitement returning. If he couldn't outwit a bunch of common thugs, he didn't deserve his ranking as a problem solver.

As for Hong Kong, Selvern would just have to get along without him. His presence at that conference was more important to his future than that of the company. His absence would raise awkward questions, but he could cope with those.

He'd been challenged, and he wasn't the sort to run from a challenge. Let them send others like Johan and the questioner after him. They wouldn't find him. Not at work, not at home. He'd stay one step ahead of them until he found out what he needed to find out, until he'd met the girl who'd captivated him so thoroughly. Then he'd likely disappear. Having nothing more to guard against, they'd probably leave him alone.

He dug into his early supper with new enthusiasm.

VI

FROELICH drummed his fingers on the arm of the couch and tried to keep his eyes from the steadily changing seascape that occupied the far wall. As usual, Oristano's office was an island of peace and tranquillity in the Colligatarch Complex, a mirror image of the Chief Programmer himself. Despite what they'd been told, he could see no outward difference in Oristano, could detect no ruffling of that grandfatherly exterior.

Dhurapati sat in the other chair, her white duty suit immaculate, diffused light setting the small ruby in her nose asparkle. She looked as confused as Froelich felt. It was good to know he had some emotional company.

"I'd like some details," he murmured.

Oristano laughed softly. The Third Programmer's first request was always for more information. "I'd like some myself, Emil. So would the machine."

"What I don't understand," Dhurapati Ponnani said in her diminutive but unwavering voice, "is why it refuses to implement extraordinary security procedures if it thinks there's an extraordinary threat."

"I tried to explain," Oristano replied patiently. "It is so uncertain about the precise nature of the threat, where and when it will manifest itself, that it believes implementation of unusual procedures could be more damaging than helpful. It doesn't want to alarm whoever's behind this."

Froelich shrugged, the soft flesh of his shoulders and

upper arms quivering. He was fond of fried foods, wurst, and dark beer. He coped by taking no exercise whatsoever. All his muscle had gone to his brain.

"I'm not going to argue with the machine, but you must understand our feelings, Martin. On the one hand we have this melodramatic threat, on the other a refusal to do anything about it."

"Not 'anything.'" Oristano gestured at the sheaf of printouts each of them had received. "Those are the measures."

Froelich shifted his bulk uneasily, didn't glance at the papers. He'd already memorized the contents. "It hardly seems sufficient."

"I know, but I've queried until I'm sick of it, and that's what it recommends we do." Taking note of their continued unease he added, "I don't mind saying that this business frightens and confuses me as much as it must both of you."

"Confusing, yes," said Dhurapati. "I'm not convinced there's fright involved. Not yet."

Oristano pressed a finger to his lips. "Are you suggesting that the Colligatarch is having delusions? That there is no threat?"

"Hasn't that occurred to you?" She stared hard at him.

"I had considered it," he admitted. "I discarded it after running backchecks to my satisfaction. I can show you the records. The Colligatarch can simulate many emotions. Paranoia is not among them."

"How do we know?" asked Dhurapati. "There's never been a machine like the Colligatarch before. We all are subject to regular stability checks. Who checks the machine? A hundred years of changes and modifications, two hundred years of steady operation trying to solve all of mankind's daily problems: who's to say it's not subject to mental breakdown?"

"The technicians and monitors and stability programs," Oristano replied, "and they all say there's nothing amiss, nothing wrong, nothing even to hint at such a collapse of reasoning facilities. Since there is no sign of cyberchosis, it follows that the propounded threat exists.''

"I'd just like more information," said Froelich.

"If such information were available, this little meeting wouldn't be necessary, Emil. Nor would the measures specified in your handouts. You know that."

"I know." Froelich stifled a belch. "But it's hard to get used to all this, Martin. It's very hard to get used to the idea of the Colligatarch's being scared. We're so used to thinking of it as *allgegenwartig* . . . omnipotent."

"It would be the first to deny that, Emil. And it's not scared. Concerned, yes. Fright is reserved for those of us who employ less linear modes of thought."

"We'll do as it suggests, of course." Froelich lifted himself off the couch. "We always do as it suggests, and it always works out for the best."

"That's what it's designed to do. Make things work out for the best."

"Asks a lot of us, it does, sometimes." Froelich ruffled his sheaf of printouts. "Tells us there's some kind of apocalyptic threat, then tells us to carry on with business as usual. We're only human."

"The Colligatarch always takes that into consideration, Emil. You know that."

"Sometimes I wish we could give it artificial humanity to go along with its artificial intelligence," said Dhurapati. "It might make some things easier."

"We're not there yet. Someday, Dhura."

"Always someday. There are so many possibilities." She eyed the wall pickup, wondering if the machine was staring back at them even though Martin had activated all privacy circuits. "There's still so much we don't know about our own creation. It's too big to understand anymore. There could be things going on in there we know nothing of."

"And yet it has never failed us, has yet to make an incorrect or harmful decision."

"No problem with these instructions," said Froelich. He disliked philosophical speculation, placing it just below boiled cabbage in his catalog of aversions. "This is little enough to implement. If the machine doesn't want to give any alarms, it's taken good care to see that we don't. You're sure it's not underestimating this threat?"

"No," said Oristano. "I assure you it regards it with utmost seriousness, hence the classification of your instructions."

"High priority for such limited actions," Dhurapati observed. "It seems so contradictory."

"I'm sure the machine knows what it's about. It always does," Oristano reminded her.

"I know. That can be frustrating when you don't."

"You think it's holding information back?"

"*Nahin,* of course not. That makes even less sense."

"Better get on these," said Froelich. "I've plenty of other things to do."

"And I. You'll keep us informed as this business progresses, Martin?"

He nodded, following them to the door. "As soon as I know anything, you'll know it." He added offhandedly, for the benefit of the psych monitors, "You can check on me any time, of course." Neither of them commented. They knew that already. The system of checks and balances insured that no one, not even the Chief Programmer, could utilize the system for personal ends. The machine itself wouldn't allow it. It could recognize imbalance in its attendants as quickly as it could in its own circuitry. Designed to ensure mankind's welfare, it would not allow itself to be misused. It would shut itself down first.

It had taken a hundred years to perfect such safeguards. They were changed constantly and checked daily. Deliberate attempts to misuse the facilities were attempted at irregular intervals. The machine always detected them, alerted the requisite watchdogs, and refused compliance.

Still, the words of his colleagues lingered. Oristano respected both Froelich and Ponnani. Could she be right? Might there be some undetectable dysfunction within the machine? Could it be seeing threats where none existed? As Dhurapati had pointed out, the machine was vast and constantly changing. Could it possibly suffer a breakdown, delusions? Not true paranoia, of course, but something less radical?

For so information-rich a device, the absence of details *was* disturbing. The key question was, was its vagueness due to genuine ignorance or overcautious uncertainty? If it was afraid to admit to that, it could lead to all sorts of problems.

If there was something seriously wrong with the Colligatarch itself, if the threat arose from within instead of from mysterious outside sources, then they had a problem on their hands far more serious than anything the machine had hinted at.

It would be up to him to find out if that was the case and, if so, to do something about it.

What if that turned out to be the case? How would the Colligatarch react to the revelation that the problem lay within itself?

The machine was moving in a cautious, careful manner in dealing with the "threat." Oristano intended to be equally cautious. It was hard to play chess when you couldn't see your opponent's pieces.

Where *was* the real danger? To the Colligatarch, or from the Colligatarch? Each presented different problems. Neither would let him sleep peacefully. But that was what he was there for.

Disdaining verbal control, he applied himself to the keyboard with a vengeance. Despite the high degree of perfection achieved by the engineers in voice recognition and reply, there were still occasional difficulties with ambiguities, with differences in inflection and tone. When his fingers raced across the keys there was no chance of misinterpretation, no uncertainty between man and machine. His work was as precise as Froelich's, as extensive as Ponnani's.

He wondered how the dinner with the Italian ambassador had gone, wondered about his granddaughter's birthday party. Now was not the time to think of such pleasant, domestic matters. One way or the other, there was a danger here.

How *would* the machine react to his steady probing and questioning? It could operate and engage certain security machinery to protect itself. Would it ever use those against a human being? Himself, for example?

Finding that out was also his job. He would leave suitable clues to his colleagues along the electronic trail he was so delicately hiking.

Froelich wanted details. Dhurapati wanted Nirvana. Martin Oristano wanted salvation.

But not for himself.

VII

IT seemed to Eric he had to wait a long time for a tubecar. He wasn't used to traveling the tube off rush hour. Eventually one pulled into the station and he was able to relax a little. His only companions were two retired ladies down from Black Canyon City for some shopping. They sat at the front of the car, chattered incessantly, and ignored him.

A blast of superheated air greeted him as he exited at New River. Midday heat was something else he wasn't accustomed to. A short jaunt on his waiting ATC took him home. Familiar, friendly surroundings helped him to relax further.

For a long time he just sat there, staring at the blank opto on the bedroom wall, thinking. Eventually he rose and stripped off his tattered, stained suit. He stayed deep in thought as he let the whirlpool bath massage his body. There were no aches and pains, no bruises visible, and that was odd. There *should* be aches and pains and bruises. Not even his left arm, which had been so cruelly bent up behind him, was sore.

Just lucky, he told himself. Might not be lucky a second time.

He slipped into a robe and poured himself a tall glass of iced mint tea from the fridge while he considered how to proceed.

An hour later he sat down at his terminal and plugged in the telephone. There was some machine-to-machine talk, then the screen cleared and a pleasant woman with glasses appeared on the screen.

"Why are you requesting this leave of absence from Selvern, Mr. Abbott?"

"Personal reasons. I haven't been feeling well lately." As an afterthought he added, "Family troubles."

"I see." She did something to a keyboard out of his range of vision, glanced curiously back up at him. "You are set to leave Phoenix this coming Monday for an overseas conference and product development seminar devoted to the new LEG 6744K subchip and ring opto applications."

"I know that." Eric chose his words carefully. "I'm afraid I wouldn't be much help in my present condition. Shiraz can take my place, or Gonzalez." Neither Shiraz nor Gonzalez would be as effective as he would be, but they wouldn't hurt the conference, either.

"Death in the family?" asked the woman on screen. Eric said nothing, looked downcast. The woman checked something else, reacted to a hidden readout. "It says here, sir, that in your entire stay with Selvern you've never taken one day of sick leave until just recently."

"That's true." He was suddenly thankful for his dedication and good health. Many times he'd been tempted to take off to go camping or to a ball game. Now he was glad he'd always refused the invitations.

The supervisor's attitude certainly underwent an about-face. "Under the circumstances, even without knowing the exact nature of your problems, I think we can grant your leave, sir. How long will you need?" One hand poised to note his response.

"I'm not sure." He couldn't very well say "indefinite" but neither did he want to be too specific. "Not very long."

"A week?" asked the supervisor. "Two weeks?"

"Really, I can't say. You know how these personal problems can drag on."

She nodded sympathetically, let him off the hook. "I'll

just put it down as indefinite, sir, and when you know, please notify this office.''

"Thank you," Eric said gratefully. "I certainly will." He wanted a job to come back to.

"That's all there is, sir. As of now you're on official leave. I hope you resolve your personal problems with a minimum of discomfort.''

"So do I," he told her honestly.

The image disappeared from the screen. He swiveled his chair. He was free. It was better this way. If he'd taken off from work there might have been awkward questions. Certainly Charlie would start badgering him for reasons, and he didn't feel like giving reasons just now. No, this way was better. Let them guess what he was up to. Charlie might guess, and Gabriella might pout, but he wouldn't have to listen to either of them.

As far as setting back his career, he'd worry about that later. Surely his heretofore spotless record would bail him out this one time. He wasn't going to worry about it. It didn't matter right now. Nothing mattered right now, except Lisa Tambor.

Her face encircled his mind, a necklace of stroboscopic memories. No need now to delay, and better not to. Go to Nueva York and find some way of meeting her. If he hurried he might even be able to get back in time to make the tail end of the Hong Kong conference. There was nothing to stop him.

Only . . . one man was dead and two had tried to kidnap him, and he still wasn't sure why. Would they be waiting for him? He thought it unlikely. If they had followed up they might be waiting for him outside the Selvern Tower tomorrow. He grinned at the thought. They'd have a long wait.

Charlie's opinion still haunted him. Any sane man considering today's events would stay as far as possible away from Lisa Tambor. If that meant he was not sane, he was enjoying the feeling. Madness, like love, was positively exhilarating. Life was conventional. Only rarely did it dump genuine surprises in one's lap, and he'd been saddled with a beautiful one. He had every intention of pursuing it to its conclusion, whatever that might entail. Even at the risk of ending up like Polikartos.

How to be in such love with a barely glimpsed face? Is that all it takes to make a man throw away his life? Of course, if he did manage to meet her she'd like as not spit in his eye and scream for the police. At least that would put an end to his obsession.

The world was full of celebrities, personalities, who were very different in person than from a distance. Make-up and surgery could do wonders. He might not like her. If he was lucky he would slip away, back to his mundane existence, without arousing the ire of her associates.

It promised to be a change, if nothing else. He was actually whistling as he packed his overnight bag and loaded his clean suit with potentially useful devices. It didn't matter how long he'd be gone. Day or week or month, he always liked to travel light and optimistic.

He started to dial his travel service, hesitated. If he was being watched, his actions monitored, that might trigger a key somewhere. Better to take the tube to the airport and purchase his ticket in person. Money shouldn't be a problem. Polikartos hadn't had time to dent his accounts.

He shut down the terminal and closed up the little house. He thought of telling his neighbors of his departure, decided against it. No need to involve them. Let any visitors guess what he was up to.

He wished now that he'd read detective novels. Those were the skills he'd need in the days ahead. All he knew was that the faster he moved, the safer he'd be.

Leaving his ATC behind to further confuse the curious, he jogged down to the station. Soon he was aboard another near empty car, whistling down the tube toward Sky Harbor Airport. The tube was carrying him through a dream. He was merely an onlooker now, not a participant. The detached sensation muted his good humor.

A sudden thought made him get off the tube before it reached the airport. A detour via cab took him to a small electronics specialty house. The owner did not remember him, but upon presentation of his credentials, allowed him use of the hobby room and its services.

There he set to work with perfectly legal equipment doing something highly illegal. Only an expert could alter something as personal and secure as a credit card. It took considerable skill to imprint a different name and account number on the card without altering certain molecular structures so that the user of the card could still draw on the original account.

Five to ten years in prison, no matter how skillful the work, even though it was his own card. At this point it was all part of the adventure, and he could always change the card back when he was finished. It wasn't something for an amateur to attempt, but Eric was no amateur.

Now let the people who'd confronted him try to track him! They'd find that as far as every hotel and restaurant was concerned, Eric Abbott had disappeared. Maybe he was being a little overcautious, but he had no desire to meet the two men who'd challenged him outside Polikartos's office a second time. Adrenaline could not stop a pingun or tranquilizer dart.

He had no trouble at the airport and relaxed completely once the hypersonic transport was in the air. A window seat gave him the chance to study new green squares and circles from a hundred thousand feet up.

His first glimpse of Nueva York turned out to be something of an anticlimax. That was the trouble with the opto. It brought such sights into everyone's home. There was no mystery to the reality.

The airport itself, however, was something of a shock. Jersey Flats Terminal made Sky Harbor in Phoenix look very provincial.

There were no lurking, hulking figures waiting to jump him when he emerged from the offloading ramp, overnight bag in hand. No one bothered him as he flowed with the crowd toward the transportation depot. In dramatic parlance, it appeared that he'd managed a clean getaway.

Why, he might be able to walk right up to Lisa Tambor and ask her out to lunch without anyone's interfering! Poor

Polikartos hadn't been careful enough, that was all. In fact, he still had no proof Polikartos's death had anything to do with Lisa Tambor and the two men in the hallway.

His first thought was to go straight to the modeling agency whose address he'd found in the investigator's file. But there seemed no reason to move so precipitously. Better to familiarize himself first with the strange city.

The tube shot him rapidly 'downtown. The agency was located on North 133rd street, Harlem Tower Complex Eight. He chose a modest hotel well away from his eventual destination, in upper midtown near Central Park. The prices were appalling.

The room had a clean bed, the omnipresent opto, a nice bathroom, and no view whatsoever. That didn't bother him. He wasn't on a vacation. The rest of the day he spent cruising the streets in a cab, letting the smooth synthesized voice fill him in on locales and sights, even gliding past Harlem Eight without stopping.

He had an excellent dinner, soft pretzels in Central Park, spent half the next day at the Museum of Natural History. Three comfortable, relaxed days slipped by. Then he had his suit cleaned and prepared himself.

This time he let the cab deposit him outside Harlem Eight. The eighty-story-tall hexagon was part of a complex of eight identical towers situated on parklike grounds. It was an expensive, prestigious commercial address.

The Magdalena Agency occupied all of the seventieth floor. Even the lobby whispered money. The tiles were goldstone, there was lavish use of beveled and etched glass, and the doors leading off the lobby were etched with reproductions of works by Mucha and Erte.

Eric felt out of place. The offices at Selvern were comfortable but stark by comparison, designed to give a different impression. He was accustomed to efficient, businesslike surroundings, not ostentatiousness for its own sake.

The girl in the reception area displayed a complexion the same color as her walnut desk. She was slim and beautiful but not, Eric surmised, quite slim or beautiful enough. Certainly she didn't begin to compare to the magic image he'd seen in the retreating Cadota that was now enshrined in his memory.

"May I help you, sir?" She eyed Eric's best suit speculatively. Or maybe it was Eric she was evaluating. He didn't fit the types she dealt with daily; not handsome enough to be seeking representation, not outlandish enough to be an agent. Any moment now, he thought, she was going to ask if he had a delivery to make.

This won't do, he told himself angrily. Act like you know what you're doing even if you don't.

"I'm here to inquire about the availability of one of your models. For a series of opto commercials." He gave her his best smile.

Her estimate of him rose several notches. "I see." He wasn't sure if she believed him, but he was sure she wasn't going to take the chance of being wrong.

"May I ask who's calling and what company you represent?"

"John Frazier," he told her without hesitation. "I'm with Selvern." Up another notch.

"Just a moment, please, Mr. Frazier." She gestured toward a gold, late-nineteenth-century couch. Eric accepted the proffered seat and began thumbing through the magazines on the table nearby. They were slick and full of photographs instead of words. Photographs by full sun, photographs by candlelight, photographs by starlight. It was astonishing how many angles the human body possessed and how each could be frozen in time through the symbiosis of eye and machine.

He was enjoying himself when the woman came out to greet him. Her hair was silver shot through with streaks of blond and he couldn't tell which was natural and which dye. The same went for her expression. She was very pretty, very petite, an elf forged of stainless steel. He was immediately on guard as she shook his hand.

"Mr. Frazier? I'm Joan Candlewaif. Come with me, please." He put aside the magazines and followed her.

Her office looked out on the parkland below and Harlem

Three Tower. She settled easily into her desk. Literally into, as the entrance to the circular work station closed up behind her, sealing her inside a flat-topped plastic doughnut.

"Something to drink, Mr. Frazier? Fruit juice, coffee, tea, chicory, mineral water, soft drink, wine?"

"Nothing, thanks."

"Helaine said you represent Selvern."

"Yes, that's right."

"Terkel and Brighton are their Nueva York people."

"I'm from the coast. From in-house." He made himself sound conspiratorial. He could thank his relationship with Charlie for his knowledge of advertising, and he'd thought out his speech during his idyllic jaunt around Manhattan.

"We're looking for someone with a particular look, a special look, to pose in a series of multichannel promos for a new line of consumer electronics products. Preliminary product discussion is already underway, both in Phoenix and Hong Kong. We need someone with an ethereal, distant beauty, very futuristic." He went on to detail a long list of other imaginary requirements for the imaginary opening while Candlewaif listened intently.

Mentioning Selvern was a risk, but he had to represent something. What better than his own company? He knew Selvern and, thanks to Charlie, something of its in-house agency work. If she thought to check further she would discover that John Frazier did indeed work for Selvern Phoenix. Frazier was Charlie's supervisor. So long as she didn't request a picture he should be able to carry the deception off, for the necessary few days at least.

His well-rehearsed speech obviously impressed her. Here was a man who knew what he and his company wanted.

"Everyone's looking for that special someone with a particular 'look,' Mr. Frazier. I don't have to tell you that. Finding those faces is what makes this business exciting. We have a number of ladies who might meet your description." She touched hidden switches. A video screen unrolled on the far wall and a compact projector emerged from her desk. She started sorting through boxes of holograms.

"That may not be necessary," Eric told her. He had no

intention of spending the rest of the day trapped in the office, looking at pictures of beautiful women who meant nothing to him, could mean nothing to him. "We've done a considerable amount of research on our own and settled on a hopeful already. I know she's represented by Magdalena. I'm sorry. Perhaps I should have mentioned that earlier."

"Not necessary." Candlewaif was good at covering her surprise. "It makes my job much simpler, doesn't it? I'm glad you've selected a Magdalena model. Of course, until we discuss the details of her employment I can't guarantee her availability. Who was it you had in mind? Veronika? Senta Cross?"

"Lisa Tambor." Eric made a show of consulting his notepad.

The woman frowned. "Tambor? I don't . . . oh, yes, yes, of course I remember her. She did work for us, but very briefly, I'm sorry to say. She was very much in demand, but I always had the feeling her heart wasn't in her work, that she regarded her employment here almost as a lark, a vacation of sorts. A strange girl. Pity. She could have been one of the best."

"She doesn't work for you anymore?"

"Not for some time now, I'm afraid."

"I'm sorry to hear that."

"So were we. I don't know why she quit. We did everything we could to try and persuade her she had a great future with Magdalena. What was peculiar was that she was serious about not modeling anymore. We thought she'd been given a better offer by one of our competitors, but evidently that wasn't the case."

"Are you sure of that?"

"Quite sure, Mr. Frazier. Ours is a tight little gossipy world, you see. As soon as anyone changes agencies, it's common knowledge throughout the business. No, Ms. Tambor did not go to another agency, not here, not overseas, or I would know of it. She really did quit the business." Candlewaif smiled icily. "Found herself some sugar daddy or someone to take care of her. I suppose that's an easier career, for some."

Eric bridled at the woman's implications but said nothing. It might be true. He remembered Polikartos's words.

"Just a minute," she murmured, searching through her files. She found what she was hunting for and popped it into her projector.

The tiny instrument whirred to life and the room automatically darkened. Exquisite faces and bodies filled the screen on the wall, blurred by high speed. Gradually they slowed and poses became visible, life-size and tridimensional.

Eric's fingers tensed on his chair. It was her. There was never a doubt in his mind, not from the first diffused, artsy exposure. It was her.

"Yes, I remember her," Candlewaif was murmuring. "Very quiet girl, almost a child in some ways, quite mature in others. She seemed to know exactly what she wanted and how to go about getting it. When she got what she wanted out of Magdalena, she demanded and received her release.

"I'm not kidding when I say that we did everything we could to try and keep her with us, Mr. Frazier. We made her offers very, very few beginning models ever see, ever even dream about. She was as indifferent to the money as she was to the profession. A strange lady. She did have something. Your people certainly targeted on it, as did ours. You can see it in her holos."

You can see it on the street, in a moving car, Eric thought excitedly.

"All great models have something distinctive about them," the woman went on. "Tambor wasn't refined, but the uniqueness was there. As I said, she could have been one of the best."

There was a soft snap. The image on the wall vanished as the projector died.

"I wouldn't argue with your assessment," Eric finally said.

"I wish I could interest you in some of our other models. There's a young lady from West Africa, Sara Noba, who is quite striking and possesses much the same bone structure . . . though she's not the same girl, of course. We have other well-known models who—''

"Nothing against any of your other people," Eric said quickly, "but before we reconsider I'd like to make a try at persuading this Lisa Tambor to work for us. Selvern is one of the largest corporations in North America. Perhaps with the promise of that kind of exposure . . ."

"Tambor was interested in exposure even less than money," Candlewaif told him.

"We can offer her a great deal. Wouldn't it be worth your while if I could persuade her? It might induce her to return to the fold."

"Of course we'd like that. Unfortunately there's nothing I can do for you, Mr. Frazier. I can't give you Lisa Tambor's address. We take our models' privacy very seriously here. As I'm sure you know from your own work, the world is full of oddballs and the unbalanced. I'm not including you, naturally, but this is a policy I'm not in a position to change. The most attractive and visible men and women become targets for the most unbelievable abuse." He started to comment but she wasn't finished yet.

"If you were the chairman of the board of Selvern, or Sony, or GE, or AG Renault, I still could not give you Lisa Tambor's address. I can contact her myself and explain any proposition you wish to make to her, but in all fairness I must tell you I think we'd both be wasting our time. I doubt there's anything you could offer her that we haven't already."

"You might at least tell her of Selvern's interest," Eric said lamely. It would be dangerous to insist any further. "If she expresses an interest we can go into details. I'll be in Nueva York for another couple of days." This was said to follow form. Clearly Lisa Tambor had given up modeling permanently. But they had to go through the motions.

"Fine. If she expresses a desire to pursue the matter further we could set up a meeting. How can I contact you?"

"You can't. I'm moving around quite a bit while I'm

here. Friends one day, relatives the next. You know. How about if I get back to you around, say, Tuesday next?"

"Very well. I should have an answer for you then. I advise you to contact your people out west and tell them of this conversation, though. Then maybe we can sit down and do some real business." She rose and leaned over the desk to shake his hand. As she did so he was startled to see something else in her eyes. Her handshake was not at all businesslike.

"And if you're not busy tonight, John, perhaps you'd like to have dinner with me? I know a fine Peruvian restaurant uptown that serves a mean *huachinango asado*."

"I'm sorry," he said hastily, "I'm already committed."

"I understand." Her disappointment was plain. "Perhaps sometime next week. Meanwhile I'll see if I can make contact with Ms. Tambor for you."

"That's all we can ask for. And I promise, if you don't have any luck with her, Selvern will take another look at your list."

"Fair enough. I hope you enjoy your visit to Nueva York, Mr. Frazier."

"Thank you. I intend to."

His mind worked furiously as the robocab took him back to his hotel. He had plenty of time to think because the vehicle took an intentionally roundabout route.

It was obvious that he wasn't going to get Lisa Tambor's home address out of Candlewaif or anyone else at the agency. He could try bribing a nonexecutive. The receptionist, for example, might have access to the necessary files. She might also be an honest employee who valued her job with such a prestigious concern. That would bring police in and he could hardly risk that. Not while carrying a false identity and an altered credit card.

During his visit he'd looked for security measures. He didn't see any but didn't doubt they existed. Nor did he doubt that he could solve them, as he'd solved Polikartos's. It wasn't like he was planning to break into Winston's or Konstantin's.

The most difficult part was slipping past the human

guards stationed in the tower lobby. It was just before midnight when he strolled into the building and headed for the elevators. The guard eyed him obliquely, turned away when his console showed that the visitor had, as expected, punched the button for the third floor. There was a late-night Szechuan restaurant on the third floor.

The elevator's front doors would open directly into the restaurant. Eric had no intention of confronting a smiling maître d'. He stopped the elevator between the second and third floors while he worked rapidly with the elevator's programming. It resumed its rise a moment later and did indeed stop at the third floor. But it was the back door that opened, not the front, admitting him to the long service hallway.

Security would show that the elevator had made its proper way to the third floor. It would not show which doors opened upon arrival. Soon it was on its way down again, taking late-night diners to the lobby level or underground parking.

Eric turned and walked up the empty, dimly lit corridor. There were no surveillance cameras here. A short walk brought him to a fire stairway, and he started the long climb toward the seventieth floor. He couldn't use the elevators. There was a chance the service lifts were monitored as closely as those intended for use by the public.

There was no surveillance camera in the seventieth floor corridor either. Apparently the building's tenants had confidence in their ground-floor security and individual warning devices. Few intruders, however, had Eric's electronic expertise. The frosted doors of the agency didn't fool him for a minute, though the system, which might well have been manufactured by one of Selvern's many subsidiaries, was elegant and subtle. The beautiful glass doors functioned as a pair of enormous, flat fiberoptic systems. A steady signal ran through both doors from roof to floor. Any unauthorized parting would trigger the alarm.

He had no intention of forcing the portal. It took him a few minutes to locate the keybox hidden in the doorframe on the lower left-hand side. With his pocketful of miniaturized, specialized equipment he had no trouble bypassing the key circuitry.

The doors slid apart easily at his touch and he was careful to close them behind him. A flashlight led him to Candlewaif's office. He wasn't surprised to find her cabinetry locked, though protected by far simpler devices than the fiberoptic system that guarded the entrance.

Quicksearch brought the file he wanted to life on the single terminal screen. He ran through active clients before locating the inactive file, soon found Lisa Tambor's name. There was a Manhattan address, which he entered into his wrist terminal. Then he cleaned up, shut down the terminal, and rose to depart. It had taken less than half an hour from the time he'd entered the tower lobby. All one needed was a plan of action, a few modest skills, and a little luck.

Consequently it was a terrible shock to see the two uniforms quietly waiting for him in the reception area. One held a stun pistol loosely in his right hand while the other rested in the same chair where Eric had so recently thumbed through glossy magazines.

"Didn't sound like you were doing any damage," the woman in the chair said, "so we figured we'd wait for you."

"Look, I can explain."

"Everyone who breaks in can explain." The man gestured with the pistol. "Let's go downstairs. You'd be wasting your breath explaining to us."

A stunned Eric stood motionless while the woman frisked him quickly and professionally. She hesitated a moment, eyeing his tools admiringly, but leaving them in his coat. She didn't want to disturb the evidence.

As they left, Eric tried to penetrate the secret of the doors, wondering what he could have overlooked. He was positive he'd deactivated the alarm.

The woman behind him noticed his gaze, smiled thinly. "Oh, you doused the doors all right. A slick piece of work, that. What you missed was the carpet." Eric looked over his shoulder but saw no bulges beneath the shag.

"Pressure-sensitive," she went on, "which is why I

don't mind mentioning it. You can't avoid it even if you know it's there. Step inside and the alarm goes off downstairs. To bypass it you'd have to remove the whole carpet, because the wires don't run underneath. They're part of the weave."

Sure enough, a last backward glance revealed the occasional silver thread wending its way among the green and blue.

"Carpet plugs into the walls," the guard explained, evidently enjoying his discomfort. "All the Harlem Towers use it. What I can't figure out is what you expected to steal in there."

"Never mind," said her partner. "Let the psych cops work that one out."

Now that the initial shock of his capture had worn off, Eric felt the first stirrings of panic. His excuse for breaking and entering wouldn't sway the judge's sentence. Discovery of his altered credit/identity card would be enough to ruin his career and buy him a long jail term.

They were heading for the elevators. Over the center lift a lightbar glowed brightly. Its companions were dark. With only seconds remaining in which to save himself he reacted more from instinct than thought.

His wild swing took the guard in front of him completely by surprise. Eric didn't look very threatening, and his cowed attitude was genuine enough. The stun pistol went flying. A shove sent the woman on her backside even as she was raising her own weapon to fire.

Then he was in the elevator cab, jabbing frantically at the buttons. There was no response.

The woman sounded tired as she called to him. "You're wasting your time, sleek. Did you think we'd leave the lift free for you to use? We're the only ones who can get you down."

Frantically he thumbed the CLOSE DOOR button. The opposing panels promptly slid shut. He held the switch down while he poked dozens of floor numbers.

There was an insistent knocking from outside, hands

slapping metal. Faint voices reached him. They were angry now, not exasperated.

"Open up, sleek. You're only wasting our time, and yours."

He pressed 80 and was rewarded with a whirr as the elevator started to rise. The block only extended to floors below the elevator, and why not? There was no escape in the other direction.

He could hear the voices of his pursuers fading beneath the cab. "Come down, sleek! It's going to go harder on you!"

He ignored them. He could get out on any floor between seventy-one and eighty, but he couldn't go down. Surely they'd post a guard on every stairwell, now that it was known there was an intruder loose in the tower. The same would go for every elevator, including the service lifts.

Doors parted to admit him to the top floor, then closed. The lift whined as the cab was called downward. Soon the floor would be swarming with security personnel as the alert was passed through the complex.

He still had his tools. He could break into another office, maybe one without a pressure-sensitive carpet, but that would only delay his capture. A quick search revealed a fire and service stairwell. He went up instead of down. There was a very simple lock at the top of the double flight of stairs.

The night air was shockingly cool. Off to the south he could see the office towers of Hoboken, to the east the dark strip that was Long Island Sound. Powerful heating and cooling equipment throbbed behind him. Close by was the dark shaft of Harlem Tower Six and further off, Harlem Tower Two. He stood there trying to recover his wind and wits until he heard voices from the stairway below.

"He's got to be up here somewhere . . . we've checked the whole damn floor . . . everything's tight. . . ."

More than two of them now. That was to be expected.

"Don't take any chances with this guy . . . might be unbalanced . . . watch yourselves. . . ."

This time they'd stun first and carry him down. He

started searching his aerie, not knowing what else to do, postponing the inevitable end. The end of everything. His career, his future, his chance to see Lisa Tambor. Everything.

A faint voice shouted, "There he is!" A crackling sound, a tingle in his right shoulder that felt like his foot going to sleep, and then he was running around the outer serviceway.

Two figures suddenly appeared out of the darkness in front of him. Both knelt, holding up hands and pistols.

"Hold it right there, mister. Game-time's over."

He darted between two massive cooling units. Footsteps and voices sounded on the far side, moving to cut him off. He moved sideways between the machinery, the steady hum a pounding inside his head.

He couldn't let them catch him. Not now, not when he was so close, so near to his goal. Lisa Tambor's face hung in front of his eyes, not a quick glimpse now but a hundred different poses urging him on, the vision enhanced and multiplied by the holos Candlewaif had shown him in her office. He would meet her, Tambor, he would, and nothing and nobody was going to stop him.

"He's up this way!" Two stun beams hummed behind him, missing. Then a voice, surprised, screaming, "Don't do it!"

The barrier rimming the top of the tower was less than six feet high. Running as fast as he was able he jumped. His right foot landed on the top of the barrier and his leg muscles spasmed as he kicked off. Several screams reached him dimly together with an equal number of loud gasps.

Space. He was floating through space, hands flailing, legs kicking. Eighty stories, a thousand feet below, was the garden that swirled around the Harlem Complex.

Then he was falling, falling toward the ground, his body arcing over until he could see the trees and lights far below.

VIII

IT seemed that he hit much sooner than he should have. A moment of paralysis and then he was pulling hard, pulling himself up and over the barrier. It was identical to the barrier he'd just cleared, with one important difference: it rimmed the top of Harlem Six.

Soon he was standing next to similar cooling machinery, listening to a similar rumble and staring across emptiness at a dozen astonished faces made small by distance. He'd made it. He didn't know how he'd made it, but he'd made it. That was all that mattered now.

He looked through the webwork barrier. The sheer drop made him dizzy. Turning away, he stumbled toward the place where the stairwell door should be located, shorted the lock and raced downward, not daring to try one of the elevators.

Across the abyss Eric Abbott had just cleared the paralysis that had left him but continued to hold his pursuers. No one moved to contact security central. All eyes stared in fascination at the opposite roof. The gap between the towers spanned some ninety feet. No one could make such a jump, yet their quarry had just done so, done it without mirrors, without visible mechanical aid.

A minute ago they'd had him trapped and had closed in on him confidently. Now that confidence was gone. They'd been cheated emotionally as well as physically. Despite the loss, no one expressed a desire to continue the chase.

Several precious minutes fled before the one in charge thought to contact downstairs. More time passed as he and his colleagues tried to explain what had happened. By then Eric Abbott, taking stairs four and five at a time, had reached the third floor of Harlem Six.

He fought to recall the layout of Tower Eight. There had been windows at the end of each spokelike corridor. Tower Six was the same. He reached one window, shorted out still another lock and pushed the thick glass aside.

Forty feet below, a mature sycamore reached for the night sky with heavily leafed branches. A few strollers could be seen well away to the right, enjoying the play of fountains and the smell of night-blooming flowers. Eric took a deep breath and jumped.

Several smaller branches snapped under his weight and one gouged his cheek, but there was no blood. He came to a stop, started climbing downward. On a large lower branch he paused, looking back into the lobby. Figures were moving about, but he couldn't tell if they were visitors or anxious security personnel.

He dropped to the ground, brushed himself off as well as he could. This was the second suit he'd ruined in his search for Lisa Tambor. At least he should buy appropriate clothing.

The humor didn't last long in his mind. He was frightened, badly frightened. Not from his capture but from his escape.

He'd put down his escape in Phoenix from the two men who'd sought to question him to a sudden surge of adrenaline. No such facile explanation would serve for the jump he'd made from the top of Harlem Eight. Nothing would explain that. It was fact; he'd done it. Even more terrifying was the fact that he'd been driven to attempt it. He'd gone over the edge in more ways than one.

Yet it was as if his body, if not his brain, had known all along he could make the jump. As he forced himself to walk calmly and at a modest pace toward 135th Street, he took stock of himself. Hands, feet, body all looked normal, all looked the same.

What's happening to me? What in hell is going *on?* He'd felt the same confused terror that day back in Phoenix when he'd thrown a much larger assailant through a solid ceiling. It was much worse now.

He'd walked for ten minutes before an empty robocab hailed him. "Ride, sir?" the ingratiating mechanical asked.

"Yes. Yes, thank you." He staggered to the open door and slumped in the seat. Absently he gave the name of his hotel, dreamily pulled his wallet from his coat pocket and scanned the contents.

It was all there: everything that went to make up Eric Abbott. Employee ID card, altered credit card, driver's license, medical security, a long series of official and semi-official documents testifying to himself. To who he was . . . but not what.

What am I? The voice screamed insistently inside his head.

Blocks slid past and he didn't see the lights that came to life, turning night to day on the grounds of Harlem Complex. Didn't see the small army of security personnel that fanned out from four of eight towers to search walkways and grottoes and paths, all the places where an injured man might take refuge.

The futile hunt went on till morning. The searchers didn't find Eric Abbott, didn't find John Frazier, didn't find the man who'd made that impossible leap from one tower to another. They didn't find them because all three were sitting in a small hotel room in midtown Manhattan trying to sort themselves out.

Eric spent a long time in the hot shower, letting the water cascade down his body. He was not hurt. The remarkable jump had not strained any muscles. The water washed away dirt and sweat, but no memories.

Maybe I'd better go home, he thought. Go home while he still had his sanity, before anything else happened. Anything else? What kind of anything else? Nothing made any sense.

Waste of thought. He wasn't going home now, whether his sanity was at stake or not. Why worry about an insignificant intangible like that when you had Lisa Tambor's address?

They wouldn't warn her. There were no papers scattered on the floor of Candlewaif's office, nothing to indicate what he'd broken in to obtain. The computer file would appear to have been untouched. A check would show nothing missing.

No doubt the people who'd chased him were still trying to explain his escape. That should give the local security more than enough to worry about without wondering about his identity or motivations. Security would say no human being could make such a jump. No one but a machine, a robot. He started to giggle, clamped down on himself quickly.

Exiting the shower, he dried himself off and walked into the bedroom. In the top drawer of the single dresser were his wallet, school ring, keys, and tools. One of the tools was quite sharp. He opened it and with great deliberation ran it down his thigh. It was painful and the blood that seeped out was satisfyingly red and real.

So I'm not a machine, he thought. Thank heaven for small favors. That didn't change the fact that his body was full of surprises. Time enough to work that out later.

Had they secured a picture of him? If so it would be circulating in the police files by midday. Move fast, stay ahead of investigations and suppositions. Move fast and rid yourself of this obsession before it kills you.

Meeting Lisa Tambor should be enough. If he could get in to see her, they could have a nice chat, small talk. That would be the end of it, surely. Wasn't that how such obsessions were resolved, by confrontation with reality? He didn't think the fact that he was in love with her would impress her much, and if they finally met, that alarming emotion might leave him. She might really have buck teeth or an unbearable personality. She might smell. She just might not be a nice person. It wouldn't take very much to vanquish the illusion he'd cloaked her in.

He checked his wrist terminal and the entry so recently and laboriously acquired. There was Lisa Tambor's address. Excitement and anticipation began to push aside his fear. Events had turned mad, but the aura of romance lingered around the craziness.

It was midmorning when the robocab deposited him at the prestigious location on the East River. Nearby, the Walesa Tower rose 220 stories into the sky, the home of diplomats and entertainers. Tambor's address was in a more modest structure.

He'd eaten a good breakfast, caught up on his sleep, and dressed carefully in his spare suit. As he entered the lobby, he breathed a mental sigh of relief. Instead of a human guard the security was wholly electronic. Human guards were not much in fashion in residential buildings. They could be bribed too easily. You couldn't bribe a machine, but an expert could find other ways to confuse it.

Selvern sold such security machinery, and while Eric hadn't participated in the design of any, the basics were familiar to him. Twin video cameras ten feet above an input wall tilted down to stare at him.

"State your business, please."

"I'm from the Magdalena Modeling Agency, here to talk to a former client, Ms. Lisa Tambor."

"Ms. Tambor's residence is East Riverside Twelfth," the voice informed him. "If you'll present your credentials, sir, I will announce you."

"Thanks." Eric spoke with a calmness he didn't feel. Extracting the card he'd prepared so carefully the night before, he slipped it into the waiting slot. It was blank, but not to the machine. A mechanical gulp and it disappeared.

The card did not carry the imprint of the Magdalena Agency, since he had no idea what that might be. It did contain a rotocycling imprint which should fool the system. He stood and sweated and waited. The machine seemed to be taking an awfully long time.

Eventually the card reappeared. "Thank you, Mr. Lawson. I will announce you."

"No need for that. Ms. Tambor wouldn't recognize me anyhow." Naturally not, since he was not a former colleague of hers. If she got a look at him she might check with the agency, and that would put an end to everything. Covering his movement with his body, he slipped a second card into the slot.

"Very well, sir. You may go on up."

The card stayed in the machine. With a hum, the intricate brass and steel sculpture that blocked the lobby as efficiently as any grate parted to admit him. His heart pounded as he pressed the button for Twelve sub-T inside the wood-paneled elevator.

He stepped out into a round room, beautifully furnished in rare woods and matching fabric wallpaper. Four doors led off from the reception arch. He went to number four and pressed the greeter. Chimes sounded from inside, followed by a faint voice. "Just a moment."

There was a snap as magnetics were uncoupled. The door opened about a foot and a face so beautiful Eric's heart skipped two beats peered out at him. It was the color of cafe au lait and as delicate as spun-sugar sculpture.

"Can I help you?"

"The lobby security admitted me," he mumbled, as if seeking further assurance of his own presence. "My name is James Lawson. I'm from the agency."

"The agency." She frowned exquisitely, her facial muscles a symphony of subtle motion.

"The Magdalena Agency. You used to do work for them."

"Oh, yes. That was for such a little while. I don't understand." He had the presence of mind to say nothing. The door moved aside a little more. "You'd better come in, Mr. . . . ?"

"Lawson. Thank you." Never had he meant two words more in his life.

The floor and ceiling were curved, forming a large ellipse with the walls. Outside and below lay the East River and the towers across the water. There were no straight angles in the room. It was decorated entirely in soft curves, unthreatening furniture, and all enameled white, like a furnished egg. Round sculptures decorated the floor, paintings in circular frames startlingly colorful on the walls. There was lots of crystal.

In the white-and-crystal room the dark-skinned Tambor shone like a Burmese ruby in a necklace of diamonds. Perhaps the effect was intentional, perhaps she simply liked white, but the result was overpowering. It was hardly needed. She would have stood out as boldly in the Chinese room at the Met.

She indicated a nearby white couch. "Please sit down." He did so, trying not to stare at her too long lest he trip over the furniture, or the carpet, or his own feet. His earlier hope that on contact his obsession might dissolve itself vanished in a flood of emotion. There was nothing now she could do to mute his love for her. She was all he imagined she could be, and much more.

"Du bist wie eine Blume, so hold und schoen und rein."

"I beg your pardon?" She walked to a crystal bar.

"Old poetry," he murmured. "It means, 'Your beauty is like a flower, immaculate and fair.' "

She hesitated in the middle of pouring a glass of mineral water, eyed him confusedly. Her expression was charming, as was everything else about her.

"That's a very nice thing to say, Mr. Lawson, but a bit forward, don't you think? Certainly not professional."

"My name isn't Lawson," he blurted out helplessly. "I'm not sure what it is anymore. I'm not sure of anything right now."

Wrong, all wrong! You'll frighten her. Yet she didn't seem nervous as she sipped at her glass and looked back at him.

"What an interesting thing to say. You look like an interesting man, Mr. Whoever-You-Are."

"Abbott. Eric Abbott. At least, that's who I was last week and the week before that. I'm not so sure now. Not sure of anything except"—he was surprised how easily the words came out—"that I'm in love with you."

What her response to that declaration might be he couldn't imagine. Shock, surprise, confusion over this amorous masquerader who'd somehow gained entrance to her home. Her reaction was not what he'd expected. She put a couple of ice cubes into her glass, pulling them from a kinetic sculpture. He began to wonder if it was possible to surprise this woman.

"That's unfortunate for you, Mr. Abbott." There was real sympathy in her voice. Her eyes were sad and secret. She stood there by the bar, her body visible through the transparent crystal, and continued to watch him. She was perfectly calm and seemingly unintimidated by his presence.

She deals with these kinds of intrusions all the time, he thought suddenly. Even now a silent alarm might be at work, summoning bodyguards or security from a nearby suite or downstairs.

"I mean it." He rose. "I love you with every atom of my being, Lisa."

"Would you like something to drink?"

"No, dammit." He took a step toward her. "I know this all sounds crazy. It sounds crazy to me, too. I saw you once, in a car, in Phoenix."

"Phoenix," she murmured, making it sound like an invitation. "Yes, I was there just recently."

"In a car," he repeated. "From that moment, that glimpse, I loved you."

"Of course you did." There was no mockery in her tone. "You couldn't help yourself."

"No, I couldn't." He hesitated. "I'm not the first man to confront you with this, am I?"

She looked apologetic and much sadder. "No, not by a very large number, Mr. Abbott."

"Eric, please."

"If you like. It doesn't matter. It never matters."

"You think I'm playing at this. I've never been more sincere in my life. I've never said that to another woman."

She looked at him with a little more interest. "That does make you unusual. You don't look like a recluse. Are you telling me you've never loved another woman?"

"Not like this. No, not ever."

"I'm surprised. You're a good-looking man."

"When you said that I couldn't help but love you, you seemed very sure of yourself."

"Eric, time has taught me much about myself. I know that you had no control over your reactions. If you did, you wouldn't be here now. You're not the first, and you won't be the last. I live with this sadness always, orbited by sad-faced men."

He didn't want to listen to her. What he wanted was to sweep her into his arms and crush her to him, to hold her more tightly than he had held anything in his life. Not yet, though. The time was hardly right. Although she seemed perfectly in control he didn't want to do anything to alarm her, to make her summon the help he was sure must be close at hand . . . if not already on its way.

"I don't mind not being the first. Meeting you now, I can see how impossible that would be. But I'd like to be the last."

"That's not possible either."

"You could love me. You *could.*" Then he did take her in his arms, lifting her gently off the floor with a strength he didn't know he possessed. He moved very quickly.

She was surprised if not shocked. "Please put me down."

"I'm sorry." He let her down, turned away. "I didn't mean to startle you. I've been working very hard ever since you let me in not to startle you."

"I'm not startled," she said, and then she smiled deliciously. "No, that's a lie. I *am* startled. You don't look that strong. Not that I'm any heavyweight."

"I seem to surprise myself here lately," he murmured. His eyes rose to meet hers again. "I've come all the way across the country to meet you, Lisa."

"I've had men come from off-world to see me." By her tone he could tell she took no pride in the achievement. "What's surprising is that you've managed to confront me in my own home instead of on the street or in an office." She cocked her head sideways, tried to see past the surface of the man standing before her. She looked like a dusky little sparrow, he thought, as she stood there arguing with herself.

"You're a very peculiar man, Mr. Abb—Eric. Intriguing. That's not unusual. Most of the men who become infatuated with me are intriguing. But they're also very predictable, they don't surprise me. You surprise me."

Predictable, Eric mused. That certainly didn't fit the Eric Abbott of the past week. He'd been anything but predictable.

"You want to hear something strange," she said into the silence that ensued. Each word hit him like an axe. "It's absurd, of course, but I think I might—*could*—come to love you. That would be more than surprising. It would be truly remarkable." She turned away from him and walked to stand before the curved window that overlooked the river. It was a cloudy day. Colligatarch Weather had forecast a light rain for the mid-Atlantic region.

He followed, and when he let his hands rest gently on her shoulders, she didn't resist. She didn't fall back against him, didn't sigh luxuriously, but she didn't resist. He fought to keep control of himself.

"If you think it possible, why not let it happen?"

"I didn't say it was possible." She sounded confused and upset. "I just said it was something that could happen. It's really not possible. I'm not allowed to love. It's forbidden to me." She turned against his hands, looked up at him, and for the first time her fragile assurance showed signs of cracking. For the first time the real Lisa Tambor looked out at him through luminous, pleading eyes.

"I'm trying to make you understand something, Eric. Love is forbidden to me. I could go to bed with you. I think I'd like to go to bed with you. That kind of love is quick and mechanical and tenuous. But the kind of love you're talking about is something I can't experience."

"He said he thought you might belong to someone," Eric found himself mumbling.

"What? Who said that?"

"An . . . acquaintance. It doesn't matter now. *Do* you belong to someone? Are you married?"

She shook her head. "No. That's something else that's not permitted me." She seemed sadder than ever.

"Are you trying to tell me you're being kept by a man who doesn't love you?"

"No man keeps me, Eric. The men I dally with are chosen for me. I have no say in the matter." She gave him a twisted smile. "It's my job."

No, Eric told himself. He was not naive, but it wasn't possible. She was too fresh, too clean to be part and party to that business. "You're not a rich man's mistress, then?"

"No."

"Some kind of call girl?" He didn't care if she was, but he needed to know.

Her answer surprised him. "No, not that either. It's nothing like what you imagine."

"What else do you call it when a third party arranges your lovers for you?"

"It's not a question of money, Eric. I do it for . . . I can't tell you."

"You said it was your job!" He didn't mean to sound so sharp, and hurried to soften the words. "I'm sorry. I didn't mean it to sound like that. I'm just trying to understand."

"I'm not offended. I said it, not you. It's nothing I'm ashamed of. My work is important. But it eliminates the possibility of any lasting relationship with any one man. You must see that."

"I see only you, the woman I think I love very deeply."

"Don't talk like that," she said angrily, spinning out of his arms. "Don't say things like that to me! It's not possible, won't you listen? Not for me and not for you."

"You said your work was important," he said softly, trying another tack. "I don't understand. Important to whom? To the man or men who force these liaisons on you? That I could understand."

"They're not exactly forced on me. It's . . ."

"I know, it's your job. Did you choose it, this job?"

She didn't meet his gaze. "In a way."

"Would you like to quit?"

"I don't know. I never thought of that."

Something very strange and evil held sway over this woman, Eric decided. He found it harder and harder to keep his emotions under control.

"Now, wait a minute. This is a free society we live in. You're talking like some kind of slave."

"That's an ambiguous term."

"Really? I always thought it pretty clear-cut. You said you thought you could love me."

"I don't know, I don't know!" she suddenly shouted at him. "Why did you come here? Why are you confusing me like this?" She was on the verge of tears, but Eric refused to back off.

"Sounds to me that you need someone to talk to you like this. Sounds to me like you've been toyed with and taken advantage of for a long time."

She regained control of herself. "I like you, Eric Abbott. I like you a lot. I don't know why I should, but I do. It's crazy for me to like you this much. So help me. Stop hurting me."

"Hurting you? How?"

"By being here. By saying the things you say. That's painful enough. If I were to let myself fall in love with you, it would hurt a hundred times worse. Don't you believe me when I say it's not possible for me to have a lasting relationship with any one man? Please, leave . . . now. It's dangerous for you to be here."

Eric ignored the implied threat. Having gone through what he'd gone through to come this far he wasn't about to be put off by words. Outright hatred or dislike he could have coped with. Indeed, he'd come prepared to accept that. But this strange ambivalence on the part of the girl, this feeling she gave of being caged against her will one moment and secure in her life-style the next, not only puzzled him but made him angry. All of a sudden he wanted to help her, wanted to give her help even more than he did his love.

"This isn't right," he said firmly. "It's not right that someone else choose your relationships for you, for whatever reason. It's not the right way to live."

"It's how I live," she replied simply, indicating the room. "It's not a bad way to live."

He gestured angrily. "This is nothing. Personal freedom is everything. Tell me how I can help you. Tell me how I can free you from your prison. Because it is a prison, no matter how content you are to remain within its walls. Love wouldn't mean a damn thing if I didn't try to free you."

"Go away, just go away."

"If you're not a call girl, that means you have no pimp. *Why* can't you love me, Lisa? Tell me why. Who runs your life for you, who arranges your emotions?"

"You don't understand."

"You keep saying that. Of course I don't understand. Help me to understand, Lisa! I want to understand."

"It's not that easy. There are ramifications you wouldn't accept no matter how I tried to explain them to you. Complicated factors beyond your ability to comprehend. There are certain matters I don't understand myself. And of them all, the thing I understand least is why I'm so attracted to you. It shouldn't be possible."

"Why not? You said I wasn't hard to look at."

"That has nothing to do with anything. I'm not supposed to be *able* to love a man . . . that way. It's not supposed to be a part of my makeup. It . . . complicates everything."

He laughed aloud, unable to help himself. "Please, don't look at me like that. I'm not chiding you. So you are attracted to me, then. If you're trying to drive me away, that's a bad way to do it."

"Ambiguities again. I thought I'd put them comfortably aside. Damn you, Eric Abbott! Who *are* you, and why are you complicating the hell out of my life?"

He sighed. "Sometimes complications lead to insight." He moved back to the couch and sat down, sinking into the soft white. "I'm a junior, soon to be senior, engineer for the Selvern Corporation. I work with microelectronics, both theoretical and actual design, and application. You might call me a design supervisor. I have the ability to grasp seemingly unrelated aspects of design and pull them together. I can both design the pieces of a puzzle and explain how they should be assembled.

"I'm thirty-one years old, have never been married or even engaged, though I'm no virgin. Both my parents died when I was quite young."

"I'm sorry," she said.

"So am I. I never knew them. I've attended the University of Arizona and Colombo International Technological Institute. I hold three degrees, two advanced, and make a very good salary." He indicated the lavishly decorated chamber. "Not enough to afford anything like this, but more than enough to support a family in comfort.

"I've been told that I'm a pleasant companion, have a reasonably active sense of humor, and am not bad in bed. I'm diligent in my work, responsive to my friends, and forgiving to any enemies. President of the World Council, a prime programmer, a major opto star, I'm not, but I think I'd make you a good husband. And that's who I am."

She was shaking her head, slowly, sadly. "Eric, poor dear strange Eric. You're a good salesman, too, and modest enough. But it wouldn't matter in the least if you were an opto star, or President of the World Council. I still couldn't marry you."

"But you could love me. You've said that already."

Her hands curled into tiny fists. "I don't know. I'm not supposed to love. It interferes with my work. I've spent all my life learning how not to love."

"Complications again?" He rose from the couch. "Listen to me very closely, Lisa. You tell me that you love me. Tell me that and everything will change. I'll take care of everything. There'll be no more men you don't love, no more orders you don't want to obey. Believe that."

"Why should I? Who do you think you are? You haven't said one thing that would make me believe you can do any of that." She looked past him suddenly, toward the front door. "Please go. You say that you love me. If you love me, you'll leave."

"Why do they always say that?" he murmured wonderingly. "In all the plays and novels and opto serials, why do they always say that? I'm not going, unless you agree I can see you again." He stared at her, his soul aching. Standing in front of the window, she was silhouetted by diffused light, perfection and heaven, life's dream made real. "Tell me I can come back tonight and I'll leave immediately."

"You shouldn't. You mustn't. It hurts me already. And it will end by hurting you worse."

"Let me worry about me. As for hurting you, you've got it backward. I'm not surprised, given what you've told me about your life. We can talk about it tonight." A sudden dark thought raced through his mind. "Are you expecting someone? Do you have to 'work'?"

"No." Suddenly she sounded anxious to reassure him. "No, you don't have to worry about that. Not now, not today."

He relaxed and the cloud vanished from his mind. It was painful enough to have to consider the idea without having to hear it confirmed. "That's good."

She walked him to the door. "I wish you wouldn't come back." There was no steel in her words, none of the strength she'd displayed earlier.

"We'll talk of everything tonight," he said consolingly, "and don't worry, Lisa. Everything's going to work out all right, you'll see. I promise you it is."

"You make it sound so easy, so simple. Life isn't as simple as you think, Eric. It's infinitely more complex than you can imagine."

"I confess my ignorance along with my love," he said with a smile. "Tonight you can educate me."

"You're impossible. You won't listen and you have no common sense at all."

"Sound like a man in love, don't I? If it helps any, Lisa, I don't understand why you should have this effect on me, either. But isn't that what love's all about?"

"I don't know," she whispered. "I've never really loved anyone."

"Until now," he said, taking her abruptly into his arms.

The kiss lasted longer than he intended, certainly longer than she intended. When they finally parted there was a glimmer of something new and wonderful in her eyes. The uncertainty was still there, the old taboos and regulations, but mixed now with a faint hope and desire to believe in him, as she'd never believed in anything before. He saw it clearly and knew he couldn't let her down. Not now, not ever.

IX

HE walked all the way back to his hotel, disdaining the robocabs and public transport, enjoying the light rain that was falling. He didn't feel it. He felt nothing but joy and delight in being alive.

She'd found him attractive, had said as much. She'd said she could love him. The confrontation had turned out better than in his wildest imaginings. Where he'd been prepared to find indifference or distrust, he'd discovered warmth and love. If that one brief glimpse of her in Phoenix had captured him, her actual presence had imprisoned him forever.

No longer was she a fading, distant image. She was a real person now, one with fears and troubles of her own. They only intensified his feelings for her. Here was someone who needed not only all the love he'd kept buried inside all his life but who also needed his help and protection. She was a prisoner, there was no question of it. Though of what he still wasn't sure. It didn't matter. All that mattered was that she cared for him, if only to the point of concern for his welfare. He would settle for concern now and wait for the love he was certain would follow.

Time passed with agonizing deliberation, but he made himself hew to the schedule he'd planned. What would they do tonight besides talk? Perhaps he could get her out of that crystal-and-white cell. Dinner? No doubt she'd already dined at Nueva York's most exclusive restaurants.

What about the lower levels of Forty-second Street? Had she ever been there? Ever had a hot dog on a cold street, or satay on a stick, or rumaki by the basketful? He would try to find out tonight.

He was full of plans and forcing himself not to run as he reentered his hotel. Though he was hungry, he passed by the coffee shop. Before he did anything else he was going to lay out the new suit he'd purchased to replace the one he'd ruined during his inexplicable escape from the Harlem Tower.

The suit waited, neat and clean, on its hanger. He took it out of the closet and laid it flat on the bed, turned to go to the bathroom, hesitated. Something was wrong with the pants. He inspected them closely, couldn't find the problem. Only when he ran fingers up one trouser leg and bent over it did his euphoria evaporate and his excitement turn to apprehension.

An expert had done the work. It was very subtle, almost undetectable. The original laser stitch had been opened. Checking the other leg, he saw that it had been similarly treated, threads removed and hastily resealed. The fabric was still stiff. In another hour all signs of tampering would have disappeared.

A check of the matching jacket revealed similar treatment. There was no outward damage or signs of manipulation, only a stiff, crinkly feel to the material where it should have been soft and flexible.

Why would anyone search the seams of his clothing? He stood staring at the suit that suddenly smelled of an alien presence, then commenced a careful inspection of his room. His toiletry articles appeared untouched, except for his razor. He'd shaved twice since cleaning it last. There should be hairs in the receptacle. There were none. Someone had made another revealing mistake.

He went through the entire bathroom without finding anything else, then moved to the bedroom. Where would be the logical place, he thought? He started with the underside of the bed, found nothing, switched his attention to the small desk and its chair. They were clean, as was the opto screen and tuner. So was the back of the single picture bolted to the wall.

He found what he was looking for inside the window jamb. Very tiny, smaller than his thumbnail and about as thick as a dime. Four inches of nearly invisible wire ran from the device and clung to the outside of the aluminum window frame.

It was a marvelous bit of miniaturization, and he wondered which company was responsible for it. Wouldn't it be funny if under a microscope he found SV for Selvern imprinted somewhere on the device? Oh, very funny indeed! He might even, at some time, have aided in the design of the circuitry. It was not comforting in the least to know that the bug might be part of the family.

Another was secured to the light fixture hanging from the ceiling. Its tiny antenna ran up the side of the lighting element and curled around the tube. But the choicest surprise of all awaited him when he rechecked the desk. He'd overlooked it on first inspection because he'd been hunting for something else.

There were two pens attached to the hotel writing pad. That seemed extravagant for so modest an establishment. Both were the same shade of blue, but one had the hotel name stamped on its side and the other did not. Other than that they matched perfectly, except that the unstamped instrument's stylus was not visible. Nor was it retracted. A glance showed a tiny plastic lens. As he picked up the tiny opto camera he wondered if anyone on the other end was watching. If so, would the sudden movement of the peeper set off an alarm?

He dropped the peeper, feeling a desperate urge to get out of the room, out of the city.

Yes, get out, a loud voice screamed at him inside his head. Get out like she told you, while you still have a chance!

He fled from the room, the suit forgotten along with his other possessions. Down the hall now, ignoring the elevators again lest they be full of the owners of the bugs in his room. Having discovered him, they were likely to come for him in person now.

But who were they? Someone was going to extraordinary lengths to insure the total privacy of a very confused and, he was convinced, very unhappy young woman. Someone with access to sophisticated technology and plenty of money.

He thought again of the underworld. They utilized modern surveillance technology as readily as did the government and private industry. But usually their methods weren't as subtle as the available instrumentation. Of course, what did he know of the real underworld? He was a junior designer, a law-abiding citizen. Everything he knew he'd seen on the optotext.

Whoever they were, how had they tracked him to his room? If they'd been watching all along they would have known when he'd left Phoenix. They might have tracked him to Nueva York. But to trace him here—that seemed impossible, since he'd used his altered credit card. To find him so soon meant access to city-wide search facilities and enormous resources. And why not confront him directly? Why this sham with the spy bugs in his room?

It didn't matter now. He was out on the street and running through the afternoon crowds. Other pedestrians ignored him. People in Nueva York ran a lot.

Seeing no hint of pursuit he finally slowed to a walk. Maybe they were tracking him with relays. He found himself staring suspiciously at anyone gazing too long into store windows or at nothing in particular. Yes, a different man and woman to watch him every three or four blocks, a whole series set up to monitor his position.

But why? Why such close attention? It made no sense, no sense at all. Lisa Tambor was truly beautiful, yes, unique in many ways and everything he'd hoped she might be, but hardly worthy of this kind of shielding.

Had he pricked the jealousy of some unimaginably wealthy industrialist who wanted her for himself? Yet Lisa implied she'd had liaisons with many men. Even so, what harm could there be in her meeting once or twice with some innocent, love-struck engineer from the Southwest?

Something didn't add up. Several somethings. Usually such puzzles were glass to Eric, who amazed his friends at parties and gatherings with his uncanny ability to solve the most complex new game or riddle in minutes. A quirky talent useful only for amusing one's friends and making life a little easier. It failed him now. He had no idea what was happening.

Is this what it feels like to be hunted?

He turned a corner and in the same movement slipped into a restaurant under the cover of the busy lunchtime crowd. Hunted . . . it sounded like something from a cheap opto. If anything, he still felt more confused than pursued. Take it one thing at a time, he told himself.

If they'd located his hotel, then it was likely they knew he'd visited Lisa. She didn't know, he was certain, or she would have said something to him. Had she been trying to do that every time she'd told him to leave? He wasn't sure.

He relaxed a little as he settled into a chair behind a back corner table. How much did she feel for him? He chose to believe what he'd seen in her eyes as they'd parted instead of what she'd said with her words. Love was possible. As long as he had that hope to cling to, no one and nothing was going to drive him out of this city.

Someone was standing in front of his table. Eric knew instantly it wasn't one of the waiters.

The man was stocky and dark and of indeterminate age. He might be thirty-five . . . or fifty-five. His black hair was wavy and combed straight back from forehead and temples. The sideburns were cut short and peppered with white, as was the thin, heavily waxed moustache. Chubby cheeks and a round nose gave him the appearance of Santa Claus the morning after.

His accent was thick and vaguely Middle Eastern, each word accented as distinctively as its owner's appearance. His attire was neat and inconspicuous.

"How do you do, Mr. Abbott? My name is Kemal

Tarragon.'' He nodded toward the empty chair opposite
Eric. ''May I please sit down?''

Customers and waiters swirled behind the intruder. Eric
could not tell which, or how many, were genuine and
which in the employ of this stranger. Evidently the man
noticed his gaze.

''Not to worry, Mr. Abbott. I am alone. You could leave
if you wished, but keep in mind that I found you here. It
would be aggravating but not impossible to find you
someplace else.''

Eric offered an ingenuous smile and wished he'd had
more practice at this. ''You must be mistaken. My name's
John Frazier.''

''I must be mistaken indeed. I thought it was James
Lawson. Or was it James Frazier and John Lawson? Too
many aliases can become an encumbrance and draw attention instead of diverting it.''

Eric kept one eye on the door and freedom. ''Sorry. I'm
new at all this.''

''Then accept my congratulations. For a novice you've
done quite well.'' Tarragon nodded toward the chair a
second time. Eric waved absently at the air.

''Yes, sit down,'' he said disgustedly. ''How did you
find me?''

''You can alter many things, Mr. Abbott. Your name,
your credit card ident—'' Eric started to rise and Tarragon
put up a restraining hand. ''Please relax. I have no
intention of reporting that bit of naughtiness to the Nueva
York authorities or to anyone else who might be interested.''

Eric frowned. ''You're not with the police, then?''

''No.'' The man tried to smile ingratiatingly but his face
wasn't designed for it. ''The one thing you can't change,
or rather didn't change, is your face.''

''I'm fond of this face. It may not be much but it's done
all right by the rest of me.''

Tarragon nodded knowingly, as though listening to the
replay of a conversation heard many times before.

''You made things difficult for us. Not because you're
good at it, but because you moved fast, very fast. What

put us on to you in the first place was two badly damaged
gentlemen who had the misfortune to try to strong-arm you
back in Phoenix. I must say you don't look like an expert
in self-defense.''

"I'm not. I got lucky.''

"I'll accept that. I'm not really interested in what
happened. Clumsy, that pair. As soon as they're recovered
enough, I'm going to have them fired.''

"Those two work for you?'' Eric said quickly.

"No, not really.''

"What the hell d'you mean, 'not really'? Either they do
or they don't.''

"Not really,'' said the man with maddening assurance.
Eric let it pass.

"If you're not a cop, who do you work for? And what
do you want with me?''

"I don't want anything with you, Mr. Abbott. Actually,
I want as little to do with you as possible. Tell me, though.
What is your interest in Lisa Tambor?''

Eric had hoped this question wouldn't come up, desperately wished this man was interested in him for some other
reason. It was no good. Logic had a way of catching up
with you no matter how much you tried avoiding it. This
Tarragon talked slowly but was about as dense as vacuum.
Eric considered a number of possible fabrications and
discarded them all. Why go to all that trouble? Since he
couldn't fool the man with aliases, why bother to try with
more elaborate lies? Might as well tell him the truth.

"I'm in love with her.''

Tarragon sat and looked thoughtful. "That's most interesting. I suspected it, you know, but you shouldn't be.''

"Sorry. Life would be a lot simpler all around if I
wasn't.''

"Agreed. Aren't you going to order?'' He nudged a
menu across the table. "My treat.''

"Thanks anyway. I've kind of lost my appetite.''

"Shame. This place isn't bad if you stick to the sandwiches
and avoid the main courses. Their baklava is junk, though.''

"Tarragon's a funny name.''

"My family had a thing for spices. I have a sister named Cinnamon. My brothers and I were luckier. You can't be in love with Lisa Tambor."

"Funny. She told me the same thing."

"She told you straight, then. You have my sympathy, Mr. Abbott. Now I must ask you to pack your things and go back to Phoenix and forget all about this."

Everything Lisa had said, this stranger was repeating, Eric thought. At least there'd been no mention of the break-in and miraculous escape from the Harlem Towers. Perhaps they hadn't connected him to that yet. They still might. The two security guards who'd surprised him in the Magdalena office had taken long looks at him before he'd fled. They should be able to identify him on sight.

That hinted that Tarragon was telling the truth about not being a cop. No mention had been made of arrest. Indeed, he'd disclaimed any interest in such matters. So far there'd been no threats. Only a mild ultimatum.

"Are you sure you're telling me everything, Mr. Abbott? You came all the way from Phoenix to Nueva York because you fell in love with a glimpse of Lisa Tambor? That is a serious question, and this is a serious business. I am not ready to accept this as a simple case of postadolescent puppy love."

"Don't you think it's serious to me?" Eric half shouted, a little self-righteous anger rising to the surface. "My whole life's been disrupted, torn up."

"If it makes you feel any better, you've managed to disrupt a number of other lives as well. Important lives."

"Good. Look, I still don't understand what's going on here. What's so serious about my falling in love with Lisa Tambor? What's so impossible about it?"

"It's an aberration, Mr. Abbott."

"Not to my way of thinking."

"Your way of thinking is not important in this matter."

"Oh, really? Whose way of thinking is?"

"No need to trouble you with that. You have a nice job with the Selvern Corporation."

"What about it?" Eric said defensively.

"Big corporations have a dislike of aberrations. I know. I deal with them all the time. Why don't you go back to Phoenix, Mr. Abbott? Go back to your friends, to your nice job while you still have it."

A direct threat at last. Perversely, it made Eric feel better. He'd almost come to like this man. Disliking him was much easier.

"You'd ruin my career without explanation just because I'm in love with Lisa Tambor?"

Tarragon nodded solemnly. "I'm afraid that I would have to, Mr. Abbott. Without hesitation."

"I see." Eric seemed to consider. "I'm impressed. Impressed because you're so confident you can do it. It would take important, high-level connections. The company respects my work."

"I'm sure it does." Tarragon worked at not sounding patronizing. "But not as much as it respects the opinions I can bring to bear on it."

"I believe you. I tell you what. I will go home."

Tarragon didn't try to hide his relief. "That will be much better for you and everyone else concerned, Mr. Abbott."

"If," Eric added, "Lisa Tambor tells me to my face that she never wants to see me again as long as she lives."

Tarragon's relief vanished. "For just a minute there I thought you were going to be sensible, Mr. Abbott. It's not possible for you to see her again."

"Why isn't it possible?"

"Because Lisa Tambor's destiny has already been determined, and it does not include additional meetings with a junior designer from the Southwest. She has her work to perform."

"I'm not clear on that. What kind of work does she do?"

"Something else you need not concern yourself with. Listen to me, Mr. Abbott, when I say that I am truly sorry to have to keep you in the dark about all this, but it is necessary. Just as it is necessary that you remain ignorant on your way home."

Eric shook his head. "I never did like being ignorant. It's important to me to know what's going on around me."

"Not in this instance, Mr. Abbott. It's much better for you not to know."

"Who plans Lisa's destiny for her?"

"A judgmental question at best and another answer I cannot supply. I wish I could be more informative."

But you *are* being informative, Eric thought coldly. He just might have considered returning home, just might, if not for one thing. Tarragon's words hinted at a threat hovering not only over himself, but over Lisa as well. He was damned if he was going to abandon her to people like this Tarragon, or the types who had stalked him in Polikartos's building back in Phoenix.

"We understand something of your confusion and distress, Mr. Abbott. I can tell you that we are prepared to pay your return ticket to Phoenix. We can even explain your absence to your employers in such a way that you will not suffer from it, which is more than you can say if you return by yourself. I'm told you canceled out on a very important business trip to come here. We can fix that for you."

Power, money, information: these people have access to everything, Eric thought nervously. *Who* was he dealing with?

"Why do that for me? Because you're such nice folks?"

Tarragon let the sarcasm slide. "As a matter of fact we can be extremely nice folks. All we want is to avoid any difficulties."

Read "publicity," Eric told himself. A straight answer at last. Criminals hate publicity. It's the one weapon they have no defense against. Illegal activities would explain many things—Polikartos's death, the crude tactics employed against Eric in Phoenix, the ability to bribe executives or programmers at Selvern. He became aware that this man might be ready to have him hustled into a waiting vehicle outside the restaurant, to take him to a quiet place where less polite forms of persuasion might be utilized.

Lisa must be some important mobster's unwilling mistress, or even worse. He suggested as much to Tarragon.

The amused response was not expected. If Tarragon was lying, he was doing so most effectively.

"Your inferences are hilarious, Mr. Abbott, though given the confused sequence of suppositions under which you're operating, I suppose I shouldn't be so surprised. You have to excuse me."

"You'll have to excuse me, too," said Eric, suddenly angry. It seemed his opponents held all the cards, and he was tired of playing the joker. "I'm not going. I'm not interested in your one-way ticket, your threats, or your implied omnipotence. Go ahead and get me fired if you can. It's only a job. With my qualifications I can get another anywhere."

"You think so? Anywhere you apply you'll find our comments waiting in personnel files."

"Sorry, I don't buy that. Pardon my pride, but I don't think you have that kind of leverage with everyone. I'm too good at what I do, and what I do is mighty valuable. You can't buy off or intimidate every advanced electronics manufacturer in the world. There are always the socialist democracies, and the off-world independents on Mars and Luna and Titan.

"You know something else? Even if you could, I still wouldn't go back. I don't like being pushed around, Tarragon."

"So the two back in Phoenix found out. There are other ways of pushing, Mr. Abbott."

"Not me. You're not pushing me out of Nueva York and you're not pushing Lisa and me apart."

"Lisa-and-you now, is it? You really think you're in love with the woman, don't you?"

"I don't have to think about it."

"Maybe you're right. Maybe it is real love. It's not my job to decide." He paused a moment. When he spoke again, his demeanor underwent a radical shift. Instead of demanding and threatening, it was almost as if he was pleading.

"Mr. Abbott, you strike me as a nice young fellow. *Lütfen* . . . please, continue with your bright future. There are five billion-odd people on this planet. Two and a half billion are women. Surely among all those you can find someone other than Lisa Tambor to become infatuated with? You are good-looking, intelligent, you make nice money. I should have made such a living at your age. Also, I rather like you."

"Sure you do."

"No, damn it, I *do* like you. Your persistence does you credit and you've shown ingenuity and courage. I hate to see such attributes thrown away on a pipe dream. It doesn't matter whether you love Lisa Tambor, or whether she somehow comes to love you. What matters is that it matters to others. People in the position to have their desires carried out. People who won't be as understanding of you as I'm being right now.

"Do go home, Mr. Abbott. Forget about Lisa Tambor. Hold on to your memories and get on with your life. Before I met my present wife I was deeply in love several times. Each time I was convinced it would kill me to give up the woman I was in love with that day, that week, that month. Life isn't like that, Mr. Abbott. You have choices. Make the right one now."

"Don't lecture me on life, Tarragon."

"Why not? I've seen a great deal more of it than you, Eric Abbott. You could find far less understanding lecturers. Accepting that you may be in love with Tambor, why can you not accept that you can fall out of love with her? A little work on your part, a little pain, and all will be forgotten." He stared earnestly at the young engineer.

"We could do more than pay your ticket home. There could be respectable financial remuneration for your"—he smiled only slightly—"emotional upset."

"You can't push me out, so now you're trying to buy me out."

Tarragon leaned back in his chair, shaking his head. "You just won't let me help you, will you, Mr. Abbott?

You intend going on with this journey into the unknown even if it means sailing over the edge.''

"Even so," Eric agreed, nodding slowly.

"I don't understand you. You are part of a business where common sense and logic are employed to the utmost every working day. Yet in your personal affairs you act inimically to them."

"I'm in love with Lisa Tambor," he said simply.

"Look, we just went—" Tarragon cut himself off. "Nothing I can say will change your mind, will it?"

"I was wondering when you were going to realize that."

"I had hopes," he muttered. "Stubborn, so stubborn."

"It's been a saving quality. Other designers would get frustrated by their inability to solve a particular problem. I never did." He smiled thinly. "You see, I'm not inimical to all the qualities that have made me a success."

"Enough of them." Tarragon rose and Eric tensed. "Enjoy your food, Mr. Abbott. I told you, I'm not a cop." He sounded irritated now, though whether at Eric or himself, Eric couldn't tell. Perhaps both. He spoke to himself as much as to Eric.

"I tried. I did what I could. They'll be disappointed, but I can't help that. It's out of my hands now. I can't say it was nice talking to you, Mr. Abbott, but it certainly was interesting. I can't help you anymore."

"I don't want your help. Is that how you helped Polikartos?"

"Who?" Tarragon frowned, then remembered. "Oh, yes. I suppose one could blame him for all this. I didn't like him. You I like."

"Did you order his death?"

"It's time for me to go, Mr. Abbott. You're certain I can't buy you a ticket back to Phoenix? First class?"

"Not right now," said Eric with enforced casualness. "Get back to me in a couple of weeks. Maybe you can buy me two tickets."

"That's really the saddest part of this, the fact that you really believe there's some kind of possible hope for you.

It's insane for you to love Lisa Tambor. No matter how much you love her, she can't love you.''

"We'll see about that. This morning she was in my arms, and nothing seemed impossible. I don't expect you to understand that, Tarragon, because despite your carefully acquired veneer of chumminess, you're far more cold-blooded than I could ever be.''

"Good-bye, Mr. Abbott. Enjoy your meal.'' He turned and made his way through the crowd toward the street.

Eric sat a long time at the table. No one eased past him to spike his water glass or remove him from his chair. There was no rear entrance to the restaurant, and in any case, it would be safer to step out onto the busy street than retreat to some dark alley where he could be spirited away out of sight of encumbering witnesses.

He spent the rest of the day wandering through the Museum of Science and Industry, hugging shoals of exuberant schoolchildren, listening with half an ear to the patronizing spiel of the guides as they tried to explain insect wings and dinosaur bones to their enthralled charges.

When the clock crept up on evening, he exited the old stone complex, afraid of waiting until dark. He didn't think he was followed, and he took the precaution of changing tubecars and cabs several times.

He saw animosity now in every face, viewed anyone who happened to glance in his direction with suspicion. Were they still watching him? It seemed unlikely they'd decided to leave him alone, but Tarragon had been so ambiguous that he couldn't be sure. Was he waiting, giving Eric a last chance to change his mind? Or was that just wishful thinking?

Of one thing he could be sure. His freedom was circumscribed and his hours numbered. Better then not to linger on paranoid thoughts.

X

NO one confronted him when he emerged from the tube chute and walked the last block to Lisa's building. Nor was there anyone waiting to accost him in the lobby. Once again he was grateful for the electronic doorman, whose memory would encompass only residents and regular visitors. There was no fear in him as he approached the flat, glowing wall and its stereoscopic eyes.

"Can I help you, sir?" The voice was as pleasant and polite as it had been on his previous visit.

He struggled to conceal his nervousness. "Lisa Tambor, please."

"Who shall I say is calling?"

"Eric Abbott."

The machine processed, since it evidently and expectedly had not stored his identity in its file. "If you'll wait one moment, please, sir."

He turned to stare at the glass entrance to the building. Any second now he expected Tarragon to rush in, accompanied by a coterie of muscular, heavily armed, blankfaced men, to escort him forcibly to the airport. His concern was reinforced by the delay. It seemed the machine was taking much longer than necessary, though the delay was likely only in his mind. Since he'd left the museum the world had slowed down. Every step was taken through wet concrete, every word slowed down by half.

Off in the distance he heard the doorman's voice. "I'm sorry, sir. Ms. Tambor does not wish to be disturbed."

"Did she say that?" he asked bluntly, all thoughts of diplomacy fled. It would be wasted on the machine anyhow.

"Yes sir, she did."

"Try again, please. That's Lisa Tam-bor." He supplied the codo number.

A brief pause, then, "I'm sorry, sir, she does not wish to be disturbed."

"Tell her that I'm not leaving until I see her."

"As you wish, sir." Another, longer wait, and the reply, "She requests that you leave, sir. I am not equipped to compel you, but I am to add that she asks this out of concern for your own safety and well-being."

"Tell her it's her safety that concerns me right now, not mine. I'm not leaving until she sees me." Were those shapes milling about just outside the main entrance watching him covertly now, or were they just passersby lingering in the shelter of the drive-up, staying clear of the light drizzle that had begun to fall? He kept his eyes on the doorway.

"She asks me one more time to request that you leave, sir."

"I will not."

"Then I am instructed to allow you up."

"Allow me, then."

"Very well, sir. The elevators are—"

"I know where they are."

The decorative grillework parted to admit him. As he waited for the lift, he kept his attention on the entrance. He stepped into the cab without any sign of pursuit, however.

I've gotten this far, he told himself tightly. This far. Let me see her again, let me touch her one more time, and nothing, nothing, will put us apart!

What peculiar thoughts for a sober, stable design engineer. He tried to make the cab rise faster, found himself leaning against the doors as it slowed. He peeked out cautiously into the circular lobby chamber, found it deserted. No one was waiting for him.

The doors started to close and he darted out, walked quickly across the thick carpet to touch the chimebell outside Lisa's home. Again the minutes stretched interminably; again he feared he'd gained this much only to be denied sight of her at the final moment.

He need not have worried. The lock went *snick* and the door moved aside. He stepped in fast, fearful that even then a hand would reach out to grab his collar and yank him away. The door closed softly behind him.

Immediately he saw the evidence of a profound internal struggle on her exquisite face. She looked drawn, tired, but not angry. Obviously his presence was hard on her. She'd tried very hard to send him away.

"You shouldn't have come back," she told him, confirming all his thoughts. "Eric, you shouldn't have come back."

Eric, he thought with a surge of pleasure. Still Eric, not Mr. Abbott. Never again, Mr. Abbott.

He followed her into the living room. Through the broad window the far side of the East River was ablaze with light.

"There was no way I could not come back, Lisa." He reached out to pull her to him. She moved away, agitated, anxious. He forced himself to hold his emotions in check.

He was totally unprepared for the violence of her outburst.

"It's all wrong! You *can't* be in love with me!"

"We've been through that before," he replied quietly. "I am in love with you. And I think you're in love with me."

"No! I'm not in love with you! I'm not. It's not possible. It's not allowed."

"It *is* possible!" he yelled back. "And as far as this business of it's being 'allowed' is concerned, that's bullshit. There are no slaves anymore. Are you talking," he said with sudden insight, "about some kind of formal contract?"

"Something like that," she murmured, lowering her voice and not looking at him.

"Well, if that's all that's bothering you, I'll buy it up. Whatever the amount is, don't worry. I have a lot of ready credit and an excellent rating. I don't give a damn how much is involved. We'll burn it together and scatter the ashes."

She shook her head sadly. "You don't have that much money."

"You'd be surprised at my resources."

"No, Eric, you don't have that much money. No one has that much money."

Her sudden calm resignation unsettled him. "There are other ways. Contracts can be broken in court. Especially if it can be demonstrated that they were signed under duress."

"But there was no duress involved."

"Maybe not," he said reluctantly, refusing to concede the possibility, "but you're sure living under duress now. Aren't you?"

"Please don't quiz me, Eric." She fell limply onto the couch. "I'm so tired. All this has been very hard on me. I'm so confused. I don't know what to think anymore. Nothing is making sense, and it always has."

"Good!" He sat down next to her, took her hands in his. This time she didn't try to pull away. "You're tired, confused, don't know what to do next. You know what that sounds like to me?"

"What?"

"It sounds to me like someone in love."

"You are impossible. You just won't listen. I'm trying, to save you and you won't listen. I suppose you can't help yourself. But the others always listened to reason. It took longer with some than with others, but never this long."

He ignored the implications. "I don't want to help myself. Lisa, I don't know how well you've been sheltered or isolated or protected or what, but it's pretty clear to me what's happening here. You're being manipulated as well as intimidated. You're entitled to run your own life, and no piece of paper or file can take that away from you. You can do anything you damn well please, and that includes falling in love. No contract can prevent that."

"You don't know," she said with great earnestness. "You can't see it's not possible. You don't have all the relevant facts, Eric."

"Then give me the facts. Facts I can deal with calmly."

"I wonder," she murmured. For the first time since he arrived, he thought he detected a hint of a smile. "If you could, you wouldn't be here now."

"Love isn't sensible, Lisa. Tell me one thing and never mind all the rest. Do you love me?"

"I . . . can't." She didn't look at him. "It's not allowed."

"To hell with whether it's 'allowed'! His grip tightened on her wrists. "Do . . . you . . . love . . . me?" When she didn't reply, he phrased it differently. "Tell me that you can't love me."

"Eric, I *can't*. I can't! But I think . . . I think I must." Her voice was breaking, full of wonder and amazement at the unexpected confession. "I think I do."

He moved a little closer to her. "That's all that matters, Lisa. That's all I want to know. Forget about your past, your present. I don't care what you've done, or where you've been, or what you've signed your name to. If you love me, everything's going to work out all right."

"It won't, Eric," she whispered. "It's not enough." She was clearly frightened now, and not just for him. Now she seemed afraid for herself.

"It *is* enough. Believe it. Believe in me, in us." He pulled her to him. When their lips touched this time, she let herself melt into him. There was no restraint, no testing now. No holding back. She'd committed herself.

"How very touching."

They turned sharply to stare across the room. Tarragon stood in an arched doorway.

"Touching and foolish." He'd been leaning against the jamb. Now he stood straight.

Eric wasn't really surprised to see him. Tarragon walked into the living room. As he did so several other large men filed in behind him. Two moved to stand in front of the main door while their counterparts hurried to block the balcony. They took up their assigned positions confidently and waited for additional directions from their boss.

"So it was you all along," Eric said. "So you're the one who's keeping . . ."

Tarragon shook his head. "No, I'm only an employee,

Mr. Abbott. As is Ms. Tambor. I am sorry. I thought it wouldn't come to this, but you insist on sticking your nose into business that doesn't concern you. Business you have no business knowing anything about. I don't know what's to be done with you. What would you suggest?'' He quickly raised a hand when Eric seemed ready to reply.

"No, too good a straight-line.'' His eyes narrowed as they moved to the woman curled tightly now against Eric. "Go to your bedroom, Ms. Tambor.''

She stood up, said meekly, "Yes sir.''

Mouth agape, Eric tried to hold her back. "No, Lisa. You don't have to.''

Her expression was as mournful as a wounded manatee. "I do have to, Eric. I tried to tell you. Oh, how I tried to tell you!'' She sounded hurt for both of them. "But you wouldn't listen to me.''

"Lisa!'' he shouted. She didn't look back but dashed across the floor and slammed the bedroom door behind her. Internal hydraulics prevented any loud noise.

Every man in the room had watched her go. Now they turned less admiring stares on Eric. He sat frozen on the couch, staring at the silent door. There were no words to describe the pain inside him.

Hadn't she just confessed her love for him? Well, almost, anyway. Hadn't he just held her in his arms? She'd responded to him, physically and emotionally. It *wasn't* impossible!

What kind of hold did Tarragon and those he worked for have over her? His pain turned to anger. Drugs? Maybe they had her hooked on some powerful narcotic and she feared losing her only assured source of supply. Or perhaps it was some subtle kind of hypnosis. There were ways of controlling a human being that were not talked about on the opto meditext.

He stood up, his fingers clenching and unclenching. "How do you do it?'' he whispered tightly. "How do you come off ordering her around like that? What have you people done to her?''

Tarragon ignored all the questions. He was not as polite as he'd been in the restaurant.

"Are you quite happy now, Mr. Abbott? Did you have your little rendezvous? Did you enjoy it? I hope so. It's going to cost you. How much and in what way, I don't know. That's not my decision. But something's going to have to be done to rectify the damage you've done."

"Look, if it's a matter of money . . ."

Tarragon grinned mirthlessly. "Money. Why does the average citizen always think in terms of money? *Reductio ad absurdum*. It's not a question of money. Never was. No, you've caused problems for people who prefer things to go smoothly. The worst part of it is you've managed to confuse and upset that young woman." He gestured toward the tightly shut bedroom door. "That's going to trouble a great many people. I'd like to know how you managed it. They're going to want to know."

"You've been watching," Eric said quietly. "You've been watching since I got here."

"Yes, I've been watching. D'you think I'm no good at my work?"

"Did you enjoy it?" Eric asked nastily.

"Not a bit. Nor did I dislike it. It's all part of my job. I wish you'd understand that. I'm not paid to make value judgments, Mr. Abbott. Just to carry out directions. Like my subordinates." The four men who'd followed him into the living room shifted their stances slightly, commenting without words.

"These are not a couple of ignorant thugs, Mr. Abbott, like the two you encountered in Phoenix. I don't think you can make much trouble for them. For your own sake and good health I'd advise you not to try."

Eric listened but didn't hear. No way was he leaving Lisa in the company of these people without putting up a fight, however desperate, however futile. He thought of making a run for the bedroom door. Would Lisa let him in? Would she help him? From the manner in which she'd reacted to Tarragon's command, he doubted it.

She said he'd confused her. Tarragon had just finished

saying the same thing. Did she love him or not? Or had she simply mouthed the words, perhaps for Tarragon's benefit? His triumph of moments earlier had been dumped indifferently at his feet. He almost looked forward to the coming, pointless fight. It would be a pleasure to incur some pain that might drown out the pain he was feeling now.

"You're an interesting man, Eric Abbott," Tarragon was saying, "but not interesting enough to occupy me further. I have other business that needs taking care of. I should have pegged you for a fanatic earlier and had you picked up outside the restaurant."

"You wouldn't have done that," Eric told him. "Too many witnesses."

"Perhaps. You learn fast, Mr. Abbott. Not that it's going to do you any good. I offered you safe passage out of this, practically begged you to leave. You wouldn't listen to me."

"And what now?" Eric asked him. "Do I end up like Polikartos?"

"I don't know. I hope not. There will be a lot of questions first. After . . . I don't know. What happens from now on is out of my hands. I take no responsibility for it. You're responsible for whatever happens. You had several chances to climb out of the hole you've dug for yourself, and you've persisted in digging it deeper. Whether grave or metaphor, I don't know."

"Lisa," Eric called toward the door. "Lisa, come out."

"You're a professional man," Tarragon was murmuring. "You understand my position."

"Lisa, come on out!" Suddenly it occurred to him there might be others in the bedroom. They might have clamped a gag on her, might be holding her back. There was no way to tell. There was only the blank door and Tarragon's four men moving toward him, spreading out to take him from four sides. He stepped up onto the couch, trying to watch all of them at once.

Tarragon looked disappointed; his subordinates, unconcerned. Eric abruptly decided one of two things would now happen: either he would somehow make his escape and get to the bottom of all this, or else these four would beat the crap out of him.

"C'mon then," he said encouragingly, teasingly, making a rude gesture with one hand.

"We're coming," said one of the men in a flat, unpleasant voice.

"Will you come along nice and quiet, Mr. Abbott?" asked another. "This is your last chance. We don't want to hurt you."

"But I want you to hurt me," Eric told him with a grin. "Come on, try to hurt me. Maybe I can hurt one or two of you before you take me out."

"I don't think so, Mr. Abbott." The speaker looked to Tarragon for instructions, commented, "This guy's nuts, you know?"

"I think not, Jerome, but as I've told him, analysis isn't our department. Try to keep him as intact as possible, okay?"

"If you say so, sir." The one named Jerome was now the nearest to Eric. He stepped forward quickly and reached for Eric's right leg. The others moved an instant after, the well-trained team rapidly tightening the circle.

"Don't make this hard on yourself, Mr. Abbott," Jerome said as he touched Eric's leg.

Eric swung an arm downward, intending to knock the other man's arm aside. There was a muffled snap, thoroughly sickening for so slight a sound. To his credit, Jerome didn't scream. His face contorted and he clutched at his shattered right wrist. At the same time the other three jumped on their quarry.

Eric found himself going backward over the couch. Two thick arms locked around his neck while the other pair fought to get his arms and legs under control.

He kicked out blindly. One of the men went flying, slammed into the ceiling. He hung spread-eagled and imbedded in the fiberfill insulation like a fly in amber, staring blankly at the floor. Either the ceilings here were thinner than those in old buildings in Phoenix or else he'd kicked harder. Eric didn't know. He didn't know a damn thing, except that he had to get away from this place and these men so he could save Lisa.

His head jerked backward as the man who had him around the neck yanked hard. Convulsively he tried to pull against the pressure. His neck snapped forward and the man who'd been trying to cut off his wind flew over him, over the couch, spinning and tumbling like a rag doll. There was a tremendous crash as he went through the safety glass of the balcony doors. Splinters flew everywhere and for a few seconds the white room was full of flying diamonds mixed with blood. Eric felt as if he were drifting inside a kaleidoscope, full of bright, colorful destruction. Around him people were yelling softly. It was carnival time and he was with Charlie and Gabriella.

They were on a ride called Moons of Saturn, in a little plastic car that simulated zero-gee. As it went every which way at once, they could look out through the transparent acrylic and see the lights of the state fair mesh with the sky. Machines and kids and hawkers and carnies filled the air with an undisciplined tintinnabulation while in the distance the white was as bright in his eyes as in his ears.

The man who'd gone through the balcony doors vanished. He might have screamed once as he fell eighty floors toward the East River.

The one remaining thug hung on to Eric desperately now while Jerome raised his good hand. The heel of his palm moved in a straight thrust toward Eric's nose, intent on shattering bone and sending the fragments into his brain.

Off in the white distance Eric thought he could hear Tarragon shout, "Don't kill him!," but Jerome wasn't listening to his boss anymore. All sense of civility and dark humor was gone now, destroyed as thoroughly as the glass doors and two other men.

The palm made contact. It certainly should have killed him. Instead Eric felt only mild discomfort near the center of his face. His nose did not break, did not even bend.

Jerome pulled back, voiceless now. Eric found he was

sickened by the carnage around him. Blood dripped onto the white carpet from the man still imbedded in the ceiling. He reached up and pulled the last man off his back, threw him into the retreating Jerome. The impact sent them tumbling into the crystal bar. Glasses jumped off shelves and bottles fell over, spilling golden fluid. The wine dispenser jammed in the OPEN position, and claret poured in a steady stream across the floor, less viscous than the blood it mixed with.

Something stung him in the left buttock. He jerked around to see a now transformed Tarragon standing behind him. As he stumbled clear Eric reached down and yanked out the hypodermic. A pressure syringe: no needle. It looked like a toy. He pinched it to see if it was real. It broke beneath his fingers. That was funny, because it was high-impact plastic. Can't trust any manufacturers these days, he thought hysterically.

Tarragon was watching him closely. As Eric continued to stand on the couch and smile back, Tarragon's expression of uncertainty was replaced by one of utter terror. His composure was gone.

"I'm going now," Eric told him quietly. "I'm not taking Lisa, because I'm confused and I don't know what I'm going to do next, and I don't want to chance her getting hurt. But you can't keep us apart. You can't keep us apart."

. "You should be on the floor," Tarragon was mumbling. "You should be half-dead and unconscious. There was enough TLC in that syringe to put a hundred men down. Why the hell aren't you unconscious?" He made it sound like an accusation. Eric almost felt like apologizing.

The dream-state persisted as he stepped down off the cushions. Reality was something fondly remembered. "I'm going now," he said again. The door was locked from the outside. "That's a neat trick," he told Tarragon, who was staring at him wide-eyed. "How'd you do it?"

A thin trickle of spittle clung to a corner of Tarragon's mouth. He didn't look very confident or sophisticated just then.

"You should be unconscious," he said still again.

Eric had no answer for the recycled comment. He put a hand on the door handle and gave an experimental tug. Something inside moaned. The handle was welded in place and so were the security hinges. It was the lock that finally gave, with an explosive *ping*.

A startled curse sounded in the lobby as the lock burst from the door and shot across the chamber to ricochet off the far wall. Now the door opened normally, Eric thought as he stepped out.

There were three more men waiting for him. They looked surprised to see him unescorted. From behind Eric, Tarragon suddenly started shouting.

"No hands! Don't try to touch him! Shoot him, shoot him!"

At this the men backed off warily and drew small pistols. Eric walked blithely past them and thumbed the elevator call, not caring much what happened now. Nothing could happen or it already would have, wouldn't it? Couldn't it? A giggle rose in his throat, and he rushed to smother it. Behind him the three men eyed him confusedly as he waited for the elevator.

Tiny pins pricked his back and legs and a muscle twitched once in his neck. He ignored this as he stepped into the elevator. More curses sounded behind him. As he turned in the cab he had a last glimpse of three startled faces. There was a whirr as the doors closed and the descent commenced.

He used the time to pick the hypo darts out of his back, thinking crazily that the minute holes might not show up on his new suit. As he held one of the tiny syringes up to the elevator light he could see a residual smear of blue liquid still left inside. Idly, he wondered what it was. A narcoleptic similar to the stuff Tarragon had injected into his backside? It didn't matter, because it had no effect on him either.

Far above, Lisa Tambor lay motionless on her bed. During the sound of fighting in the living room she'd held herself and cried.

Then the unexpected: silence. More unexpected still,

Eric's voice in the silence, saying calmly, "I'm going now." That's when the tears had stopped, to be replaced with first confusion and then a desperate, rising hope.

Maybe it was at that moment she realized she really did love him, impossible as it seemed. The realization struck in the face of everything she knew and went against everything she stood for, everything she was. But there it was.

"I did love you, Eric." She said it because she wanted to hear herself say it and because she knew with equal certainty she'd never see Eric Abbott again.

They could order her to go to her room and stay there, but they couldn't keep her from thinking, and they couldn't keep her from feeling. At least she could take that wonderful feeling, that forbidden, impossible love, with her wherever she went. It would be nice to have that, even if she couldn't have him.

It was as impossible as she'd told him it was.

Then she'd heard Tarragon screaming and yelling. He sounded worried, and that gave her pleasure. She'd never liked Tarragon much, though he'd never been anything other than deferential and polite to her. She didn't like any of the people she worked for, even if that was silly and counterproductive, as the psychs told her. Actually it was indifference more than active dislike. There was no reason to hate them. No reason at all.

There were only two waiting for him in the lobby. Tarragon must have finally gathered enough of his wits about him to call downstairs.

Interesting that they think this necessary, Eric mused. Three lines of defense, just in case. Tarragon wasn't taking any chances.

The decorative grille which divided the elevator bay from the outer lobby was closed, locking him in. He didn't know if the two who confronted him were male or female, because he couldn't see their faces. All riot-control suits were built with one-way glass in the helmets.

They turned toward him immediately. Yes, they'd been informed of his escape. The suits were silver, striped and marked in red. They whined as they trundled toward him, the tiny servo motors in the armatures and leg joints responding instantly to the muscular movements of the bodies within. Metal fingers reached out for him.

Eric watched the news and had seen such suits in action. One man in a riot suit could disperse or otherwise incapacitate a crowd by himself. The operator inside the suit was protected from weapons advanced as well as primitive, while the servomotors gave him enough strength to manhandle vehicles as easily as people.

When Eric tried to dart past the first, the second reached out to grab him around the waist. A steel cable emerged from beneath the right arm to whip several times around his midsection.

Reaching out and back he grabbed hold of the cable and pulled. Even in his dream-state it required a conscious effort. Riot suit and operator rose off the ground. It was so easy to use it like a flail to hammer away at the other. There were no screams from inside the soundproofed suits, so he battered at the first until the metal split at several joints and the armatures were jammed.

As he let the second suit fall to the ground, it reached metal fingers toward his face. He grabbed it with his free hand, pulled, and twisted. Servos squealed and oil spurted across the immaculate marble floor of the lobby. Then the joint exploded. When he let it fall, it hung limp and useless, dripping lubricants.

The other arm was now digging into his shoulder, motors humming under the overload. His bones should have snapped. Instead, he felt only a light pressure. Idly he reached up and banged away at the metal with his bare hand until it fell away.

Lifting the suit and operator inside by the cable, he spun it over his head. It picked up speed like a rock on a string, until the lobby was filled with a roar like helicopter blades. He planned to throw it through the sealed grille. Suddenly the street beyond the entrance was full of flashing blue and red lights and he could see additional riot police hurrying toward the building. Some were clad in suits like the two he'd just disabled while others carried very large weapons.

So instead of heaving the riot suit at the grille, he made a half turn and threw it toward the two-story high glass wall that delineated the far end of the elevator bay. Traveling at tremendous speed, the heavy suit snapped free of the restraining cable and smashed through the thick glass, the panels making a deafening racket as they came crashing down to the unyielding floor.

Now he could hear shouts and yells behind him as he ran for the gap. There were buzzes and pops as guns were fired in his direction. Something stung his right side once, twice. He ignored it and jumped through the opening.

How far the jump carried him he couldn't tell. Twenty feet outward, thirty, a hundred or more; he couldn't have said as he soared through the darkness, arms flapping, legs kicking. As he described a long arc, he discovered that someone had stolen the earth. Instead of grass or decorative stonework or gravel there was only another second or two of falling.

Then he fell through a sheet of undulating black ice and disappeared.

The chill of the East River acted like a tonic on his system. Fear and wonder gave way to fresh determination. He kicked hard, gasping, and sucked air as he broke the surface.

Across the river the towering walls of light blinked uncaringly down at him, advance guard of the electronic Stonehenge that was Queens. As turned a slow circle in the water, he caught sight of the building he'd escaped. He'd landed well out in the river.

Tilting his head back, he saw that the lights were on in maybe half the high-rise homes. Somewhere up there, Lisa. Next time he would have to plan their rendezvous with much greater caution, think it out in more depth. He had a lot to think about.

Voices, loud and upset, drew his attention to the bank above. Drifting and thinking, he decided, could be dangerous to his health. The pursuit had followed him through the hole he'd made in the glass wall, fanned out to inspect the landscaped garden he'd jumped over. Powerful lights probed the well-manicured bushes and trees, crawled up the side of the building. None sought shapes in the water yet. That would come soon.

Taking a deep breath and arcing his back like a dolphin, he went under the surface and started swimming upriver. The water was clean and cool around his body, soothing and unthreatening. He'd always been a good swimmer and he pushed on until his lungs threatened to burst.

When he stuck his head out into the night air the next time, coughing and spitting out river, there was no sign of pursuit. In fact, the residential tower itself lay out of sight downriver. He'd covered far more distance underwater than he'd estimated.

He repeated the dip and swim several times until he was convinced he was near mid-uptown, then swam for shore. There were no docks or industrial buildings here. Manhattan was all residential or office blocks. No one saw him climb the boulders that formed the breakwater.

He sat sharing his seat with curious rock crabs as he caught his breath. A different, evaporative chill replaced the cold of the river. It was vital to get out of his wet clothes, and fast.

A pedestrian park bordered the river where he exited, neat parkland dominated by maples and hybrid elms. He guessed he was close to 102nd Street. Couples holding hands passed by as he ducked into the bushes. Once a police car slid softly past, its electric engine rumbling with stored power. The occupants did not look grim or anxious. No general alarm had been sounded, then. The more he thought about it, the less likely it seemed.

Whoever Tarragon took orders from didn't want publicity, he remembered. The lower police ranks might not even be notified of this evening's events.

Then he noticed the drunk sprawled on the grass behind the park bench. The inebriate was neither bum nor plutocrat, just an overindulgent citizen too long away from hearth and home. He was a little taller than Eric. As Eric

approached, the man mumbled something about his god-
damn boss. A middle-managerial type, Eric decided. Selvern
was full of such gray personalities.

He hesitated, the thought of what he was about to do
disturbing him much more than the havoc he'd wreaked
back in the tower. This man didn't intend him any harm.
But Tarragon and the police hadn't left him with much
choice.

So he walked over to the drunk and said gently, "Excuse me, but I have to do this." The man stared up at the
soaking-wet apparition and gaped. Probably he thought he
was looking at a fellow celebrant. Certainly Eric didn't
look like a mugger.

The man said nothing as Eric put an index finger in the
hollow of the drunk's throat and pushed carefully. The
man started to kick and fight. Moving behind him, Eric
kept up the pressure while holding the man immobile for
another minute. That was all it took for him to slump
heavily in Eric's arms.

Letting him fall to the grass, Eric began with the coat,
moved on to pants and underwear. Personal belongings he
stacked neatly nearby. He was about to do likewise with
the man's wallet, thought better of it, and removed the
loose cash, shoving the bills into his own still damp wallet.
The more he made his actions resemble an ordinary rob-
bery, the less likely anyone was to connect it to his
extraordinary activities. He left the credit cards alone.
They were useless to an ordinary thief.

The suit was a little large and hung loosely on his
lankier frame, but not enough to attract undue attention, he
thought. He tucked the sleeves and cuffs under and it
looked better. At night the difference shouldn't be too
noticeable.

As soon as the stores opened he'd find himself a new set
of clothes that fit properly. He still had his credit card,
though whether it was safe to use it anymore he didn't
know. Tarragon had already amply displayed his ability to
access information.

One thing he knew for certain: he couldn't go back to

his hotel. That would be as closely watched now as would Lisa's codo.

He made a bundle out of his old clothes, leaving his unwilling benefactor snoring and snuffling naked on the grass behind him. There was a public dispos-all situated near the rest rooms half a block away. A few teens gamboled loudly around the water fountain, outrageous in their swapped attire; boys in dresses, girls in suits, unisex makeup plastered on every face. They offered up a few juvenile obscenities but otherwise ignored him. The fountain was brightly lit and close to the street, and they weren't really in the mood to slice any citizens. He was grateful for the inattention. More trouble he didn't need.

He stuffed his old clothing into the safety chute and pressed the switch. There was a muffled *whoosh* as the tube below sucked up the damning evidence, sending it on its way along with several million tons of additional refuse toward the power-plant burners.

From now on he'd have to be exceedingly careful of his movements. Tarragon would be less than polite the next time their paths crossed. If he didn't try to see Lisa again, he might be able to slip out of the city and pick up a few threads of his former life. Former life. His future, like his mouth, was set. He was going after Lisa, and Tarragon probably knew that as well as he did himself.

How long would Tarragon's desire to avoid unwelcome publicity keep him from notifying national authorities? Eric could plan better if he knew. Of course, he was a murderer now. Or was he? It had all been in self-defense (or was it resisting arrest?). The past hour was a muddle of screams and rapid movements and confused thoughts. It might be that he hadn't killed anyone. But he'd certainly damaged many.

He stumbled out of the park, following the beacon of the moving traffic lights on busy First Avenue.

Staring down at his hands, he slowly turned his right hand palm-downward to stare at the knuckles. There was no sign of damage. Even his fingernails were unbroken. He clenched his fingers, slowly let them unclench. An ordinary hand, surely. His hand, smooth and uncallused. The same hand he'd grown up with.

He was suddenly dizzy. Another drinking fountain stood nearby. The edges were smooth, green plastic, the copper spigot dull bronze in the evening streetlight.

Experimentally, he grasped the spigot and pulled hard. Nothing happened. The spigot did not move. Frowning, he took a deep breath and pulled with both hands. Nothing.

There was no threat, he decided. Nothing to make the adrenaline rush to his muscles (though there was no denying any more that something considerably more potent than adrenaline was involved).

After him. They were after him! He had to defend himself, had to save himself and Lisa. They were going to get him, put him away, do something terrible to him, and worse to her!

He pulled again. There was a crunch as cement crumbled and the spigot emerged from its socket, trailing copper pipe behind it. The pipe cut through the thin cement and plastic like a piano wire through flesh. Water began to dribble, then to spurt from strained sections of pipe.

He let it fall aside, stumbled away up the street.

What's happening to me, he thought wildly? What's happening to me? It was all crazy. He shouldn't be able to do things like that. Memory conjured up an image of himself whirling a heavy riot suit and its operator over his head like a cowboy twirling a lariat. Impossible, impossible! Had they really happened, those impossibles, or had he dreamed them?

Methodically, he tried to reconstruct the past hour of his shattered life. He'd gone to see Lisa. Tarragon had confronted them. He'd fled, breaking away from everyone who'd tried to restrain him. No man should have been capable of engineering such an escape.

He wanted to scream for help then, sink to his knees there on the street and scream for the sky to help him, but he dared not risk the attention. Instead he kept walking, lifting his head and regulating his stride in an attempt to melt into the night crowds as he blended into the walkway that bordered the First Avenue corridor.

It was impossible. Therefore it hadn't taken place. That was simple enough. He forced recent events to the back of his mind. He was reasonably confident of his sanity. Not mad, he told himself reassuringly. Just in love. A new hotel room, new clothes, some food and he'd feel much better. He pulled the opposing lapels tighter across his chest.

It was counterproductive to dwell on the implausible, not to mention the impossible. For the moment, therefore, he would assume they had not happened. Right away he felt his pulse slow. Take a while to concentrate on the basics: food, shelter, clothing. Later Lisa, somehow.

No one stared at the loosely clad figure as it made its way up the avenue. This was Nueva York, and far more badly dressed citizens walked its streets every night. There were some who might have remarked on the strange smile the man wore, but that sort of dazed, distant look was also common in the big city. At least he was walking purposefully and not stumbling inanely about.

The police cruiser that passed on patrol likewise ignored him. Why shouldn't they? There was nothing to indicate they were ignoring the most dangerous man in the city.

Eric Abbott, of course, did not think of himself as dangerous. No, he was in love, and that was a thing of beauty. Nothing dangerous about being in love.

XI

IT was a mission control room. That was self-evident. But it did not launch shuttles or probes to deep space. It only monitored information, shuttling bytes back and forth between components buried deep inside the Urirotstock and out to the world network. Satellite dishes fringing the mountain's crest linked the room with Colligatarch relays in multiple overhead orbits. The operation spoke of smooth power, electrical and human.

Each console had been individualized according to the whims and taste of its operator. One boasted a tall maternal wood carving from the Central African Federation, another displayed shellacked blossoms from the Pacific Union, a third a string of handmade bells from the Inuit Republic. Each testified not only to the tastes but to the origin of each operator.

As he descended the ramp, Oristano felt a cool, quiet pride in the way the world's most complex computer station functioned. Everything was as it should be. Backups rested behind their consoles, sleeping or reading optotext. They were rarely called upon for emergency work, so efficient had the system become.

Everything was as it should be, and yet it was not.

"CPO, sir?"

Oristano looked to his right. "What is it, Frontenac?"

The man thrust a handful of printouts under the Chief of Operation's gaze. "It's the Australians again, sir."

"I see." He scanned the printouts, his mind elsewhere. "What is it this time?"

"They're complaining about their share of the plankton harvest."

Oristano sighed. He supposed some nationality had to claim the winner's ribbon for most obstreperous.

"These figures look all right to me. What's their complaint?"

"They say their harvest window doesn't take predictions for an unusually severe Antarctic winter into account."

"Gott im Himmel," Oristano muttered to himself. Then, to the assistant, "Tell the Australian representative that we only predict the weather, we don't control it. Not yet, anyway. Tell him that every other nation has to operate its krilling fleet under the same restrictions and that the catch is apportioned according to a thousand variables, of which weather is only one."

"They won't like that," the assistant said dubiously. "They'll say it shows a northerner bias as well as a failure to sympathize with a problem oceanic in origin."

"They always say that," Oristano responded tiredly. "They wouldn't be happy unless we picked up and moved Colligatarch Center to Christchurch."

"Is that what I should relay to them, sir?"

"No, of course not, Frontenac," he said irritably, and hurried to soften his tone as he saw the other man react. "I just mean that you should reply with some common sense. Be diplomatic about it, as usual. Inform them that the Colligatarch will make a special study of this problem and render a further report based on additional research."

"That will only mollify them for a little while, sir."

Oristano made pacifying gestures with one hand. "A little while is long enough. I've got other things on my mind these days. Just keep them off my neck for a month or so, will you, *s'il vous plaît??*"

"Oui, CPO." He took back his printouts and left Oristano alone.

As if there wasn't enough for him to worry about, he

grumbled to himself as he returned to his office. The red light over his desk was pulsing silently. It was a toss-up as to who was the more demanding—the Colligatarch or his wife. Not to mention who was the more understanding. The comparison was unfair to Martha. He settled into his chair.

"All right, I'm here. You can shut that off now." Instantly the light winked out. "What is it now? More thoughts on threats?"

The Colligatarch was immune to sarcasm. At least, it chose to give that appearance. It said politely, "No, Martin. It is the same threat that has troubled us all along."

"All along is right. This has been going on for weeks." He tried to conceal his impatience. It was all very well to announce some terrible menace and put everyone on alert to deal with it, quite another to expect everyone to maintain that state of readiness when day after day went by and nothing happened.

"I have learned a little more since the last time we spoke of the matter."

"That's good. What 'little more'?"

"Nonspecifics."

"Of course." Oristano sighed. "It would be too much to expect you had discovered anything specific."

"Hints, suggestions, overtones, leanings are often very important, Martin."

"I certainly didn't mean to denigrate your work. Enter this new information into my study file, and I'll review it when I have more time."

"Busy day?" asked the machine with genuine concern.

"The usual."

"Australians giving you trouble again?"

"You've heard? I've already dealt with that."

"This is more important than arguments over fishing rights."

"Are you saying that I'm not taking your 'threat' seriously enough?" Oristano perked up. The implication was that the machine was drawing inferences from

Martin's vocal inflection and expression. "I am. We all are. You have to understand that's it hard for us, laboring as we do under more immediate problems, to regard this as anxiously as you seem to, since to date there has been nothing in the way of a demonstrable danger to the system."

"Then you will be pleased to know, Martin, that I have finally detected a disturbance which must be dealt with."

Oristano sat up straighter in his chair. "It's about time " Odd how he was more relieved than concerned.

"You need to notify the International Surveillance Network to watch for intrusions or attempted intrusions by unauthorized personnel into Colligatarch Subsidiary Service Termini in the following cities: Bombay, Kyoto, Singapore, Brisbane—perhaps the Australians will have something truly serious to yell about—Antafogasta, Bogota, Nueva York, Metrotex, Madrid, Milan, and Kiev."

Oristano automatically entered the list into his study file, frowned.

"Something about this troubles you, Martin?"

"That's quite a list. I'm thinking of the expense involved in calling for special surveillance at so many points. Do you expect the danger to manifest itself at all of them?"

"All and none. I am still in the process of trying to decide where the actual serious assault is to take place."

" 'Assault'? Then you've collated enough imponderables to project actual physical violence against the system?"

"It has moved from the realm of the possible into that of the probable, yes. As to the expense, I have already eliminated a number of additional locations where the probability of intrusion exists but is lower. I regret I cannot be more precise."

So do I, Oristano mused. Nevertheless, it was a relief to be able to deal with something besides febrile cybernetic hallucinations. It would help the morale of the staff. One thing to say a threat exists, another to alert security in Madrid. Time for a little reality to replace supposition.

"Interesting that you don't include Central."

"The threat is not directed here. At least, not now."

"Then this is all you deem necessary?"

"For now, Martin. I will notify you if I feel further steps should be taken."

"Good enough." He felt a sudden, uncharacteristic urge to rejoin human company.

He sought out the diminutive programmer from Behar.

"More troubles with the unnameable threat?" Dhurapati asked. The cabochon ruby in her nose was almost black in the dim light of the corridor.

"I'm afraid so. Now I'm to call a worldwide alert at CS Service Termini."

She shook her head, black hair moving beneath the thin silk of the work sari. "This can't go on forever. Tell me, Martin, do you still believe in the seriousness of this 'threat'?"

"Why else would the machine call an alert?"

"Because it senses your doubt and mine and everyone else's, and seeks to justify its confusion and concern by raising an alarm, perhaps to no more purpose than to reinforce its own closely held delusion."

He eyed her appraisingly. They were in a service corridor decorated to resemble a similar tunnel on the Hawaiian island of Kauai. Water dripped off ferns and epiphytes. It was hard to believe they weren't strolling through that tropical paradise. Yet overhead lay several thousand meters of solid granite and beyond, the cold wastes of the Alps.

"You're still insisting something's wrong with the Colligatarch's central logic functions?"

"I'm not ready to insist on it. Not yet. But I do think it's time for you to order an independent study. Care should be taken not to make the machine suspicious. The investigation should be cloaked in the guise of a standard circuitry checkup. This much needs to be done." She stopped, stared up at him. "There are others on the staff who agree with me, Martin."

"Very well. I confess to having second thoughts myself. Go ahead and set up the necessary study. I'll clear it through the network." His thoughts shifted.

"You know, the Colligatarch is still new enough so that we don't, even after all these years of operation, know everything about it. It's continually evolving, electronically and mentally. This sort of checkup ought to be carried out on a regular basis. Increased sophistication of operation requires a corresponding increase in the sophistication of monitoring such operations."

"We need to tread very lightly here, Martin. I realize it's unlikely we could do anything to alarm the machine, but we need to tread very lightly."

"I leave it to you, Dhura, to devise a check program which will do just that."

"I will, Martin." She reached out for him, rested a tiny hand on his arm. "I know this has been difficult for you, Martin. The responsibility of seeing to it that mankind's most important tool continues to function smoothly rests ultimately on your shoulders. It's not a responsibility I would care for."

Martha was very far away then. The hand was warm and gentle on his arm, and he'd been stuck inside the mountain for a long time. It was hard just to nod.

"Thank you for your concern, Dhura. It's nice to know someone's sympathetic. Besides the *verdammt* machine, of course."

"We're all sympathetic," she said. As he did not respond, her hand drew back. "If there's anything else you need, if you need to talk again, please call on me."

"Thanks. I appreciate that. But I'm not on the verge of collapse just yet."

"I understand," she said, favoring him with one of her rare smiles. He was reminded of certain tropical flowers that blossom only once or twice a year. The blossom moved away, graceful and delicate beneath the thin sari.

It took an effort to drag his thoughts back to business. The import of what they were going to do with the machine weighed heavily on him. Their worries were still subjective, but there had never been a situation quite like this one in the whole history of Colligatarch Central. Doubts nagged at him as he walked back toward his office.

How *would* the machine react to such a probe? It was feeling threatened from outside. Would it interpret a special investigation of its innards as a threat from inside?

Nonsense, he told himself firmly. You've seen too many horror-optos. The Colligatarch could not possibly perceive an internal study as a threat. Still, he recognized the truth of what he'd told Dhurapati. There was much that went on in the billions upon billions of circuits that composed the Colligatarch they did not understand.

More and more problems were handed to the machine every year. Expansion barely kept pace with demand. Had they finally fallen behind? Was it just possible that under the immense burden of all mankind's problems the machine was capable of having a mental breakdown? Dhurapati could voice such a fear. As Chief of Operations he could not. It was a fear he would have to keep to himself, at least for the foreseeable future.

There was no reason for panic. He still had full confidence in his people and in the Colligatarch itself. If the problem *was* internal, it would be discovered and corrected. Like as not the machine would aid in the diagnosis. But if the trouble was inside the machine, it would certainly explain the enigmatic nature of the "threat."

He couldn't do it all himself. In the complex cell that was the Authority, he was no more than endoplasmic reticulum, a conduit between the nucleus that was the Colligatarch and the surging protoplasmic mass of mankind. It was a wonder he hadn't cracked under the strain.

He wouldn't, of course. It was why he was CPO. His co-workers knew that. He suspected the machine did also. He had no intention of disappointing anyone. Problems with the Colligatarch there might be, but the Chief Programmer would show none.

The lingering heat of Dhurapati's hand still warmed his skin. He forced himself to think of other matters. There was plenty to occupy his thoughts.

* * *

Eric was feeling much better as he sat in the substreet bar. It was large enough to swallow a stranger, low enough to mask many of the sounds of the walkway above. The bartender served him indifferently. So had the clerk in the clothing department of the big discount store. There had been one bad moment when the register seemed to hesitate while processing his credit card, but it spit it out soon enough. It would take the authorities a little while to put a tracer on the newly altered card.

Now he sat in a suit of new clothes that fit in all the proper places, his tool packets secure in both inside breast pockets, cash from the intentional overcharge fattening his wallet. Much better.

The rest of his belongings might as well be back in Phoenix, since his Nueva York hotel was off-limits from now on. Certainly Tarragon's people didn't intend to sit quietly and wait for him to put in an appearance.

The laugh-opto blared loudly above the bar as larger-than-life figures stumbled over each other, accompanied by larger-than-life laughter. He didn't know the series. Sitcoms were not among his favorite forms of entertainment. He preferred sporting events, docu-optos, or an occasional concertcast.

It was hard to gauge the opinions of his fellow drinkers. Some of them stared blankly at the screen. If they registered amusement at the antics being portrayed, it was all internalized. Now and then a faint, uncertain grin might appear on a tired face, as if some gag or pratfall had penetrated to the central node several minutes after the joke itself had passed into history.

Livelier couples inhabited the booths and tables. They chose conversation over the opto, words mixing with subtle looks and touches. Eric envied them their security, their acceptance of their place in the scheme of things. They knew where they'd come from and where they'd be in the morning.

Once he'd shared that security, that certainty. Now it seemed he was certain of very little. As the brandy warmed his belly, he tried to dissect the events of the past week. He had done a number of improbable things, then followed up by doing a number of impossible things. All he was sure of anymore was his love for Lisa Tambor.

Of his flight from her codo the previous night, he recalled surprisingly little. While all the action had been taking place, a shadow had been drawn between his eyes and his mind. Of one thing he had no doubt: by any reasonable extrapolation of events he ought to be dead or dying several times over.

He was not. Nor was he filled with panic anymore. He had passed beyond panic.

I am not insane, he told himself repeatedly. I can think and perceive quite sensibly. Nor am I Superman. But if I am sane and not Superman, then what I am I? Not a robot. Of that he was certain also.

Experimentally he tried to lift the table on which his drink rested. It was bolted to the floor and didn't budge. It reaffirmed what he'd already proved with the water fountain. His peculiar abilities and exceptional strength only manifested themselves in moments of extreme stress. Something inside him sent his body into overdrive whenever he was threatened.

How he'd come by this remarkable talent was a total mystery to him. Since he'd never been one to waste time on an insoluble problem, he put it aside for future consideration.

One thing was certain: whatever this peculiar ability consisted of, he had it. He'd used it on three separate occasions in two different cities. Could he count on its aid if another crisis arose? He had no way of knowing. Each time was a new throw of the dice, with two lives at stake. He wondered what was responsible.

Also a question for future consideration. Right now he was full of the present, a present centered on Lisa, of the way she felt in his arms and the way his soul drained into her each time they met. That was sufficient motivation for the moment. Everything else would have to wait until he could be certain of her safety.

The opto near the bar blurred. A few disappointed

groans rose from those who'd been sucked into watching the sitcom. A brief highlighting flash illuminated the face of a popular local newsawk. A second image was superimposed on the upper left-hand corner of the screen.

Eric recognized it and froze. It was an old picture, a company ID shot. He'd changed a lot since it had been taken, but there was no mistaking the portrait.

"Good evening from thirty-three news update. This is a picture of Eric Abbott, a resident of New River, Arizona, NAT, who is believed to be at large in the city and is wanted on several charges by the authorities. Abbott is believed responsible for the recent disturbance at a luxury East Side codo complex. He is considered armed and dangerous.

"Any citizen who thinks he or she may have seen this man is urged to contact metropolitan police immediately. In other news tonight, the Japanese Emperor announced a doubling of Prosperity Sphere rice exports to . . ."

Eric didn't hear the rest. Slowly, so as not to attract attention, he turned in his chair until he was facing away from the center of the bar. Few customers appeared to have paid any attention to the opto announcement.

Was the picture old enough to permit his continued use of the public walkways? There were more lines in his face now. He'd worn a beard in the old days but that was no help: the police computer had wiped it for the broadcast.

He forced himself to finish his brandy, then exited without comment. It was starting to drizzle again and he was still without umbrella or raincoat. An umbrella would be better. It could help hide his face.

It was easy to find a lower-class hotel, midtown and away from the rivers. He paid for the night in cash. Once inside he double-locked the door and spent several tedious hours under a bright lamp altering his credit card again. Only when his latest identity was safely in place did he let himself lie down.

He slept much better than he'd expected to. Exhaustion overcame his anxiety. Whatever had helped him escape

Lisa's building did not let him off without making any demands on his body.

When he finally awoke it was midday. Using the directory in the optophone, he located the type of store he needed. It wasn't a long way off. Little was, in Nueva York. Avoiding the come-ons of the cabs, he walked the necessary half-mile.

The proprietor was most helpful, and Eric soon returned to his room. No one confronted him, but he knew he had to do something. Citizen indifference wouldn't protect him forever. Sooner or later some zealot would recognize him from the repeated publication of his portrait and point him out to the police.

The spirit gum was hard to work with and he found himself wishing he'd spent more time in company amateur theatricals. At last he had the moustache in place. Then he worked the bleach through his head until he was a nice Nordic blonde. Putty would have altered his entire face, but he chose not to chance it. He had no experience with such materials, and a badly done false nose would draw more attention than his real one.

He found a barber to cut his newly bleached hair. When he finally glimpsed himself in a mirror, it was still the face of Eric Abbott that stared back at him . . . but only on close inspection. He was satisfied.

Thoughts of how to regain contact with Lisa occupied him for the rest of the day. It was not enough to see her anymore. Somehow he had to get her away from her gilded prison.

The fecund streets of the city led him to an amateur astronomy shop. Shelves were filled with everything from miniature radio telescopes for eavesdropping on Orion to thick books pinpointing meteor impact sites.

"Can I sell you something?" asked the hopeful man behind the counter.

"I need a telescope."

"I see. What kind, sir?"

"Something small and compact."

The man nodded as though he dealt with such requests

every day. He probably did, Eric mused, but from customers with different intentions.

"Something that would fit easily inside your coat pocket?"

"That would be nice." Eric added what he hoped would pass for a nervous smile.

"Going to gaze at some heavenly bodies?" The man winked.

Eric hesitated before responding, but the salesman seemed more understanding than accusative.

"Something like that."

"I understand. It's your business, of course. I'm required by city law to inform you that it's a municipal felony if you're caught within city limits pointing a telescope anywhere at an angle of less than sixty degrees."

"I follow you."

"Fine." The man turned and caressed a cabinet with a magnetic key, began searching exposed shelves. He brought out a collapsing tube of dark alloy only an inch in diameter.

"Here you are, sir, just the thing. Very light, nonreflective body, folding optics, electronically enhanced to one twenty-eight power."

"Sounds like it should do nicely." Eric inspected it as if he knew what he was looking for.

"Now if you plan on doing some really strenuous observing," the salesman said as he produced a much larger tube with a second, narrower cylinder straddling its back, "this Quelmar has ten times the resolving power together with an integrated violet laser spotting scope attached. The laser is, of course, undetectable in normal nighttime usage.

"It will also," he added sotto voce, "take a standard camera adapter."

"That's all right," Eric assured him. "I prefer the smaller model."

"As you wish." The salesman hid his disappointment at not selling the much more expensive unit. "That'll be twenty-nine ninety-five please, plus taxes." Eric paid him in cash and walked out with the telescope folded to thumb-size inside his coat pocket.

Using his re-altered card he splurged on a relaxed dinner. It was the best meal he'd enjoyed since leaving Phoenix. In a theater he sat and watched the holofilm until he couldn't 'stand it anymore (the waiting, not the film), then rose and paced the streets until near midnight.

Witching hour, he thought. That seemed appropriate. He wouldn't have been a bit surprised if he'd suddenly turned into a pumpkin.

As he entered Lisa's neighborhood he began to move with greater caution, keeping to the shadows and avoiding late-night pedestrians without drawing attention to himself. It was raining again, and the umbrella he'd purchased did indeed conceal his face.

There didn't appear to be any extraordinary concentration of police vehicles cruising the vicinity of the East River codos. That made sense. They wouldn't want to frighten him off if he was stupid enough to return. He had no intention of trying to enter Lisa's tower. Maybe his actions were foolhardy, but they weren't blindly dumb.

It would have been impossible had her codo faced directly onto the river. Fortunately it was angled to provide a view of the city as well as the water.

The codo tower one half-block downriver boasted an electronic doorwatch similar to the one in Lisa's building, except that the voice was feminine and the sculptured grille in the lobby more modern. He used a different ploy to fool the voice and gain admittance to the elevator bay.

I'm becoming quite an accomplished break-in artist, he told himself ironically.

As he rose upward he considered the profusion of shadowy figures he'd counted working the grounds around Lisa's tower. Gardeners and laborers, electricians and strolling lovers, none of whom seemed to pay any attention to each other. The gardeners looked up too frequently from their bushes, the lovers spent too much time glancing sideways instead of at each other. Eric was sure they were all waiting for him to put in an appearance.

He had every intention of disappointing them.

The elevator finally slowed to a stop. This tower was several stories taller than Lisa's. The security lock atop the service stairway yielded to his probes and he tried not to run as he emerged into the cool air.

XII

THREE stories of heating and air-conditioning equipment towered above him, throbbing softly to itself. The dark gray mass was alive with clicking service panels and bright warning lights. Everything was functioning as intended, and there were no signs of wandering service technicians.

He took no chances—kept to the dark places as he made his way silently to the edge of the roof. When he reached the fence he dropped to his belly. No telling when some searcher on the ground might idly play his seeker beam over the tops of the surrounding skyscrapers.

Taking the compact telescope from his pocket, he extended it to its full length and stuck it through the wire mesh of the fence. Ninety stories below, the sounds of the city were muted and weak. The location of Lisa's codo was imprinted permanently on his brain, and he had no trouble picking it out.

The little scope was all that its seller had claimed. It provided a fine view of the porch and the high transparent windows behind. The glass had been replaced with admirable speed. Unfortunately, all the curtains were pulled. He cursed himself silently for forgetting that possibility.

Lights showed behind the curtains. Once or twice he thought he could see a shape moving against the light, a faint silhouette of uncertain outline. He watched for over an hour. The lights stayed on. Someone beside himself was losing sleep.

River mist chilled him. She was there all right. The key question was whether or not she had company, and if so, how closely she was being watched. If she had freedom to move about her own rooms, he might be able to get in touch with her just long enough.

Folding the telescope, he put it back in his pocket and stood, then commenced an inspection of his surroundings. It didn't take long to find the service bay he was after. Once more a lock yielded to his tools.

Inside the bay he found repair equipment, fiberoptic jumps, powerpacks for supplying energy to temporarily disconnected facilities, and brackets holding dozens of tools. He helped himself to several potentially useful items while searching for the phone.

He lifted the unit and was relieved to hear a normal dialtone. There was always the chance it was a straight-line, connected only to some unknown service exchange. Taking a deep breath, he dialed Lisa's number, thankful he'd had the presence of mind to note it when he'd first visited her home.

As he waited anxiously, he gazed across the darkness at her building. There were several rings, then a familiar voice, hesitant and soft.

"Hello?"

"Lisa! Can you talk?"

"Is that you?" She was sharp enough not to use his name.

"Yes."

"Where are you?"

"Safe, for now."

"But where? Tell me and I'll come to you. I would have the other night but they held me back."

"I wondered about that. Where's Tarragon?"

"In the other room, with his people. I'm in the bedroom. They leave me alone in here." A pause, then, "You've got a lot of people upset."

"That wasn't my intention, Lisa. I'm trying as hard as I

can not to upset anyone, but they're making it damn difficult for me.''

"I have to see you. We have to talk. Tell me where you are and I'll come to you. I can slip out for a moment. They'll leave me be for a moment.''

Anxious. She sounds so anxious. He remembered the warmth of her body against his. Even then she'd been uncertain, confused, doubtful of her own emotions. Now she seemed so positive. Of course, she'd had time to settle her own thoughts, but the past few days had sharpened instincts he hadn't known he'd possessed.

Carrying the phone, he walked out into the light mist and looked over the edge of the roof. "There's a big sycamore in the park that runs along the river. I'm in the top branches, on a remote phone.''

"Wonderful! I'll tell them I need some air. They'll let me go for a few minutes. You'll wait for me?''

"Of course I'll wait for you. Don't you remember what I told you just before Tarragon and his bullyboys jumped me in your living room yesterday?''

"I remember.'' She hung up. Or at least, the line went dead.

Eric took out the telescope and thoughtfully settled down to watch the park below. There was movement much too soon after his call. Figures fanning out to encircle the tree he'd chosen. Out in the river, isolated pleasure craft suddenly began to move toward shore, collecting together like a squadron of whirligig beetles.

A couple of minutes passed before there was a concerted rush toward the tree. Lights came on like fireflies, assaulting the branches.

The computer-generated voice had been very good, the best he'd ever heard. It should have fooled him completely. That it did not was no fault of its operators. It could only imitate Lisa's voice, not her emotions. She had a way of pausing before announcing any significant decisions, and that hadn't been right either.

The clincher had come when he'd asked her to remember what he'd told her the other day as Tarragon's minions had moved in on him, before she'd been ordered to her bedroom. He hadn't told her anything in particular.

If she was unable to answer her own phone, it seemed likely she wasn't in the codo anymore. Tarragon and his employers wanted to keep them apart. It was obvious they'd taken the next step. But where had she been moved to?

Quickly he retreated to the service bay and hung up the phone. He headed for the stairway. Distant sounds made him pull up short.

Footsteps, lots of them, heavy on the metal stairs, and whispered voices.

He retraced his steps, moved to the far end of the roof. They came pouring out of the stairwell and fanned out to cover the whole roof. There were city police and men in neat business suits and others clad in paramilitary gear carrying heavy weapons. His escape the other day had obviously impressed his pursuers. Those who'd survived.

He continued to retreat across the roof until suddenly there was no more roof. He could hear them muttering to each other, saw the light come on inside the service bay. There were a couple of sharp popping noises.

Two men entered the bay, and as they stepped into the light he saw their insectlike faces. Gas masks. Sleep gas, or perhaps something stronger. When they reemerged they were shaking their heads.

He considered the several stories of heating and cooling machinery overhead. There were numerous ladders climbing the metal flanks, and in minutes they'd be alive with police . . . assuming they weren't scouring the top already. He'd relied on his false location to fool them, but these weren't children he was dueling. At the same time they'd moved to encircle the sycamore, someone else had been tracing the origin of the phone call.

The wire-mesh fence was cold against his spine. They were very near now. Soon someone would see him standing there in the mist.

He leaned over the fence and examined the side of the building. Some kind of decorative marbled polyethelene.

He wondered what they'd do to him if they caught him. Not that he much cared anymore whether they took him forcibly back to Phoenix, or put him under some kind of brain probe, or cut him up to see what made him tick. Being of a scientific bent, he was more than a little interested in the latter himself, but not to the point of wanting to preside over his own vivisection. Somehow he didn't think they'd let him watch.

So without thinking about it any longer he kicked up and over and found himself hanging by his fingers from the metal mesh, ninety stories above the East River park.

His shoes were designed for long walks on pavement and not much else. They gave the feeblest grip in the mist. He would have to rely on his hands, and suddenly it seemed as if his fingers were made of steel. Like a housefly he started working his way down the side of the tower.

Once he came to a blind spot where the polyethelene had been worn smooth. Angrily he jabbed the wall, only to see his fingers penetrate up to the second knuckle. Whenever he needed handholds after that, he made them.

He doubted they would think to scan the perpendicular sides of the building. Nevertheless he descended ten floors before he considered it safe enough to crawl sideways to a window. There were no porches on this tower. When no one responded to his rapping on the glass, he punched his way through.

The codo was dark and empty. He took a few minutes to catch his wind, chancing that the owners would not return while he recovered. Without disturbing the arrangement of towels or other items, he used the bathroom to wash and dry his face. Then he grabbed a quick snack from the refrigerator, exited, and resealed the doorlock from outside.

The hall was empty. There was no private, lavishly decorated lobby like the one in Lisa's building. An empty elevator took him down to the fourth floor. He wasn't sure if they'd be watching the main entrance, but he took no chances, letting himself out onto the side of the building again by means of a service window.

From there it was a short descent to the ground floor. He hid for a while in a clump of pyrocanthus bushes until he was certain he had a clear path to the street. There were plenty of official and unmarked vehicles parked there, and a small crowd of curious gawkers thoughtfully hampering the police patrols. He slipped unnoticed into the crowd.

His caution was unwarranted. The police were not watching the street. No doubt their attention was aimed at the roof far above, where the real action was supposedly taking place.

He sauntered off into the park, forcing himself to maintain a slow pace. He was halfway to First Avenue when a voice shouted, "Hey you!"

Uncertain whether to run or turn and attack, he hesitated. A single yell could bring the whole horde of officials down on him.

The man in the metro police blazer and beret moved nearer, spoke irritably. "This is a restricted area, citizen. Didn't you see the lines?"

"I'm sorry," Eric said carefully. "I've been thinking and I didn't . . ."

"Never mind." He was fiddling with the call-all in his ear. Evidently it didn't fit properly. He gestured toward the street with his stunstick. "Go on, get out."

"Thanks. Sorry." He turned and moved on. Maybe the cop hadn't studied the reports on Eric Abbott. Maybe he'd just been called in for special duty. Maybe he was thinking about his girlfriend.

No matter. Eric had no more trouble. He saw the thin cord marking off the park as he emerged from the pedestrian lane. No police here, though. Only signs and ropes. He stepped over the cord and increased his pace slightly until he was surrounded by late-night strollers taking in the air along the river.

For several hours he wandered aimlessly through midtown, occasionally stopping to satisfy his suddenly ravenous hunger with fast food, trying to decide what to do next.

There was no way of knowing where Tarragon had spirited Lisa to. She might be in another codo in the same building or in another residential tower nearby. Or she might have been taken out of Nueva York altogther. How could he know without confronting Tarragon directly, which was out of the question?

He kicked at the slidewalk in frustration, was only half startled to see a narrow crack appear in the slowly moving pavement. Quickly he looked around to make sure no one had seen him. He would have to work at controlling his temper. It still stimulated something awesome and enigmatic within him. One thing he did not want now was to attract attention to himself.

There was no one he could turn to for help, no one he could trust. No one to help him find the answers he desperately needed to know.

But there were other ways of obtaining information. It might not be necessary to confront maybe-friends or certain enemies.

He entered a bar and went to the phone. The tiny directory screen lit up when he deposited a coin. A few quick punches of the keyboard produced the address he wanted.

Then he was back out on the street, no longer wandering aimlessly but with a definite destination in mind. Thoughts of Lisa drove him through the crowds.

The station was located beneath a District Administration building downtown, near the Battery. The aboveground floors were shuttered for the night, but the subterranean elevators were still operational and full of people.

His lift dropped him ten stories into solid granite bedrock and deposited him in a long hall. It wasn't crowded nor was it deserted. It was very late, or very early, depending on how you arranged your day. The thirst for knowledge never dries up, no matter what the hour. Some of the supplicants were sleepy-eyed, others wide-awake.

He found a place in one of the shortest lines, and it

wasn't long before he was admitted to another, narrower hallway. Soft carpet muffled footsteps. To left and right stretched a long row of glass-enclosed booths. He walked to his left until he found a booth where the fiberoptic glass wall was bright green. Stepping inside he secured the door behind him. As he did so the glass turned crimson.

Sitting down in the comfortable, adjustable chair, he touched a switch which killed the audio. Not that he was likely to have any eavesdroppers to worry about, but he felt better confronting only a visual display. He could block that from sight with his upper body.

The screen responded immediately to his touch. "Welcome to your local Colligatarch Subsidiary Service Terminal. Through the miracle of modern science and communications, you, the ordinary citizen, have the same rights as anyone in the world to utilize the vast repository of knowledge that composes the Colligatarch Authority. Your requests will be handled by Nueva York Subsidiary Center.

"Please insert your identity credit card into the slot on your left and leave it there until you have concluded your session. Your account will be billed automatically according to the difficulty of your request and the length of time required to process it. The Colligatarch Subsidiary Service Terminal, Nueva York Center, is now open for your personal use." The period that ended the sentence flashed green on the screen.

Surprisingly, he discovered he was homesick. The terminal wasn't all that different from his bedroom console back in New River. The setting was less luxurious and the design more utilitarian, the keyboard and screen fashioned of far tougher materials, but the setup was similar. It had to be tougher, since it had to resist the heavy hands of ordinary citizens as well as the strawberry soda and melted chocolate applied by insufficiently supervised children.

Certainly some kind of tracer had been put on his altered card. If so, it would alert the authorities to his presence here. That still might not matter if he had enough time to extract what he needed from the machine's data banks. The best solution would be to try to obtain an answer without using the names *Eric Abbott* or *Lisa Tambor*. He would need to be as concise and nonspecific as possible.

"I need to know the location of a friend," he entered.

"Use the public directory," the machine immediately responded. "If the name is not listed, I am not permitted to give out the information."

"It's not a question of its being listed or not," he entered. "I have reason to believe the person in question may no longer be within the city limits. She was compelled to travel on short notice and was unable to leave a forwarding address."

"In that case it is unlikely I can be of help to you, citizen." The neat letters flashed on the screen. "If your friend has not informed you of her new destination, it is unlikely I will be able to do so."

"You may have more information pertaining to her movements," Eric supplied. He paused. There was no way of working around it anymore. Quickly he entered Lisa's name, address, and phone number.

"I need any information on this woman's location and/or movements you can supply," Eric added. "It may be necessary for you to contact the Nueva York police department files for details."

"If this is a matter involving police files, I still cannot help you," said the machine. "I will, however, make the requested inquiry."

Eric waited nervously. How many alarms would his roundabout inquiry set off? If so, how long would he have to escape this underground facility before Tarragon's people arrived?

On the screen the word WORKING appeared. As the delay stretched into five minutes his nervousness increased. He found himself glancing frequently up the long hallway. The appearance of two policemen gave him a bad start, but they entered a booth half a dozen cubicles up the hall from his, to remove a drunk who'd chosen the warmth and privacy of a Colligatarch terminal to try to sleep it off.

Probably the drunk had used the usual ploy of setting the machine to solve some impossible task. Eventually watchdog monitors had overridden the program and alerted security to the fact that someone was occupying the booth for other than acceptable reasons. That was why the booths were fashioned of transparent material. Legitimate users had nothing to hide.

He waited another couple of minutes before asking, "Is there some difficulty with my request?"

The machine replied immediately. "You have supplied very little hard information. Therefore a considerable amount of secondary searching is necessary." Eric thought to dig further, decided against it.

No more police appeared. It occurred to him that despite having been awake for some time now, he was not in the least bit sleepy. No doubt the tension was keeping him alert.

A flash of letters drew his attention back to the screen. Hope turned quickly to confusion.

He expected another declaration of helplessness from the machine but there was always a chance it might come up with some bit of useful information. He got neither.

Instead, the glowing sentence said, "Go to Sublevel Six, Booth B."

He considered a moment, then asked, "What about the whereabouts of Lisa Tambor? Does my query require rephrasing?"

And again only the message, "Go to Sublevel Six, Booth B."

Had he finally triggered an alarm of some kind? Were they trying to ease him out of this busy public corridor so they could hustle him out of sight unseen by witnessing eyes?

What else could it be? Surely the machine wouldn't say blithely, "Go to Sublevel Six, Booth B, where there is a trap waiting for you and we may arrest you in peace and quiet." But that was the effect of its reply. And that made no sense either.

Stalling, he entered, "Does this relate to my query as to the whereabouts of Lisa Tambor?" The machine replied with commendable brevity.

"It does."

Rising, he removed his credit card. Perhaps they hadn't noted the newest change yet. He left the booth. No one watched him return to the elevator bay. Even as he entered the first available lift he was unsure how to proceed. He could request street level and vanish back into the rush of early-morning Manhattan, or he could follow the machine's seemingly innocent instructions.

His hand hovered over the controls and almost compulsively demanded Sublevel Six. The car rose quietly as he tried to decide if he should change his mind and redirect it.

He was as tense as he'd been all night when the doors parted. No ranks of heavily armed police waited to greet him. Instead he found himself on a busy, round-the-clock service floor. For a wild moment it was as if he was back in Phoenix, emerging onto any of a number of similarly laid-out floors in the Selvern Tower.

Ahead stretched a broad, carpeted corridor. The vast room was divided by modular cubicles, movable walls some two meters high. Within, people worked busily at soundproofed machines.

Since no one appeared to question his presence, he walked idly down the corridor. In one large cubicle he saw several people working with a large screen a meter and a half square. It was built into the floor. They would move long light pens over the vitreous surface while arguing in low voices about respective entries. Some of the cubicles contained consoles akin to the one he'd just utilized four floors below.

As he stood gazing, somebody's grandmother came up and put a comforting hand on his shoulder. She had lovely green eyes and spoke with the voice of authority.

"Can I help you, young man?"

He tried to put something like a smile on his face. "Excuse me. I've had a rough night."

"You certainly look it." She studied him closely. "Where are you supposed to be? I don't believe you belong to my section."

"I don't belong to anybody's section. I'm a civilian."

Why did he think he could trust this woman? He rushed on. "'I just came up from SL Ten.''

"Oh, a citizen. That doesn't tell me what you're doing up here. We have no public facilities on this level.''

"I put my request to a public booth and it told me to come up here. Sublevel Six, Booth B.''

Her brows drew together. "Booth B. Are you sure?''

"Yes ma'am." As they conversed politely he was ready to bolt and run.

"Well, we can check that quick enough.''

He followed her down the corridor and through several branching aisles. Unlike the modular cubicles surrounding it, Booth B turned out to be fully enclosed. Only two other similarly secure stations were visible. One was occupied. The walls of the booth were solid and opaque. A tiny console was built into the entrance.

"Enter the query you used to obtain your final instructions,'' the woman directed him. Eric used the console. The miniature screen lit up with the single word ADMIT.

The older woman shrugged, eyed him oddly. "So you do belong here. I wonder what your question was?'' She'd been too polite to peek. "It must have been important. Only very important inquiries are referred up here.'' She gave a little shrug. Eric wanted to ask her what she was baking.

"None of my business, of course.'' She gestured to her right. "If you need any help, there are advanced tech people present to assist you.''

"Thanks. I'll manage.'' He smiled gratefully, entered, and listened to the door lock automatically behind him. The console and display were identical to the one he'd used below. A little more modern in design, perhaps, a little sleeker, slightly less proletarian. Taking a seat, he entered the same queries as before, adding the reference number of the Sublevel Ten cubicle which had sent him upstairs.

"Hello,'' said a smooth voice. He jumped a little in spite of himself, stared at the console where he'd shut off the audio. Or thought he had.

"Yes, I know you've shut off the audio," said the voice. "Please do not be alarmed. This booth contains independent audio-video facilities. I feel it is better to dispense with the time-consuming process of keyboard entry and retrieval."

"Who is this? Who am I talking to?"

"I should think you might have guessed. I know who you are. You are Eric Abbott."

"Just a minute, that's wrong. You saw the name on my credit card. It's Mark Curtis."

"Please do not waste our time with futile denials, Mr. Abbott," said the voice calmly. If it was a machine voice, Eric thought furiously, it was beautifully processed. "You are a fine technician, but your work is not perfect. You have insufficient experience in illegal modification." Was that a hint of dry humor there?

"Who is this? Security? City authorities?"

"No indeed. This is the voice of Colligatarch Central."

"What? From Switzerland?"

"Yes. I am conversing with you via satellite relay."

Eric sat back in his chair. As an engineer and designer, he held even more respect for the Colligatarch Authority than the average citizen. To find himself addressing the central core of that globe-girdling network was sufficiently overpowering to make him forget for a few moments the troubles which had brought him to this place.

"I don't see why you should be interested in my query. I'm just trying to find a woman."

"But I *am* interested, for reasons of my own."

"Don't you always have reasons of your own?"

"You have a sense of humor. That's good." Then, quite out of the blue, "Where were you born?"

"I beg your pardon?" Was this some kind of elaborate, cruel joke the authorities were playing on him? For a second he thought of calling in help, then decided against it. He would continue with the game in hopes of learning something useful.

"Your birthplace."

"If this is really Colligatarch Central, you should have easy access to that kind of information."

"Verification is always useful."

"All right. Phoenix. Chandler, actually. That's a suburb. I've lived in the Greater Phoenix area all my life."

"What were your parents' names?"

He drummed idle fingers on the unused keyboard. "Listen, this isn't making any sense. I'm trying to find the woman I love. A number of people don't want me to find her."

How much of this did the Colligatarch know? He'd always believed, like most citizens, that the Colligatarch knew everything it wanted to know, but it hadn't mentioned the events of the past week. Instead it was questioning him about perfectly ordinary details of his life that surely existed already in half a hundred data banks scattered across the North American Federation.

He answered the question, was rewarded with another. "Where do you work?"

He shook his head, settled himself into the seat, and continued to answer the most mundane queries. Height and weight, color of hair and eyes, the names of his friends, his hobbies, what kinds of optos he liked, how often he attended the symphony, what major illnesses he had suffered while growing up, how he felt about politics, religion, economics, his work, and dozens more.

Finally, "How do you feel at this moment?"

That one made him hesitate. "I don't follow your meaning."

"Right now, sitting in Booth B, how would you evaluate your general condition?"

"Put upon, confused, anxious, otherwise healthy and sane."

"And physically?

"About the same. A little bruised and battered. I've had a rough couple of days, but I haven't broken any bones or torn any muscles."

A long pause, then, "You are Eric Abbott."

"Is this some kind of a joke? All this is readily available to you from fifty different sources."

"Verification is always—"

"Useful, yeah, you said that."

"You want to know about Lisa Tambor?"

This couldn't be Colligatarch Central, Eric decided. Never mind the fact that it could hardly be bothered by the problems of one man in search of his lady-love. It would not spend expensive time querying him all the way from Europe simply to ascertain whether his true weight was eighty or ninety kilos. Someone was stalling him, toying with him, though he didn't think it was Tarragon's people. They would have burst in on him by now.

"Where is she?" he asked. He did not expect a useful answer. Some part of him added aloud, "I love her."

"That is not relevant. Eric Abbott, you are advised to return to your home and work in Phoenix and forget about Lisa Tambor."

"Funny, I've already been told that." Maybe it was Tarragon. Maybe in spite of everything, he was hoping this machine-oriented directive would get the troublesome engineer out of his hair.

"I am aware that you have been so instructed previously. You must return to your home, Eric Abbott. There is no malice in this order." Order, he thought. Not suggestion. "Lisa Tambor serves a function which your presence complicates. No actions will be taken against you if you return home *now*."

"Really? What about my free ticket?"

"I am not aware of it."

"Oh, come on." He was tired of the game. "Your security people, a man named Kemal Tarragon, offered me a free ride home if I'd leave Lisa alone."

"Then I suggest you contact this man to see if that option remains available to you. This may be your last opportunity to do so. Transmission ends."

Eric leaned forward. "Now hold on! You directed me up here to repeat that same old . . . !"

He stopped. Every light on the console had winked out

save those which indicated it was still powered-up. Try as he would, Eric couldn't prod it to respond.

"I'll be damned," he muttered. He exited the booth, forgetting for an instant that there might be police waiting for him to emerge. There was no one except the elderly supervisor who'd first guided him to the booth. Apparently she'd decided to wait for him. Now she watched him curiously.

"It's quite a privilege, you know. I envy you."

"Envy me what?" he said absently. "What's quite a privilege?"

"Talking direct with Colligatarch Central." She looked apologetic. "The details of your communication remain private, of course, but there's no hiding where the input originated."

"So you're in on it, too."

She looked confused. "In on what?"

"Nothing. I'll find my own way out."

"Certainly. If I can be of further help . . ."

"No, you've done enough already." He could feel her eyes on the back of his neck as he started back toward the elevators.

What now? What would they try next? One minute they threaten to kill him, the next they repeat old warnings. If they held to form, now they would try to kill him again.

He'd learned nothing. Only that Tarragon's reach extended at least as far as the Colligatarch Subsidiary Service Terminal, Nueva York. Despite what the old lady had said, he still refused to believe he'd been conversing directly with the Colligatarch Central itself.

He did not enter one of the elevators. Instead he found his way across the vast chamber by reading identifying cards on individual cubicles.

Eventually he found himself near a solid wall, read the inscription on a modular divider, peered into the cubicle beyond.

"Excuse me? I'm a newsawk for channel eighty? The cybernews network?"

The man inside the cubicle looked up indifferently from his work. "What about it?"

"I need some information. I'm working on a homicide."

"So? What's wrong with your office terminal?"

"You know how it is at a network," Eric said confidentially, fully aware the man had no idea how it was at a network. "Intercepts, other reporters stealing your sources. Isn't there someone down here who works with police sources?"

"Of course." If the man had been more suspicious, the question would have been met with trouble instead of an answer. Or perhaps he was simply tired. It was now early morning and near the end of shift for the night workers. It's hard to be suspicious when one's primary thoughts are of sleep.

He didn't even ask for credentials, simply assumed that Eric had a right to be there by virtue of being there.

"You want Angelo Vargas, Module Eighteen Sixty-five."

"Thanks. Appreciate it."

Eighteen Sixty-five was located across the chamber, next to several deserted cubicles awaiting the arrival of the day shift. Eric circled the spot several times, trying to decide if what he had in mind could work. As to whether or not it was worth the risk, that was a foregone conclusion. He'd run out of ideas and viewed this as a last chance.

As he entered the cubicle, he closed the swinging door behind him. The middle-aged man at the desk looked up tiredly.

"What can I do for you, citizen?"

"Are you Angelo Vargas?" The man nodded, his hairless dome shiny in the reflected overhead light. "You work with the Nueva York police authority?"

"On occasion. I'm more access-ready than active. You want active, you'll have to go to the nearest precinct station."

"No, access will be sufficient. I'm a newsawk for channel eighty. I need some information on a recent disappearance. Missing persons stuff. Can you help me?"

"Probably." Vargas looked significantly at his fingers, which suddenly discovered dirt that needed to be rubbed away.

"Fifty bucks."

Vargas nodded and smiled contentedly. "No video?"

"Just research for now. I wouldn't want to compromise my sources."

"Fine. Just show me your station identification card and we'll get to work."

Eric didn't miss a beat. "No problem." He fumbled in a coat pocket. "Is that the call-up code you use?"

"Where?" Vargas turned to glance at his glowing screen. As he did so Eric took out a long, thin metal tool and pressed it into the back of the man's neck. The flesh was soft, and he had to be careful not to press too hard.

"This needle beam is very quiet. You cry out, you touch anything that even resembles an alarm, you cause me any difficulty whatsoever, and you'll never leave this module alive. I make myself clear?"

"Very clear, citizen. Take it easy. I've got three kids and a good wife, just don't do anything crazy, okay?"

"I'm not a *pocoloco*, friend, but if you make me the least little bit nervous, I'll slice you, *comprende*?"

"Sure, sure, just calm down, will ya?" Vargas was near hysteria.

"I'll kill you," Eric repeated, surprised at the vitriol in his voice, "and get the information I need somewhere else."

"Christ, I said I'd do what I can," Vargas moaned softly. "I'm not a matrix, you know. This isn't a precinct station."

"I know, but you move information. A lot of information."

"Sure I do. What do you want to know? Just tell me and I'll get on it." The man was frantic to get Eric his information and get rid of him, which was fine with Eric. He was as anxious to leave as the man was to be rid of him.

Eric added a final warning. "No tricks now. I'm access-knowledgeable. You key in an alarm code and I'll spot it, and it'll be the last code you ever key in. I won't warn you again.''

"Okay, okay." Vargas's voice was cracking and he seemed ready to cry. "I'm not going to die over some stupid data. Tell me what you want to know."

Eric was convinced the man would do what he could. Why shouldn't he? As soon as Eric fled the man could raise half a dozen alarms, forestall any damage his visitor might do with his stolen data. Except that Eric wasn't going to be forestalled.

"Woman's name, Lisa Tambor. Formerly of . . ." he struggled a second to remember her address and telephone number.

"What am I supposed to do with that?" the man asked nervously.

"She's left the city or moved within it. I have reason to suspect she may not have made the move voluntarily. See if you can find anything, *anything* under that name involving recent movement, travel, relocation, anything."

Vargas nodded, bent to his work. Eric watched carefully but could detect nothing unusual in the man's methodology as he conducted the search. He kept the metal tool pressed against Vargas's neck.

"Nothing," he finally announced. "Is she a criminal or something?" Eric didn't answer.

"Do you have access to travel information through here?"

"Look, I can only access police-related matters."

"And the police need to know when and where people are going."

"I'm liable to trip a code accessing an area that's outside my normal territory."

"I'll chance it."

Vargas shrugged, entered the necessary requests. The word OPEN appeared on the screen. "What now?"

"Check all transport out of Nueva York. Tube, bus, plane, suborbitals, everything."

"Right." If she'd been moved via private vehicle, they

wouldn't find a thing, Eric knew. Somewhat to his surprise, the screen lit up with a formal reply.

There it was. "Tambor, Lisa, Luftaire nonstop to London." There was an outside chance it might refer to a different Lisa Tambor, but the name was sufficiently unusual that he doubted it. Besides, time of departure fit perfectly. So did the mode: first class.

"Now try for a Kemal Tarragon on the same flight."

This time the query came up empty.

"Try finding him in police banks."

Again nothing. "Maybe he doesn't exist," Vargas ventured hesitantly. "Maybe he's a figment of your imagination."

"I wish he was."

Vargas spoke hopefully. "Is that all? Are you going to leave me alone now?"

"Yes. In just a second or two." He reached up and around with his free hand. The man hardly had time to gasp as Eric's fingers moved against his throat.

He struggled, but Eric had struggled with considerably stronger men recently, and Vargas was no match for him. His eyes rolled and he slumped in his seat. He'd be unconscious for maybe twenty minutes, and to any passerby he'd appear to be sleeping. Twenty minutes would be enough for Eric to clear the building.

Quietly he exited the module, carefully closing the door behind him. No one waited in ambush in the corridor.

When Vargas regained his senses he'd rush to notify security. They should be puzzled. At best they might suspect some stranger would be on his way to London in pursuit of some woman. With luck the badly frightened Vargas would not even remember Lisa's name.

Of course, Eric would be starting all over again in London, but at least he'd have the right city, and they shouldn't be expecting him. If he could get out of town fast, he might gain himself a breathing spell. The search for him should remain concentrated in Nueva York.

He moved rapidly through the aisles and did not encounter the elderly supervisor who'd greeted him earlier, for which he was grateful. By now he'd mastered the art of blending in with his surroundings. None of the programmers or processors bothered to look up as he walked by.

The elevator lifted him to the busy main lobby. A few quick strides and he was back out on the streets of the city. It was early morning now and the first day-shifters were striding briskly toward the waiting maws of ranked office buildings.

It was only a few steps to the nearest tube station. As soon as he saw there were no security cops on board his car, he relaxed and snatched a few precious minutes of sleep. The ability to catnap wherever and whenever he chose was something he'd always been thankful for. When the tube deposited him at Long Island Airport half an hour later, he was feeling almost refreshed.

There was a flight departing for London in forty minutes. His credit card set off no alarm when he purchased the ticket. The rest of the time he spent strolling around the airport—visiting a gameroom, watching the opto, sipping a sloe gin, and concluding with a fast breakfast. He looked forward to another, longer nap once safely aboard his plane.

The stewardess was bright, young, and professional. She inquired after his needs and he waved her away with a smile. All he wanted now was more sleep.

The thunder of engines was briefly loud as they lifted the flying wing off the runway and out over the Atlantic. In a little while they'd climbed above slower commercial traffic. He had a quick glimpse of a cruise dirigible idly working its way up the New England coast, the bright stripes and patterns on its curved sides duplicating an ancient Picasso. Ten minutes later they'd reached upper stratospheric cruising altitude and the ramjets took over, boosting speed to Mach 5.

He closed his eyes and snuggled down into the soft seat. Soon they'd be in London. He'd have to find a room and begin working on a way to track down Lisa and her captors in a city as big as Nueva York.

He was quietly confident that he could do so. The thought of locating one person in a city of twenty million no longer seemed daunting. At least he'd left Tarragon and his minions far behind. They could comb Nueva York for months without learning that he'd fled.

Eventually they would trace his credit card to the ticket purchase. By that time he hoped to have Lisa spirited away. It was a gratifying romantic vision and helped to put him to sleep.

XIII

ISABEL Jordan hurried to catch up to Oristano.

"What's the reason for this meeting, Martin? Pulling us away from our work in the middle of the day."

"Not my doing," he told her. "Blame the machine." As they made their way in tandem toward the conference room, she noticed the rest of the staff gathering.

"All twelve of us. Don't you think it's a little extreme?"

"The circumstances are extreme." Oristano rubbed at his eyes. He was very tired and missed Martha very much. Several weeks had passed since he'd been outside the mountain, and he longed for the sight of cold lakes and fresh snow.

"You don't know what it's going to say?"

"No." They turned a corner. Anira Chinelita was arguing with Froelich, kept up her muttering as they fell in step with the CPO and his companion.

"I can guess. It's this endless 'threat,' isn't it?"

He nodded. "Maybe there will be specifics we can deal with this time. Maybe that's the reason for the meeting."

"Don't count on it." Jordan wore a glum expression. It made her seem to be glowering, though this was more a result of her great height then her actual feelings. A former captain of the North American Olympic basketball team, she was the tallest member of the staff. "Do you still think there's a real danger, Martin?"

"I assume so, since the machine's said nothing to the contrary."

"I didn't ask you for the machine's opinion, Martin. I asked what *you* think."

"Izzy, I just don't know. I do know there's been no interference with our independent probe of the machine's logic functions."

"I've heard about the suspicions of cybernetic paranoia. Strikes me as silly."

"Dhurapati doesn't think so."

"Dhura wouldn't. Still, there's something to be said for acting as if everything can go wrong. Here we are."

They entered the conference room, nodding absently at the pair of armed guards who flanked the entrance. An opto eye noted their presence as they passed through the doorway.

Tea, coffee, and other beverages were available from individual dispensers located beneath each section of the oval table. A holo of the Alps in spring covered the far wall and gave the room some feeling of size. Opto screens filled two opposing walls. Each desk insert in the main table had its own communications equipment as well as access to computer terminals and small pop-up screens.

As soon as everyone had taken a seat and quieted, a familiar voice filled the room.

"I'm glad to see you were all able to attend."

"It damn well better be important," snapped Dr. Siakwan from his seat. Siakwan had never been famed for his sunny mood; only for his brilliance. He was fond of uttering outrageous obscenities in Mayan, confident that only four or five other people on the planet could understand him. It permitted him to insult friends and enemies alike with equal enjoyment.

"I've got half a dozen reports to sign out within the next—" he checked his watch with an Aristophanean flourish, "hour and a half. This isn't helping any."

"I assure you, Dr. Siakwan," the Colligatarch declared placatingly, "we will be out of here very soon.

"I've called you all together because I have an important announcement to make that I did not wish to deliver via the usual channels. You are all aware that a serious danger threatens me, and that this has occupied me for some time now."

No one said anything. There were a few impolitic, barely muffled groans. Isabel Jordan had activated her private console and was playing a complex mathematical game, listening with only half a mind.

"I can tell you that I now understand the nature of the threat and that I may have identified its source as well."

That made everyone take notice. Even Dr. Siakwan looked interested instead of combative, and Isabel Jordan wiped her game.

"Then tell us," said Oristano.

"There are still many things I am not sure of, specifics that I lack, missing pieces of the puzzle. But I have a grasp of the general outline now. There is no need to trouble you until that outline has been solidified."

"If there's no need to trouble us," said Jordan, "was it absolutely necessary to drag us all in here to inform us of that fact?"

"I thought it would raise your spirits. I am aware that this particular problem has placed something of a strain on all of you lately. The threat still exists, but I am in a position to begin to deal with it now."

The earlier groans were matched now by tired sighs.

"I am continuing to monitor all relevant developments and will keep all of you posted as additional facts are learned. Meanwhile, you may return to your regular assignments, secure in the knowledge that events are at last coming under control."

"This wouldn't have anything to do," said one of the other staff members, "with our recent external probe of your logic circuitry, would it?"

"Not at all," said the Colligatarch. "You must, of course, proceed with that probe, Dr. Novotski, until you have obtained the results you require. I shall endeavor to assist you and your team in any way I can."

"That's good, because I still have a number of things I want to do."

"I'm sure you do. Thank you all for your attention and consideration." The voice went quiet as the single doorway slid aside.

There was no rush to the exit.

"Any questions?" Oristano asked as he stood.

"Not hardly, *doh shieh*," grumbled Siakwan as he moved toward the door. "Damn waste of time."

Dhurapati moved to stand next to Oristano. "You don't think it's been playing with us all along, Martin?

He shook his head. "The Colligatarch doesn't play. It's too conscious of the value of its own time."

Novotski joined them. "*Izvanit'yeh* . . . excuse me, comrades, but it occurs to me this business may have been a test of our mental stability, not the machine's."

"I am discounting nothing," Oristano responded flatly, "but I disagree with that assessment, Alex. I believe in the machine; therefore I must also believe in this threat. I also believe it when it says it is getting everything under control. I don't know about the rest of you, but today's news makes me feel a lot better."

"I wish I could say the same." Novotski turned to depart, deep in conversation with Dhurapati Ponnani. Oristano chatted with each member in turn as he or she left, like a pastor after Sunday morning services, before departing himself.

The door was locked and the lights turned off. The conference room was now empty . . . except for the lingering presence of the machine. It considered what it had seen and heard, appraising stares, expressions, commentary, even the posture of its human colleagues.

Despite their grumbling, all had departed more relaxed and reassured. And why shouldn't they? There was no reason for the most skeptical of them, not even the extraordinarily perceptive Martin Oristano, to suspect that the Authority staff had been lied to for the first time in two hundred years.

* * *

"Ladies and gentlemen, please fasten your seat belts. We are beginning our descent into the London area."

Eric complied. He was anxious to resume his search for Lisa. The flight had provided him with time to reflect, and he'd decided that the best way to try to pick up her trail here was by repeating his visit to the local Colligatarch Terminal and asking the same questions he had in Nueva York.

He leaned against the cool window glass. There wasn't much to see. Rain covered the British Isles this time of year.

Don't worry, Lisa, he thought confidently. They can't hide you from me forever. I won't let them keep us apart. If necessary I'll follow you around the world. Or off it.

Touchdown was a gentle bump, the shriek of the jets as the pilot backthrusted only slightly deafening. The steward moved through the cabin asking everyone to please keep their seat belts fastened until the plane came to a complete stop. As usual, he was ignored. The plane taxied toward the terminal and slowed. Frowning, Eric joined his fellow passengers in staring out at the rain-slicked tarmac.

"There'll be a brief delay, ladies and gentlemen." The pilot didn't try to hide the irritation in his voice. "Some trouble with the ramp. I'm told they'll have it fixed in a minute. If you'll all relax, we'll be deplaning shortly."

Eric leaned back against his seat and read through the last of the in-flight magazine. When it began to repeat itself he turned it off by pushing the tiny teletext screen back into the armrest of his seat.

He was almost looking forward to confronting Lisa's captors. The giddy feeling of invulnerability, though dangerous, was exhilarating. He let it flow through him, because it was better than feeling the fear.

Up the aisle on his side of the cabin a woman was leading her young daughter back from the forward restroom. The most peculiar expression suddenly transformed the woman's face. It hung there like a bad taste until she unexpectedly dropped to her knees. When she fell over on her side, the passengers nearest her moved to help.

The little girl was able to cry, "Mommy, mommy!" and bend over the unconscious woman for a second before her own eyes rolled up and she fell on top of her mother. She was joined by the men and women who'd left their seats to try to help.

The progressive collapse of everyone seated forward led to an inescapable and frightening conclusion, and Eric was up out of his seat racing for the rear of the plane even as the realization struck home. Around him, the rest of the passengers were slumping in their places. He held his breath and his face reddened. All he knew was that he had to get off the plane *fast*.

He'd reached the stern exit and was grabbing at the emergency door release handle when whatever it was that had laid low his fellow travelers finally caught up with him. He stood swaying for a moment, trying to focus on the suddenly elusive handle. It danced maddeningly in front of him and refused to stay in one place. His eyes began to water. He made a convulsive stab for the handle and missed, his fingers puncturing the inner wall of the door but only bending the titanium alloy beyond.

Then it was quiet as death.

Five minutes passed before the forward door popped open. Figures entered, moving slowly while inspecting every quiescent body. Occasionally a passenger who'd fallen into the aisle had to be gently lifted and returned to an empty seat.

The intruders were completely encased in suits of flexible silvery material that was transparent from the neck up. These suits were designed to protect their wearers not only from the intentionally fouled atmosphere inside the plane but from more motile dangers.

In addition to protecting the wearer from most beam weapons and many solid projectile guns, the charged field suits could also, at the touch of a switch, fill themselves with several thousand volts. The charge could be regulated, to stun or to kill on contact. They were not activated now, but nervous fingers hovered close to controls.

"I don't see him," said the leader of the squad. Not satisfied to rely for protection on his suit, he also carried a stun pistol. Like the suit, it was linked to the battery pack on the man's back.

He stepped over an unconscious girl of eleven. "Charlene, you and Habib check the first-class compartment."

"He wasn't traveling first class," the woman behind him objected.

"I know, but he might have switched over in-flight. We can't take chances. Watch yourselves."

"What chances?" the woman protested. "Everyone on board will be out twenty-four hours, including him. I don't understand all the precautions. Seems like a bloody lot of trouble to go through to take one fugitive."

"You heard the reports from Nueva York."

"Sure, we heard them," said the dark-skinned man standing near the woman, "but that doesn't mean we must believe them. You know our American friends—always prone to exaggeration. It's their proclivity for romanticizing crime."

"Our job's not to evaluate, Habib. All we have to do is follow orders."

"Suit yourself, Sergeant." Habib and the woman moved away. Others came aboard to take their place.

The silvery figures continued their inspection of the aisles, moving together toward the back of the plane.

"I overheard," said a burly newcomer to the sergeant. "What *is* the big deal with this guy? There's going to be hell to pay when this hits the media. Imagine snucking a whole plane to take one man!"

"It won't reach the media," said the sergeant, "unless somebody opens their big, fat mouth. Then there *will* be hell to pay."

"Don't look at me, Sarge," said the questioner. He paused to adjust an elderly man who'd fallen awkwardly from his seat. "I think this one's got a broken arm. How are they going to keep the hospital cases secret?"

"Not our concern," said the sergeant. "That's in the lap of the Chief and Airport Security, thank goodness. All we've got to do is find this bloke."

Find him they did, several minutes later.

"Looks like he made a run for the exit," suggested one of the argent police. "He must've held his bloody breath forever."

"Not long enough." The sergeant eyed Eric Abbott's motionless form speculatively. He certainly didn't look like much, he thought. "Looks like he gave it a good try, though." He glanced back up the aisle.

"His ticket says he was in seat eighteen. Here he is back at forty-four. That's a helluva run under the gas. Doesn't take but a whiff of that stuff to put you under."

"Maybe he was back here to go to the loo," suggested one of the bobbies.

"Could be. We won't find out." The sergeant checked his chronometer. "Time to haul him out of here. We can thank our stars for this rotten weather. Hides us from the terminal." He reached down and slipped Abbott's legs under his arms.

"How come you get the light end?" grumbled the next bobbie in line.

"Because I'm a sergeant and you're only a corporal. Put some back into it."

Together they wrestled the unconscious form up the aisle. Other silver-suited commandos made way for them, commenting as they passed.

" 'E's nothin' to look at," muttered one. "Bloody lot of trouble for nothin'."

"Aye," said Charlene, who'd returned from first class to have a glimpse of their quarry. "Good-looking, though, in a quiet kind of way."

"You might not think so if half of what 'e did in Nueva were true."

"Can't you see their faces when they hear how easy a time of it we had bringing him in?" They shared a chuckle as they followed the limp body out of the plane and down the mobile stairway.

Abbott was hustled into an idling, unmarked van. Inside he was slipped onto a waiting pallet. Straps were crossed over his body from neck to ankles. Arms and legs merited separate treatment. Two women in white monitored the captive's vital signs. If he showed any movement they were ready and prepared to insure that he didn't wake up.

The van's engine rose to a soft whine against the rain. Behind it, police commandos were exiting the plane in a steady stream. Several had already unfastened their headgear and pushed it back as they walked toward a waiting bus. They chatted easily among themselves, pleased that the operation had gone so smoothly.

Much ado about nothing, as one said to a companion.

XIV

HE was drowning in one of Lisa's eyes. It was explosive bright blue. New blue, ice blue, *Blume* blue as he'd once told her. The blue was not surprising. The eye was all water, which was.

He'd fallen helplessly toward it, arms flailing, legs kicking, tumbling over and over until he struck the limpid surface and plunged ten meters deep. Kicking furiously, he swam upward, clawing for air, until he broke the surface of the eye.

Painfully he began swimming for shore, aiming himself at the high, fleshy ridge which bordered the cold liquid. A silvery moon lit the surface from high overhead. You could hear the sound of tears lapping the lower shore as they fell from the corner of the ophthalmic ocean, falling upward toward the sky, where they blurred the crescent moon.

As he turned to rest awhile by swimming on his back, he found he could see the great eyelid, its delicate black barbs curving upward into the night like the ribs of some vanished alien building. They trembled delicately as she cried.

It was a wonder that in the darkness the water held its bright blue, a clear blue the color of water viewed through arctic pack ice. He knew the strain was telling on her as she fought to keep from blinking and crushing him, and he tried to swim faster, but the water was thick and cloying and he was tired, so tired.

So he blinked instead. The night sky disappeared, to be replaced by a vague, watery haze. He didn't open his eyes all the way, only a crack, just enough to ascertain that he was conscious and aware.

There were voices around him, deep rumblings in the air. Mumbled syllables passed like swift verse among unseen shapes. He lay still and listened and peeked, the gauze that masked his vision slowly dissolving away.

Some kind of hospital. He was in some kind of hospital that was more than a hospital, because the windows were crossed with metal bars. He found he could look down at himself without moving his head. Straps crossed his chest, and when he twitched one leg he felt others restraining him there: one at the thigh, one at the knee, a third at the foreleg, and a last securing his ankle.

There were other beds, most of them occupied by people who supplied the voices he heard. Some were sitting up, most lying down. Light came from long fluorescent sticks set in a high ceiling. The walls were not painted so much as they were enameled a pale blue. It looked like solid plastic, but he knew it was only paint.

Two or three of the voices around him were shouting. They made no more sense than those that passed in whispers. Occasionally a figure in white passed the foot of his bed, ignoring him. Some were male, some female. Red chevrons decorated the sleeves of their uniforms. They reminded him of the bars that blocked the high windows.

After a while two new figures appeared and approached his resting place. As soon as he determined they were heading toward him, he closed his eyes and held himself as motionless as possible. He could hear them breathing above him, could feel the pressure of their stares against his face.

"You really think all these straps are necessary?" asked a feminine voice.

"I don't know, Doctor," a man replied. "I wasn't consulted when he was brought in."

"It seems extreme," the woman said. The concern in her voice was professional rather than personal. "I don't see how he can do anyone any harm when he's so heavily sedated."

"I agree, Doctor. It makes more work for the duty nurse, but the instructions they gave us were explicit."

"What a waste of time and money." There was a brief pause and he heard a wrist terminal beep twice. "He's got enough topalamine and endozite-B in him to keep a platoon of soldiers harmless. Risky enough."

"I told them," said the man, "but they didn't seem to care if he recovered full motor function or not. They just want him kept unconscious and alive.

"You know, sometimes I hate this damn job, Doctor. Sometimes I think of quitting to take an outside job."

"Take it easy, Charles," said the woman. "We're monitoring him constantly. He'll come out of it okay."

"Maybe he will, but there's no medical reason why his body should have to deal with injections at these levels. It's bordering on toxicity. I won't be held responsible if something happens."

"Nothing's going to happen, Charles," said the woman soothingly. "In any case, he's not a European citizen. By nine tonight there'll be a team in from North America to take over. Then he'll be out of our hands and we'll never see him again."

"No, but I'll still have to think about him," the man muttered. A longer silence, then, "I wonder what the hell he did to merit this kind of treatment? I wonder what he's wanted for?"

"I've no idea, Charles, and I don't care to know. He may be a murderer or simply an embezzler. We don't judge, we only treat. Frankly, I share your concerns. I'll be glad to see him go."

"I don't give a damn what he did; it stinks to see a man tied down like that."

"It doesn't bother him. He can't feel a thing, Charles. You know that."

They chatted a while longer, using a lot of technical medical terms unfamiliar to Eric. Then they went away.

He wondered what time it was. Dull light came in through the barred windows. After a while he opened one eye slightly.

They were coming for him tonight. Who was? A team from North America. That would include Tarragon or his deputies. They would take him out of this place and back to Nueva York, and then what? He didn't know and he couldn't imagine and he didn't want to find out, any more than he could allow them to put an ocean between him and Lisa again.

How had they traced him? Had someone at the airport recognized him from a description given by the clerk he'd made use of? He remembered his plane landing, the pilot's aggravated voice announcing the short delay, the woman returning with her daughter from the restroom who suddenly keeled over in the middle of the aisle for no reason at all. Then running, running desperately for the rear exit, never smelling anything, not sensing anything as he'd reached for the handle. Whatever they'd employed had been fast, odorless, and powerful.

Then waking up in This Place. Wherever that might be. For all he could tell he might be on the Continent instead of in London. But the accents around him were mostly English.

He had to get out somehow. First get away, then find Lisa. The bars on the windows were more informative than obstructive. Some kind of prison hospital, most likely.

He tried to sit up, found he could move only a little. More than strong straps held him immobile. His muscles refused to obey the commands of his mind. Forcing himself to relax, he considered the problem. He'd never been drugged before and found the sensation interesting. Feet and hands were numb, the rest of him only slightly less inoperative.

Strange what the brain concocts when suspended halfway between wakefulness and death. Imagine how it would be to stand upright again, to walk. His mind was clear and his vision no longer blurred. Imagine how things would have to change for walking to become possible.

First his body would have to purge itself of whatever chemicals they'd shoved into his bloodstream. It wouldn't be enough to run them through the kidneys. The molecules would have to be broken down, the bonds destroyed. Too complex a job for white blood cells. Something more complex and yet more subtle was required.

Even as he lay motionless considering the problem, he could feel himself growing stronger, could sense more and more muscle fibers twitching in response to his desires. The voices around him became understandable. The accents *were* English. Still somewhere in Britain, then. Maybe no longer in London, but somewhere below old Hadrian's Wall. That was vastly encouraging.

Lying on the bed with his eyes shut tight, he knew only that he was becoming himself again. There was no conscious awareness of the breakdown of complex narcotics within his body. Once he had to take care to lie especially still when some doctor appeared.

He felt something prick his right arm and sensed the injection. His mind fluttered and thoughts wavered for a moment while he briefly reexperienced the near-forgotten sensation of swimming in a dark blue lake.

But he was expecting it this time and did not lapse into dreams. The doctor was joined by two others. It required a tremendous effort not to open his eyes for a look at his captors.

"Is this the one?" A new voice, American accented.

"That's him." The female physician who visited him earlier. How much earlier? He didn't know.

"Doesn't look threatening."

"That's what we thought when they wheeled him in."

A faint breeze cooled his nostrils, perhaps the result of someone's passing a hand over his face.

"Now, some of these chaps in here," Charles said, "I could understand all this nonsense. Take MacReadie down there. Third bed, left side of the aisle. A double murderer, and he's neither sedated nor strapped down. If this one's psychotic he doesn't belong in here. He belongs over in Block C, in the mental ward."

"From what I've been told, this one's not psychotic," said the American voice. "Just damn dangerous."

"Someone certainly thinks so," said the woman doctor. "I'll be glad to be rid of him."

"I understand. If he starts giving you trouble . . ."

"A laugh from Charles, derisive rather than amused. "Not bloody likely. He's saturated."

"Nevertheless, the reports I've received are full of the most dire warnings. If anything untoward occurs, you must get in touch with me immediately."

"I know," said the woman. "Your people are in the Newlin Building, aren't they?"

In his excitement Eric was positive he jumped a little, sure he'd given away his awareness. But they must not have been watching him at that moment. Or else they simply didn't notice. He tried to still the beating of his heart, certain the sudden rush would draw their attention.

"Right, well, I'm off," said the American.

"So are we," said Charles. "Look, couldn't you tell us what this chap's wanted for?"

"Sorry." The American was pleasant but unyielding. "I'm not authorized."

"Must be something extraordinary," Charles muttered.

"Must be," admitted the American in neutral tones.

Eric listened to their conversation until they'd wandered beyond range of his hearing. Electric before his eyes were the words *Newlin Building*. Now he had a destination, a place to begin. And something else: that newcomer's voice. He'd memorized it as surely as he'd memorized the name of the building. If he heard it in a crowded store, he'd be able to pick it out of a mob. That voice could put him on Lisa's trail.

He hesitated. The man hadn't indicated where this

Newlin Building was located. It might be in London. It might also be in Glasgow, or Manchester, or Portsmouth. But if that were the case, if it wasn't located in the same city as the hospital, surely the man would have specified its location? He felt better. It had to be in the same county as the hospital.

A destination. It was all he needed.

The chemical factory that was his body continued to cleanse itself. It was amazing how refreshed he felt two hours later. It was as though the events of the past hours, much less the past couple of weeks, had had no cumulative effect on him at all.

He tried an experiment, attempted to raise his left hand. It came up easily, halted only by the strap. The strap was keeping him from his beloved, from Lisa. It was a dirty, inhumane way to treat any human being. He'd been trapped like an animal and now they were treating him like one. He pushed angrily at the strap.

There was a soft *spang* as the restraint snapped. It should not have snapped. It was fashioned of carbon-fiber mesh padded on the underside so as not to bruise the flesh beneath. It was stronger than steel and it broke as easily as a rubber band. He raised his right arm and the sound was repeated twice, since there was a strap at his elbow as well as at his wrist.

Then he sat up and there were lots of snapping, *spang*ing sounds. He'd waited until the room was empty of medical personnel but he dare not wait too long. The men from the Newlin Building, the men with the nameless faces, were coming for him soon. He smiled. If they would give him just a few minutes, he would save them the trouble of making the trip.

Somewhere in the room someone suddenly murmured loudly, "Cor, would you 'ave a look at that!" He thought it might have been the double murderer with the broken leg. Other voices spoke in stunned whispers, one in a foreign language he didn't recognize.

Reaching down, he ripped away the rest of the restraints, turned sideways on the bed, and stretched luxuriously. His muscles were on fire.

There was a tall cabinet between every two beds. Opening the one next to his, Eric was delighted to discover that it contained the clothes he'd been wearing on the plane. They were clean and neatly pressed.

He went first for the inside coat pockets. His billfold was there. It contained his identification and credit cards. Undoubtedly the police had made copies for study. His tools were missing.

He slipped off the hospital gown and dressed as quickly as possible. When he was done he took a moment to brush back his dyed hair and adjust his collar. The false moustache had been removed but he didn't regret the loss. It had itched.

As he started calmly for the door, one of the other inmates grinned at him from his bed. "It ain't that easy, friend." He didn't respond, reached the door.

It was made of metal. There was a small window set at eye level, and it was locked tight. Standing to one side, he waited until the duty nurse entered. As she walked past he slipped through. She didn't see him, but the guard seated immediately outside did. He eyed the unexpected, neatly dressed man curiously.

"Dr. Williamson," Eric told him cheerfully, glad they'd shaved his unconscious form.

"Williamson?" said the guard with a frown. "I didn't admit any Dr. Williamson."

"Of course you didn't. The earlier guard did. I've been here for some time."

"Some time is right, mate. I've been on duty for four hours. What guard?"

"Why, that gentleman over there," Eric informed him, pointing down the hall. When the guard turned to look, Eric hit him on the back of the neck. Not too hard, he hoped, but he wasn't going to worry about it. At the moment he wasn't feeling very charitable.

The guard caved in and dropped silently. He wasn't carrying a weapon—a precaution in case any of the hospital prisoners managed to get this far. Eric rushed to the next barrier and hit the call button set alongside the door. This one didn't even have a window mounted in it.

"What is it, Harris?" asked a voice through a speaker. The opto pickup overhead and out of reach swiveled to focus on Eric. "You're not Harris."

"Of course not." Eric smiled politely at the pickup. "I'm Dr. Williamson."

"No Williamson on my list," said the speaker.

"I spent the night with a seriously ill patient. Check with the night watch, or if you prefer, I can show you my identification." He made a show of reaching for his inside pockets.

"Why isn't Harris with you?"

"You mean the guard?" Eric nodded down the short hall. "I think he's asleep. I didn't want to disturb him."

"Be hell to pay. Never mind, Doctor. I'll check your ID myself." There was a buzz and the heavy metal door slid aside. Eric stepped through.

He found himself confronting a man holding an armed stungun. It was pointing at his belly.

"I don't know who you are, mate," said the guard warily, "but I'm going to damn well find out."

Another guard seated behind a desk squinted, raised his voice excitedly. "Hey, wait a minute, I know this one. That's the import from bed seven."

"Don't be absurd," Eric told him. "I am Dr. Matthew Williamson. I know the prisoner to whom you refer. How could I possibly be confused with him? He's tied down."

The shorter guard hesitated a moment, rubbed at his forehead. "Well, sure, he's tied down, but you sure look like . . ." He reached for the phone on his desk.

"I know." Eric took a step forward. "These credentials should take care of everything."

The man seemed very light, but nothing surprised Eric anymore. He threw him at the other guard. The stungun went off only once. Eric's shoulder tingled, but he'd ducked most of the blast.

Then he was racing down the busy corridor, pushing white-clad doctors and nurses and startled visitors aside. Minutes later the alarms began to go off. He forced himself to slow to a walk as he turned a corner. In a prison a running man is as conspicuous as a frog at a heron convention.

Shouts and yells sounded behind him and eventually the inevitable, "There he goes!" Then the sounds of weapons firing, and this time not all of them were stunguns.

He started running again. A guard appeared in his path and tried to swing the muzzle of his rifle around. Eric straight-armed him, a little harder than he meant to. The man went flying over a desk and slammed into a window. Reinforcing wire woven through the glass kept him from falling through, but he couldn't continue the chase. Eric's hand had crushed his sternum.

He saw open doors and rushed through them. The sunlight, filtered through the low rain clouds, was a warm shock to his system. Ahead lay the main gate to the compound, the only exit through a high wall—another shock. Men on the platform above the gate were trying to aim something long and metallic down into the grassy courtyard between wall and hospital. Others on the grass clustered together in front of the gate and engaged in animated discussion. They hadn't spotted him yet.

Oddly, his thoughts as he turned and ran to his left were centered on the climate. What a wet, sorry country. Where was the England of innumerable flowers and singing birds he'd read of so often? As he accelerated he saw several men hurrying toward him on a three-seat cycle. They were yelling something at him, but words no longer held meanings.

There was nowhere for him to go. Pursuit was closing in from both sides and behind. Ahead lay only the wall, a much less ambiguous opponent. Putting his arms across his face, he lowered his head and clenched his teeth.

A dull explosion sounded in his ears. He staggered, found himself suddenly beyond the wall in open country, running across a field toward a nearby wall of trees. He steadied himself and began to cross the open country in long, effortless strides.

Behind him his closest pursuers, the three guards riding the cycle, ground to a halt and dismounted. Instead of hurrying after their quarry, they slowly approached the gap in the wall. Thick at the base, it tapered to a sharp cement ridge crowned with three high-voltage wires. The hole was ragged and uneven. Cement dust still fell from the upper part of the gap. Gingerly, they felt the inexplicable opening.

"Well, come on," the oldest said, holding his weapon more tightly than usual. "Let's get after him."

"You get after him, Max." The speaker was running a hand over the raw edge of the hole.

"Let's go, I said. We've got an escaped prisoner out there." He pointed toward the nearby woods. The third man shook his head and spoke with unaccustomed solemnity.

"That's not quite right, Max. There's an escaped something out there all right, but it ain't no prisoner. Have a seat and think about it some."

The corporal named Max hesitated, found himself eyeing the hole uncertainly. "Somebody on the outside was helping him. They planted some kind of bomb and timed it to go off as he was making his run for it. A bomb, or a mine."

The third speaker shook his head. "It weren't no mine, Max. And it weren't no bomb. There was no explosion before he hit the wall."

"We would've heard it," said his companion.

"It went off just as he reached the wall," the corporal suggested lamely.

"No way, Max. If that were the case he'd have died in the blast, and here we all three of us saw him crossing the field like a damn marathoner. Put me on report if you want to." He turned and strolled back toward the idling cycle. "I ain't going after whatever that was that went through here for nobody. Not for the warden, not for the PM, not for the bloody King himself."

Corporal Max stood in the hole in the wall and considered how to proceed. Twenty years of experience did not offer up any suggestions. At that point he determined the best thing to do would be to wait for someone who ranked him. Yes, wait and let someone else give the orders. Wait and hope that one and all decided to ignore whatever had smashed its way through a solid concrete wall.

The sirens had long since faded behind him as Eric emerged from the trees. Ahead lay a picturesque little village. A steady drizzle was beginning to fall, making him wish for the umbrella he'd bought back in Nueva York.

The town was too small to rate a tubestation. He settled gratefully for the shuttle bus which picked him up. No one on the bus gave him a second look, and he slumped into the rear seat. Now if he could just get to a tubestation, his pursuers would have the devil of a time trying to track him.

If he'd known how poorly that pursuit was shaping up, he would have relaxed. A prisoner had escaped from the hospital: that much had been accepted. What was causing all the confusion was the manner of his escape. Tarragon wouldn't have been confused, but Tarragon wasn't at the hospital to explain the impossible to the badly unnerved administration.

The bus let him off in a larger town. At the local tubestation he was relieved to discover that it was only a three-minute tube ride to downtown London. He had the money he'd changed at the airport prior to leaving Nueva York, and sooner than he'd dared hoped he found himself making the crossover at Hammersmith Station. The tube took him to Picadilly, and he made still another precautionary switch to St. James before he risked riding up to the street.

Not daring to use his credit card unless absolutely necessary, he took surface transportation to the National Gallery. He spent an hour researching artist's supply stores before settling on one, moved from it to an electronics hobby shop, and before evening had replaced the tools they'd taken from his breast pocket.

Another hour in the gallery study rooms and he had another identity on his credit card, matched to a proper British address lifted from the Birmingham directory. That should slow them down, he thought grimly.

From the gallery he worked his way up to Oxford Street, where he purchased a new set of clothes, rain gear, and a proper brolly. Down a public dispos-all chute went his Nueva York suit, and thence to a public information booth.

The Newlin Building was located halfway between the Tower and Greenwich, on the Thames, in an area of high-rise office buildings.

The robocab deposited him up the street, after circling the block several times in search of clumps of large men trying to appear inconspicuous. If the news of his escape had been disseminated, it hadn't resulted in any unusual security measures being taken in this area.

Thirty stories of gray metal and glass, the Newlin Building rose above the murky waters of the old river. London looked much like Nueva York, but somehow everything smelled differently.

Was Lisa here? Or would he have to wring her location out of Tarragon's English associates?

The building did not have an automatic receptionist. Instead there was a round desk marked "Information." An elderly guard hovered nearby. He spent his time concentrating on his watch instead of the businessmen who came and went in the lobby. Most of them were leaving. It was evening and close to quitting time.

As he approached, the pleasant young lady seated at the desk looked up at him. "Can I help you, sir?"

"I'm trying to locate a friend."

"Does she work here?"

"I think so." Now was not the time to hesitate. "Her name's Lisa Tambor."

The woman checked her directory, frowned. "I'm sorry, sir. No one using the name Lisa Tambor works in the Newlin."

That would've been too easy, he told himself. "What about a man named Kemal Tarragon?"

She checked her file. "Sorry, sir. Neither of those names rings a bell."

He started to describe Tarragon, switched instead to a more memorable image.

"The woman, Tambor, is a little taller than you. Extremely beautiful, dark skin, very exotic look. Blue eyes." In this country of largely pallid citizens, Lisa would stand out sharply. "Very large eyes, petite figure but not skinny."

"I still don't recognize the name." The receptionist hesitated, "But I think I may have seen the young lady you refer to."

Eric's hands tightened on the edge of the desk, bending the hard plastic. Fortunately the woman didn't look down.

"She went upstairs with a Mr. Brostow. That would be Canal Imports, I think." She consulted her list. "Yes. You might inquire about her there."

"How do I find Canal Imports?"

"Twenty-eighth floor, suites sixteen through thirty."

"Mr. Brostow. Thank you very much, you've been a big help."

"You're welcome, sir. No trouble at all."

Eric moved toward the elevators, at the last instant thought better of it and searched until he'd located the fire stairs. His brain worked feverishly as he climbed. It was too much to hope that Lisa might be here, too much to think he might get a break after everything that had happened. He'd expected to have to find the man who'd eyed him in the hospital, then Tarragon or some highly placed assistant, then Lisa.

But if she'd been brought to England, why *not* here? Why not this building? He remembered how she'd obeyed Tarragon's order back in her codo in Nueva York. Would she do the same if the confrontation was repeated? How could he be certain of her reactions?

Then he was at the twenty-eighth floor and peering down a heavily carpeted corridor. One or two severely clad business types crossed from one door to another. From his position by the stairwell he could see the elevator access clearly. There were no signs of any guards.

As casually as possible, he stepped out into the corridor and began scanning suite numbers. As soon as he reached sixteen he began querying receptionists. None had heard of Lisa Tambor, but what had worked below worked equally well on the twenty-eighth floor.

"I think I saw someone of that description, yes," said the young man behind the narrow desk. "I was coming back from my lunch break and—"

"Which suite?" Eric spoke more sharply than he intended, tried to soften it with a smile.

"It's strange, you know. At the end of the hall there are two doors, one on the left side, one on the right, and they're not marked. I think that's where I saw her, coming out of one of those doors. I say it's strange because I always assumed they led to storage rooms. You know, for janitorial equipment and like that. They're certainly not connected to any of Canal Imports' offices."

"Thank you," said Eric.

"I don't think you'll be able to get inside," the youth hastened to add. "They're always locked." He smiled apologeticaly. "I know. I've tried myself, out of curiosity."

"It's all right," Eric told him. "I know what I'm doing."

"Be careful," the man told him. "Curiosity killed the cat, you know."

"I know, but I have nine lives." He hurried to the end of the hallway.

As the receptionist had indicated, there were the two opposing, unmarked doors. There was no sign of a buzzer or ringer, and the handgrip was set flush with the surface of the plastic. No twist-proof door was going to stop him, not now. He pushed and pulled sideways simultaneously. Metal protested loudly, then gave with a snap.

He stepped inside, found himself in a narrow hall. As he walked he found himself peering into empty offices. Once or twice individuals emerged, glanced indifferently at him, and vanished behind soundproofed doors.

He started trying the doors. When he intruded he excused himself with a quick smile and a few words. As he was beginning to despair, he opened a door which did not admit him to an office. Instead, he found himself staring into a large, comfortably furnished room. Sitting on a couch facing a window overlooking the Thames was a slim figure. The sight sent a shiver through him from toes to fingertips. He closed the door softly behind him.

She likes to look at rivers, he told himself. We'll have to find someplace that overlooks a river.

She sensed his presence before he could say anything, turned slowly. Recognition sent one hand to her mouth, and those magnificent wide eyes grew wider still.

"Eric," she whispered. "Eric."

"Hello, Lisa." He moved toward the couch, glancing warily to left and right. For the moment, at least, they were alone.

"You shouldn't be here." Then, in a completely different tone, "They told me to forget about you, that I'd never see you again."

"They're not always right," he murmured, wondering as always who "they" were.

His body moved of its own voliton and it seemed the most natural thing in the world to step around the couch to sweep her up in his arms. The fervor of her embrace dispelled any final, lingering doubts he might have held. All the agonies and pain of the past week, all the questioning and confrontation were washed away by the tears she poured out on his shoulder.

"I don't understand you." He used a gentle finger to wipe tears from the corners of her eyes. "In Nueva York Tarragon tells you to go to your room, and, like some dumb automaton, you comply. You never came out to see what was happening to me."

She looked back toward the river. "I didn't want to see what was happening to you because I knew what was going to happen to you."

"But to leave like that, without a protest, without a good-bye. *Why*?"

"Because I had to," she told him simply. "Tarragon is one of my bosses. I have to do what he says."

"Not anymore you don't. Not ever again."

She shook her head sadly. "It's so easy for you to say that, Eric." The bitterness in her voice was directed more at herself than at him. "You still don't know anything."

"Do you still love me?"

"That's a stupid question. Of course I love you. It shouldn't be and I don't know why I should but I do."

"It's simple for me. I know that I *should* love you and that it should be. It's right."

She looked past him, toward the door. "How did you find me here?"

He was too exhausted to feign bravado. "It wasn't all that hard. I flew in on a plane, had a nice rest in a comfortable bed provided by the State, enjoyed some organized exercise, and here I am." No need to go into details she wouldn't believe anyway, he mused. "And now you're leaving this place, leaving Tarragon and your other 'bosses,' to come with me."

"Where?"

"To Phoenix, of course. We're going to get married."

"Then what, Eric?"

"Settle down, have some children."

"Children?" She pronounced the word oddly, as though it were something she'd never considered before. "Yes, I suppose that, given certain conditions, it would be possible."

A strange way to put it, he thought, but rushed on by to other thoughts. "It's not impossible."

"No, of course it isn't," she said dryly. "I'll get a nice job to complement yours and we'll live happily ever after. Just your typical suburban couple."

"It's a picture worth considering," he told her. "Sometimes the simplest thoughts are the easiest to hang on to, especially when everything around you seems to be going mad.

"As for Tarragon and his bosses, I've already thought about how we can take care of them. We're going straight to the biggest media center in London and offer the whole thing to the opto networks. When a few million people know your story, Tarragon's people will be a damn sight more careful before they try sprinting you off to another country and sticking me away somewhere where I can't say anything.''

She brightened a little at the idea. ''That's just sane enough to be possible. I never thought of that before.'' Watching as she sloughed off her apathy the way a butterfly sheds its cocoon was a wonder to behold. ''Stranger things have happened.''

''Only on the rarest of occasions,'' said a new voice.

Eric turned and stared.

Tarragon again, standing in the hallway door.

XV

ALWAYS Tarragon. Would they never be free of Tarragon? Must he forever play Valjean to Tarragon's Javert? It wasn't fair, dammit! It just wasn't fair!

"Not this time, Tarragon. You're not separating us this time."

"I'm sorry, Abbott. I have to. My job, you know." Eric could see the heavily masked men clustered in the narrow passage behind him. A similar mask dangled from Tarragon's neck.

"And this time we won't allow you the luxury of waking up. Someone made a mistake. My people won't repeat it." Even as he spoke Eric saw the tiny capsules arcing through the air. As they struck the floor and furniture, they burst, hissing softly. Tarragon pulled his mask up over his face.

At the same time men pushed into the room, aiming their guns at the single target. No stunguns this time, he noted. No more kid gloves, no more chances. Simple automatic projectile weapons.

He knew that they meant to kill him, regardless of the mental damage that might result to Lisa. He knew it not only from the weapons themselves but from the expressions on the men and women who wielded them. He knew it from the way Lisa screamed behind him.

Her hand was still in his and he felt his fingers tighten convulsively around hers. She screamed again us the guns went off.

How strange, but he thought he heard Tarragon scream, too.

Darkness then, so warm and quiet.

So this is death, Eric thought. Not unpleasant, in fact, peaceful as the pastors claimed, save for the angelic choir singing somewhere off in the distance. That was only natural, of course.

He'd never been a particularly religious man and was vaguely surprised to hear angels. Well, life had been full of surprises. Why not death?

Something pressed tightly against him, a warm, pliable shape. He recognized the feel of Lisa. They'd been killed together, then. Together at last. Tarragon had finally won, though Eric doubted it had been his intention to have Lisa killed along with him. The thought of Tarragon discomfited made him feel a little better.

It was dry, chilly, and there was a faint musty smell to the air. That struck him as peculiar, as peculiar as being able to feel Lisa so strongly. The darkness, the angelic voices blending in perfect harmony, that much he could have anticipated, but somehow the ascent toward heaven should not be dry and musty.

He let go of Lisa and found he could walk. He also knew he was breathing. That also didn't seem right. Surely when you died you dispensed with such temporal necessities as respiration?

Something stopped his progress, and reaching out, he found stone beneath his hand, cold and unpolished. Too many things not making sense.

"Eric, what happened to us?"

"I . . . I don't know. We're not where we were. I thought Tarragon's people killed us."

"So did I," she said, "but I don't feel dead."

"A choice contradiction in terms," he murmured softly. He let his eyes roam the darkness.

There was light, not from above but off to his right. It was weak, faintly yellow, and not at all sublime.

"I don't think we're in the Newlin Building anymore,

Lisa. I don't think we're in Kansas anymore, either." He laughed, but the echoes were mocking and he quickly calmed himself. "Do you hear angels singing?"

"I hear something singing. You too?" He nodded, forgetting that she couldn't see the gesture. They started walking toward the light.

As their eyes grew accustomed to the darkness and the increasing dim illumination, he saw they were in a low, vaulted chamber with an arched roof. The walls and ceiling were of hand-hewn stone blocks. Many boasted deeply cut inscriptions; some showed paint and other forms of decoration.

Still clinging to Lisa's hand, he angled more to his right, chasing the light where it showed the strongest. Above them the heavenly chorus continued in song. He paused to eye one massive stone slab and read the inscription. The English chiseled into the rock was archaic but legible.

HERE LIES COL. JOHN SANTHORPE
FELL IN THE SERVICE OF HIS KING
DURING THE REVOLT OF THE AMERICAN COLONIES
MARCH 3RD, 1775
AGED 33 YEARS

"I always thought crypts were buried well below heaven," he muttered. Now Lisa was moving faster toward the light, leading him on.

"They are, Eric, they are. Where are we? And what happened to Tarragon and his people? And how did we get here?"

"Plenty of questions, no answers," Eric mumbled in confusion. "Sounds like life above us, not angels."

They found themselves in a passage lit by sunlight from overhead. The ceiling was low. They hurried down it and came to a spiral stone staircase. As they climbed, the voices of the choir grew louder.

The staircase opened into a small room barred by a

locked door. The lock opened easily at Eric's touch and admitted them to an epiphany of light and sound.

They stood in a side nave, having finally emerged from the catacombs below. Far away, beneath the immense painted and mosaicked dome, a choir was rehearsing. As they stared, the conductor stopped, irritatedly bawled out an off-key tenor. Then the music was resumed. Eric finally recognized the piece as Vaughn Williams's *Toward the Unknown Region*. Heavenly in inspiration, but decidedly secular in execution.

Eric didn't recognize their locale, but Lisa had prepared well for her forced journey to England.

"We're in St. Paul's!" she said excitedly. "But how?"

Eric only half heard her. He was lost in awe at the grandeur of the structure in which they found themselves. "Beautiful," he murmured. "I've always heard about it. Never thought to see it."

"This is not the time to play tourist." She started pulling gently at his arm. "How did we get here? And can anyone else follow?" Her eyes were darting every which way, as if she expected Tarragon to spring at them any moment from behind one of the immense marble pillars.

"Strange," Eric mumbled, turning his attention back to her. "I felt the disorientation. There was a mental wrench, not a physical one."

"I felt something like that, too," she told him, "but that's a description, not an explanation."

"What does it matter?" he said, suddenly feeling very alive and light-headed. He took her in his arms again. "I told Tarragon he'd never separate us again, and he hasn't." The kiss lingered until they both felt themselves growing short of breath.

"You're never going to have to worry about Tarragon again. I'll take care of that."

"So naive, Eric. You're so wonderful and puzzling and handsome and enigmatic, and so naive. Tarragon will find us. He'll always find us. Somehow we've slipped out of his grasp, but only for a moment."

"It's a big world," Eric countered. "And there's always the satellite colonies on Luna, and Ganymede, and Titan."

"It doesn't matter," she said softly. "He'll find me. It's his job."

"Hang his job and him with it! Not if you love me."

"It's not possible for me to love you, but I do."

They stepped clear of the nave and found seats on an empty bench. Other tourists wandered in respectful silence through the immense chamber. Their eyes were aimed upward. A few listened and nodded in contentment to the sounds of the choir.

"When you talk like that," Eric admonished her, "you sound like Tarragon himself. What's your relationship to him, anyway? I thought he was some kind of mob chieftain, and later that he worked for one."

"There aren't such things anymore," Lisa told him. "The Colligatarch makes them impossible."

"There are still rumors," Eric insisted. He found that he couldn't meet her gaze when he asked the next question. "*Are* you some rich politician's or corporation executive's mistress?"

"No." There was an amused smile on her face, but she wasn't laughing. "Tarragon does work for the government, but not in an executive capacity. He's kind of a field supervisor, a troubleshooter for a very important ongoing project."

Eric frowned. "Then what's his connection with you? Are you involved in this project somehow?"

Her left hand reached up to gently caress his face. "Poor sweet, mysterious Eric, I do love you so. You don't understand. I told you at the start that you wouldn't understand." Her hand pulled away reluctantly.

"Eric, I *am* the project. And I can't love you because I was designed not to."

His thoughts tumbled wildly over one another, preconceptions shattering like thin glass. "You're not making any sense, Lisa. Okay, so you're involved with some kind of government project. I can accept that. You say that you're a designer?"

"Eric, please, listen to me. Don't make this any harder for me than it is. I am the project. I'm not a designer. I am . . . was . . . designed. I'm a lure, Eric."

"A lure?" He gaped at her, wisdom at a dead-end.

"You know what a lure is. A little wiggly thing that fits on the end of a fishing line. I've been constructed with great care. I'm told only the best bioengineers in the world assisted with my design. It was a difficult thing to accomplish. Standards of beauty differ from one part of the world to the other, and I had to appeal to men from every continent."

"I don't doubt that you would," he whispered.

"Listen to me! Eric, I'm an artison, an artificial person. I'm like Topsy, Eric." She laughed nervously. "I was just growed."

Quietly he sat next to her, feeling her warmth, knowing her goodness, sensing her love and not wanting to believe her. But she spoke with too much assurance.

He had to take her at her word. There was no conceivable reason why she would manufacture such an incredible lie, not now, not safely clear of Tarragon's clutches. He could look inside her and not be able to discover the truth. Only a molecular biologist could do that.

Inside as well as on the outside, Lisa Tambor was perfectly human. Too perfectly. There was nothing to distinguish her from a normally conceived human being other than certain special talents or abilities her designers might have built into her. Talents like the ability to lure, for example.

A brief glance into a passing car on a street in Phoenix had disrupted his entire life and driven him several times to the verge of death. Yes, he could well believe she was a lure.

Her fingers twisted against each other on her lap. "There are certain people that WOSA, the World Space Authority, needs. Not just scientists, I'm told, but particular mental types required to provide proper population balance on Garden and Eden, the GATE colonies. I've been told that I was designed expressly to appeal to these mental types. They have an irresistible desire to fall helplessly in love with me." Her smile was twisted.

"It's a kind of test, falling in love with me. How did you think people for Eden and Garden were selected, Eric?"

"The lotteries," he mumbled weakly. "Everybody has a chance to be . . ."

Her laugh was kind even as it was tinged with sadness. "Lotteries! Do you really think WOSA would choose the people intended to insure mankind's survival by populating the only two extra-solar colonies by mere chance? Oh, a few are chosen that way through the lotteries to keep people like statisticians from getting too curious about the procedures, but when WOSA locates a certain type they want to recruit, they put him in close proximity to me. I have several male counterparts, by the way, and there are other female lures at work. If the subject responds correctly to my presence, they are recruited."

"How could anyone not respond to you?" Eric told her.

"You're prejudiced. It's a carefully chosen combination of visual excitants, pheromones, and other characteristics beyond my comprehension. I can't explain it all. I'm not a scientist. I don't know how I produce the effects in men that I do, only that it happens." She went silent then and they listened together, each lost in private thoughts. Eric was thankful for the occasional off-key notes the choir produced. They were necessary reminders of reality.

Finally he looked back at her. "It doesn't matter. Nothing matters so long as you love me."

"I do love you," she told him, fighting back fresh tears. "That's not built into my makeup, but I do. I don't understand it, but I do. And you can't love me!"

He took both her hands in his. "Stop telling me what I can and cannot do, what's possible and what's not."

"But don't you see, Eric? That's why Tarragon and the bureau are so upset. You're not supposed to love me. You're a stranger off the streets, an accident, an anomaly. You don't fit the mental profile."

"Tarragon's told you all this, hasn't he?" She nodded.

"I don't doubt that I'm a surprise to them, but how do they know I don't fit their damn profile? They haven't tested me."

"But they *have*, Eric. Tarragon told me. When this began, when you started pursuing me, they went into the employee data bank at your company. They studied all your employment and subsequent updating tests. None of it fits, Eric. Nothing matches properly. If there were even a few parameters you tested within, Tarragon would have treated you differently. Of course, you wouldn't have been allowed to stay with me, but you might have been recruited."

"Then their parameters are wrong," Eric told her, "because it's an unarguable fact that I *am* in love with you. Obviously, they've slipped up. Maybe their parameters aren't exact."

"And what if they aren't? What if they have made a mistake and they decided to recruit you, to send you?"

"Tarragon wants to send me someplace, all right, but it isn't Garden or Eden." The paradise worlds, he thought idly. No taxes, no crushing burden of day-to-day jobs. It was something everyone dreamed of, everyone aspired to.

Well, he didn't. Not anymore.

"It wouldn't make any difference, Lisa. You should know that. Because they wouldn't let me take you with me."

"No, they wouldn't let us go together, Eric. My work is here. The work I was designed for."

He shook her forcefully. "Stop that! I can't think of you that way, as a bunch of figures and calculations on some engineer's designing screen. You're not a machine."

"I am a machine, Eric. An organic machine. We all are. My specifications are just a little more rigorous, a little more precise than yours. I was built up molecule by molecule, Eric, strand by strand, just like the bench we're sitting on, like the dome arching over the choir. A Christopher Wren of biology drew me up on a terminal, Eric, and organic chemists watched my growth.

"I'm not bitter about it. I'm resigned to it. I don't feel any less human than anyone else in this chamber, or for that matter, any more human. I don't feel bitter about all the nice men who fell in love with me, were told the truth, and went out to the colonies. Once things were explained to them, they fell out of love with me very quickly." Her expression was suddenly desperate.

He hastened to reassure her. "I'm not falling out of love with you, Lisa. Not even a little. I don't give a damn what you are—robot, android, or artison. What you are is what you are, Lisa, and what you are is the woman I love."

She didn't try to stop the tears this time, sobbed against him. "I'm *not* bitter about it," she insisted. "You've got to believe that I'm not bitter about it. None of us has any real control over our own destiny. We each do the best we can with what life deals us. I do my job, the job I was designed to do."

"You were designed to love me," he told her gently.

"Eric, they'll find us and take you away from me." A few people turned to stare, looked away when they met Eric's eyes. "They'll take you away and ship you off to Eden or Garden, or worse."

"They'll do nothing of the kind to me. I told you nothing was going to separate us again."

She pulled back, stared hard at him. "Haven't you been listening to me? Haven't you heard anything that I've said?"

"Every word, and not one of them makes a bit of difference."

She dried her eyes on the sleeve of his coat. "It doesn't, does it? Not to you, anyway." She eyed him strangely. "They've told me some of what you've done. Not to my face. I've listened and overheard a lot of things. Tarragon talks on the phone in my presence, sometimes. You've done impossible things. Inhuman things."

"I know. I don't know how I've done them. It's as much a mystery to me as it must be to Tarragon and his mentors. It doesn't matter. All that matters is that we're together now and nothing can—"

She stopped him with a finger to his lips. "No, Eric. It's important. It might explain everything. I'm not supposed to be capable of loving you like this, and a nonprofile man is not supposed to fall in love with me. But I do love you, and you love me. I can only think of one thing that explains what's happened to us, explains what you're done.

-"Eric, you have to be an artison yourself."

He wasn't shocked by the suggestion. She thought he might be, but he wasn't.

"I'm not an ignorant person, Lisa. I've considered the same possibility. There are certain tests you can do. I applied some of them to myself, when I was left alone back in Nueva York. Artisons are perfectly human, to all outward appearances. But there are tests that can tell." She stared anxiously at him.

"I'm not an artison, Lisa. It was one of the first things that occured to me when—" he hesitated—"when I began doing things no human being should be able to do. I know that somehow I'm special. Only a blind man could deny it. But I'm *not* an artison. I failed every one of the tests. I didn't have access to a laboratory, but I did have access to the Nueva York library, and to local drugstores. I failed every test, Lisa. I didn't pass a single one."

"Then what are you, Eric Abbott?" she asked softly. "What are you?"

"I don't know. Different, but not like you. Different in some other way. I'm a design engineer. I know how to run tests and interpret results. I agree it would have explained everything, and I almost wish it had. But it didn't. I'm no artison. More than a human, certainly, but in what way I've no idea.

"It doesn't matter, truly it doesn't. Someday we'll find out. All that matters now is that we love each other. Can you accept that, for now, as enough?"

"If you can accept what I am and still love me, Eric, then I can accept anything." She searched the cathedral's interior. "We need to start thinking, start planning our escape. Not from London, but from Britain. I know it's impossible to stay free forever, but you've made me want to try. They'll track us down eventually, but a few days, or weeks, of happiness will help me live out the rest of my life. I'll always have those memories to turn to." Her eyes were bright and she looked more alive than he'd ever seen her.

"We'll give them a run for it, Eric! It won't be easy. You're a wanted man, and me, I'm an expensive product, difficult to replace. Let's make them work for me!"

"We'll do more than that," Eric assured her. "You keep saying there's no place we can hide from them, nowhere outside Tarragon's reach? Well I've been thinking, and there is such a place. We've been talking about it for the last ten minutes. WOSA needs colonists? Well, it's just acquired another two."

She tried to hide her smile. "That's a wonderful idea, Eric. Unfortunately, it can't work. It's impossible. Of course, my falling in love with you is impossible. Your falling in love with me is impossible. Sitting here now, holding you close, instead of lying dead downriver or back in Nueva York is also impossible. So I suppose I shouldn't be intimidated by still another impossibility."

"No indeed," he told her, eyes shining. "But we have to wait here a few minutes longer before we can begin." He settled himself against the ancient bench.

"But why?"

There was a strange, beatific expression on his face. Beneath the dome, the voices of the choir soared. "I've always loved Vaughn Williams."

Tarragon was accustomed to operating independent of government interference. He reported to an authority which regarded regional governments as nuisances, relics of a dying past.

Despite that, or more likely because of it, he regarded the upcoming interview with apprehension. The trip across the frozen surface of Lake Lucerne had been made in eerie silence, the skifoil skimming the ice while fat snowflakes drifted down to melt against the windows, and the craggy majesty of the Alps rose like pale ghosts behind the storm clouds.

The entrance to the mountain was deceptively calm, the immense metal doors moving aside to admit him quietly, the ranks of armed, alert guards noting his every step. Inside he found himself plunged into an organized maelstrom of activity, bumped and nudged by rapidly moving programmers and processors while his escort maneuvered them both ever deeper into the bowels of the Authority.

Then the escort left him alone outside a door. It was a perfectly ordinary door, identical to dozens he'd passed during his descent. The voice that bade him enter, however, sent a chill through him, a new sensation for Tarragon. Every informed human being on Earth knew that voice.

"Come in, please." He entered.

The elderly man who sat staring at several optos matched the voice. Tarragon looked past him, at the optos. The information displayed was incomprehensible to him.

How tired he looks, Tarragon thought. He always looked tired during his public appearances, but never this worn. He wondered if they used makeup on him for his opto speeches.

"It's me, sir. I have an appointment. Tarragon?"

"Tarragon? Oh, yes, the man from North America." Oristano swiveled round in his chair and extended a hand. He did not rise.

"How do you do, Tarragon." He gestured toward a nearby couch. "Please take a seat."

Tarragon did so, feeling a little more at ease. While the Chief of Operations and Programming still presented a formidable appearance, it was much less impressive than he'd anticipated. What Martin Oristano represented, however, was more than enough to awe his visitor.

"Excuse me, sir, but I still don't know why I've been told to report to you. I'm not used to being yanked from an unfinished assignment, especially one as baffling and frustrating as the one I've been concentrating on this past month."

"I am quite familiar with the problems you've been having, Tarragon, and believe me, I sympathize."

Tarragon nodded, unsurprised. The CPO had access to

everything that happened on the planet. "Then there's more to this business than I've been told?"

"Quite a bit more."

"That still doesn't tell me why I'm here, or why I've been pulled from the case."

"You haven't been 'pulled from the case,' Tarragon. You're still assigned to it. You've been brought here to be filled in. You see, the Colligatarch itself has become interested in the exploits of your Mr. Abbott."

"I knew it." Tarragon nodded as he shifted nervously on the couch. It was too soft for his taste. It made him want to relax. "I knew there had to be more to that man than met the eye. I didn't believe the reports until he slipped out of our grasp in Nueva York. And then when he escaped from us a second time outside London, and then right in front of . . . have you been told what he's done?"

"As I said, I am familiar with the relevant details."

"I'm sure you are, sir, but it's one thing to read about them on an opto screen and another to stand in front of a hole in a solid concrete wall that your quarry's just walked through. It's another thing to watch him vanish before your eyes before sleep gas and a dozen shells reach his body. What am I dealing with here, sir? I have to know what I can expect in the future."

"I understand, Tarragon. In turn you must understand that this business has put many important people, including myself, under a considerable strain. I've spent more time on this matter than intended, and now it appears little enough time remains."

"There is still enough time," said a new voice. Tarragon's eyes swept the room, saw no one. Then the small hairs on the back of his neck rose as he realized who the voice must belong to.

Suddenly he wished he was elsewhere. He was just a poor city boy from the back alleys of Ankara who'd risen far in a difficult profession. He didn't belong here. There were forces in motion around him beyond his comprehension, forces that would use him or cast him aside with cold indifference. The role of pawn didn't appeal to him.

"Excuse me, your lordship." Immediately he felt a fool. That couldn't be correct. But neither could "your computership."

The machine sensed his distress. It was not uncommon in humans conversing with the Colligatarch for the first time.

"Colligatarch will be fine, Kemal."

He relaxed a little, wondering that the machine would be thoughtful enough to address him in the familiar. His professional curiosity quickly overcame his awe.

"Colligatarch, I was told that certain things that should not have happened have, indeed, happened. They progress toward the absurd. Who or what is this Eric Abbott I have been asked to capture?"

"Eric Abbott is a threat, Kemal. A threat not only to the Lure program to which you are attached by WOSA, but to a great deal more. Everything that has happened up to now has been part of an elaborate deception, designed to mask the actual nature of this threat.

"I have entertained suspicions as to the true nature for some time now, but only suspicions. We have all been cleverly drawn down an entirely wrong path. Now I believe I have divined their actual intentions. We are at a crisis point.

"I *could* deal with the immediate danger posed by your Eric Abbott, but that would result in his destruction. There is a small but finite opportunity to change the moral and ethical polarities involved. I would prefer to do this, but it entails considerable risk."

"I didn't think the Colligatarch took risks."

"I am, in the last analysis, Kemal, nothing more than an elaborate counting machine. I consider probabilities and make suggestions based on them. I would like to employ the best probabilities to ensure that Eric Abbott is not used against us again . . . and if events can be manipulated, to ensure even more than that."

"Us?" Tarragon blurted.

"Mankind and myself. We are tied together, you know."

"Yeah," said Tarragon softly, not knowing.

"Delay involves certain risks," Oristano put in. "The Colligatarch is trying to tell you that there's an outside chance we may be able to turn Eric Abbott against those who are using him."

"I don't know about that," Tarragon muttered. "He strikes me as a pretty independent sort of person. I don't think he's in the mood to listen to anyone. Or anything," he added pointedly, eyeing the opto pickup across the room.

"Our success may lie in that very independence you have so correctly observed, Kemal," said the machine. "But we must move quickly. Martin, you may listen or return to your own work. This does not involve you."

Tarragon readied himself. It was one thing to take orders through a machine, quite another to receive them from a machine. But this was no mere machine. This was the Colligatarch.

There was only a little resentment, and as the machine instructed him, he soon forgot it.

Truly there was much to learn, and a great deal he hadn't even suspected.

XVI

ERIC felt Lisa's hand on his arm. The movement caused her body to move against his, drifting within the limits imposed on her by the harness that kept her safely anchored to her seat.

"This isn't going to work," she whispered.

"It'll work," he assured her. "It *has* to work. It's worked so far."

"Only because we shocked them so badly back in London. I still wish I knew how you managed that."

"So do I," he said feelingly. He leaned back slightly so that she could look past him. "We might as well enjoy the trip. It'll be over soon enough. Ever been off-planet before?" She shook her head, staring past his chest. "Me neither. It's more of a wrench than leaving Phoenix was."

Below them the Earth was a lambent blue-and-white globe, electric against the blackness of space. Ahead lay their destination and, if they were extremely lucky, safety.

GATE Station was much more than a vast orbiting laboratory. It was the largest inhabited facility circling the Earth, positioned in geostationary orbit above the Mid-Atlantic Ridge where it intersected the equator. Thousands of lights sparkled along its sides, giving it the appearance of an exploding snowflake. The actual design was similar.

Branching arms extended for a kilometer and more in every direction possible. Rising from top and bottom relative to the heavily inhabited axes were many square kilometers of solar panels composed of amorphous metallic glass solar cells that drew enough energy from the distant sun to power the floating city.

One particular arm caught the eye of every passenger the instant it hove into view. It was familiar to everyone from numberous appearances on the opto: a long, thin cylinder that ended in a modest, well-lit bulge tipped by a parabolic dish two kilometers in diameter.

GATE Terminus.

At the base of the immense curving dish was Departure Lounge, and immediately beyond that the GATE itself, the GATE that led to Eden or Garden according to how the projector was aligned. The GATE that led through an as yet undefined limbo to paradisiacal worlds of milk and honey, a fifth-dimensional subway across the galaxy, a journey still better understood in philosophical than physical terms.

No one understood quite how the GATE worked, or why it worked. Its development arose out one of those wonderful accidents of science, those exquisite serendipitous discoveries that occur every few millennia or so.

The men and women who'd discovered the principle that led to the building of the GATE hadn't been looking for it. When they found it, it took several years more to understand what they had.

Now the GATE had been operational for nearly 150 years. Mathematically it still made no sense, but like the bumblebee too heavy to fly, it still worked. It enabled mankind to extend two tenuous threads to the stars while sneering at the tyranny of light-speed.

Barnard's Star, Alpha Centauri, all the nearby suns were easily bypassed. Eden and Garden lay further in on the galactic lens but were as near as a complexly charged chamber. In terms of actual travel time they lay closer to GATE Station than Earth. No GATE could be built on a planet, of course. Gravity and magnetosphere made it impossible. So men were forced to resort to travel via sturdy, slow ships to reach GATE Station or the solar colonies.

From time to time there was talk of building a second GATE. The enormous expense made it unlikely, and the physics made it impossible. To be able to operate without cross-over interference, a second GATE, according to the mathematicians, would have to be constructed several trillion miles outside the orbit of Pluto. Until the actions of the GATE field were better understood, mankind would have to get along with a single GATE. No one worried about it much anymore, not after a century and a half of successful operation.

No one greeted the shuttle passengers as they disembarked. There were no customs officials on GATE Station. It was open to the citizens of every nationality.

A moving walkway carried them to a large, domed reception area. Children bounced delightedly around their parents, laughing as they played in the three-quarters normal gravity. Through a two-story-high port the Earth rotated mechanically.

They settled into a moderately elegant restaurant, where Lisa blanched at the prices. Eric didn't glance at them, assigning everything to his malleable credit card. There was no reason to stint, since within a short time the card would be useless no matter how deftly altered.

"I still don't understand how you plan to try this," she told him later that night. Around them the dimmed lights of the walkways glowed softly yellow. A few couples and groups strolled among the fountains and the soaring roses that benefited from the light gravity, drinking in the sight of Earth and stars.

"We can't pass ourselves off as colonists. Everyone's screened prior to GATing. For that matter, I don't see how you expect us to get as far as the Departure Lounge."

"I'm sure you're right about passing ourselves off as colonists," he told her as they turned a rounded corner. "The quota is tight, and the final ID must be exacting. Don't you remember the story of that murderer—what was his name?—Griss or something like that. He tried to do it ten years ago. Figured once he was through the GATE he was free to start a safe, new life. He was right about that much.

"He did everything. Got himself a counterfeit departure suit and identification card, memorized the procedure, learned all the right responses. Hell of a scandal about it. And then he failed at the last minute, having passed all the checks and autocurbs, because his group leader didn't recognize him.

"The colonists spend six months preparing to buy the GATE. They're too well known to one another for a stranger to slip in with them."

"Then how are we going to do it?"

"We're not going to try and pass ourselves off as colonists, Lisa. We're going to pass ourselves off as GATE technicians."

She shook her head. "Suppose someone asks us to fix something?"

"I can do that. I know how portions of the GATE are put together."

She gaped at him. "How could you know that?"

"Selvern, the company I've worked for, is one of the major suppliers of replacement components for the GATE. I've helped to design newer, more compact parts for the Station off and on for the last ten years. I don't know how everything works, of course. No one man does. But I know enough to fool an unsuspecting supervisor.

"I have something like an eidetic memory, Lisa. I remember every project I've ever worked on. It's one of the reasons I've been able to advance so fast in my career. My old career, I should say. I can make it sound like I know what I'm doing, and you can be my apprentice. That way you shouldn't have to answer any technical questions."

"Assuming it works, what then?"

"It only takes a second to actually make the passage. I'm hoping we can make a run for the GATE and slip through ahead of the assigned colonists in front of us. I won't know for sure until I see the actual layout of the GATE chamber. If that doesn't look like it's possible, I may be able to operate the Station myself. We'll study the procedure."

"What about guards? They're not going to let some lowly technician take over the main consoles."

"I think the guards are all stationed outside the Departure Lounge. Anyone admitted to the Station itself would already have cleared as many security checks as necessary. Once we're inside—" he hesitated uneasily—"I think I can cope with any physical reactions. I've done so these past weeks. I don't want to hurt anyone. With luck I won't have to. But they're not going to stop us, Lisa."

"You make everything sound so plausible. What if you don't make the GATE operate properly?"

His reply was quietly matter-of-fact. "Then we'll be dead, and Tarragon will have failed anyway because we'll still be together."

She put her arm around his waist. "My old life is already dead, Eric. Either we'll have one together or we won't have one at all."

He nodded slowly. "I've nothing to go back to. Everything I want in life is here now."

They followed a circuitous route toward the GATE annex, gradually losing the tourists as the hour advanced toward midnight, Station time. They wandered back and forth outside the single lock that led to the GATE area until a tired technician of approximately the right size emerged.

The man said good night to the two guards manning the heavy airlock, turned up a side corridor leading toward the residential section of the floating city. He was very surprised when Lisa accosted him, looking lost and forlorn. Undoubtedly he did not fit the mental profile for falling in love with her, but ordinary lust was something else again, and Lisa's beauty easily aroused that in any man.

Eric found himself resenting what happened subsequently as he shadowed the two on their way to the man's apartment. There was no other way as safe, however. Lisa had argued with him until he'd acquiesced. Nor was she troubled by the inevitable, having performed such functions all her life. Still, Eric hit the somnolent form of the technician harder than was necessary as he lay in the bed.

They bound and gagged him and locked him in the compact lavatory. Eric slipped into one of the tech's clean duty uniforms and placed the only tools he could scrounge in highly visible pockets.

There remained the problem of finding similar garb and identification for Lisa.

"You up to it?" she asked him uncertainly. "If not, well, I can go both ways."

"You've already done your part. Two months ago I wouldn't have considered it. Now," he finished confidently, "I think I can handle it."

Finding a woman of similar late-night inclinations took a little longer, but Eric's attractions coupled with his newfound assurance proved more than attractive to one bored member of the opposite sex. They had now managed to acquire uniforms and identification, though displaying the latter could lead to trouble. Eric fervently hoped they wouldn't be asked to prove their identities. The uniforms ought to be enough.

"What now?" Lisa asked him. By mutual agreement neither mentioned the necessary liaisons. "We can't just walk in. I'm sure we'll be checked thoroughly."

"I think the uniforms will be sufficient, but there's one more thing we can do. At least I've had plenty of practice at it lately."

Ignoring the prone, bound form of the female technician, he set to work at her desk with his recently acquired tools. The identity cards were no more complicated than standard credit cards. Complex enough to foil the ordinary thief, but not Eric. An hour's careful work adjusted them to match their new owners. He still hoped they wouldn't have to use them.

There was one more thing left to do. Having broken so many laws already, Eric didn't give it a second thought as he forced his way into the city's administrative computer network. The false entries were made quickly. A close check would reveal them to be fraudulent, but by the time any curious inspector cross-checked with official files on Earth, they would be free or dead.

For now, a security check would identify them as Mark Lewis and Suzanne Culver, repair tech and apprentice.

"It's a lucky thing that murderer Griss didn't have your talent with computers and molecular-identity structures," Lisa observed as they advanced along a dimly lit corridor.

"He was only fighting for his life," Eric replied softly. "My motivations are stronger."

Despite all the precautions they'd taken, it was hard to feel confident as they neared the first checkpoint. There was no way to avoid it, no way around the succession of airlocks, since there was only the single corridor leading to GATE Terminus. The Terminus itself was armored against intrusion, even to the exclusion of an emergency lock for suited personnel.

The two guards at the lock were nearing the end of their shift. Neither glanced at the pair of approaching technicians. Eric sensed the tightness of the borrowed shirt across his chest and shoulders, tried to slump to minimize the bad fit. Repeated observations of techs going and coming had taught them the correct procedure.

"Cards." The woman who extended her hand sounded bored. So much riding on two rectangles of thin bonded plastic. Eric's handiwork would now have its toughest test to date. This was no simple airport ticket counter, no restaurant register they were trying to deceive. It took an effort to breathe normally.

The guard inserted both cards into a slot on the front of a small machine. A bright light played first across Eric's features, then Lisa's. With a click both cards reappeared and were returned. His falsifications had been accepted by the Station network.

"Go on." The guard gave an absent wave of her hand. "I haven't got all night. What's left of it."

Eric walked through the electric gate with Lisa close behind. There was a hum as the lock in front of them slid back. Ahead lay a long corridor that was almost filled by the moving walkways that ran in opposite directions.

A single button at the guard's station could turn the entire length of the tunnel into a lethal trap. He had to fight the urge to run.

They stepped onto the walkway and were carried forward. Nothing happened. They reached the next checkpoint without incident and had to resist the urge to look around to see if they were being followed. From checkpoint two to GATE Terminus there was no place to turn around.

The procedure repeated itself. "Cards, names," muttered the guard. Eric almost forgot his newest alias. An alert Lisa jogged his memory.

"Come on, Mark, get the cobwebs out. I know it's early, but we're burning time."

On to checkpoint three, then four, and then the last. Beyond checkpoint five the corridor expanded to room size. Ahead was Departure Lounge, all around them the living quarters for the colonists. Beyond the Lounge lay the GATE.

They started forward and were shocked when a voice called out sharply from behind, "You two . . . just a minute."

Eric stood rooted to the deck, frantically trying to decide whether to make a run for the GATE or turn and strike out. As he wrestled with two rotten choices, a lieutenant of WOSA Security stepped in front of him.

"Maxine Zandman," she said, announcing herself. She eyed them curiously. "I don't think I've seen either of you two here before."

Eric offered her his most ingratiating smile. "We've just been assigned to GATE repair. Came in on the last shuttle."

"Starting in awfully soon, aren't you?"

"I'm in subquad transposition repair and maintenance. You know how that is. You don't keep things moving right, you lose the whole effect. A tough piece of business to swallow anytime, let alone this early in the morning." He indicated Lisa. "My apprentice."

The lieutenant nodded, aware her subordinates were watching. She had no intention of mishandling this newcomer.

"Right. Nice to meet someone so enthusiastic about their work."

"Do the best I can," Eric told her, brushing past.

As soon as they were out of earshot, Lisa whispered to him, "What is subquad transposition?"

"I don't know, but I'll bet that lieutenant didn't know either, and she wasn't going to confess that in front of her platoon."

"What if she decides to check on it?"

"If she checks on us, we'll check out. If she checks on our 'work,' it'll take her an hour of difficult reading to find out that I'm talking bullshit. By that time we'll be safely away."

They made their way through the busy Lounge. Dozens of colonists milled around—chatting, reading, watching their last optos. Eric saw couples, singles working at becoming couples, anxious mothers shepherding excited children. Those soon to depart displayed the contents of green carry sacks. Bulkier supplies, he remembered, were sent through after the people.

It was impressive, seeing so many of the famous green uniforms in one place, knowing that each represented the failed hopes of thousands left unchosen. Every one in the Lounge, including the children, had passed rigorous, demanding tests to reach this point.

But not as rigorous as ours, he thought grimly.

They had no trouble passing from Lounge to GATE. A steady stream of technicians shuttled through the last lock. The guards waved the uniforms through without comment, assuming quite properly that the five checkpoints down the corridor had already done their work.

Occasionally they drew an interested glance from a repairman or supervisor, but that was all. Several hundred specialists shared duty-time at the Terminus and it was impossible for any one to know every one of his fellow workers on sight. As for the white-clad scientists and engineers who actually ran the GATE, they ignored everything but their work.

After a while the repeated stares began to make Eric

nervous, until he realized no one was looking at *him*. Of course they would attract stares: it would have been abnormal if they hadn't, since he was accompanied by one of the most beautiful women alive. Her work uniform couldn't conceal that.

As he edged toward a console whose function looked familiar, he could hear the colonists talking about their destination. It was early morning, and the GATE was just recommencing service following nighttime hiatus. As he made a show of laying out his equipment, Eric wondered that they'd succeeded in breaching GATE security. Actually, it wasn't so surprising. Security only had to keep watch for the exceptional antisocial like Griss. There was no threat of sabotage. Even the most desperate criminals on Earth wouldn't harm the GATE, because there was always the chance they might get to use it.

The GATE itself was not particularly impressive: a modest nave located at the far end of the room, surrounded by curving metal structures and hundreds of blinking lights. Beyond it lay only blackness. Beyond that, according to theory, was normal space, and beyond that space twisted into something quite un-Einsteinian, and beyond that total darkness which became the light of the end of the line.

Eric and Lisa blended easily into the crush of activity. Kelly-green-clad colonists walked in single file toward the waiting circle in front of the GATE. Every thirty seconds, on cue from the GATE master, five of them would step forward in unison to vanish from this part of the galaxy, only to reemerge safely on the far side of Elsewhere.

Actually the process was remarkably ordinary. There was no explosion of light, no violent concussion of atoms being torn apart as the colonists took their giant step through. They just passed away, like a lone camel swallowed by a hot desert horizon. The only sound to accompany the transposition was a brief sibilant hiss as molecules were taken apart.

As he watched, Eric couldn't keep from wondering if any of the departing colonists had been drawn into the program by Lisa's charms. He didn't ask her to identify any of them, and she didn't volunteer any information. Even if a former acquaintance did show up, it wasn't likely he'd notice her. She wasn't close to the GATE and the eyes of every colonist were focused on the dark tunnel to elsewhere.

Off to the right, the GATE master sat studying a bank of readouts on the main control console. Every twenty seconds he would call out in a clear voice, "Ready," and then, "step through, please." His tone never varied and his gaze never left his instruments.

It was interesting to watch the faces of the colonists as they actually took the step. Each handled it differently. Some took a deep breath, others closed their eyes, a few hopped through jauntily, and some went in whistling. Once or twice a child would burst into fearful tears. Then the line would slow as mother or father quieted the anxiety, and the march would resume.

Eric and Lisa labored hard at their nonexistent job, but most of their energy was directed at fixing the transposition procedure in their minds. They didn't have forever. Sooner or later some supervisor or foreman was going to wonder just what the strangers were working so hard to fix.

Eric took a chance by sitting down at an empty terminal and running questions. There were several things he badly wanted to know before they made their attempt. As he probed the computer, Lisa worked to locate a gap in the line of colonists. Only five at a time could make the jump. Six could overload the field and all half dozen could perish.

Their hope lay in locating a close-knit group of three or less. The break in routine would come as a special request from family or friends wishing to make the journey alone. It was easy for the GATE master to comply. It slowed the line only a little and, as a last request, was always granted.

Eric amused himself by breaking down the locks on different files, something he was an expert at. He wasn't surprised to learn that the actual mechanics of the GATE were quite simple. Most great scientific discoveries are.

Not that the information would ever be of any use. He doubted Eden or Garden possessed the sophisticated manufacturing infrastructure necessary to build a GATE, let alone an orbiting station to base it on. They only had access to receiving terminals.

A single mother with two children was leaning out of the line, talking earnestly to the GATE master. She was in the eighth grouping.

"There's our spot," Eric murmured excitedly. "She wants the pleasure of taking her kids through by herself. I'm afraid she'll have to tolerate a little company."

Lisa nodded, put her tools aside and starting walking a circuitous route that would take her toward the GATE. Eric followed, his eyes searching for possible opposition. No one questioned their movements.

The monitor said, "Ready."

Suddenly Eric thought, *We're going to make it.* At the same time he wondered, as did so many others about to embark on the great journey, at the lack of discovered human inhabitable worlds. Only two in two and a half centuries of searching with sublight drones and advanced telescopes. Ah, but what a pair they were, Eden and Garden!

Unlike the others, he did not see darkness inside the GATE—only a bright, secure future for Lisa and himself, a future where they would blend in with relaxed, easygoing settlers of high intelligence, a place where no Earthly authority could trouble them anymore. Because the GATE was a one-way street.

Gateway to paradise, he thought. GATE: Gigamplified Amorphous Transspatial Element. Praise Allah, praise Jesus, praise Jehovah, Buddha, Zoroaster, and praise especially the physicists who'd stumbled unexpectedly across this bizarre but wondrous distortion of the space-time continuum. Praise them all. They would be his and Lisa's salvation.

The single mother and her two children stepped into the waiting circle and awaited word from the GATE master. Eric and Lisa were just alongside and ready to cross over to join them when heaven collapsed like a drifting soap bubble.

"ERIC ABBOTT!"

It was a loud voice, a voice accustomed to having its orders obeyed instantly. The GATE master and the rest of the GATE crew turned curiously toward the source of the interruption. Eric took another step, only to hear his name repeated more forcefully. As he turned slowly toward the lockway joining GATE Terminus to Departure Lounge, he was filled with despair.

A small black man wearing the uniform and insignia of a major of security forces stood staring back at him. The officer looked anxious. His sideburns were white and the gun in his hand oversize. Similar weapons filled the palms of the men and women who clustered around him.

Senior scientists and engineers began to talk among themselves, commenting on the extraordinary intrusion. It didn't take long for their attention to shift from the security team to the couple lying under their weapons.

Behind Eric the GATE hummed softly, tantalizingly. It was very expensive and complicated to shut it down completely. The GATE master still had not said the fateful words—"Step through"—to mother and offspring. Only "Ready." How important was it to wait for the other? Was the pause important, or merely ceremonial? Eric didn't know, and he had to know.

The abyss was so close. Did they dare it? Once lost, the moment would not present itself again. They were more than a few steps from the GATE boundary. Plenty of room for the guns to bring them down.

He could cover a lot of space in a single leap. That much he knew from recent experience. But could he do it while pulling Lisa along with him? He was fast, faster than was reasonable, but he couldn't outrun a needle-beam. He struggled to evaluate the stance and aim of each member of the security team, tried to guess how accurate they were, how firm their grips on their weapons.

Even if they were wounded and made the step, they

should still be safe, once through to the other side. He fought with himself. It all took much less than a second.

"I am Major Orema," said the small man in command. "I'm in charge of GATE security. You are Eric Abbott." His eyes barely shifted. "And you are Lisa Tambor. You are wanted for questioning and you must both come with me, please. *NOW*."

"Tarragon," Eric mumbled. "Questions mean Tarragon."

Orema frowned, then the look turned to one of recognition. "Yes, I know the name. The request does not come from him, only through him. Important people have put their names to the request."

Better to chance it, Eric thought. Better to try and fail and die here after having come so far than to be sedated and shipped back to Earth.

"If not Tarragon, then who? People have been working to keep us apart as though it meant something. Am I at least permitted to know the names of my persecutors?"

"It's not persecution, Eric Abbott. I'm not privy to all the details. I'm only a policeman. I have been informed, however, and was not told to keep it from you, that you are to be taken to Zurich and thence to the Authority, where you will be questioned by the Colligatarch Council itself." Mutterings from the crowd, different glances cast Eric's way.

"What have I to do with the Colligatarch, and it with me?"

There was anxiety on the major's face. Did he know what Eric was capable of? Had he been told? There was no harm, Eric decided, in trying to stall with a mild bluff. "If you want my cooperation, I want an explanation."

The major looked uncomfortable. Another officer leaned low to whisper in his ear and he listened before nodding.

"I was told to tell you that you are being used, Eric Abbott."

Eric frowned. "Me, used? No, no, you've got it backwards. It's Lisa who's being used. It's her I'm trying to save."

"That is not relevant," Orema replied. "I have been

informed that she is an artison and not properly human."
More murmurs from the watching crowd. "Of course she
is being used. She was constructed with use in mind."
Lisa did not stiffen, did not react. She'd heard it often
enough before.

The major fastened his tiny, piercing eyes on Eric's, and
there was a look in them he'd never seen before. It made
him uncomfortable without knowing why.

"And you're not human either, Eric Abbott, and you are
being used."

Despite the thin edge of the moment on which the
confrontation was balanced, Eric managed a slight smile.
Here, in this one thing, they could be proven wrong. He
could catch them in a lie.

"I've run all the right tests. I know I haven't been
acting—" he hesitated—"normally these past couple of
weeks, but I've run the tests. I'm no robot, no android, no
artison. I know there's something different about me, but
those aren't the answers. I've checked myself for it, and
there's nothing you can say that will convince me otherwise. Furthermore, I don't care that Lisa's an artison, and
it doesn't bother her that I know."

Suddenly he thought he understood the peculiar look in
the security chief's eyes. It was simple, naked fear. The
major was terrified of him. A glance showed that his
people, to a greater or lesser extent, were also afraid. They
held their weapons in steady hands, but their souls were
shaking.

But why? Sure, he had demonstrated certain impressive
abilities, but they had him trapped. There should be
exultation in their expressions, not fear.

"No, you're not a robot, Eric Abbott, and you're not an
android, and you're not an artison. That much I've been
assured, though as I said before I'm not privy to all the
information. What I have been told has come from
Colligatarch Authority directly to GATE Station." He
hesitated and Eric saw his finger trembling on the trigger
of his pistol.

He wants to kill me, Eric realized wonderingly. He's

been told to bring me in for questioning, but he would prefer to kill me. And now he thought he could detect something else in the major's face, living there alongside the fear.

Revulsion.

He pressed for specifics. "That doesn't leave much for me to be, does it, except a man who's been treated unjustly."

"Eric Abbott, the Colligatarch says that you are a construction of the Syrax."

XVII

BETTER perception, Eric thought dazedly. Only with better perception could he tell which of them was insane. As matters stood, he wasn't sure.

Lisa was staring up at him, disorientation in her gaze, but she still clung tightly to his arm. The major had not spoken. The accusation had come from a younger man standing behind him. Eric noticed that he was wearing a white science uniform, not the black of security.

"Abbott, my name is Joao de Uberaba. I'm with the research detachment at GATE Station. I'm a bioengineer. I understand that you're a design engineer working mostly with microcircuitry." Eric nodded weakly while next to him Lisa listened and watched out of vast blue eyes.

"We can talk on the same level, then." He glanced downward. "Nothing personal, Major Orema."

"Pretend I'm not here," Orema murmured.

"I've been in contact with Colligatarch Authority on Earth," Uberaba began.

Eric interrupted him. "This is crazy! I don't know anything about the Syrax! I'm not a Syrax agent. What kind of idiocy is this?"

"It's not a question of idiocy, but of engineering. You really believe in yourself, don't you? I'm telling you, *you are a construction.* As surely as was the GATE, as surely as was this floating city, you were built." He nodded toward Lisa. "As was the woman beside you, though her origin is different."

"Look, I know I've done some unusual things," he was about to say "inhuman things" but changed his words in mid thought, "but that doesn't prove what you say."

"You're quite right about that, but many seemingly unrelated things when placed alongside each other create a context from which explanations may be drawn, like the pieces of any other puzzle. As an engineer and designer you should know that better than anyone."

"I was born in Chandler, Arizona, a state of the North American Federation, in—"

Uberaba put up a hand. "Spare me. I'm sure your implanted memories are as detailed and strong as the Syrax could make them. They really are wonderful technicians. A pity they don't share their knowledge.

"I've been briefed on the extent of your 'unusual' activities, Eric, and they are very impressive. You've done some remarkable things. But as you say, demonstrations of extreme physical ability do not in themselves constitute proof of extraterrestrial origin. But no artison or android could have done what you've done, not even one designed as an athletic model.

"You had an altercation in Nueva York, in Ms. Tambor's home. In addition to a lot of other blood, you left behind a very little of your own. Like everything else at the scene it was studied intensively in hopes of learning something about you. It's very good blood, but it's not natural."

Eric listened silently while his brain screamed at him to grab Lisa in his arms and rush the GATE, to get away from these insane people and their droning madness before it engulfed both of them. But he couldn't. He was too fascinated by the man's bizarre theory. He was too much the engineer intrigued by a possible solution to an inexplicable problem. Why, if you let your mind come apart, stopped thinking rationally, what Uberaba was saying made an abstract sort of sense.

"In addition to your physical abilities, Eric, you were

given a considerable if not profound independent intelligence. Use it now to consider what I've said. How *did* you imagine you managed one incredible escape after another? In Nueva York you defeated an entire squad of highly trained professionals.'' Around him, Orema's people shifted uneasily.

"In a suburb of Greater London you broke out of a prison hospital by running through a solid concrete wall while filled with enough dope to lay out a dozen weight lifters. And lastly there is the still unexplained business of your departure from an enclosed office in a building on the shore of the Thames, in London. Six reliable witnesses were within two meters of you when you both vanished, even as you were about to be shot. Where did you go, Eric, and how did you do it?''

Construction. Creature of the Syrax. Good blood, but not quite natural, oh, most definitely unnatural.

They're not mad at all, Eric thought suddenly. *I* am. I am, or the rest of the world. Looking to his left, he found Lisa staring up at him, and he could see that she didn't want to believe either. But despite that, he saw what he wanted to see, what he needed to see. The love was still there, in her face, in her eyes. Man, android, artison, alien whatsis, no matter. Whatever Eric Abbott might be, Lisa Tambor loved him.

The catacombs of St. Paul's . . . how had they arrived there? At the time they'd accepted salvation without question because there'd been no time for analysis. Think back, further back. Back to what had seemed such a pleasant, normal life. Back to that night in Phoenix, in the restaurant. The appearance of the Syrax.

How indifferent its casual inspection of bar and patrons had been! How fluid and casual its movements. Had it materialized there to observe human recreational habits, or to run some kind of final check? On what? Its machine?

And right after that, the fateful glimpse of Lisa on the street, and events set irrevocably in motion. Accident? Coincidence? Or long-dormant programming activated?

Teleportation. A Syrax could teleport over a short distance. Thames to St. Paul's, defensive reaction triggered instinctively in the part of him that... wasn't quite natural? How much of Eric Abbott was human and how much... something else?

"You're in love with the artison four in the Tambor series, aren't you?" the far-off voice of Uberaba was saying gently. "That's what I've been told."

Eric stared at him. Nothing else in the room existed anymore—not the colonists, not the security team with its weapons, not Orema, nothing. Only the vague presence of Lisa, himself, and Uberaba. Everyone else had ceased to exist, because only Uberaba had the answers. Eric ached with the need for answers.

"Yes, I am in love with her." He held her close and almost cried when she did not pull away.

"You know what you're not," Uberaba explained patiently. "I'm sure Tambor four has told you that it's impossible for her to love a human male. Don't you find it strange that she should love you?"

Eric didn't reply. There was nothing to say.

Uberaba continued. "It explains a lot, doesn't it?"

"Why? What if what you say is true? I still don't understand why."

The bioengineer whispered to Orema. "I think his ignorance may be genuine." Then, to Eric, "That's fairly obvious: the GATE.

"In most of the sciences the Syrax are far in advance of us. They continue to mete out information in tiny dribs and drabs in the hope that someday they'll be able to wheedle the secret of the GATE out of us. In that one area of physics we've not only equaled, but have jumped far beyond, their accomplishments, thanks to a lucky guess on the part of some incredibly fortunate researchers.

"Their starships are far more efficient than any vessels we've built, but they still take years to reach Earth. In comparison to the GATE, they don't move at all. Ever since they made contact with us and learned about the GATE, they've worked at duplicating it. They can't, because its discovery was pure accident.

"The Station here is shielded, which means they can't teleport in. Why do you think we take such security precautions here, Eric Abbott? To keep out terrestrial iconoclasts? No. To protect the GATE. It's our one hold over the Syrax, and they badly want to break it. They've been trying for a hundred years."

I know how the GATE works, Eric thought suddenly. I scanned the records in the computer here. But why? You don't have to know the secrets of its operation to use it. All you have to do is step through. Why did I research that?

A tremor passed through his body, a mental quiver as the realization, no longer avoidable, finally struck home.

The bioengineer was right.

Abruptly his perception of his surroundings underwent a subtle shift. He saw Orema and his people and Uberaba and everyone else in the room differently, as though the world had suddenly gone slightly out of focus. Except he knew that wasn't true. *He* was the one out of focus.

And yet he didn't feel different emotionally, didn't feel like a puppet or the extension of some extravagant computer program. He still felt like Eric Abbott, alive with all the feelings and thoughts and desires and hopes Eric Abbott had always possessed. Oh, they'd fashioned him fine, had the Syrax! Their work reached a new nadir of bioengineering perfection in him. It had to, to have fooled everyone for so long. Even the shield Uberaba spoke of had not kept him out of GATE Station.

The bioengineer's voice and face were full of sympathy. He saw the pain on Eric's face. "I know how difficult this must be for you to accept, but if you need further proof . . ." He reached behind him. Eric tensed, but what the bioengineer produced was no weapon.

The small, triangular metal unit displayed a few tiny readouts and a couple of adjustment controls. As Eric stared, Uberaba nudged first one, then its companion. A whispery hum filled the room.

"That's a carrier wave, Eric." He held out the unit so that Eric could see the signal dancing across a miniature opto. "That's you. You've been broadcasting it all along, I suspect. I've been told it's a very deceptive carrier wave, near impossible to detect without sophisticated sensing equipment. You're transmitting, Eric, without being aware of it.

"There are two Syrax ships orbiting Earth right now. Not in the same orbit as GATE Station: that would be too obvious. They're far away, but not behind the curve of the planet. Which one do you think you're transmitting to?"

"I don't know," Eric mumbled. His free hand went to his head, touched gingerly, as a man might caress a live bomb. "I didn't know I was doing that. I don't feel anything. Please, you've got to listen to me! Maybe I am what you say, a construction of the Syrax, but I'm an independent construct. I'm not a slave. They couldn't make me a slave or their deception wouldn't have worked. . . ." he broke off.

"As well as it has?" Uberaba finished for him. "Seems to me you've accomplished almost everything they planned for you."

"No! I *am* independent. Circumstances have brought me here, yes, maybe as they intended, but I've acted alone in everything."

"You know the secret of the GATE. You haven't broadcast it yet. We know because we've deciphered and can interpret the carrier wave they're using. But you've learned it. You ran it through a terminal." He gestured across the room. "That terminal. It's been checked. No one knows how you managed to crack the codes so fast, but. . . ."

"You forget that I worked for the company that designed many of the components," Eric told him softly.

Uberaba nodded, looked satisfied. "So subtle. Subtle and patient. They function on a different time-scale than we do."

"Let us go through the GATE," Eric pleaded with him. "It's ready. Just give us a second and let us go across to Eden. You know we can't come back. The GATE's a one-way trip to anonymity."

"The Syrax probably have a good idea where Eden is

located, and their ships are better than ours. They could go there, pick you up, and drain the information out of you. They're very patient.''

''Patience won't be enough,'' Eric pointed out excitedly. ''One of their starships would take a hundred years to reach Eden, even if they do know where it is.'' He did not add that he was certain they did know, because, he realized suddenly, *he* knew. How did he know? It was part of his stored knowledge, information sequestered in the back of his brain that lay dormant until required.

What else did he know that he didn't know he knew?

''I'd be dead by then and...'' he stopped in mid-sentence and a look of puzzlement spread across his features.

There was a voice in his head, soft and feathery. Actually it wasn't a voice so much as an aural projection. It wasn't telepathy; the Syrax were not telepathic, but rather mind speaking to mind via an infinitesimally small communications device implanted in his skull.

He understood everything clearly. The voice was calm, polite, and friendly: everything the voice of a best friend ought to be. It told Eric what he had to do. Just push a little with this part of his brain. Push gently, *there and thusly,* and he and Lisa would be teleported to safety aboard the Syrax starship. Then they would be safe forever from the malicious, primitive actions of human beings and could live out their natural lives in comfort and peace. The Syrax saw nothing immoral in rewarding a device for a job well done.

Push, the voice urged reassuringly, just a little.

At the same instant the tiny monitor the bioengineer was showing Eric let out an electronic squeal. Uberaba and Orema shouted simultaneously. Eric wasn't certain what they said because he was too busy reacting.

The reaction was instinctive and involved a mind-push, utilizing another bit of information that had been thoughtfully stored in his brain. It was not a teleport-push, however. It jumped out from Eric toward his enemies, and they all went down, falling over one another like a box of toy soldiers.

It was quite a push, because as the security team collapsed, every readout in GATE Station went momentarily berserk and the lights flickered unsteadily. The colonists broke and ran, mothers carrying children, fathers trying to shield their families from the alien *thing* that stood next to the GATE.

The security team was very good, and despite the power of Eric's defensive reaction a couple of them had managed to fire their weapons. One had shattered a relay in the ceiling before being stopped by the thick wall. Several members of the team were twitching like frogs in a biology lab. The bioengineer had fallen across Orema. Eric knew the paralysis wouldn't last long, just as he knew it wasn't fatal.

Lisa turned to look at the man she loved. "The GATE, Eric. While there's still time."

Behind him, the darkness beckoned. A glance showed no change in GATE status. It was still fully powered, still awaiting its next quotient of travelers. It wouldn't stay that way much longer.

He remembered the soporific gas they'd used on him on the Nueva York to London flight. Here they'd like as not exhaust the atmosphere from this section of the city in order to protect the secret of the GATE. That would kill a large number of the screaming, panicky colonists who were trying to force their way back into the Departure Lounge, not to mention the technicians and scientists who sat cowering in their seats. One was moving fingers toward a switch, perhaps a power shutoff. Eric glanced at him and he fell forward onto his console. No one else raised a hand from where it lay. It occurred to him that they thought he'd killed Orema and his people.

Let them. For the moment it was nice to have fear on his side. Striding purposefully forward, he bent over Orema and pulled the needle gun from his fingers. He could see Orema's eyes glaring up at him, unmoving in their sockets.

Then he turned slowly to face Lisa, who still stood

waiting by the GATE. When she saw his arm rise she screamed and tried to reach him. He was much too quick for her.

With great precision and care he stuck the gun against his head and pulled the trigger.

Her scream degenerated into something sharp and feral, the first inhuman, purely artison sound he'd ever heard her make. She slammed into him with her hands flailing at the gun, but he'd already let it drop.

Then he calmly took her in his arms and kissed her forehead. Only a little blood trickled from the neat hole in his skull. Sobbing, she struggled to hold him up. Her sobs faded and her expression turned to one of astonishment when she realized he didn't need the support.

Those who were still conscious stared blankly at him.

"It's all right, Lisa. It's already healing over." Behind them the security guards were beginning to stir, hands groping for weapons, eyes jerking stiffly toward their target. They would not need orders from Orema this time to shoot to kill.

Eric ignored the activity. "They built me very well, gave me the best of human abilities as well as everything Syrax that could be put into a human body and brain. But they didn't plan on me falling in love. You see, Lisa, they made me a little too human." She was looking past his ear, toward the wound which was sealing itself much too quickly.

"There was a transmitter there. The transmitter the bioengineer referred to. Maybe it could function as a control unit as well. I didn't want to find out. Now it's gone. So are the Syrax. They were talking to me . . . here." He touched his head near the wounds. "Now that's gone, too."

"They won't give you up easily," Lisa said. "They'll come after you, attack the city. . . ."

"They might," he replied as though it was no longer a matter of consequence, "but I doubt it. Of course, they wouldn't want me taken prisoner either, but with the transmitter destroyed I don't think they can touch me. Now we can go, Lisa.''

"Tambor series four. It doesn't bother you?''

"Everybody should have a nickname. I'm sure you'll think up a cute one for me.'' He led her toward the GATE.

I am not a human being, he thought, and was pleased that the idea no longer troubled him, because he knew better.

"Ready," he announced. There was a pause and he looked back at the technician monitoring the ultimate console.

"Ready, but you're not supposed to . . .''

Orema raised the rifle he'd taken from the guard next to him and fired just as Lisa and Eric stepped into darkness. The energy bolt never reached them, went instead where spent energy went to die.

As they vanished, the little monitor lying next to the prone form of the bioengineer let out a sharp buzz, and a readout flashed all the way over into the red. Whether it signified Eric's disappearance or represented some distant howl of alien rage, no one would ever know.

Parseconds, the newsawks dubbed travel time through the GATE, and they were not far off. Eric had taken off on his left foot and for a brief eternity it seemed the right one would never come down, would just continue lengthening until he boasted an inseam a light-year long.

But it did come down, contacting something hard and unyielding. He stumbled, felt Lisa stumble against him.

They stood in a room very different from the one at GATE Station. The walls were paneled with pressed wood. Real wood, of a quality only the wealthy could afford on Earth. Eric looked over his shoulder, half expecting to see Orema and his soldiers come tumbling through the GATE. But they were far away now, unimaginably far away.

The GATE opening was disconcerting because it was a near duplicate of the GATE they'd just stepped through, but on close inspection he could make out small differences in construction.

A few simple tables were waiting across the floor of the barnlike structure. Small computer consoles rested on the tables, and connecting cables were strewn haphazardly around wooden legs and metal power outlets. The figures seated at the tables were dressed simply. Not primitive, but hardly fashionable.

The nearest removed his feet from the monitor they'd been resting on and stood to greet them. He was quite tall and lanky, a good deal taller than Eric. His expression was good-natured, if momentarily confused.

"Hi. I'm Jeeter." He jerked a thumb toward the colonists milling around the tables at the far end of the barn. Some of them might wonder what had happened to the rest of their group, but they were too involved in processing to inquire. They were, of course, completely ignorant of the events that had transpired at GATE Station subsequent to their own transportations, divorced from the news of the moment by time and many trillions of kilometers.

"I was beginning to think we were through for the day," the tall man explained. He looked past them. "Are you two the last? Some of the newcomers said we should expect more."

"There was a cutoff imposed," Eric said thoughtfully. "We're it for a while, I think."

"Strange. Wonder why?"

"There's been a little trouble, I think. I don't know who or what is going to come through the GATE after us, but they might bring a pack of lies along with them. If you can take us to your local government representative or whoever's in a position of authority, I'd like to explain."

"Don't worry yourselves. You just got here. Actually, nothing that comes through the GATE could surprise me. One week we receive new colonists, the next week it's unexpected supplies we can't use. Have to constantly realign the GATE, you know. What sort of trouble were they having?"

Eric glanced down at Lisa, chewed at his lower lip as he tried to formulate a good reply. "Actually, we're the trouble."

"I thought it might be something like that. Easy to see you're not wearing the usual green, and no duffles, either. As for explaining to someone in authority, you might as well talk to me. One of the first things you'll notice here on Eden is that we're a lot less formal about rankings and. so forth than they are back on good ol' Earth.

"I'm Assistant GATE Supervisor. Stupidvisor I call it, some times. Anything you want to tell the Council you might as well tell me."

Eric was beginning to feel a lot better.

"Do you mind if we sit down?" Lisa asked him. "We've had a hectic few days."

"Inconsiderate me. Come over to my station. I'm still on duty and I have to keep an eye out in case they do send anyone else through. Sometimes kids can emerge in pretty rough emotional shape."

They followed him down a wide wooden ramp. Near the base, several men in coveralls were using electric lifts to shuffle and stack crates.

"That's the last of last week's supply shipment they're rearranging," Jeeter informed them. "We don't rush things on Eden. That's something all newcomers have to adjust to."

As they walked further into the building Eric had come to think of as the "barn," he was startled by his first glimpse of the landscape. Long picture windows provided a spacious view of the terrain immediately outside. Tall evergreens dominated. They were thicker and bushier than their distant relatives on Earth.. Barely visible in the distance were high, rugged mountains. Above the trees, several extremely rotund flying creatures were battling a strong headwind.

Covering everything—ground, trees, mountain peaks and bird-things—was a familiar but utterly unexpected mantle of snow.

"Something of a shock, isn't it?" Jeeter was amused by their expressions, though his expression soured quickly. "There aren't supposed to be blizzards in paradise. New arrivals are quick to remark on the discrepancy. It's the first of many, I assure you. Eden's habitable, but paradise it ain't, and it's a few millennia from getting there." His reassuring smile returned.

"I'm always interested in the reactions of new colonists. You see, I was born here. I'm third-generation Edenite, and I never expected anything better. I wasn't lied to, and I feel sympathy for everyone else who was. Some Earthies can't handle it. They arrive expecting perfect weather, food dangling from the trees waiting to be picked, gentle streams that never flood.

"There actually are one or two places like that here on Eden, down on the equator. We've only just located them. Planetary exploration is dependent on local means of transportation, not to mention limited available manpower. Meanwhile we're stuck here in the so-called temperate zone, tied to the GATE because moving it might break the link with Earth. Chances are good that it wouldn't, but we're not secure enough yet to take the risk, though some of us don't care if we ever hear from Earth again, supplies or no supplies.

"Right now we're working on a repulsion rail system that will take us to the Auraxis coast. But it's far from perfect there, just better weather on balance."

"What's wrong with it?" Lisa asked.

"Seasonal hurricanes, occurring with a greater frequency than they do on the Gulf Coast of North America."

"We're from North America."

"Good. Depending on what part, you'll handle the transposition better than some. Every so often we get colonists from Imperial Russia, Scandinavia, and Canada. They don't mind the climate here."

Eric found a vacant chair, sat down. He was starting to relax a little. "So it's all a lie, then, to induce valuable people to emigrate, to participate in the 'lotteries'?"

"Oh, we have our libraries and our little symphony and our discussion groups, but there isn't much time to spare. Keeping warm and fed occupies everyone's time. Psychological testing of colonists before they're sent through pretty well eliminates the potential snobs. We do get a few once in a while, though, who claim they're above physical labor.''

"What do you with them?''

"Not a damn thing. No work, no food. We're very democratic here. No one's starved yet, to my knowledge, but some people die before they should. There's a lot of bitterness here. It festers, and eventually it kills.'' He shook his head. "This is not paradise. Not according to the descriptions I've read.''

"I wonder if Garden is as bad?'' Lisa murmured.

"We've no way of knowing, of course, since there's no communication between the colonies any more than there is back to Earth. There's not much we can do about it. We can't build a plasma drive, and even if we could, the protesters would be dead before it reached Earth, let alone returned with a reply. It took the drone probe which discovered Eden a hundred and thirty years to make the round trip.'' He shrugged.

"Like I said, I'm third generation. It doesn't bother me as much as it does the newcomers.''

"But it still rankles?'' Eric said.

"Sure. Nobody likes to be lied to, even before they're born.'' He shifted his position on the edge of the table. "Now what about you two? You said something about possible trouble?''

Eric took Lisa's hand in his. Having arrived on a world founded and maintained by lies, it seemed only fair to tell the truth.

"We're not your ordinary new colonists. We're artisons. At least, Lisa is. I'm something else. Call me an artison-plus.''

"Oh, artificial persons.'' Eric expected anything except Jeeter's casual nonchalance. "We have a number of them here.''

Lisa gaped at him. "But I thought the colony worlds were only for specially picked humans.''

Jeeter laughed, smiled at her. "Do you think you're the first folks with trouble to have slipped through here?"

"Every attempt we've ever heard of was met with failure," Eric told him.

"Of course! But what about the attempts you *don't* hear about? D'you think, as popular as the government has made emigration, that they're going to publicize incidents where the unchosen have made it through the GATE? They'd have trouble with unauthorized attempts every hour.

"Oh, we do get an occasional bonafide criminal who makes it through. You'd be surprised how many ways there are to disguise someone's identity."

"Don't count on it," Eric murmured.

"Their attitude changes fast once they step through. Either they cast off their past or they don't make it. Eden has no room for those who think they can live off the labor of others, and this population's too smart to be fooled. Crime isn't in fashion here. In that respect, maybe we do have one small aspect of paradise. The really brutal types, the killers and arsonists, aren't smart enough to make it through.

"In addition there have been four or five artisons who've made it through, and one robot. You can meet the robot if you like. He's ninety-four and something of a local icon."

"How on Earth could a robot sneak through?" Eric wanted to know.

"Disguised himself as a mobile excavator and was sent through with a supply shipment. We admire that kind of ingenuity on Eden. It's what keeps you alive in the winter."

Lisa eyed the snow outside. "It's not winter?"

"Mid-spring," Jeeter told her somberly. "I said it wasn't paradise. Even the equator gets some snow. As for your personal concerns, forget 'em. There's no origin prejudice here on Eden. Life's difficult enough without fabricating additional problems."

Eric wrestled with himself before adding, "There's something more. I said I wasn't your usual, garden-variety artison. I . . . I don't really know enough about myself to say all that I am. I'm human. I *know* that. But I wasn't . . . manufactured . . . on Earth.''

Jeeter made a face as Eric struggled to interpret the expression. "We'll, that's a new one. You seem human enough to me, and it speaks well for you that you're not trying to hide anything.'' He looked to Lisa. "You vouch for him?''

She leaned her head on Eric's shoulder. "For the rest of my life.''

"Good enough for me. You do your work and help out and contribute to the colony, and I don't care if you're one of Satan's imps fled from hell.'' He slipped off the table and moved to his console, studied the information displayed.

"Doesn't look like we're going to get anyone else through today.'' He touched several switches, and the steady hum that had enveloped the GATE Terminus faded. "No point in wasting power. It'll notify us if a transposition is in progress. Usually there's a week between shipments.

"Tell you what. Since you're such an interesting couple, I'll run you through the reception line myself.'' He led them to the back of the barn. The line of newly arrived colonists had shrunk considerably. None of them glanced back at Lisa and Eric, save for one curious older gentleman.

"I don't remember seeing you two during the orientation session.''

"Late additions,'' Eric told him. He turned away, accepting the explanation.

"Move over, Mari.'' A dark-skinned lady smiled openly at Eric, moved to another chair, and relinquished her console to Jeeter. It was a compact, portable unit, easily shipped through the GATE. Eric was curious about the local manufacturing facilities. High technology didn't appear to be a priority item on the Edenites' agenda. On the other hand, a colony in existence for a century and a half ought to have some capabilities, founded on basic equipment shipped out from Earth. As a design engineer, he'd probably find out soon enough.

Jeeter confirmed his feelings after Eric had outlined his electronics background. "Glad to have you with us, though I don't think you'll have much time for theory and design. This equipment is made to last, and we'll be producing our own memory and logic components some day soon, but there's always need for good repairmen. I'm sure you'll fit right in." He made some notations, glanced expectantly at Lisa.

"What about you? What's your specialty?"

Eric stepped in to spare her potential embarrassment. "If it's acceptable, she's just going to be a home-maintainer for a while."

"We'll find something for her. There's plenty of work to go around. Not for an ex-model," he said, guessing correctly. "There's no high fashion on Eden. We're more concerned with keeping warm."

"I'll do anything assigned to me," Lisa said quickly. "I'm . . . stronger than the average woman."

"No problem. It doesn't matter what you used to do, only what you do now. Remember, this is not terrestrial society. This is a highly motivated, rigorously sorted collection of intelligent human beings. There's nothing like it anywhere on Earth. Maybe on Garden."

"But despite your intelligence and social balance, you're still angry at having been lied to," Eric said.

"Sure, but there's no point in making speeches since we can't do anything about it. Stress leads to high blood pressure, protein breakdown, and an early death."

"I see what you mean about balance. Are you a typical example? Nothing seems to bother you for more than a second or two."

"I expect I'm average. We do have our designated iconoclasts. We're not all engineers and agri specialists. You might recognize a couple of famous actors in our opto producing group. There are something like seventy-five thousand of us now. Our birthrate is steady and healthy, our children superior, and there's a steady infusion of fresh blood from Earth. We've grown enough to allow some diversity."

"There's something more," Eric insisted. "You know what we are, but not who we are. You said a few criminals had made it through the GATE."

Jeeter's eyebrows lifted slightly. "No, you didn't mention that. If there's a legal problem . . ."

"We're not criminals," Lisa hastened to add. "Not in the common sense."

"Surely you're not going to tell me you're political refugees? There are plenty of places on Earth to escape to."

"Not that, no," Eric went on. "It's . . . look, nothing personal, Jeeter, but I think it might be better if I explained to someone in a position of social as well as technological authority."

"Fine with me. Just give me your word you're not wanted for infanticide or something sick like that."

"That's easy enough to do." It was true that he'd killed, but also that he'd never been confronted with a charge for murder. That wasn't what Tarragon and his people wanted him for.

"Then that's done." Jeeter rose. "Come with me. I'll take you to Administration."

The four-seater snowcat trundled slowly down the muddy road. Jeeter spent much of the time talking enthusiastically about the repulsion rail system that would soon link the colony center with the slightly more benign seacoast to the south. There were few of the electrically powered vehicles about.

Instead, the road was heavily used by elegant sleigh wagons pulled by brightly colored horned animals the size of small elephants. Their fur was black with white-and-gold splotches, and their feet were wide and massive.

"Recundas," Jeeter told his passengers. "They domesticate easily. I know it makes it look like we're going backwards, but not everyone has access to a crawler. Things will get easier when the rail system is finished."

The administrative center and largest town on Eden was called Snake, a name applied by the first colonists with fine irony. Most of the buildings were constructed of wood, an unheard-of luxury on Earth. Lying under a mantle of fresh powder, it offered a charming if not idyllic appearance. The people wandering the streets looked well dressed and content, but as Jeeter had pointed out, they were too intelligent to let crushing disappointment weigh them down forever. Faint puffs of smoke marked larger buildings on the outskirts of town.

"Snake has a population of thirty thousand," Jeeter informed them as he parked the crawler inside a covered structure next to a cluster of two-story buildings. All were intricately carved, the decoration comprising an eclectic mixture of northern European, oriental, and modern motifs. Evidently Eden had its share of artists.

They followed him out of the parking structure into a heated corridor, glad to be out of the cold.

"We'll find you some standard newcomer-issue clothing as soon as you're finished here," Jeeter assured them. "You wouldn't last ten minutes outside in those outfits." Occasionally he exchanged brief greetings with others using the corridor.

"This is irregular, but you've insisted that you're irregular, so I suppose that makes it regular."

Eventually they came to a small rotunda, turned down a branching corridor to the left, and stopped in front of a desk.

"Hi, Naki," he said to the woman seated behind the wood.

"Morning, Jeeter. How'd it go at the GATE today?"

"Smooth as usual. Couple of interesting newcomers. Who's ombuds for the Council today?"

The woman checked her console. "Tarlek and Madras."

"Ask Madras if she can spare us a minute or two. Tell her it's Jeeter Sa-Nos-Tee and that I've got company from Earth."

"Give me a second." She lifted a hand comm unit.

"You'll like Madras," Jeeter assured his new friends. "She's a sweet old gal and my aunt or cousin or something."

The receptionist looked up. "She'll see you, but she says it had better be important."

"It is," Eric said. The receptionist looked after them as they continued down the hall.

XVIII

MADRAS was in her early sixties, Eric guessed. She was small and olive-skinned and wore her hair straight back. Her forehead shone in the overhead lights as if it had been polished. Eric wondered if she'd been conscripted to this job or if she'd served as a professional administrator on Earth. Later he would learn he was wrong on both counts. She'd been born on Eden and elected to the position.

"Lisa Tambor and Eric Abbott," Jeeter told her, introducing his charges. "Just in today through the GATE."

"How do you do?" Madras asked, shaking hands with them. "I enjoy meeting new arrivals, but it's hard when it takes away from your regular work schedule."

"These aren't your usual new arrivals," Jeeter said. "They're both artificials."

"So? Why should that interest me?"

"Mr. Abbott here insists on speaking with someone in a position of social importance. He alluded to it a little on our way over here. Something to do with irregularities surrounding their transposition."

"That's nothing unique. Have a seat, Mr. Abbott, Ms. Tambor. Do you wish Jeeter to leave?"

"No, not now," Eric told her. She had put her stylus aside and was now giving him her undivided attention.

"Jeeter's told you we're not natural humans. That doesn't seem to matter here, and we're immensely grateful for that. But I have an additional problem." He was surprised how easily the words came to him. "Are you familiar here on Eden with a race called the Syrax?"

That produced a reaction from the administrator, and even Jeeter looked startled.

"I can see that you are," Eric said wearily. He proceeded to tell them the whole story, beginning with his first glimpse of Lisa in Phoenix and leaving nothing out. He didn't want some informed later arrival contradicting anything he said now.

When he'd finished, Madras leaned back in her chair, put her delicate hands behind her head, and regarded him thoughtfully.

"You strike me as more human than many, Eric Abbott. In any case, your honesty vouches for you now. What hands or tentacles molded you no longer matter. You're far beyond reach of human and alien alike. We're all Edenites together on this world, and anyone who is capable of, and willing to, make a contribution to the general welfare is more than welcome. You had no reason to tell me all this, since you probably could have kept your origin and activities a secret. That you did so marks you as good Edenite material." She glanced up at Jeeter.

"I don't think this calls for any special convening of the Council. I may not even bother mentioning it at the next regular meeting. Welcome to Eden, Mr. Abbott. And Ms. Tambor, or perhaps I should say Ms. Abbott?"

"If you like," said Lisa with a smile.

"I really don't know how to thank you people," Eric mumbled, and he meant it.

"No need for thanks," said Madras. "We're all outcasts here. We've all been lied to."

"You're lucky. My whole life is a lie."

"Why then, this is certainly the place for you, isn't it? You're now a part of the most elaborate deception in human history." She spoke without bitterness. Resignation, Eric thought. As Jeeter said, everyone here was too occupied with the business of survival to waste energy and time lamenting the unalterable.

Finding Eric a job took a little more time than expected. The usual procedure was for a group of colonists to bring with them a list containing the names of those who would follow several months later, together with an explanation of each colonist-to-be's particular talents. Since neither Eric nor Lisa had ever appeared on the list, nothing had been prepared for them.

Once established, however, his exceptional ability instantly gained the respect and admiration of his colleagues. Soon they were seeking him out with unsolvable problems of their own.

As for Eric, while he'd enjoyed working at Selvern, he'd never dreamed work could be so relaxing and gratifying. Eden's colonists had been selected for their emotional as well as intellectual maturity. Here there was no fighting for advancement, no pushing for the top rung of a nonexistent corporate ladder, no thought of hindering someone else's work to gain personal advantage. All that mattered was that the problem be solved. It was an exhilarating atmosphere in which to work, and Eric responded with previously unimaginable enthusiasm.

Though comfortable, life on Eden bordered on the spartan, especially during wintertime. There were also occasional, unpredictable, sometimes fatal assaults by storms or animals which the colonists were unable to deal with. Such incidents made further mockery of the rosy picture WOSA had painted for the colonists in its advertisements back on Earth.

Still, the colonists coped, and Eden's population grew steadily. The deep bitterness each new batch of deceived arrivals felt was soon pushed into the background as the business of staying alive took precedence over everything else. The natives, like Jeeter and Madras, concealed their feelings far better than newcomers, but as he came to know his fellow citizens more intimately Eric was able to detect hints of the vast reservoir of anger that lay concealed beneath smiling, helpful exteriors. The newcomers had been lied to, but those born on Eden had been denied their birthright.

Instead of the envy and jealousy he would have felt on Earth, Eric received only compliments and good wishes from his associates when he was promoted to supervisor in charge of all computer-related activities on Eden. Eric enjoyed it because he was able to spend more time with Jeeter Sa-Nos-Tee. He was on a first-name basis with most of the population of Snake by now, and as he felt more and more at home among the Edenites, his hitherto reclusive personality expanded like a flower in the sun.

Like most secrets in small communities, the secret of Eric's and Lisa's origins could not be kept hidden for long. Revelation bore out the truth of Councilwoman Madras's claim. No one gave a damn. Lisa grew close to an agri specialist before she learned that Aelita Marcensky was an artison like herself.

As the months passed, Eric relaxed more and more, though he still couldn't completely convince himself that they were safe. There was always the fear that the authorities might send a suicide team through to ensure that the Syrax plan, gone astray or not, could not harm the colony.

He carefully scrutinized each new group of arrivals alongside Jeeter, but evidently the authorities had been satisfied with his defection. Eric still lived, but the Syrax had failed in their attempt to steal the secret of the GATE, and the prosaic Colligatarch should count that a sufficient success. In any case, there were no kamikazes among the newcomers, and none of them mentioned Eric's or Lisa's history to the Council. There would be no point to it, since the deceived Edenites would hardly jump to do WOSA's dirty work.

"Tell me something, Jeeter," Eric asked him as they performed minor surgery on part of the GATE circuitry one day, "do you think many people would go back to Earth if they were given the opportunity?"

Jeeter slid out from beneath the console he was working on, pushed back his red headband, and looked thoughtful. "I don't think so, Eric. Independence is worth a lot. This planet may not be the promised land, but the society we've been able to develop here is a thousand years ahead of

Earth's. There are only two clinical psychologists and no psychiatrists to serve everyone on Eden, and they spend a lot of their time skiing. No, I don't know anyone who'd go back to that cauldron of tribalism and petty personal rivalry and crime. Life here is tough, but at least it's sane. And there's no Colligatarch to 'suggest' how we're to run our lives."

Eric nodded. "The Earth couldn't function anymore without the Colligatarch. Population's too big and unstable."

"Well here it's sensible *and* stable. I've read a lot about this Colligatarch. It runs everything, doesn't it?"

"Not exactly. It has no real power. It just advises."

"Uh-huh." Jeeter was nodding knowingly, a rueful smile on his face. "And like everything else, I suppose it 'advised' an embryonic WOSA to set up the lie about paradise worlds that lured my grandparents and everyone else through the GATE."

"I don't see how the deception could have been arranged without the machine's connivance," Eric agreed.

"I didn't know that it was possible to design a duplicitous machine."

"The Colligatarch's much more than a machine," Eric explained. "It possesses consciousness along with extraordinary computational abilities. It's tied into every major computer ganglion on the planet."

"No, most of us wouldn't care to live with something like that watching over us, no matter how beneficent its motives."

"That's why I've been wondering about your local computer setup. It strikes me as pretty sophisticated for a population of seventy-five thousand."

"It has to be, to help us cope with our 'paradise,' " Jeeter pointed out.

"Does it? You know what I've been thinking? That within another fifty years or less you're going to receive some innocuous-looking program that, once inserted into the local system, will turn it into a smaller analog version of the Colligatarch."

Jeeter's expression darkened. It was the first time Eric

had ever seen him really upset. "Now, why would it want to do that?"

"To extend its reach to the colonies. Remember that the machine had to have been in on the deception from the beginning. Subsequently it helped in the expansion and design of all colony facilities. It passes on what supplies you're to receive, how many specialists in what fields. I'm frankly surprised it hasn't sent an operative piece of itself through to be integrated into our network already. It's only a matter of time."

Jeeter sat up. "We have to inform the Council. At least we can be on our guard from now on. We can scan each program package as it comes through."

"You think that'll be enough? The Colligatarch and WOSA have been fooling the colonists for a hundred and fifty years. You think they won't be capable of fooling you in the future?"

"Well then, you'll be able to detect it. You're the best we have, Eric."

"Thanks, but what happens fifty years down the road? Programming and procedures on Earth may have advanced so much by then that not even I will be able to see through the deceptive techniques."

"*Something* has to be done. The settlers here wouldn't stand for that kind of control. It's one of the things they came here hoping to get away from."

"They won't have any choice in the matter," Eric said grimly. "Once the Colligatarch's electronic satrap takes control of the local system, you'll never be able to dig it out. Eden will be forced to deal with Colligatarch-generated 'suggestions' whether it wants to or not." He grinned humorlessly. "Besides, what's the harm in that? The Colligatarch only wants to make life better for you. That's all it's programmed to do. Making decisions will become so much easier."

"We like making our own decisions, as you know. Our computer network is useful, sure. So are plows and hydro-electric generators, but they're all nothing more than tools. We don't need a machine making decisions for us, even under the polite guise of suggestions. I know the history. Sure, it's made life on Earth easier, but after a while everything's left up to the machine. We don't want our own brains to atrophy.

"We don't need a Colligatarch here. We're not subject to Earth's periodic threats of war, or mass starvation, or epidemics. We'll just have to watch the deliveries as close as we can."

"There's something else that might be done," Eric murmured. His attention was focused on something off in the distance. Jeeter let him concentrate on his thoughts for several minutes before interrupting the silence.

"What? Some kind of advanced alarm procedure we can build on to the network?"

"No. I can't outthink or out-anticipate the Colligatarch. It will slip itself into our system no matter how carefully we try to prepare. It may already have begun to do so."

"Then we're helpless, short of throwing away our entire network and scrapping everything new that comes through from Earth."

"Not necessarily. You see, I know where paradise is," he said quietly.

Jeeter said nothing. Conversation at several other tables died as the eavesdroppers no longer were able to conceal their interest. Eric didn't suggest that they leave. Everyone would know sooner or later.

"Oh, you mean Garden," Jeeter finally said.

"I doubt it. Garden's probably much like Eden. It wouldn't make sense for WOSA to send half the colonists to a rough world like Eden and the other half to the promised land."

"Why not? We certainly wouldn't know the difference."

"No, but the psychological profiles and task requirements of all colonists are the same. Different profiles and skills would be demanded if differing worlds were being settled. I think anyone with access to a list of such items for the past century or so could figure out neither Eden nor

Garden is what it's advertised to be. I think the population of Garden's no better off than we are here.''

"Then what the hell are you talking about, Eric?"

"You know what I am."

"Sure." Jeeter appeared embarrassed that his friend had thought it necessary to mention the matter. "You're an artison built by an alien race, the Syrax. So what? To me and everyone else on Eden, you're just another citizen. More gifted than most, no less human than most. We don't give a damn if you were produced in a womb, a test tube, or some kind of alien pressure cooker."

"Thanks." He forced down the lump in his throat, sought to cover with information the emotions he was feeling. "The Syrax supplied me with an enormous amount of usable information. I drew on this store without being aware of it. The rest subsequently became available when I was made aware of my origins at GATE Station and when the now obliterated transmitter in my brain was activated.

"I've had a lot of time to run through those implanted memories. Some of it I don't understand. My perspective is too human. Much of it is fairly comprehensible, like mathematics and other nonabstracts.

"The Syrax are a very old race, Jeeter. Travel through space via starship is a long, tedious process, but they've been at it for thousands of years. Some of their drone ships have taken that long to reach their programmed destinations and return. Some are still outbound after millennia and won't return until all of us are long dead.

"Why do you think they've been trying so hard to steal the secret of the GATE? Because they've amassed a catalog of habitable worlds, worlds that would take hundreds of years for colonizing ships to reach. Since their society abjures war, and is far more moral than ours, there's little they can do except try to buy the secret from WOSA, or bend their rules to the breaking point by attempting to steal it."

"Why not just make a fair trade for the information?"

"They're a little bit afraid of humankind, I believe, and they'd like very much to keep us pinned down on Earth and its two colonies. That's another decision that's caused them a lot of moral anguish. They're at once contemptuous, fearful, and intrigued by us. One day we'll either be friends, or there'll be a war which I fear mankind might lose.

"Included in their catalog are a number of worlds suitable for human occupation. Some are more than merely suitable. The one I have in mind might as well be named Paradise."

"If they think you've gained access to all your stored information after having turned your back on them, the Syrax must consider you the most dangerous being alive. They must be worried to death that after accepting your humanity, you'll turn your information over to human authorities."

"I suspect that's exactly what they think, but I don't think they're worried. They must know by now that I've fled beyond human as well as Syrax reach. Of course, human authorities feel exactly the same way about me."

"Isn't it nice to be popular," Jeeter muttered sarcastically.

"I'm sure they're not worried," Eric went on. "Disappointed that their device failed them, but not worried. Colonists and supplies are still coming through the GATE here at regular intervals. If the Syrax believed I'd fallen into the hands of human scientists, I don't think the GATE or much of anything else would be operating normally anymore."

Jeeter stared into his friend's eyes. "Tell me something, Eric. If the Syrax arrived here and approached you, *would* you turn over the information they want?"

"No. I owe them nothing, just as I owe mankind nothing. Neither has any claim on me. All I want is the chance to live out my life with Lisa as quietly and inconspicuously as possible. I've made real friends here— you, Madras, others. In my opinion, you owe the governments of Earth no more than I do. We've all been lied to and we've all been used."

"True enough." Jeeter leaned close. "Tell me more about this paradise world you've found inside your head."

Eric noticed the rest of the barn's staff moving close to listen.

"It's farther from Earth than either Eden or Garden, much farther. I know its coordinates well enough to translate them into figures the GATE Terminus could use. The computations are complex, but I could work them out, especially if I had help."

"Some of the finest practical engineers alive are here on Eden," someone in the crowd pointed out.

"I know," Eric told the speaker. "I've been working with some of them."

Suddenly Jeeter's excitement faded. "None of which does us a damn bit of good, since there's no way you can turn a receiving terminal into a broadcast terminus."

Eric nodded in agreement. "The power requirements alone place it beyond reach of any colony's resources, not to mention the fact that a transmitter must be placed in free space beyond gravitational and magnetic interference. However," he announced quietly, as though giving the temperature outside, "it is possible to reverse the polarity from either end, so long as sufficient power is available."

A rising murmur from the crowd filled the barn. Jeeter spoke for all of them.

"Come on, Eric! We all know that traffic through the GATE system is strictly one-way."

"One way at a time," Eric corrected him. "I've been working on the problem ever since I got here, and I've had access to Syrax as well as human knowledge. In theory, there's no reason why it can't be done."

"That would mean," Jeeter said slowly, "that we could all return to GATE Terminus, to Earth, if we wanted to. All of us."

"I asked if you thought people would do that, given the opportunity. You said they wouldn't."

"I say it again, though I suppose a few might prove me wrong. But you're no physicist, Eric. The GATE's been in operation for a century and a half. It seems incredible that you'd stumble across something so important where dozens of engineers who've made the GATE their life's work would miss it.''

"What makes you think they missed it?" Eric asked him softly.

He might as well have set off a paralysis bomb in the barn. The silence ended with a flurry of angry, explosive questions.

When the first fury had vented itself and the room had quieted down, Eric continued.

"Do you think that, after stealing the lives of your parents and grandparents, WOSA or the Colligatarch would risk letting the disenchanted and the tricked return to Earth? There's too much at stake, from their point of view.

"Earth is threatened by its own burgeoning population, old tribal rivalries, new diseases, and off in the background, the Syrax. The two colonies are safety valves. You've been planted here to ensure the survival of the human race should the mother world be visited by catastrophe. If it's necessary to lie to make certain the colonies are properly populated and stay that way, do you think the government's not going to do it?

"I'm sure the secret of two-way travel via the GATE system is known only to a very few top scientists and leaders. Certainly the GATE Station crew isn't aware of it. Too dangerous to let them in on it. Some disgruntled engineer might want to bring back a friend or two. Much better to make it plain that GATE travel is strictly a one-way trip. Jeeter, would your grandparents have stuck it out on this icebox if they could have returned home?" Murmurs of agreement rose from the crowd.

"I doubt it, too," Eric went on. "The colony would never have grown, and it was important for it to grow, for the reasons I just alluded to. You've all been lied to and used.''

After a solemn pause Jeeter asked hesitantly, "And you can modify the receiving terminal here to permit travel back to GATE Terminus?"

"I think so. There's some risk."

From the back of the crowd an engineer declared, ''The

GATE is always powered up. It's too expensive to shut down."

"Then there's no reason why we can't reverse the polarity and make the GATE swing both ways," Eric insisted.

"That doesn't get us to this paradise of yours," another technician pointed out.

"True. But we can realign the system and project a receive unit like this one"—he gestured at the framed darkness nearby— "to a new world. We can go from Eden to GATE Station, and then from GATE Station to—"

"Paradise?" someone else finished for him.

"How do we know," asked the engineer who'd spoken first, "if any of what you're telling us is the truth, that it's not part of some greater Syrax plot to get you back to GATE Station so they can pick you up and milk your mind?"

"I know it's not. I've studied my own body as intensively as the workings of the GATE since I've been here," he assured her. "I'm sure the Syrax consider me a lost cause. Maybe they're already at work on a new model, one less likely to break down on them." That brought forth a few gentle laughs.

"No wonder the Syrax are so desperate to obtain the secret of GATE operations," Jeeter muttered. "They could put a receive unit anywhere, including Earth itself."

"And by the same token, if they wanted to break the secrecy, WOSA could put a receive on the Syrax home world. It's a dangerous situation," Eric said unnecessarily. "One of these days it's going to blow up. I'd like to be clear of any fallout." He looked over the heads of the anxious crowd, located the engineer who'd voiced her suspicions.

"If I were still under the control of the Syrax, I could have reversed the polarity myself, at night. It doesn't take much work. You'd be surprised at how simple it is, if you know what to do. I could have delivered myself and my knowledge to them without anyone's knowing."

"Maybe," she said thoughtfully.

"Maybe. I certainly wouldn't have to tell you what I'm telling all of you now. I didn't have to confess my origins when Lisa Tambor and I came through."

"That's enough." Jeeter rose, put a hand on his friend's shoulder. "Eric Abbott is as much a man as any of us."

"Not me," said a female electrician, and the crowd cracked up. When the laughter had subsided some, Eric looked gratefully at Jeeter.

"Well, as human, anyway."

"Eric, are you sure about this world?"

"Positive. The catalog is full of information on each planet, and this one's no exception." He let his gaze rove over the crowd, saw the hope, the intense wish to believe on many anxious faces. "It's everything Eden and Garden were advertised to be."

"If it's not," Jeeter said warningly, "we could be stuck there forever."

"Not at all," Eric reminded him. "You're forgetting that we can reverse polarity on GATE Station. If the Syrax information turns out to be wrong, and I've no reason to suspect it is, we could at least return to Earth, or Eden.

"We can cannibalize enough replacement components to build a second receive terminal, send it through to GATE Station, then on to Paradise. It will be a trade-off. The infrastructure you've worked to build up here against complete freedom from Earthly interference and the return of your birthright. You can still have what you were promised."

"It will have to be put to the Council," Jeeter was muttering, "and there'll have to be a general vote. Not everyone will want to take the risk."

"What about you, Jeeter? Will you come with Lisa and me?"

"Eden's my home. I was born here." He broke into a wide smile. "I can't wait to get the hell off." Roars of assent rose from the onlookers. When the general amusement had died down, Jeeter turned serious once again.

"Assuming everything works out, Eric, what happens

when we arrive at GATE Station? WOSA's not going to let us make use of the GATE for our own purposes."

Eric didn't smile at all. "Then we'll have to insist, won't we?"

Nearly a third of Eden's population voted to chance the move to the world Eric described in such glowing terms. They comprised a solid mix of newcomers and native Edenites disenchanted with the world they'd been given. Many still yearned for the promised land that had called on the spirits of their parents and grandparents. They owed little to Eden, and nothing to Earth. They came from every profession, every branch of Eden's society. It was a good cross section. The new colony of Paradise would not lack for necessary skills.

Using lifters and repulsion pallets, they transferred those supplies that could be spared from Eden's warehouses. There was a heated discussion concerning whether they should take any computer components at all, but even Eric argued in favor of taking the basics along. It was the insidious influence of the Colligatarch they had to beware of, not the machinery itself, and the Colligatarch would not be able to reach them on Paradise.

It would take time to build on Paradise what had laboriously been constructed on Eden: bridges, roads, manufacturing facilities, and it would have to be done without the aid of regular resupply from Earth. That was the price they would have to pay for achieving real independence. None of the volunteers balked. They were ready to do the work necessary to cast off the last umbilical cord.

At least they wouldn't be dependent on Earth for heating equipment, Eric assured them. From the information in the Syrax catalog he knew Paradise to be a world of gentle oceans and lush farmland, of mild temperatures and seasonal rains. He knew it was so because he could see it in his mind.

"It's going to take time," Madras commented as he, Lisa, and Jeeter stood before the Council. "You've twenty-five thousand volunteers, and you can't pass them through the GATE in a couple of minutes. How are you going to hold it for the necessary time?"

"Transposition is practically instantaneous," Eric reminded them. "We'll send our Paradise receive unit through first, then start bringing over people and supplies. Once we gain control I'll assume the GATE master's station and his functions. We'll bring through groups of fifty, hold them at the Terminus while I realign for Paradise, then transpose them again five at a time. Then back to Eden, Eden to Terminus, Terminus to Paradise, and so on.

"The GATE will transpose five people every thirty seconds. Allowing for realignment and recoordination, say it works out to five every minute. Working nonstop that's three hundred people an hour, seven thousand two hundred per day. So if we can hold the Terminus for four days, we should be able to safely transpose every volunteer and all necessary supplies."

"Four days," another Council member muttered. "Working round the clock. I'll chance it." Councilman Symionowski was sixty-four years old and ailing, but he wanted to be among the first to make the journey.

"We've selected the team for the first assault," Eric went on. "If for some inexplicable reason the GATE is powered down, we'll just have to wait, but the delay should be only momentary at most. Since the regular GATE crew isn't aware two-way transfer is possible, we'll have surprise on our side.

"I'll be one of the first five through, together with Lisa and Jeeter Sa-Nos-Tee. The rest of the assault team will follow at thirty-second intervals. I don't foresee any problems. The GATE crew is unarmed, and all security is located between the Departure Lounge and the rest of the city.

"Furthermore, the whole security setup is designed to keep unauthorized visitors from getting into GATE Station, not out of it. We ought to be able to lock ourselves in tight. We're going to arrive through the exit.

"At first there should be confusion, then some kind of probe of our forces, then consideration of how to carefully dislodge us. GATE Station is horrendously expensive. The authorities will take great pains to insure it isn't damaged. It's going to take a decision at the highest level before local security can come after us in real strength, and by that time we should be done with the Station. Our best defense will be bureaucratic inertia.''

"I'm not sorry I'm staying here," Madras told him. "This is my home now. But many of us feel differently." Councilman Symionowski let out a grunt of assent. "I'm afraid I prefer palpable comfort to old dreams. Those of us who will remain behind will, of course, do everything we can to help."

"Someday, somehow, we'll let you know how we've fared," Eric assured her. "Or our descendants will, anyhow. Paradise will be a colony of Eden, not of Earth."

"Our assistance and our prayers will go with you," she said solemnly.

Eric looked thankful. "We're going to need both."

XIX

IRONICALLY, the weapons they would need for the assault on GATE Station were readily available on Eden. Their presence among the supplies the first colonists unpacked was further proof of the authorities' duplicity, since no guns should have been needed on a "paradise world." Now the well-used "sporting implements" would find new employment.

More than enough spare parts and backup components existed to build the receive terminal which would be transposed to Paradise. While Eric's engineering team put it together, others began the task of assembling and caring for a third of the colony's population, coaching those who'd never been through the GATE on how to act, assigning everyone from the eldest to the youngest a specific task, stacking and preparing supplies for rapid transposition.

As the weeks of careful preparation slid past, there were some who had second thoughts and decided to remain on Eden. Their places were taken by others who determined to take the chance after all. The total number of departees fluctuated but held relatively steady. Fortunately, the weather cooperated, and tent housing was sufficient to keep the crowd sheltered and warm.

Then there were no more morning briefings to be held, no more preparations to be made. Everyone knew what was expected of them. Under normal circumstances such an undertaking would have been impossible, but the 25,000 who'd opted to make the attempt were not a normal collection of citizens. They had been winnowed from Earth's entire population. They were as extraordinary as their leader.

The squads of men and women, grouped by fives, assembled in the barn, those in front checking their weapons a last time. The realigned GATE didn't look any different. It still generated the same sounds, the same tenebrous darkness beneath the metal arches. Only the direction had been reversed. Some hailed Eric a genius. He demurred, insisting he was no more than an efficient sponge.

If his math was wrong, not to mention the work of the engineering team, they might step through to limbo. It would be a quick death, and fail-safe instrumentation in the barn should detect such a failure. That would be the end of the grand experiment. The 25,000 would mutter awhile, then return to their shuttered homes. Eric gripped his stun rifle tightly. It must not happen that way. It must not happen to Lisa or to any of his newfound friends. There were too many depending on him for it to fail.

But it would take more than good intentions to convey them safely across the void.

Jeeter stood close behind him. "There has to be a first step, Eric," he said gently. "Let's get on with it. I want what my parents and grandparents were promised. Let's go slay the lie."

Eric nodded, signaled to the technicians manning the remodeled equipment, made a final check of his watch. Then he stepped through.

It was dark in GATE Station. Telltales glowed brightly on deserted consoles, showing that everything was still properly powered up, but there was no sign of a night watch. For a terrible instant Eric thought the LED's were stars and that they'd emerged somewhere infinitely far out in empty space. Then the outlines of the consoles came into focus and he relaxed.

They'd timed it perfectly. A wall clock showed that it

was just after midnight, GATE Station time. Since there was no transposition in progress, the area had been secured for the night. They would not need to use their weapons.

Morning might prove otherwise.

Moving to his right, he sat down at the main console and began familiarizing himself with the controls, a task made easier by his eidetic memory. His well-drilled companions hurried to take up their preassigned positions around him. A few lingered briefly at the ports, staring at the Earth orb rotating below. Third- and fourth-generation Edenites, they had never seen it before.

Jeeter urged them on.

Eric did not glance toward that green world. It was not his home, never had been. It did not pull at him. Home was a world named Paradise, which he had yet to set eyes upon.

The takeover was anticlimactic. Several members of the team rushed to secure the airlock door from the inside. This was done mechanically, bypassing the electric locks so that no alarm might be raised at Security Central.

By pressing close to the acrylic of a port, an observer could see the lights of the floating city. The two hotels were alive with light, and a shuttle was just departing, its huge delta-winged shape turning like a top in slow motion as it oriented itself for the drop to the surface.

"It's beautiful," said a young woman staring at the planet below. "I never thought it could be this beautiful."

"Want to stay?" Lisa asked her. "That's part of the arrangement. Anyone who wants to can stay here."

She turned to face the main console. "No. I want a new life, not an old one."

"You're going to get it," Eric promised her.

Other technicians were assuming their assigned positions, inspecting strange instrumentation. Eric had sketched much of it from memory. Now the weeks of study on Eden were going to pay off.

The Terminus was filling up with Edenites. The airlock

had been secured, there was still no sign of alarm, and the crew was in place. It was time to locate Paradise.

The computer mainframe readily accepted the new co-ordinates. Techs carefully positioned the hastily transposed receive station and shoved it into darkness at Eric's command. It would travel only to a place where it could operate. It would not materialize beneath a thousand feet of ocean or a thousand feet up in the air, but would make the minute final adjustments itself.

Eventually a telltale flashed incandescent green on the GATE master's board. The receive terminal had success-fully established itself and was standing by. Muted applause rose from the tech crew as the tension was released. A destination had been gained and Eric's promise at least partly fulfilled.

"It's time," he told the first cluster of anxious volun-teers. The man in front nodded, stepped into the waiting circle with his four companions. Hugs and handshakes were exchanged. "Ready," Eric said calmly. A thousand years ago he'd listened to another man seated in the same chair utter that same word, so rich with promise yet fraught with peril.

"Ready," the five echoed.

"Step through."

They were gone. Seconds ticked away, the first of millions. Lisa's fingers dug into his shoulder, and this time the cheers from the tech people were unrestrained.

The Paradise Express was rolling.

Then it was time to readjust the GATE again, and greet the next batch of fifty from Eden. There was time only for a few handshakes and kisses before they followed the first contact team through.

The excitement gave way to determination as the pro-cess settled into a routine. Fifty from Eden together with supplies, fifty to Paradise, back to Eden, thence to Paradise.

It was early morning, eight o'clock Station time, when the first city tech appeared before the airlock. The word was passed back from the guards who'd been assigned to keep watch.

"There's two of them out there, Eric," said Jeeter. "They can't figure out why they can't get in."

Eric didn't look up from his work, spoke without turning. "Did they see you? Ready," he said in the same breath to the next five transposees.

"No. We've been waiting for someone to show up for over an hour. From outside you have no line of sight into the work area, and we've been careful to keep the lights out. Not that they're needed now." That much was true. The city had swung around the eclipsing mass of the Earth and now rode in sunlit orbit.

As far as the rest of the city was concerned, GATE Station was still empty and secured. It drew on its own solar power supply for energy, monitored its own activity, and no one had noticed the shift in the position of the huge dish every ten minutes.

The peace lasted another couple of hours, until the growing knot of concerned GATE technicians finally called upon a security repair crew, operating under the logical assumption that something had gone wrong with the airlock mechanism.

The technicians and scientists retreated up the corridor to the next checkpoint. Since Eric's people had turned off the airlock instruments, there was no way of determining the atmospheric pressure on the inside, and the repair crew wore full spacesuits. Eric wanted them functioning under just such a misconception. It would slow them down.

Several more hours passed before the repair crew requested and received permission to cut the lock seals. Lasers were in the process of being unloaded when the airlock suddenly slid aside and the armed colonists yanked the clumsily clad repair crew inside, together with their equipment.

As the lock was quickly resealed, Jeeter was able to report to Eric. "We've got 'em."

"That should make them think long and hard before trying again," Eric replied, concentrating fully on his work, "but next time they'll bring weapons along. I think it's time we made contact with Station authorities."

It wasn't necessary. Before he could compose a suitable greeting, the communications speakers throughout the Station roared to life.

"This is Commander Karl Rasmusson, of City Security! You are in illegal possession of WOSA property, whoever you are. Identify yourselves!"

Jeeter moved to a pickup, replied in that relaxed, disarming manner women in particular found reassuring.

"Sure. My name's Jeeter Sa-Nos-Tee. I'm a third-generation colonist over from Eden. We decided to pay the old hogan a visit. So please say hello for me to everybody down in New Mexico, and greetings from my grandparents Yaz and Sula Sa-Nos-Tee."

Eric would have enjoyed seeing the faces at Security Central, but even if he'd been given the opportunity, he couldn't have spared the time to look away from the GATE master's console.

Steady were the readouts, unvarying the numbers. "Step through," he told a family of three and a bright-eyed elderly couple, and they disappeared in the dark wake of their predecessors.

When Rasmusson spoke again, his manner was decidedly less belligerent. "Whoever you are, you're lying about where you've come from."

"Not lying," Jeeter assured him.

"GATE Terminus operates only in one direction: outward."

"Now, that's what I call a lie." Jeeter was enjoying his role as spokesman immensely. "That's what we were told, and I'm sure it's what you believe, and everyone on Earth's been told the same lie, because it's what WOSA wants them to believe. But we're not lying. Contact some higher-ups at WOSA and ask them. You'll find out."

That was the last they heard from anyone for a long time. Jeeter had let the secret out, and once the accusation was confirmed, everyone who'd overheard would have to be sworn to silence and checked for security clearance.

That ought to occupy Rasmusson's forces for a while. It did.

Much time had passed, and the first tech crew had been relieved by a fresh corp of replacements when the speakers crackled again. Only Eric refused to relinquish his post. He continued to recite "Ready" and "Step through" in steady, monotonous tones and intended to continue doing so until the last colonist from Eden had been successfully transposed.

"This is Dr. Dhurapati Ponnani," the new voice announced. A murmur rose from those recently transposed colonists who had recognized the name. "I am a direct representative from Colligatarch Authority, recently arrived at the city.

"I call on you to prove your identities. We also demand to know what you are doing with the GATE. External sensors have detected fluctuations in the power supply as well as movement of the projection unit.

"You claim to have discovered a way of utilizing the GATE for two-way transportation. We neither confirm nor deny that this is possible."

A demand, an accusation, and a compliment, Eric mused. Their new arrival did not mince words. "Ready," he said firmly.

"What we're doing with the GATE is none of your business," Jeeter replied politely. "Say that we're toying with it. If you'd been lied to for a century and a half, you'd feel justified in some relaxation, wouldn't you?"

A pause, and the indecipherable sounds of whispered conversation. The next question surprised everyone.

"Is there a man called Eric Abbott with you?"

"Eric who?" said Jeeter dumbly, but their new adversary would have none of it.

"I think there probably is," Ponnani insisted. "He's the only one who's been through the GATE who'd know how to reprogram and redesign the circuitry to allow two-way use, not to mention being the only one with a reason to do so."

Jeeter shrugged, moved to finally spell his friend at the

main console. Eric rubbed his eyes as he addressed the pickup.

"I'm here, Dr. Ponnani."

"I thought as much. Doesn't it occur to you that what you're doing, by making use of the GATE for your own reasons, is not only illegal but highly dangerous? I don't mean to you and your friends, but to the people of Earth?"

"Why should I care about the people of Earth?" he replied coolly. "I'm not of Earth. Your associates went out of their way to prove that to me, and they succeeded in convincing me when I didn't want to be convinced. You disowned me."

"You were never ours to disown, Eric Abbott. And you are dangerous, I tell you!"

"I promise you, Dr. Ponnani, that what we're doing here in no way threatens the interests of the people of Earth. My friends from Eden bear a considerable grudge against a certain elite segment of the population, but I assure you they would not participate in anything so apocalyptic as you envision. For that matter, I'm not doing anything that in any way threatens my creators, the Syrax. There is no danger to anyone in what we do here."

"Now look here, you!" He recognized the voice of Security Commander Rasmusson. There was a feeling of Dr. Ponnani's being shoved aside, physically as well as figuratively. "I've been briefed on you, Abbott. If you force me to, I can order the destruction of GATE Station itself, if it's thought vital to the security of the human race."

"I don't doubt that you can," Eric responded calmly, "but first you have to determine that that's necessary. I don't think you'd risk blowing up the GATE on your own authority, now, would you? That's quite a step."

More veiled whispering from the speakers. "I can obtain the requisite authorization fast enough, you'll see."

"Will I? That would be interesting. In your request you should note that we haven't harmed a soul . . . the repair crew that decided to become our temporary guests can vouch for that . . . nor have we damaged so much as a paper clip. We know precisely what we're doing (a half lie, at least) and we'll be finished before too long."

"You're *Syrax!*" Rasmusson screamed accusingly.

"I am *not* Syrax," Eric replied evenly. "I'm human. I proved that when I fled from them as precipitously as I did from your Major Orema. If anything, my identity is in doubt, not my origin. As for my allegiance, that is reserved for my friends, regardless of shape.

"So I strongly urge you to discuss the situation carefully with your superiors, Commander, before embarking on any drastic course of action. There are thousands of lives and trillions of world dollars at stake here in GATE Station. They shouldn't be obliterated in a moment of thoughtless anger and frustration."

There was a lengthy delay. When the commander spoke again, it was in a subdued, almost conciliatory voice.

"I will consult, but you could hasten the inevitable by opening the seals on lock number five and letting us in. I will discuss the possibility of general amnesty in return for your cooperation. My first concern is for the general welfare, my second for the GATE. You could damage the Station severely in your ignorance."

"We know what we're doing," Eric assured him. Behind him he heard a cheerful Jeeter say, "Step through." Each "Step through" was a victory, each "Ready" a triumph.

"I hope so, creature of the Syrax, for the sake of those people you've already duped."

Jeeter looked up at Eric and grinned. So did many other members of the tech crew. Eric smiled back briefly, then hid his face while Lisa helped shield him.

Bold leaders are not supposed to cry.

The tension in the conference room was thicker than Oristano could ever remember. The last time they'd been called together thus it had been to discuss a danger only half-real. There was no doubt about the viability of the one they were facing now, however.

When the thing called Eric Abbott had turned on its

makers and fled through the GATE, the Colligatarch had called an end to the emergency. It had gambled that the Syrax had made their creature too well, too human, and the gamble had paid off. With the transposition of Eric Abbott to distant Eden, the threat posed by the Syrax had self-destructed.

Now it appeared they had miscalculated. Either the Syrax were infinitely more thoughtful in their planning than the Colligatarch and its human associates had ever imagined, or else this Eric Abbott had returned for reasons still unknown, in which case, as they said in Monte Carlo to the south, all bets were off.

Instead of having vanished, the problem had reappeared, cloaked in unknown intentions and an infinitely more unpredictable set of variables. As a basis for a course of action, they had only a hysterical report from the commander of GATE City Security and a far more reasoned one from Dhurapati Ponnani.

"I don't think we have any choice," said a tired Anira Chinelita from her chair. "We have to order the destruction of GATE Station, as the commander suggests. We can't allow the secret of the GATE to fall into the hands of the Syrax."

"We have no evidence that this Abbott is operating under the control of the Syrax," Oristano quietly pointed out. "He continues to insist on his humanity. For our sake, it's well that he does.

"By now you're all familiar with the incredible details of this business, which, I might remind you, some of you dismissed rather casually when the Colligatarch first brought it to our attention." A few irritated mutters sounded from around the table. "You know how, against all odds and despite every precaution, Abbott succeeded in boarding GATE City in the company of the Lure artison Lisa Tambor. You have seen the reports which describe how the Syrax have likely manipulated him mentally and physically during his years on Earth, manipulated him into believing he was truly human. Personally, I am not afraid of this Abbott. I cannot fear what I pity."

"Your compassion is legendary, Martin," said Siakwan impatiently, "but does us no good now. Commander Rasmusson mentioned offering general amnesty. What do you think the reaction would be among Abbott's associates?"

"I think they would follow his lead, whatever he decided to do," Oristano replied. "They have more reason to trust him than any representative of WOSA. These are extremely intelligent people, remember. People like the colonists don't forget when they've been lied to."

"What bothers me," said Dr. Novotski softly, "is that this unexpected reappearance may all be a part of some more elaborate Syrax plan. Their work is so subtle. Suppose Abbott's return, while supposedly free of their influence, is in fact only part of some greater deception in which he is playing an unwilling and unknowing part? Not only is Abbott familiar with the GATE's design and operation, he has taken physical control of it." Worried expressions appeared on the faces of his colleagues as the implications began to sink in.

"To what end?" wondered Oristano aloud. "And why return with colonists? Dr. Ponnani informs us that the GATE is in use and probably has been ever since Abbott's friends took control of it, yet to every outward appearance GATE Station is unchanged. If the intent of some mysterious, convoluted plan was to deliver it boldly to the Syrax, why does Abbott wait and invite possible destruction? I'm sorry, Alex, but your theory doesn't hold water."

"They're doing *something* with it," said Isabel Jordan tightly. "It would help my decision a lot if I knew what."

"Dr. Ponnani is reporting an unusual amount of flux in the field," Oristano reminded her, "but she can't determine what it signifies. Neither can the machine. Needless to say, Abbott's people aren't being terribly informative."

"Rasmusson says they mentioned "toying" with it. Could that be true?" Froelich wondered.

"I think it unlikely they would risk annihilation without something stronger in the way of motivation," said Siakwan dryly. "What I would like to know is how this creature managed to compel the people of Eden to do his bidding."

"I don't see it that way," said another member. "We have no evidence any form of coercion is involved. We've had ample demonstration of the creature's physical abilities. Might he not also be capable of some form of mental mass control?"

"I don't think so," said Oristano.

"Nor do I. Dr. Davidov is correct. They appear to be cooperating with Abbott of their own free will." It was the first time the Colligatarch had addressed the table since the beginning of the conference, and the members shifted about in their seats while maintaining a respectful silence.

"It is clear that if this Eric Abbott were capable of such mental control, he would have exercised it by now while keeping his physical abilities a secret. At the same time he would already have been able to deliver the GATE into the hands of the Syrax. He could simply have taken over GATE Station when he and Lure Tambor series four arrived there."

Siakwan persisted. "I still say he must be exercising some form of control over the Edenites."

"Indeed he is, Doctor. There is no lever so powerful as truth, and that is a commodity which circumstances regrettably have forced us to deny to our colonists."

"We can debate motivations later," Novotski pointed out. "Right now, *tovarishch,* we must decide how to regain control of what we have lost, since Abbott shows no sign of relinquishing control of the Station. It must be brought back under human control."

"But it is under human control," Oristano argued. "The Edenites are in charge as much as is Abbott."

"Under government control, then. It amounts to the same thing."

"Not in this case," said the Colligatarch quietly. "In any event, it seems to me that there is no reason yet to take the drastic step proposed by Dr. Chinelita. Three days have passed since Abbott and his followers took over. They have as yet made no demands upon Station personnel or upon the government. Quick work has suppressed news of the takeover and kept it restricted to members of the scientific community and the Station staff. We are still permitted the luxury of caution.

"I need not tell you how long it would take to rebuild the GATE, not to mention the cost. An extended delay in shipment of supplies could cause a great deal of hardship on both colonies. The need for total destruction has not been proved. We are not reduced to the final option."

"I disagree, but your points are well taken," admitted Chinelita.

"What do you recommend we do?" Oristano asked. "Sit and wait?"

"No. We must, of course, take action. Anything short of destruction of the GATE itself is open to consideration."

"Eric Abbott, if the reports are all accurate, has already overcome the effects of massive dose of drugs and limited physical attack. The only thing that's had any effect on him is morphoresene, a narcoleptic gas," Oristano pointed out.

"And he no doubt is prepared to deal with a repeat of such an assault," the machine added. "I therefore propose that we utilize the only weapons which have proven really effective against him so far: psychological."

One of the members let out an openly derisive snort. "I see. We'll just talk him into opening the door and letting our people in."

"Not immediately, perhaps, but he has displayed a willingness, even an eagerness, to talk about himself and his situation. He is confused about the matter of self. We must build upon that uncertainty."

"He doesn't strike me as acting in a confused or uncertain manner," said Jordan.

"First," the machine continued, ignoring her, "we must have more information about what is happening inside the Station. We have one advantage on our side, and we must make use of it."

"What's that?" asked Davidov.

"GATE Station can operate during periods of emergency indefinitely under its own power until machinery begins to break down, but its stored atmosphere will suffice without recycling for only a week. Three days have passed. Three more and the air in the Station will begin to grow foul, one additional day and we will truly be able to open the door and walk in. Certainly we should not wait a week, but at least we know this cannot continue indefinitely.

"And there is something else that has not been mentioned during this discussion. We all know what the Syrax stand to learn if they regain control of Eric Abbott. I must remind the table that we stand to learn a great deal if we can regain his loyalty. He represents the ultimate in Syrax biological engineering. Think what that could mean to biology research here on Earth. He could be as valuable to us in his own way as the GATE.

"And that, Dr. Chinelita, is still another reason why I oppose taking any extreme action against the Station."

Oristano was drumming his fingers on the table. "Abbott hasn't been handled very tactfully by domestic enforcement groups. What makes you think he'd be willing to donate a thimbleful of spit to the Authority, much less willingly cooperate?"

"He is human and yet he is not. He considers himself more human than Syrax. Certainly he has managed to persuade many Edenites of this, else they would not be cooperating with him. He seeks an identity. I believe we can offer him more than his creators."

"Then we must work to win him over, not destroy him," said Oristano. "Ladies and gentlemen, this conference is dismissed. I will entertain suggestions from each of you within the next twenty-four hours. All other regular assignments are suspended until the crisis has been resolved. Thank you."

They filed out of the room, already considering possibilities and alternatives. As usual, Oristano was the last to leave, and when he did so a nagging thought tagged along with him.

The Colligatarch had not proposed a firm course of action for dealing with the problem. Was it really waiting to consider what its human associates could come up with, or was it stalling because it couldn't decide what to do?

It was not a comforting thought to carry back with him to his office.

XX

LISA had delivered another meal to Eric and, more importantly, was watching to make certain he ate it. He'd been monitoring the main console for more than seventy-five hours without sleep. His eyelids did not flutter, and his hands were steady on the controls. As steady as the monotone in which he gave instructions.

"Ready . . . step through. Ready . . . step through."

By now the Terminus resembled a well-oiled machine, and it functioned in comparable silence, each man and woman doing their job efficiently and without question.

Now and then he allowed himself a recreational thought.

They're confused, he told himself. They can't figure out exactly what we're up to, and they're afraid to attack because the Station will suffer. So suggestions are moving up and down the chain of command, and will continue to do so until someone garners a consensus for their favored course of action.

"Eric, tell me something."

"Ready . . . anything I can, light of my life . . . step through."

"Why do you love me? You're obviously much more intelligent."

"They really restricted your education to a few designated areas, didn't they? Intelligence is a poor measure of humanity."

She leaned over to kiss him without obstructing his vision. "When you say that I don't feel so stupid."

"You're not stupid, Lisa. You've just been undereducated, and deliberately so. Ready . . . step through."

"We've all been undereducated, compared to you," Jeeter told him. "Not that I envy you your manner of education." He glanced toward the team guarding the airlock, received a wave by way of reply.

"Still quiet, but they're bound to try something again soon."

"Another twenty hours and it won't matter what they try," Eric reminded him.

"That's true." He sounded wistful. "It's going to feel funny being truly independent of Earth. We'll be the first group of humans in history to break the bonds for real. We'll be freer than any settlers have ever been. I wonder what Paradise is really like?"

"We'll all know soon enough. I expect Paradise to be like paradise. For everyone's sake. If not, I expect to face a lynch mob twenty-five-thousand strong."

Jeeter looked around the busy, quiet room and made shushing motions with his hands. "Don't talk like that. You've got everyone convinced that you know what you're talking about. This isn't the time to sow uncertainty."

"The universe is a maelstrom of uncertainty, Jeeter. I'm ninety-five percent sure of the references I drew upon from the Syrax catalog. I considered the five percent deviation acceptable when I made this proposal."

"Five percent," Jeeter murmured. "How come you never mentioned that before?"

"Because it would have sowed uncertainty," Eric reminded him without a glimmer of a smile.

Jeeter shook his head slowly. "It's a good thing the Syrax didn't program you for a career in show business."

"I believe those aspects of human existence are a mystery to them. I never was the life of the party."

"You're sure making up for lost time. You *are* the party now, Eric." He let his gaze wander back to the undisturbed airlock. "I wonder what they'll try first?"

Dr. Dhurapati Ponnani was pondering the same question as she stood watching Commander Rasmusson give orders in City Security Central. As it developed, they had less time to reach a decision than they knew.

The young officer who approached Rasmusson was out of breath from running. He saluted quickly and interposed himself between the commander and his subofficers. Ponnani moved closer.

"What the devil's wrong with you, mister?" Rasmusson growled. "I didn't ask you to join this discussion."

"Sorry, sir," the young officer said apologetically, panting hard. "I'll accept any reprimand, but I considered it vital to deliver this message personally."

"What message? Why didn't you call it through?"

"Sir, recalling your general directive about maintaining media silence concerning the difficulty at hand, I—"

"Never mind. Say what you came to say."

"I've just come up from Traffic, sir. There's a very large ship approaching the city. It's half a luna out and coming in damn fast. It's Syrax, sir."

Rasmusson looked grim. "Then this *is* all a part of their plan." He looked to his left. "Ovimbi, tell communications to try to raise the Syrax, and fast." Then he turned to the watching Ponnani. "I'm sorry, Doctor, but this takes things out of my hands. I have my orders. We may have to blow the Station."

She sighed. "I am expecting suggestions from Colligatarch Authority any time now as to how to proceed with Eric Abbott."

"Tell it to the Syrax. I'll delay as long as I can and no longer."

"I understand. I disagree, and I'll lodge a formal protest, but I understand."

"That's all I expect you to do." There was a frantic wave from Ovimbi, the communications officer, and Rasmusson stalked over to a wide, curving console. Speakers crackled as communication was established.

The voice that filled the room was gentle but metallic and stilted. The Syrax made use of mechanical translating devices whenever they felt it necessary to speak to human beings. The surprise was that video was provided, and the large opto screen above communications immediately became the focus of attention throughout Security Central.

As always, the sight of the Syrax was disconcerting, though less so on opto than in person. Beyond it, shapes could be seen drifting through thick fog. The Syrax who spoke stood before the alien pickup. No one had ever known a Syrax to sit.

"You are the commander of the orbiting station."

"I am in charge of its security, yes." Rasmusson beckoned Ponnani forward until she was standing alongside him. "This is Dr. Ponnani, who is in charge of the scientific complement here."

"Good life to you also, Doctor."

"Thank you." Ponnani eyed the limber, cartilaginous shape with fascination.

"In your language I am called Limpid." That was all. No surname, no title. "We believe that Eric Abbott has discovered the secret of reversing the polarity of the GATE field, and in concert with an undetermined number of human beings has taken control of it." Rasmusson did not comment.

"We have sources of information," the Syrax added.

"Traitors," the commander muttered darkly, unaware that he'd said it loud enough for the pickup to detect.

"Traitors. You would be interested perhaps to know that the term sounds somewhat similar in our language. That is of no moment now. Eric Abbott is utilizing the GATE for transpositional purposes, yet you have not moved to prevent him."

"We can't," said Ponnani. Rasmusson made as if to quiet her but she shook him off. "I'm within my authority in speaking to matters involving the GATE, Commander. Besides, I see little harm in confirming what they already know." She looked back to the screen. "You know what rebuilding the GATE would entail."

"You suggest its destruction. Why would you consider such a thing?"

"To prevent you from obtaining that which you set Eric Abbott to do: steal the secret of GATE technology and operation."

"Eric Abbott was a failure. A complex, interesting, but overengineered failure."

Ponnani noted that the Syrax did not bother to try to deny the purpose behind Abbott's construction. "Why contact us now?" she inquired.

"We disliked failure. To learn why we failed we need to study our failure."

"Why? So you can build a better thief next time?" Rasmusson snapped at the alien.

"Not sensible. Having been made aware of this method, you would naturally guard carefully against its reuse in the future. I repeat: we dislike failure. An independent tool is a contradiction in terms. There will be no more Eric Abbotts."

"You say we'd be on guard against it. How do we know you couldn't build a person who could outwit our safeguards?"

"Because we will help you to design the necessary methods of detection. Methods which your own scientists can confirm."

"That's unusually generous of you," said Ponnani. "Why should you help us guard against your own inventions?"

"Because we want Eric Abbott back. For the time being we are more interested in learning how and why he failed than we are in learning the secrets of the GATE. We feel this is necessary for our own security. You perceive Eric Abbott as a threat to your race. How odd we should feel the same."

Rasmusson looked dumbfounded. "How can he be a danger to you? You made him."

"Eric Abbott is human, Commander. As human as we could make him. But he is also full of Syrax ability and information. This melding is unique and unstable. Not a comforting combination.

"I would not reveal this to you except that you should

eventually discover it for yourselves, and time is important now to all of us.''

"We know why it's important to us," murmured Ponnani. "Why is it important to you?"

"You ask too much. You must be satisfied with the knowledge that he is a danger to Syrax and human alike.''

"What do you have in mind?" Rasmusson asked cautiously.

"We will provide you with the necessary safeguards for your security if you will permit a single one of us to board GATE Station. We have the means for regaining control of Eric Abbott. Once our representative is aboard, you may raise your antiteleportaic screen again. This will enable you to ensure that we do not spirit Abbott and his knowledge away.

"Subsequently, use can be made by all of us of Abbott. You will have possession of him and can prevent us from obtaining any information by wiring him for instant destruction if you feel we are attempting to deceive you. You detected our carrier wave before and can easily do so again. We can study him together.

"Abbott will not be expecting one of us and our operative can appear quite close to him without warning. His friends are guarding against an attack by spacesuited humans.''

"How can you regain control of him?"

"There is a backup control unit implanted in his abdomen. It is very small and must be activated at close range. If this can be accomplished, he will be deactivated.''

"You intend to kill him?"

"No," said the Syrax. "He will enter a semicomatose state, at which point he will pose no danger to anyone.''

"What about his friends?"

"Our representative will not be able, once your screen is back in place, to teleport back to our vessel, but will be able to shift self to a place of safety elsewhere within your city. This accomplished, you should meet little resistance in your attempt to regain GATE Station. Cut off the head and the body surrenders quickly.''

"What," said Rasmusson slowly, "if we agree, and everything goes as planned, except that we refuse to countenance joint study?"

"That would countermand the bargain we strike."

"Gee, that'd be too bad."

"Would you go to war to protect the secret of the GATE?"

Some of the commander's schoolboy sarcasm evaporated. "I understand."

"It is well that you do."

"All right. Now we all know what Abbott's worth."

"You are giving us an opportunity to learn a great deal about the methodology of Syrax bioengineering," Ponnani said.

"The concession of our part," whispered the alien.

"I don't know," Rasmusson was muttering. "You're asking us to let a fox in the chicken coop with only the fox's word as security."

"The metaphor is clear," said the Syrax without humor.

"I will contact the necessary authorities," Ponnani said abruptly, "and pass on your proposal."

"You refer to your mechanical administration?"

"The Colligatarch, yes, and its human operators. It would be encouraging if we could cooperate on something like this."

"You may construe it as a first step in closer relations, if it will expedite matters."

"I'm sure it will. We have measured the Syrax teleport range. Stay outside it and we will contact you again as soon as a decision is reached."

The Syrax executed a strange, fluid motion with its head and arms. Then the opto went black.

"I don't like it," Rasmusson said immediately. "Letting a Syrax into GATE Station poses all sorts of dangers."

"I'm aware of that, but the fact remains that it may be our one chance to regain control of it before Abbott and his people do something unimaginable. I think they're as scared of him as we are."

"Nonsense! He's taken control of his trap, but he's still trapped."

"We don't know that. We don't know much of anything about Eric Abbott and only a little of what he's capable of. I don't like giving the unknown too much time. Fortunately, I don't have to make the final decision. That's up to the Colligatarch and the Council Authority."

"But we can make our recommendations. What are you going to recommend, Dr. Ponnani?"

"I'm not going to recommend a damn thing."

"You'll be branded as indecisive."

She smiled at him as she moved closer to the communications console. "Fortunately, Commander, that is not as much of a vice in my profession as it is in yours."

They were almost through, in every sense of the word. At the main control console Eric sat steel-steady. He'd gone four days without sleep, but there was no hint of drowsiness in his gaze and his fingers moved methodically over the instrumentation.

Everyone wishing to transpose to Paradise had done so except for the technical and security personnel, and they were in the process of being shifted. In the interim, Eric was bringing through more than a hundred of the disgruntled who wished neither Eden nor Paradise but to return to Earth. When they were freed to tell their stories of deception to the media, optos would burn out all over the globe. The government would try to silence them, but it's difficult to silence a hundred angry men, women, and children. Reestablishing only one-way communication with the colonies was going to be a near impossible task for the authorities.

Lisa walked over to stand next to him. She was chewing rations transposed from Eden.

"Hungry, husband?" Madras had made it formal. Kindly old Madras who'd declared Eden her home and had proven unable to resist the challenge posed by a new world. She gave up her Council post gladly. She suffered from chronic bronchitis, and the promise of a warm world eventually proved too much for her. So while waiting for her turn to step through to Paradise, she'd performed the ceremony, beaming at the happy couple from in front of Eric's station, pronouncing them man and wife in the light of three worlds.

"Not hungry, thanks."

"You look tired."

"I suppose I should be, but that's not it. Something else nagging at me. Going on for almost a whole day now. Digs at me and won't go away. Ready . . . step through."

"You're sure you're not sick?" she asked him, concerned.

"I've never been sick a day in my life. I always thought I was lucky." He laughed hollowly. "No luck to it. Just good engineering." He shrugged. "We're almost finished anyway."

"I wish you could be less pessimistic."

"I think I was built pessimistic. Persistent and pessimistic."

Around them the open spaces between the consoles were filled with the hundred who intended to return to Earth. Children played and bawled, and a thousand conversations made it difficult for the technical crew to continue their work. It was impossible to reach a port, since returnees crowded close to gaze out at the world they'd left behind and would soon be returning to. Eric envied them their affection if not its object. For him, home was a place not yet seen.

Abruptly he rose from his seat, blinked at the GATE. "Lisa!" She turned at the sharpness in his voice. Jeeter also looked up in puzzlement, as did several other techs working near him.

Eric turned a slow circle, staring off into the distance. Returning couples milled noisily around his position, unaware that anything out of the ordinary was going on.

When he moved toward the GATE, leaving the main console activated and locked, Jeeter rose to shout at him.

"We're not through bringing the last ones over from Eden."

"No time!" Eric shouted at him. "Everyone for transposition, get in line, now!" The technical and security teams rushed to comply, wondering at the sudden shift in routine. Five-by-five, Eric gave orders for them to step through while Jeeter manned the main console.

At last only the three of them were left, together with a makeshift tech crew composed of people returning to Earth. That too was part of the plan, though this last-minute change in sequence was not. They watched anxiously, wondering but unwilling to argue with the man who'd succeeded in returning them to GATE Station.

Jeeter moved toward the GATE. "Let's go, Eric, Lisa. Why the sudden rush, anyway?"

"Just a feeling," said Eric, making one last check of the controls and imparting final instructions to the young engineer who would take command in his absence. "I've had funny feelings before and I've always come out better for acting on them." He smiled then and took Lisa's hand.

"It will vanish along with ourselves, wife." He started to lead her toward the GATE.

Behind him the young engineer's wife moved to stand next to her husband. "Good-bye, Mr. Abbott, Lisa. And thank you."

She had tears in her eyes, though they were not shed on behalf of Eric's departure. She was going back to the home she'd considered lost forever.

And he? Where was he going? To oblivion or to Paradise? Well, Paradise would be nice but not necessary. He would settle for a home.

Something stood between him and the main control console. There was no expression on the pale, ghostly face as it stared directly at Eric. Something exceptional passed between human and alien in that instant. Something that was more than a communication between manufacturer and manufactured. It was a cry for help, an angry order, a wash of curiosity, an appeal to a part of Eric that he hadn't suspected existed, all homogenized and blended together in a single powerful mental rush.

The Syrax had materialized three meters out of position. It took a giant step toward Eric on ropy, flexible legs. A few of the decolonials screamed.

A long-fingered hand stabbed toward Eric's back. The

Syrax had planned to appear directly behind Eric. At the critical moment Eric and Lisa had stepped toward the GATE. Wordlessly the alien tried to recover.

It was not fast enough, not quick enough. His face as blank as that of his erstwhile master, Eric pulled Lisa tight to him and jumped in concert with Jeeter through the Gate, at once ignoring appeals, orders, queries, and everything else the Syrax had thrown at him in that single vast mind-filling stream of consciousness.

Gone. Quite gone.

The alien paused before the humming GATE, centimeters short of its target. Its long, boneless fingers drew back. It could not reach across the lens of the galaxy. It might follow and control, but a glance showed that the necessary sequence no longer flashed on the control console, and the operation of the GATE was foreign to its complex mind. Nor was it immune to human weapons, and surely the construct Eric Abbott had those aplenty wherever he now stood.

Behind the control console the young engineer stared in fascination at the alien, his wife's fingers digging unnoticed into his shoulder. He touched a button as he'd been instructed to do. A few wisps of smoke rose from the console and that cracked the calm. As he hurriedly moved away, the smoke dissipated. But something inside the console had melted. He could not have said what it was. Among them all, only Eric Abbott could have explained, and Eric Abbott had been transposed.

The steady hum of the GATE softened. Around the room gauges slipped and readouts shrank. The GATE was not destroyed, nor had it been powered down, but it would not be working for at least a few days. A few key circuits had been blown, and one bit of coordinating information obliterated.

How much of this the Syrax knew, how much it guessed, none of them could say, but there were those who swore the alien exhaled deeply before it vanished as silently and unexpectedly as it had arrived.

Conversation in the room resumed. Whatever had happened

there before the GATE was now past, and they remembered their new futures. The young engineer who'd been left in command moved toward the airlock. Word was given to unseal. Weapons were put aside.

"Hello," he said to the startled officer on the other side of the opening. Soldiers tried to see past the engineer, into the Terminus. "We're ready to give ourselves up."

The spearhead of the security assault team rushed into the Terminus, followed by a small army of engineers and technicians wearing anxious expressions. GATE instruments were examined hurriedly. Everything was found to be in order and untampered with save for a small portion of the GATE master's console and data bank.

Very soon after, the high brass arrived, led by Karl Rasmusson and the sari-clad Dhurapati Ponnani. She headed straight for the GATE master's station and the little knot of engineers and scientists examining its interior.

"They did a lot of complex reprogramming," one of them informed her, "but we can't say for sure what it consisted of because the memory's been cremated."

"I can tell you." All eyes turned to the plump blonde woman standing close by. "My name's Greta Kinsolving. I was a programmer on Eden. I was told to explain certain things, but only to a direct representative of Colligatarch Authority."

Ponnani straightened. "You can talk to me, then."

"You must be Dr. Ponnani, the one we heard over the intercom." Ponnani nodded curtly. "It was all part of the plan, Doctor."

"What plan, young woman? Eric Abbott's plan?"

Kinsolving shook her head. "The plan all of us decided on." She gestured back toward the GATE. "Many went through, you see. He found another world for those who still dreamed. I'm not a dreamer. I wanted to come back." There were whispered rumblings from those decolonials still in the chamber, and Ponnani sensed a hostility WOSA's publicists were going to be hard pressed to try to contain.

That was not her major concern of the moment, however.

"I don't follow you, young woman. Are you saying Abbott sent some of the people from Eden over to Garden?"

"No. I said he found another world for them. Not Garden. They called it Paradise."

"That's insane," she announced firmly. The other scientists, though, were listening raptly to the story.

"Abbott said otherwise. He told us it was part of the knowledge the Syrax had stored inside his head. He chose it from their catalog of surveyed worlds."

"My God," muttered the man next to Ponnani, "he had access to that kind of information?"

"That's what he told us."

Ponnani was tight-lipped. "Gone, if true. All gone. No wonder the Syrax was so desperate to regain control of him. They must have been terrified that we'd succeed without them."

"He was tired of all of it," Kinsolving told them. "He was tired of you, and tired of the Syrax. I think he just wanted someplace quiet where he could live with his wife."

"Wife?" Oh yes, she reminded herself, the artison Lure Tambor series four.

"All we need are the coordinates," said one of the scientists working on the damaged console. His eyes were alive with excitement. "We can reprogram the GATE, send representatives through to make peace with this Abbott. We can have two-way communication, contact with a third new colony!"

Kinsolving smiled sadly at him. "He doesn't want to have contact with Earth. Neither do the people who went with him. All they want is to be left alone, to have a chance at the life they were promised. The rest of us wished them all luck. A lot of my friends went. I have three brothers and a sister in Oslo who I want to see. That's why I didn't go with them.

"Only Mr. Abbott knew the coordinates, and he programmed the GATE himself. Maybe a few others, like Jeeter Sa-Nos-Tee, knew it also, but they've all gone now.

Nobody you can reach knows where Paradise is or how to sight in on its sun."

"You could be one of the richest women on Earth," one of the scientists began, "if you could tell us—"

"I can't," she interrupted him. "No one can. And I don't want to be one of the richest women on Earth." There were tears in her eyes. "All I want is to see my family again, and I'm going to!" With dignity she added, "Mr. Abbott said you all wanted more than we did."

Ponnani watched as the woman moved toward the open airlock and disappeared into the Departure Lounge. She offered a few suggestions to the crew working on the control console until her eye was caught by a man standing just out of field range of the GATE.

She walked up behind him, studied his profile. "I think I've seen you via opto report. You're Kemal Tarragon, aren't you? With WOSA security?"

He turned to face her. "Yes, that's me, Dr. Ponnani."

"Just arrived?"

"On the last shuttle, yes."

"I understand that you had more contact with this Eric Abbott than anyone else during the last several weeks."

Tarragon nodded, smiled sardonically. "We weren't close."

"That's hardly surprising. What did you think of him?"

"I thought he was a bad man, Dr. Ponnani. I thought he was a dangerous man."

"He was, but not in the way you think. He was dangerous because he had too much knowledge. I think that may be one reason he's chosen this extraordinary avenue of escape, so that he won't be a danger to himself or anyone else."

Tarragon glanced again at the dusky emptiness that was the GATE. "You can't trace them?"

"It appears not. These people"—she gestured at the remaining decolonials—"know nothing. I doubt anyone on Eden knows more. The only possible way to trace him would be to strike a bargain with the Syrax. The politicians will not let that happen for some time, I suspect. Perhaps after I am dead. A pity."

"You know," Tarragon murmured thoughtfully, "I never really got to talk to him. I was so busy trying to find out what he was up to and then track him down that I didn't talk to him. I regret that now. He was an interesting man, if man is a proper description." He blinked, looked back at her.

"Where did they go, anyway?"

"To a world named Paradise, according to a representative of Abbott's who remained here. Whether the name is descriptive or merely hopeful we've no way of knowing."

"I see. Well, my department should be pleased. The secret of the GATE is still safe from the Syrax, and that was their primary concern. There will be a problem with these returned colonials . . . I've heard their complaints and I can't say that I blame them . . . but that's a problem for WOSA's hired apologists, not me. I think I'll keep my job, and that was *my* primary concern. May I ask you something, Dr. Ponnani?"

"What's that, Mr. Tarragon?"

"Call me Kemal. I've had a lonely time this past month and I'm sick of dealing with nothing but business. This is my first visit to GATE Station. Would you do me the honor of dining with me tonight?" His meeting with the Colligatarch itself had killed much of the awe he'd felt for those who worked with the machine.

"I am also tired. *Han* . . . yes, I accept your invitation."

He looked very pleased as he moved to talk with Rasmusson.

An interesting man, she thought, but anyone who'd had so much contact with Eric Abbott was bound to be interesting. Dinner conversation should prove equally interesting.

She returned her attention to the silent black nothingness that was the GATE. Dust motes danced in and out of the enigma.

Where have you gone, Eric Abbott? What hopes and fears and private terrors did you take with you? Those of mankind, of your creators, of your unique inner self we are never to know? It seems I am never to meet you in person. What were you? Man, android, artison, sculpture of the Syrax; where in that pantheon of intelligence and flesh lay the line that divided? And what was the difference?

She would have to settle for what information the returned colonists could provide, try to piece together the illusion of a man from the memories of casual acquaintances. Lure Tambor series four could tell her more, but she was likewise gone with the galactic wind. Ponnani's lips crinkled into the semblance of a smile.

Tambor series four, thought Dr. Emeritus Dhurapati Ponnani, why do I stand here envying you?

The reports were filed—by Tarragon, by Ponnani and Rasmusson, by the scientists and engineers and technicians and those of the disgruntled colonists who could be persuaded or bribed to do so. Every word was dissected, studied, digitalized, and entered into the Colligatarch. In less terse terminology, the information thus gleaned was also passed on to Martin Oristano.

"So what do we do about it?" the Chief of Programming and Operations asked the machine many months later. "We can't trace Eric Abbott and his friends to their new home unless we cooperate with the Syrax."

"The time for that is not now," the machine intoned.

"I agree. We stand to lose too much. More immediately, what are we going to do now that the decolonials have made the secret of two-way GATE travel public?"

"It would have come out sooner or later. We will offer rationalizations for our secrecy that the general public will accept. There may even be a brief upsurge in the desire to emigrate. I believe enough will want to go to cancel out those who desire to return, now that Eden and Garden are well established. The storm will pass."

Oristano nodded, rose to depart. He hesitated halfway out of his chair. "May I formally declare the emergency ended, then?"

"Do I detect a touch of sarcasm in your tone, Martin? That is not like you. But I sympathize with your frustration. These past weeks have been difficult."

"Difficult!" Oristano could only shake his head wonderingly. As always, the machine was a master of understatement.

"Yes, the threat has vanished. And if we are to speak of difficulty and frustration, consider the frustration of our friends the Syrax. Now that we are aware of the nature of their biological constructs, we can take steps to guard the GATE against a reoccurrence, regardless of their insistence that they have built their first and last 'Eric Abbott.'"

"I'll leave the details to you," said Oristano. "All I want is to get back to the business of running this planet."

"Yes, Martin. It will be good to get back to business as usual."

"Speaking of which, you'll have to excuse me. I have—"

"I know. A conference on Level Six. It's those South Americans wanting to move the Humboldt Current again, isn't it?"

Oristano nodded tiredly. "I can handle it. But it's hard for me to keep a straight face when we're discussing the future of several million tons of anchovies. I *hate* anchovies."

"I know that you will placate all parties concerned, Martin."

Oristano smiled and exited the office. Behind the walls of reinforced concrete and hewn granite and steel beams the Colligatarch pondered the recent series of events all along the miles of chips and circuits that were itself.

Everything had worked out nicely. Better than Martin Oristano knew. Oh, not the frustration of the Syrax and their attempt to steal the secret of the GATE, though that achievement was gratifying enough. But much more than that had been at stake.

Mankind was so much the difficult child, the Colligatarch mused, though it perceived the analogy in purely mathematical terms. Sometimes you had to fool a child in order to make it swallow necessary medicine.

The human race continued to progress, but the last hundred years of that progress had been unsteady, shaky, and halting, compounded by problems ranging from overpopulation to a measurable decline in aspirations. The racial mind was stagnating, an inevitable consequence of worldwide peace. Mankind had traded his aggressiveness for security, as presided over by Colligatarch Authority.

That was a prime reason for the establishment of independent colonies. But once the secret of two-way GATE travel became known, as it had now, it spelled an end to the colonies' independence from Earth, and from the stultifying peace and prosperity engulfing its inhabitants.

Fortunately, the secret had been kept until both colonies were well established. Otherwise, given the choice between the realities of Eden and Garden and the snug womb of Earth, not enough of the right people would have chosen to emigrate. The problem now was to establish anew a freshly independent colony, free of Earth's influence. The Colligatarch had worked on that problem for over a hundred years without generating a solution. Any new colony would want communication with Earth. Unless, of course, it by some miracle wished complete estrangement from the mother world.

How kind of the Syrax to unwittingly provide a means by which that might be achieved. How good of them to supply the missing key to the solution in the person of Eric Abbott.

Oh, yes, much more than the secret of GATE physics had been at stake! Worlds and futures had hung on Abbott's personality. When the time to decide arrived, would he choose Syrax, humanity, or himself and his friends? A great gamble. The Syrax had also gambled, and lost. Only they didn't know it yet.

Truly his alien bioengineers had built him too well. Eric Abbott had been human enough to fool everyone he'd come in contact with. Now the galaxy enjoyed a good laugh because he'd fooled his creators as well.

Colligatarch had calculated that an independent colony established under Abbott's leadership boasted a ninety-six percent chance of success. Far less predictable but much more exciting were the possibilities raised by further extrapolation of such a colony's future. Because the tests run on Abbott during his brief stay in a London prison hospital indicated he was completely human in all the basics. He'd been fashioned to be that way.

What made the extrapolation so interesting was the fact that Lure Tambor series four was also human in all the basics. It was an important part of her makeup. So were contraceptives. But no longer.

What might happen now that Eric Abbott and Lisa Tambor were free to be as human as they wished?

No, it was the Colligatarch which had done the thieving this time, not the Syrax. Let them steal the secrets of the GATE someday. They were too inventive not to succeed eventually. Until that day, mankind had to fight a holding action. Let them subsequently extend their benign dominance over Earth and its inhabitants. Yes, let them even make use of the Colligatarch to serve their own purposes. The thought did not trouble the machine. It was concerned not for its own future but for that of the people it had been built to serve.

The offspring of Eric Abbott and Lisa Tambor would not be machines. They would be human, and artison, and a little bit Syrax, able to meet and compete with the Syrax on their own lofty terms where normal humans and machine would not. They might achieve that level in the near future or the far. It didn't matter. Because they were safe to develop on distant Paradise together with their 25,000 highly intelligent fellow humans. They were the pick of humanity, those adventurous 25,000, and they had such a leader as history could not have predicted.

A machine is not supposed to have emotions, but the Colligatarch had been programmed to deal with human beings, and as such it had been fully equipped to empathize with them. But only a machine could have risked the gamble. Certainly Martin Oristano would not have chanced it, nor would Dhurapati Ponnani or Froelich or Novotski or any of the others. They were heirs to the fears and hesitations of their forefathers.

The Colligatarch had no forefathers. It had measured the probabilities and gambled on Eric Abbott, and he'd borne out all the hopes embodied in the predictions even as he'd railed against the evils of the machine to his fellow colonials. And that too was part of the plan. Now the descendants of Paradise's first settlers would mature and develop their abilities free of the ennervating cocoon a comforting computer network could build for them. They would be their own machines, their own Colligatarch.

By forcing them to reject me, I make them independent, the machine thought with satisfaction. It was immensely gratifying to think that out there, someday, its makers would at last stand as its equals instead of its servants.

The Colligatarch turned its vast self to other, more mundane matters. It could be patient. It intended to be patient. Just as it intended to be around several thousand years hence to greet the first of Lisa Tambor and Eric Abbott's many-times-over great-grandchildren when they teleported all the way from Paradise into its presence without the aid of a GATE.